"Well, Lady Elizabeth? Shall we dance?"

Lady Elizabeth paused, shook her head slightly, and pulled her hand free. "No, thank you."

He lifted his brows. "No? Are you certain?"

The lady's mouth curved into a faint smile and she said in a smooth, rich voice, "We have not been properly introduced. Therefore, I cannot dance with you."

The chit was hiding behind convention. That was a challenge, indeed. He risked a glance at the lady's companion and found the woman regarding Lady Elizabeth with an astonished air, as if she could not quite believe the words she'd just heard.

Christian hid a smile. Perhaps the lady was not usually such a high stickler?

"No, my lady. We have not been properly introduced. We are, in fact, *illicit* strangers." He let his voice linger over the word, caressing with seductive intent . . .

By Karen Hawkins

Karen Hawkins

Her Officer And Gentleman

AVON BOOKS
An Imprint of HarperCollinsPublishers

This is a work of fiction. Names, characters, places, and incidents are products of the author's imagination or are used fictitiously and are not to be construed as real. Any resemblance to actual events, locales, organizations, or persons, living or dead, is entirely coincidental.

AVON BOOKS
An Imprint of HarperCollins*Publishers*
10 East 53rd Street
New York, New York 10022-5299

Avon Trademark Reg U.S. Pat. Off. and in Other Countries, Marca Registrada, Hecho en U.S.A.
HarperCollins® is a registered trademark of HarperCollins Publishers Inc.

Printed in the U.S.A.

For Jim and Beth Hobart,
a fairy tale among us.

Congratulations on your marriage!

Love like yours inspires writers like me.
Thank you for providing such a lovely muse!

12/10/2005

Chapter 1

Good manners do not necessarily prove good breeding. Oddly enough, this is true of both gentlemen and horses.

A Compleat Guide for
Being a Most Proper Butler
by Richard Robert Reeves

$\mathcal{I}$t all started with Lady Findercombe's rather impressive bosom.

Born of rather common parents and less than passable beauty, Miss Lucilla Trent was delighted when, at the tender age of sixteen, she developed what can only be described as "a woman's figure."

Lucilla, never a romantic sort, was overjoyed when her womanly figure caught old Lord Findercombe's rather jaundiced eye. The jaded bachelor was entranced enough to toss caution to the winds and beg for Lucilla's hand in marriage without regard for either her lack of dowry or the fact that her left eye had a rather disturbing tendency to wander.

Naturally, Mr. and Mrs. Trent were enthused. Though Lucilla found Lord Findercombe both old and dull, he was well connected, was invited everywhere, and was willing to set her up with an indulgent amount of pin money. They were, many said, a perfect match.

Once married, Lord Findercombe bestowed a wealth of heavy decorative brooches and necklaces on his wife that drew attention to her finest features. The combination of bountiful bosom and jaunty jewels soon became an accepted sight in society.

All was well and good until the night of the Hearsts' Grand Ball. The ball was held every year two weeks prior to the beginning of the season. Located only a half day's ride from town, the event was a stopping place for all the best of the best on their annual move to their London town houses.

It had become something of a tradition; the large sitting rooms and the impressive ballroom crowded to the fullest. Every year, Lady Hearst flitted from guest to guest, gathering and passing on gossip like a bee pollinating a colorful garden.

Normally, the Hearsts' Grand Ball was held up as an example of a well-thought-out and unique entertainment, a fact that delighted Lady Hearst no small amount. However, this year things were not going as planned. Within an hour of beginning, the ball was, in fact, in dire danger of falling apart.

The wonderful orchestra Lady Hearst had hired had come down with the ague. At the last minute, she'd been forced to replace them with a smallish local quartet, which was hardly the thing for a large, crowded ballroom. Then she discovered that the long sheers she'd ordered draped around the ballroom to add an air of gaiety had an odd smell—rather musty and barn-like—a fact she did not discover until too late to order their removal. But the worst disaster was the ices.

A spate of unusually mild weather had caused the front hallway to be far warmer than usual, and all the lovely ices she'd ordered specially from London had begun to melt before the first guest had arrived. She'd been so excited about those ices, too. They had been shaped to look like Admiral Nelson on board the *Victory* to commemorate the glorious Battle of Trafalgar, a topic much on the minds and tongues of the ton.

As the ices melted, hundreds of small Admiral Nelsons began to shrink. Worse, his left arm, extended and holding a sword to the throat of a panicked Frenchman, fell off completely and landed on the upturned face of his vanquished foe, giving the entire scene a rather cannibalistic air.

The real Admiral Nelson had indeed lost an arm in battle, and Lady Hearst feared her guests would think her insensitive or, worse, unpatriotic. Her fears were quite justified when she caught not one but three spiteful women whispering just such a thing to one another during the evening.

All in all, the ball was filled, which made it acceptable, but the rooms languished with yawns and desultory small talk. The guests were bored, which was the worst thing that could happen to a society hostess, even over the advent of a fire or a fatality of some sort. At least *that* would have been interesting.

Into this listless event came the noisy entrance of Lord and Lady Findercombe. It was well past midnight, and Lady Hearst had long since abandoned her post by the door, but at the suddenly animated bustle, she and her husband hurried to see who had just arrived and in such an excitable state. Lady Hearst reached the entryway first and found the Findercombes standing amid a rapidly growing crowd.

"We," Lord Findercombe said, his voice trembling in outrage, "were robbed!"

In a flash, the ennui that had held the company at bay for the past four hours disappeared.

"Good God," said Lord Hearst over the noise of the now-buzzing crowd. "Lord Findercombe, how did this come to happen?"

His Lordship turned to his wife. "Lucilla, show them!"

Lucilla untied the bow at her neck, tossed open her cloak, and exposed her low-cut gown. Her magnificent décolletage was framed for viewing, the object of all attention.

For a moment, the busy hum of voices abated.

Lady Hearst's cheeks heated, while a rather inebriated gentleman by the door leaned forward and squinted. After a moment, he said, "They look just fine to me! Both of 'em!"

A wave of laughter arose from the crowd.

Lord Findercombe glared at the young buck. "Not her bosom, you fool! Her jewels! Gone, all of them! A highwayman stopped our carriage and stole everything!"

"You don't say!" Lord Hearst exclaimed.

"Yes, and the ruffian had the audacity to tell Lucilla that she might keep one of her brooches did she give him a kiss!"

Lady Hearst gazed anxiously at Lucilla. But the younger lady did not appear at all outraged. A faint, very secretive smile touched her lips. For a moment, Lucilla's rather plain features assumed a very attractive and somewhat sensual look.

The gathering swarmed with excited whispers. More people tried to crowd into the narrow entryway, many craning their necks to see who was speaking. Lady Hearst could have burst with pleasure. Every single person in the ballroom must now be glad he'd been invited. Nothing could have been more wonderful.

She bustled forward and put an arm through Lucilla's. "Oh, you poor child! Whatever did you do?"

"Do?" Lucilla's smile never wavered. She slowly lifted her left hand. There, in the center, rested a huge emerald brooch.

Lady Hearst burst into laughter and hugged Lucilla. "Oh, you naughty puss! A kiss for a brooch!"

Lucilla looked at the brooch, a sense of wonder in her eyes. "I have never seen such a highwayman. His voice"—Lucilla closed her eyes a moment, the smile still on her lips—"so smooth, like silk. And deep. I have never heard such a voice. And he was so cultured, so handsome, so polite—"

"My dear!" Lady Hearst exclaimed. "You were held up by none other than Gentleman James!"

Lucilla opened her eyes wide. "Who?"

"Gentleman James—or Gentleman Jack, as some call him—is our local ruffian. He holds up only the plumpest pockets."

"Gentleman James?" cooed a lady who was standing nearby, her eyes wide. "Is he a *bad* man?"

"I don't believe so," Lady Hearst said. "He seems quite civilized and he has never harmed a soul."

"That's true," Lord Hearst agreed. "They say he's the devil with a rapier and a demmed fine shot, too."

Lord Findercombe fisted his hands and said rather enigmatically, "Ha!"

"The Gentleman has the most impeccable manners," Lady Hearst continued, ignoring Lord Findercombe's outburst. "Some think he may be the illegitimate son of a nobleman."

"Whatever he is or isn't," Lord Findercombe fumed, "the lout deserves to swing from the end of a noose!"

"Not an easy trick, that," Lord Hearst said bluffly. "No one has ever caught him, try as they might. He comes, he parlays, and then he disappears like a puff of smoke."

"I hear he is tall," Lady Hearst said. "Very tall, with black hair and—"

"Oh no," Lucilla said. She flushed, then glanced

at her husband from under her lashes. "The thief was not tall. I did, however, get a glimpse of his eyes. They were as blue as—"

"Lucilla!"

Everyone turned to an apparently shocked Lord Findercombe. "He was indeed tall! Quite tall! And his eyes were gr—"

"Nonsense. Gentleman Jack was of short stature and his eyes were blue. My lord, you have had too much to drink."

Lord Findercombe's mouth opened, his eyes bulging wildly.

"You heard me," Lucilla said stoutly. "You were drunk. You had two glasses of scotch before we left the house. Then, in the coach, you were sipping from your flask the entire way."

Everyone looked at Lord Findercombe, who flushed. "I am not drunk and you know it!"

Her Ladyship merely raised her brows. Those watching wondered if perhaps Lord Findercombe's outraged reaction was fueled by brandy.

Lord Findercombe seemed quite aware of this. "You, madam, have a lot to explain yourself!"

Lucilla's lips thinned. "Just what do you mean by *that*?"

"What I mean," Lord Findercombe snapped, "is that you were very quick to kiss that man, and all for one little brooch."

"It isn't one little brooch; it's one *large* brooch. And why shouldn't I kiss him? At least *he* doesn't smell like onions!"

Lord Findercombe stiffened. "My doctor recommended I eat onions to help with my digestion!"

"They might help your digestion, but they do not assist your other parts!"

Tittering erupted from the guests. Even Lady Hearst had to turn aside to keep from giggling in a most unseemly manner.

Lord Findercombe turned so red it appeared he might explode. "It was a mistake to come here so soon on the heels of a disaster. Neither of us is as we should be."

"Speak for yourself, my lord; I am perfectly fine. Better than fine. In fact, I have never felt finer than now, having met a *real* gentleman!" Lucilla threw off her cloak and handed it to a nearby footman. Then she turned and took Lady Hearst's arm. "My lady, might I request some ratafia? I am quite parched."

"Of course, my dear!" Lady Hearst cooed. "Come this way and tell me all about your horrid evening!"

The other guests watched enviously as Lady Hearst led Lucilla toward the refreshment table, leaving Lord Findercombe loudly complaining in the foyer. This spectacle soon palled, and slowly, one by one, the guests returned to the ballroom.

To Lord Hearst's chagrin, Findercombe continued to lament the loss of his lady's jewels until a gentleman appeared at the top of the stairs.

"Westerville!" Hearst said with obvious relief.

The gentleman in question smiled and continued his leisurely stroll down the stairs. Fashionably attired in a multi-caped coat, his riding boots exquisitely shined, he was the epitome of fashion. Handsome in an almost classical way, tall, with broad shoulders, he paused at the foot of the stairs, regarding the two older lords with an air of faint amusement.

Lord Hearst hurried forward. "Westerville! Leaving so soon?"

"Urgent business calls me to London."

"Demmed! I wish you'd find a way to stay another week. There is some top hunting to be had hereabouts."

Findercombe harrumphed loudly.

Hearst started. "Oh good heavens! Almost forgot. Lord Findercombe, have you met Viscount Westerville?"

"No," Findercombe said in a testy voice. "Nor do I wish to at this moment. I am too upset to—"

"He's a fine fellow," Hearst said, beaming at the newcomer. "A bruising rider to the hounds!"

The viscount grinned, his teeth flashing in a face lightly tanned. "Hearst, I would stay if I could, but I must get to London to file for my inheritance. I have hopes of purchasing that bay hunter of yours as soon as I have matters in hand."

Hearst's booming laughter filled the hall. "By all means, then, make haste to London!"

The viscount bowed. "I shall." His amused gaze flickered over Findercombe's flushed face. "Lord Findercombe, you look upset. Is something amiss?"

"Oh lud, yes," Hearst said. "A highwayman importuned poor Lady Findercombe and forced her into a kiss. Worse, the minx looked as if she might have enjoyed it!"

"Hearst!" bellowed Lord Findercombe. "How dare you suggest Lady Findercombe—that she— how could you say—"

"There, there!" Hearst said, eyeing his friend a bit nervously. "I just said she *looked* as if she enjoyed it. For all I know, she detested it and was only being polite."

"My lady is quite young," Findercombe said, sending a red-faced glare at his host. "She doesn't know what she likes. She was quite aghast when the knave forced himself upon her and—"

"Forced?" The viscount's brows lowered over his pale eyes, which in the uncertain light appeared to be an unusual shade of silver-green. "The man must have been a complete cad."

"He was," Findercombe said stoutly. "He importuned my lady in a most unchivalrous manner."

The viscount pursed his lips, a dark humor in his gaze. "I am surprised you did not call the man out. Or perhaps you did?"

"I would have, had the coward stayed! But he was away with my money before I could collect myself."

"Yes," the younger man said reflectively. "It is always so difficult to collect oneself whilst cowering on the floor of one's own carriage."

Lord Hearst gave an involuntary exclamation at this, but Findercombe merely blinked, his gaze riveted on the viscount's face. "How could you know I hid on the floor of my carriage?"

The viscount smiled gently. "Your knees are muddied."

The older lord bent over. "Oh. That. I slid to the

floor, hoping to distract the man from—not that it matters, for I did not have my pistol with me, which will not happen again!"

"Of course," the viscount said soothingly.

"A horrid happening, but over now, thank heavens," Hearst said in his bluff manner. "Westerville, you've a distance to travel this evening, so we shall not hold you further. Send a letter when you're ready for the bay and I'll have her brought to you."

"Thank you, my lord. I shall do that."

"I hope you will!" Hearst opened the library door. "Come, Findercombe! Try some of my port. It's the best to be had. Westerville himself brought it all the way from France!" He winked over Findercombe's head at Westerville and then shut the library door behind him.

The viscount grinned. Whistling softly, he left the house and made his way to his waiting carriage.

"There ye be, Master Jack," said a large, red-haired Scotsman, heaving a sigh of relief. "I've been waiting."

Christian James Llevanth, Viscount Westerville, shrugged. "I apologize, Willie. I would have been here sooner, but there was a bit of a disturbance at the ball."

"Aye," Willie said, a twinkle in his eyes. "I seen the gent and his lady arrive. A puddin' heart, if I ever seen one."

"Indeed," Christian agreed. "I thought he was—"

A dapper figure dressed in the sober black coat and neatly pressed breeches of a butler walked from around the carriage. Tall and thin with an elegant air, he bowed to Christian. "Ah, my lord! I did not hear you approach."

"I just arrived, Reeves," Christian said. The butler had been with him for only two months, and it still felt a bit odd. After years of an existence consisting of no one but Willie for company, of living in taverns and never staying anywhere longer than was necessary, now there was Reeves, a complete entourage of servants, and a luxurious house in London. All of it Christian's.

He flickered a smile at the butler. "I apologize for being late. There was a bit of drama at the ball."

Willie snorted with humor. "Aye, a bit of drama! Seems someone held up a coach belonging to a snot-nosed gent and—"

Christian sent a warning glare at Willie and then hoped the sharp-eyed butler had not witnessed it.

Reeves's attention was locked on poor Willie. "Tell me more, Master William, about this 'snot-nosed' gent? How exactly do you know the gentleman to be so, ah, predisposed?"

Willie shifted from one foot to the other, casting a wild look at Christian.

Christian took pity on poor Willie. "Reeves, we should leave. Tell the groomsman—"

"My lord," the butler said, disapprobation thick in his voice, "is there something *you* wish to tell me? Something about the gentleman who entered the house not long ago, claiming he'd been robbed?"

"No."

Reeves sighed. "One day there will be a reckoning."

"Och, now!" Willie said. "We were just out havin' a wee bit of fun. No need to get your snood in a snocker."

"My snood is not snocked," Reeves said severely. "Lord Westerville just came into a vast inheritance. These little wayward contretemps are no longer necessary."

"No one said they were necessary," Christian said. "But they are certainly enjoyable."

Willie chuckled. "The lady was properly stocked in the miff, was she not, Master Jack?"

Reeves winced. "My dear William, pray at least *try* and call His Lordship by his proper title of Lord Westerville."

"I'm proper," Willie huffed, wiping his nose on a none-too-clean sleeve. "But I won't be a-callin' Master Jack 'me lord' whilst we're upon the High Toby, I won't."

Reeves eyed Christian with a resigned air. "My lord, when your father sent me into the world upon his death to locate you, I never thought to find you so dangerously employed."

Christian's smile froze a bit. In order to survive, one had to stay focused, clear-minded. Even now, just hearing someone mention Father sent a wave of . . . fury? Sorrow? Something cold and powerful, racing through him, making him both frightfully strong and yet painfully weak at the same time. He gritted his teeth. If he wished to find Mother's killer, he had to become more accustomed to hearing Father's name. At one time he'd desired to hear Father's name over all others. But that time was long gone.

Christian caught Reeves's speculative gaze. "Had my father wished me more gainfully employed, then while he was alive, he should have bothered himself a bit more with me and my brother. He paid us so little heed that I find it odd he thought of us at all while upon his deathbed."

Reeves sighed a bit. "If you would allow me to explain—"

"It does not matter. I want the fortune; I will use it to further my search for the man responsible for betraying Mother and causing her death. *That* is what is really important."

Willie spat into the dirt. "Revenge," he said with relish.

"Revenge never served anyone well," Reeves said coolly.

"Och, there! How can ye say such? 'Tis the Highland way."

Reeves shook his head. "My lord, I implore you to retire Gentleman James to become the legend he deserves to be. It cannot help your plans if you are caught and thrown into gaol."

Christian knew Reeves was right. But . . . before he'd gained his title and the possibility of a fortune, he had never thought himself enamored of his chosen profession as highwayman. Oh, he'd enjoyed it well enough in the cold chill of the inky black nights and the uncertainty of each exhilarating encounter. But the real reason he believed he'd found it so satisfying was that every time he outwitted someone wealthier than he—someone perceived by society to be more powerful— Christian was really triumphing over someone like Father. Someone cold. Arrogant. Uncaring.

Lately, it had been borne upon Christian that perhaps he enjoyed being a highwayman for other reasons. The painful freedom that came with it. The taste of excitement that flushed his body when he and Willie approached a coach. The feel of a woman's excited mouth beneath his, as today.

He smiled. Often as not, unbeknownst to their husbands and lovers, the gently born women he'd won kisses from had given him other tokens— rings, ribbons, items that could, and sometimes did, gain him entrance to the boudoirs of the mistresses of some of the greatest houses in England.

Now he was a lord in his own right, and access to those very boudoirs was his for the asking. He was now an equal, a member of the crème de la crème.

Christian grinned. "Reeves, you have my word Willie and I have taken our last ride. From this night forth, Gentleman James is no more."

" 'Ere now," Willie protested. "Ye canna mean that!"

"I am certain he does," Reeves said, looking at Willie with disapprobation. "You, Master William, had best concern yourself with what place you will take in His Lordship's new establishment. Lord Westerville no longer has need of an accomplice to hold his mount whilst he is waving his pistols about."

Christian chuckled at Willie's outraged expression. "There now, Willie, my man! Just tell Reeves you already have a job, for you do, you know."

Willie's face cleared. "Aye, thet's roight! In fact, if ye aren't goin' to ride the High Toby, I suppose I'd best be on me new duties right away."

"Take your horse. I expect to see you within the week."

"Sooner, guv'nor!" Willie sent a hard glance at Reeves before he walked away, dignified in his own manner.

"Where is Master William off to now?" Reeves asked.

"I don't believe you want to know."

The butler sighed once more. "I was afraid you might say that." He nodded to a footman who had been hovering out of earshot. The man raced forward now to open the door and lower the steps. Christian climbed in. Reeves followed, and soon they were on their way.

The carriage swayed over the deeply rutted road. "My lord, may I inquire how you intend on accomplishing your goal, to discover your mother's betrayer?"

"I know who betrayed my mother; the Duke of Massingale. But I need more evidence."

Reeves's brows rose. "The duke is a reclusive man."

"Which is why I shall gain entry to his household by courting his granddaughter."

Reeves was silent a long moment. "I assume, my lord, that she was part of the dastardly plot?"

"No. She was but a child when my mother

died." Christian read the disapprobation in the butler's eyes. "I have waited over twenty years to right the wrongs done to my mother. I will have my vengeance one way or another."

Reeves sighed. "Yes, my lord. I can see you are quite determined. I must say, having witnessed your last profession, I find your disregard for the law somewhat disconcerting."

"I have never killed anyone."

"That is always a good thing to hear from one's employer. Pray do not become cross if I ask you to repeat that statement at various times. I find the words quite reassuring."

Christian laughed and leaned back against the thick squabs of his coach. It would take all of Christian's address to gain entrance into the duke's household. But once he reached London and spent a few weeks charming the granddaughter . . .

"Vengeance," Christian said in a low tone beneath the rumble of the carriage. The words blended smoothly with the creaking of the leather straps and the thunder of the horses' hooves.

Smiling grimly, Christian watched out the window as the inky blackness sped by. Lights flickered in the distance and beckoned him onward. Vengeance indeed. London and all her inhabitants had best beware.

Chapter 2

A true gentleman can convey the most complex of emotions with the simplest of gestures. This works well with everyone except, of course, one's female companions, be they mother, wife, or other. In those cases, one cannot be too thorough in one's communication, gentleman or no.

A Compleat Guide for
Being a Most Proper Butler
by Richard Robert Reeves

*M*assingale House was unlike other ancient houses in Devonshire; it did not suffer from dry rot or chimneys that smoked, the doors did not stick, the floors rarely creaked, and the stair railings were free of pesky wobbles. It was, as the butler liked to remind the housekeeper, a very *quiet* house.

Except, of course, for His Lordship.

Even now the Duke of Massingale's loud voice

could be heard thundering through the heavy library door, followed by the unmistakable crack and shatter of a thrown teacup.

"Gor!" said the new footman.

Jameson, the butler, sent the man a flat stare. Jameson had been with His Lordship for more than fifteen years, and he did not encourage the staff to make disparaging comments about their master and mistresses. That was solely the duty of the upper servants and no one else.

Fortunately for the footman, a lengthy pause ensued inside the library, during which a light footstep was heard upon the landing.

Jameson snapped to attention. His quick glare sent both of the footmen to their posts by the front door. Unaware she'd interrupted anything, Lady Elizabeth came down the stairs, obviously trying to stifle a yawn, the early sun burnishing her golden hair. On seeing Jameson, she smiled. "Good morning!"

Of medium height with a gentle figure, thickly lashed brown eyes, and a wide, rather sensual mouth, Lady Elizabeth was quite used to hearing that she looked just like her mother, His Lordship's late daughter-in-law, who was a noted beauty of her time. As this compliment was always followed with a sad sigh and the fervent words, "God rest Lady Ellen's soul!" the comment was never accorded much attention.

From the other side of the library door, His Lordship's voice rose yet again, along with the crisp sound of a newspaper being rent into tiny pieces.

Lady Elizabeth pulled a comical face. "Oh dear! What has Grandfather in such a taking today?"

Jameson smiled. Every member of the duke's large staff thought His Lordship's granddaughter was a ray of sunshine, though that was not to suggest she was lax in her duties as mistress of the house. As Jameson once told the housekeeper, Mrs. Kimble, whenever that *certain* look entered Lady Elizabeth's eye and her chin took on that *particular* angle, there was no use arguing, no matter how sunnily she smiled. "My lady, I fear it was the *Morning Post*. There was more than a normal amount of Tory verve today."

"Ah, that would indeed put Grandfather into a foul mood."

A noise outside the front door sent the footman scurrying to open it. Inside walked a lovely blond woman wearing a long pink pelisse, a fashionable bonnet trimmed in Russian ribbon upon her reddish hair. She was a small creature, barely five feet in height, of fairy-like proportions and a cupid-bow mouth. Accompanying her was Lord Bennington, a tall, dark gentleman with a somber expression and hooded eyes.

"Charlotte!" Beth said, hurrying forward to kiss her stepmother's cheek.

Charlotte smiled. Though quite a bit older than her stepdaughter, she did not look it. Indeed, anyone seeing them together might think the two women were sisters, though Charlotte's beauty was less memorable than Elizabeth's.

"Beth, I am surprised to see you out of bed at such an hour," Charlotte said in her soft voice, pulling off her gloves. Despite her gentle demeanor, there was a frantic air to Charlotte, as if the slightest excitement might break her into a million pieces.

Beth looked at her stepmother with a measured gaze, trying to ascertain the older woman's true state. After a moment, Beth relaxed. Charlotte seemed quite placid this morning, a fact that would please everyone in the house.

Beth smiled at her stepmama. "I would still be abed, but I was summoned by Grandfather."

"This early? Why, it is barely seven! What does he want?"

"I don't know; I haven't seen him yet. I just came downstairs and he was—"

Another teacup crashed against the door, followed by a thundering diatribe of which only the words "heathens," "radicals," and "forsaken" could be discerned.

Charlotte's smile dimmed. "Ah, the paper."

Lord Bennington glanced at the door with a grimace. "Massingale does not know what is due his station."

Beth glanced at the servants. They remained impassive, though they had to have heard Lord Bennington's comment. Beth did not like Bennington, though he'd been her father's closest companion since they'd both been in short coats. To keep the rather contentious lord from making more disparaging comments before the servants, Beth said in a sedate tone, "Lord Bennington, it is good to see you."

He made a ponderous bow. "Lady Elizabeth."

"Good morning. Are you staying for breakfast?"

He flicked a glance at Charlotte, then said in his usual heavy manner, "Not this morning, I'm afraid. I have business to attend to." He bowed at Charlotte, who stood by, threading the braided handles of her reticule back and forth through her fingers, a nervous habit she'd but lately assumed.

Beth always thought her stepmama's delicate sensibilities had come from the death of Beth's father. Indeed, several of the servants had mentioned that Lady Charlotte had changed greatly after that event. Beth could remember days after her father's death that it seemed as if her stepmama would never stop crying.

That had been years ago, of course. Now Charlotte had good days, as well as tearful ones, though fewer and fewer of those. It was rather nice to see Lord Bennington taking Charlotte about and it certainly seemed to do her a world of good. Although Beth could find no liking for the pompous lord herself, she imagined Charlotte must find his overbearing ways something of a buffer against the unpleasantness of the outside world.

Bennington frowned at Charlotte. "I am certain I do not need to remind you that the play begins at seven. As it takes an hour to reach London from here—"

"I shall be ready at five." Charlotte waved a hand, her gesture large and exaggerated. "You will not have to wait!"

"I hope not. *Hamlet* is one of my favorites." He replaced his hat. "Good day, Lady Elizabeth. Lady

Charlotte." With that, he turned and trod out the door.

Cheeks a bit pink, Charlotte whisked herself to the stairs. "Beth, I hope you don't mind, but I believe I shall take my breakfast in my room this morning."

"Of course," Beth said immediately. "Jameson, will you see to it that a breakfast tray is sent to Lady Charlotte's room?"

"Yes, my lady."

"And Jameson," Charlotte said, pausing halfway up the stairs, "Dr. Neweston is to bring a new bottle of medicine this morning. Would you let me know when he has come? I wish to speak with him. I haven't been sleeping well, and I wonder if perhaps he might order something a bit stronger."

"Yes, my lady."

Beth frowned. "Charlotte, I didn't know you weren't sleeping. Is there anything that I can—"

"No, no! Dr. Neweston knows my humors. He will find something and fix me up well enough. *You* are the one to worry about. I wish you luck with Massingale. He's been quite ill-natured of late."

"It is the warmer weather. He hates it."

"He is not easy to deal with when he's in a good mood. When he's in a bad one—" Charlotte shivered. "Well, you know him best. I will be in my room if you need me." With a nervous wave, Charlotte dashed up the stairs and disappeared from sight.

Beth sighed as Grandfather roared out again,

this time consigning the entire paper to the devil. "Jameson, please bring another pot of tea to the library. And some new cups."

"Yes, my lady." The butler cleared his throat. "My lady, forgive my presumption, but I fear Lady Charlotte is right. I have served His Lordship for almost fifteen years and he does not seem quite himself of late."

Beth paused, her smile firmly in place. "Do you indeed think so?"

Jameson nodded, his thin face lined with worry.

It was one thing for Charlotte—who was forever imagining she and everyone she knew had this illness or that—to think Grandfather might not be well. But to hear such a suggestion from Jameson, who knew Grandfather as well as, if not better than, Beth . . .

Her jaw ached, though she did not allow her smile to slip. "His Lordship is just tired. That is all."

Her voice was much sharper than she meant it to be. For a long moment, neither spoke. Then Jameson bowed and said in a careful monotone, "I shall bring more tea, my lady."

What was wrong with her? Beth wondered as she let herself into the library. She never snapped at the servants. It must be because of the early hour. Yes, that was what was wrong; she was up much earlier than usual, and all this talk of Grandfather being ill had put her on edge.

She paused on the border of the thick carpet and watched her Grandfather. He sat in a chair by the fireplace, his shoulders slumped, a thick shawl wrapped about him. For an instant, he was starkly outlined by the fire. Thin and cragged, with a shock of white hair that never seemed tamed, he scowled absently at the fire.

Beth smiled at him fondly, her unease disappearing. Laurence Jeremy Charles Westover, now the Duke of Massingale, was a tough old man. At the tender age of twenty, he had inherited his title and position along with numerous estates, all encumbered to the hilt. A weaker man would have been tempted to put his head in the sand and pretend all was well as long as possible. But Laurence Jeremy Charles Westover was not weak. He was, in fact, indomitable.

He had not been a direct descendant to the line but a distant cousin, forgotten and ignored by the wealthier side of his family until a sweeping case of the ague disposed of the other male members. The ton snickered when the new duke was named; it was whispered he was of common Yorkshire stock, his mother the daughter of a German bookbinder, his father a poorly paid rector with long-forgotten ties to the Westover family.

The new duke was not dismayed. He might be the son of a bookbinder's daughter and a poor rector, but by God, he knew how to economize and how to run a business. Within months, centuries of mismanagement were ruthlessly brought to heel. Within a few short years, he'd restored the estate to its former glory of wealth and riches.

Older members of the ton sneered that they would never accept the new duke, titled or no; he was a commoner, and a tradesman at that. But younger members—and especially those with marriageable daughters—disagreed; the Duke of Massingale was rich as Croesus and unmarried. A great number of faults could be overlooked under these circumstances. And so the duke, with all his plainspoken ways and manners, had been accepted into society.

Beth walked forward a few more steps until Grandfather turned her way. She immediately dipped a curtsy. "You summoned me, my lord?"

Hands clutched about his silver-knobbed cane, the duke sent his granddaughter a dark glare from beneath thick, white brows. "Don't stand there 'my lording' me like some ninnyhammer. Sit down!"

Beth grinned and took her place in a chair opposite his, eyeing with interest two broken cups on the floor in front of the fireplace. "Is that from our new set of Delft china?"

He hunched his shoulders even more. "Damned blue stuff."

"Perhaps we should use the gold plate. You might bend it, but you'd never shatter it, though I shudder to think what the poor firescreen might look like after another attack."

Grandfather glared. "I wouldn't have thrown anything if that damned paper hadn't been so full of foolishness." He scowled at the shredded paper at his elbow. "Jackanapes!"

"I don't know why you read it. You always get upset."

"It's important to keep abreast of the world. We are buried here in the country." He scowled down at his legs, bent with gout. He could walk, but only a short distance and only with the help of his cane.

Beth reached over and patted his hand. "Grandfather, I hate seeing you so upset. We may not be in the midst of London, but you make it sound as if we were trapped in a nunnery!"

"Might as well be in a nunnery," he replied sourly, "as secluded as we are."

"Yes." Beth sighed, affecting a sad pose. "I, for one, am so afflicted! All there is to do is run the house and oversee the servants in this luxurious manor stuffed high with books to read, horses to ride, flower gardens to design, lovely embroidery work to finish, and more things to keep me busy than I can list. It is a burden, but I do the best I can."

He looked at her. "Are you finished?"

She twinkled at him. "No. I also have you and Charlotte for company, and for that, I am very thankful."

Though he clearly disapproved of her answer, he could not keep a quiver of affection from his face. "I am glad to have you; don't think I'm not. I just don't wish you to be trapped here, your life wasted." Grandfather gripped the shawl tighter, his face tight with a myriad of emotions. His brow lowered, his mouth pressed into a tight line. After a moment, he turned a concerned gaze her way. "That is why I sent for you. Beth, you deserve a husband, someone to see after you when I'm gone."

For an instant, she could only stare. Though

Grandfather had mentioned such a thing occasionally over the years, he'd never spoken so directly. "What has brought this on?"

His face darkened, and he began plucking restlessly at the blanket covering his lap. "I have been thinking a lot lately. I have not done well by you. Your father would not have wished you to rot away here."

"I am not rotting away. I am perfectly happy."

"How do you know you wouldn't be happier with a husband?"

"How do you know *you* wouldn't be happier with a new wife?"

He scowled. "It's not the same! I'm eighty-one!"

"Well, I'm five and twenty and I know exactly what I want and when. I don't need your help in directing my life, thank you."

He eyed her morosely. "You could at least give it a try."

She sighed. "Perhaps you are right. Shall I begin interviews today? I had planned to go on a picnic but I suppose I could put that off until tomorrow."

"Don't try to wheedle your way out of this with a chuckle, Miss Priss! You should have been presented on your seventeenth birthday, but your uncle Redmond had the bad sense to die of some silly childhood complaint. Then your cousin Gertrude went the same route and we had to go into mourning all over again!"

"How rude of them, to be sure. I hate them both."

Grandfather eyed her with a flat gaze. "Cheeky, ain't you?"

"Only with you," she murmured with a smile.

"Ha!" Yet he did not smile back as he normally would have. Instead, he fidgeted with his shawl, his brow lowered.

The clock ticked loudly; the birds outside the windows sang sweetly. Usually Beth would have been fine sitting still and enjoying the day, but after Jameson's rather odd comment about Grandfather's temper, she instead found herself watching him from beneath her lashes.

He *was* a bit more stooped than usual, and there was no denying the heavy circles beneath his eyes. But it was the tinge of blue to his pale skin that worried her the most.

"Beth, I've made a decision," Grandfather said abruptly into the silence. "And I will not allow an argument; it is time you were presented."

Beth blinked. "Grandfather! I am too old! I'd be the laughingstock of London."

"Poppycock! You might be a bit long of tooth, though no one would ever countenance it to see you. You're my only grandchild. The family title may have to go to that twit Theakeliam, but you will inherit everything else, including this house."

"You cannot mean to separate the title from the house!"

"I'm eighty-one and I can do what I damned well want," he said testily. "Your father was to have inherited the title and the house. I wish he had lived to do so."

She heard the faint quaver in Grandfather's voice and reached over to pat his hand. "I miss Father, too."

Grandfather grasped her hand tightly, meeting her gaze almost fiercely. "It's what he would want, Beth. What I should have done but—" His brows lowered. "I shall not rest until you have had at least one season."

The determined gleam in Grandfather's eyes sent a wave of alarm though Beth. He was deadly serious, almost as if he thought this was his last chance—

She couldn't finish the thought. Grandfather had been parent, mentor, family, friend, and more since Father's death. She looked down at Grandfather's hand where it was clasped over hers. White and heavily veined, it appeared remarkably fragile. When had that happened? When had he grown so feeble?

She bit her lip against an onslaught of tears. Beth suddenly knew she could not let him down. She didn't wish to go to London, but if it would make him happy and set his mind at ease, what would be the cost? It wasn't as if taking a season meant she *had* to marry. And that was the one thing she did not wish to do.

When her responsibilities here at Massingale House were no more, she'd be free to taste real freedom, perhaps travel a bit and have adventures of her own. A husband could hamper all her plans.

Still . . . if it made Grandfather happy, she supposed it wouldn't hurt to *pretend* to look for a husband.

He must have sensed her capitulation for he gave a grateful sigh. "You will be the belle of the season."

"I am far too old for that."

"Nonsense. I met and married your grand-mother at your same age, God bless her soul." Grandfather's face softened as he looked at the portrait over the fireplace. It was of a tall, slender woman, wearing a costly gown of red silk, her blond hair adorned with flowers. She was a beauti-ful woman by any accounts, her face heart-shaped, her expression sweet.

"I loved your grandmother from the moment I saw her." He tilted his head to one side, smiling up at the portrait.

The door opened and Jameson came in with a tea tray. Beth put a finger to her lips and nodded to the table. The butler, upon seeing the elderly duke gazing upon his wife's portrait, quietly set the tray on a side table and then withdrew.

Beth poured two cups of tea and placed one at her Grandfather's elbow.

He pulled his gaze from the portrait with obvi-ous difficulty and picked up his teacup, the dish rattling slightly against the saucer. His eyes twin-kled over the cup at her. "I have to say that I ex-pected you to argue."

"Me? Argue?"

He cackled. "You certainly took your time com-ing. I thought you'd guessed what I wished to ask you."

"No. I fear it was nothing so prescient. I was merely reading. Had I known you were down here, tossing crockery and planning my launch into society, I would have slipped out my window and gone to live in the stable."

Grandfather chuckled. "Cheeky wench."

"Crotchety old man," she returned, grinning over her cup.

A tremulous smile touched his mouth. "Ah, Beth! You'll enjoy London, see if you don't! With your looks and spirit, not to mention the dowry I plan to put behind you, every duke, earl, and marquis will be tripping over his feet to win your favor."

She replaced her cup into the saucer so quickly, the china clacked noisily. "Dowry?"

"Of course you'll have a dowry!"

Beth sighed. Why was it that the simplest of plans was never really simple? The idea of hordes of suitors panting after her dowry made Beth wince inwardly. She would have to be very crafty to turn the tide of *that* enticement. "At least it will be good for Charlotte to serve as chaperone. She will—"

"No." Grandfather's mouth took on a mulish twist. "Your stepmother will have nothing to do with this."

"You are much too severe on poor Charlotte." Grandfather had never liked Charlotte. Beth was at a loss to understand why; Grandfather was not usually so judgmental.

"I rue the day your father married that woman. She was not fit for that position. And now look at her! Flirting shamelessly with that man—" His lips folded with disapproval.

"Charlotte has been a widow for a long time. Father would not have wished her to remain alone.

She seems quite happy with Lord Bennington's attentions, and surely she deserves that, at least."

"Bennington! Pah! I don't trust him. Either of them!"

"When Father was alive, Charlotte was completely devoted to him. You told me yourself that she made herself ill taking care of him the last few months of his life—"

"I don't want to discuss this anymore."

Beth sighed. She'd been young when Father had died, but she remembered Charlotte's haggard expression and the way the woman had practically lived in the sickroom. After his death, Charlotte had taken to her own bed and hadn't risen for months. If it hadn't been for Dr. Neweston, Charlotte would probably still be abed. "Grandfather, Charlotte has not—"

"Is she still seeing Dr. Neweston?"

Beth frowned. "Yes. He is to bring her medicine today."

"Good. Now enough of Charlotte; I don't wish to speak of her. Beth, you will set up residence in our London house as soon as possible. Your cousin Beatrice is returning to town to be your chaperone."

"Cousin Beatrice?"

"She will be the perfect chaperone. She's a bit older than you, but young enough to have the energy to gallivant about town. I wrote her a month ago, but she was on the continent with her husband. She is to return to town in two weeks."

34 *Karen Hawkins*

"So I have two weeks—"

"No. You will go to town tomorrow. You've fittings for gowns, shoes to purchase, all that frippery stuff. Until Beatrice arrives, Lady Clearmont will escort you." He didn't allow Beth to protest, but began issuing orders with bewildering speed about letters of credit and accounts.

When he paused for breath, she quickly said, "Grandfather, there is a cost to my capitulation."

He cocked a wary brow.

"I am willing to go to London, but for this one season only, whether I find a husband or not."

Grandfather's shoulders slumped. "You are a difficult child."

"And you are a difficult old man, which is why we deal so well together. I want your word that if I have this season in London, you will cease speaking of it. Forever."

"And if I don't agree?"

"Then I won't even go this one time. I shall stay at home, instead, and make life miserable by cosseting you until you scream for mercy."

He scowled. "It wouldn't hurt you to find a husband."

"I said I would go," Beth said with a laugh. "You will have to be content with that. Now, what were you saying about a bank draft?"

Grandfather reluctantly began to explain how he'd arranged financing for her trip, his voice strengthening with enthusiasm with each word.

Beth listened with but half an ear. She would go to London and set Grandfather's mind at ease, but she would not countenance a horde of suitors panting after her dowry. That would not do. So as Grandfather set about describing his plan for her, Beth began to weave one of her own.

Exactly four weeks later, in the Smythe-Singletons' glittering ballroom, a small group of men waited near the door, eyeing the newcomers with impatience.

Beth saw them as she entered. She muttered an imprecation under her breath and turned away so they would not see her.

"Pardon?" Lady Clearmont asked, yawning behind her fan.

Beth planted a smile on her face. "It's a bit hot in here, isn't it? I wonder if it might be cooler in the card room."

Lady Clearmont brightened immediately, her fingers tightening visibly over her stuffed reticule.

Beth hid a smile. Though she had a large heart, Lady Clearmont was a horrid chaperone, disappearing into the card room each evening within moments of their arrival. If there was no gaming, she would simply find a comfortable chair and doze away the evening until Beth asked to be taken home.

Fortunately, this all worked in Beth's favor. She found an absentee chaperone the best kind, and it was quite a good thing that Beatrice had been held up an extra two weeks. Already in the month since Beth had arrived in London, the group of men waiting for her at any gathering had steadily lessened. From twenty or so eager fortune hunters, there were now only five.

Beth eyed the group with a martial light in her eye. If she could discourage but one of them from trying to win her favor, then her evening could be considered a success.

A dapper young gentleman walked by and accidentally caught Beth's eye. She smiled and waved. He gaped, gulped, looked wildly about as if trying to find an escape before whirling on his heel and almost running in the opposite direction.

Lady Clearmont blinked. "That was Viscount Poole-Stanton!"

"Yes," Beth said, trying hard not to let her smile burst into a full-fledged grin.

Lady Clearmont turned to look at Beth. "Why is he avoiding you? He seemed quite taken at first and called nearly every day. Then he quit. So, too, did Lord Silverton, Mr. Benton-Shipley, Sir Thomas, Lord Chivers—all of them!"

"It's an odd thing, isn't it?" Beth said, shaking her head. "Gentlemen today are so undecided."

Lady Clearmont considered this. "So true! Just look at the prince. Such a sad state of affairs."

Beth lifted up on her tiptoes. "I vow, but is that Lord Beaufort going into the card room?"

"Is it? I won forty guineas from him yesterday. Perhaps he's ready for another trouncing!" She turned to go to the card room, then paused. "Do you—"

"I will be right here when you return." Beth looked at the small knot of gentlemen hovering just out of earshot. The second her chaperone left, they would descend on her like locusts. A plague, that's what they were.

"Very well. You know where to find me if you need me." Smiling, Lady Clearmont eagerly made her way to the card room.

Beth did not allow her admirers to swarm. Instead, she walked directly toward them. The group of fashionably dressed men straightened, hands going to cravats, tugging on shirt cuffs, smoothing back already smoothed hair.

"Lady Elizabeth!" the Duke of Standwich said, stepping forward with an eager bow. "How delightful you look this evening!" An older gentleman, he dyed his hair an unfortunate shade of brown, which had a tendency to turn his shirt collars an odd reddish color.

Viscount Longwood took her gloved hand and pressed a heated kiss to it. The youngest son of a destitute earl, the viscount was desperate for a wife with funds. "I was just telling the comte that you are the loveliest woman in all of London."

"And I," Comte Villiers hurried to add, "told *everyone* that you were the loveliest woman in the entire world!"

Beth suspected that the comte's tales of escaping France with his fortune intact were largely that—tales.

She glanced over her shoulder to make certain Lady Clearmont was well away before she sank into a graceful curtsy. "Y-y-you are all t-t-t-too kind. Th-th-thank you, C-C-C-Comte V-V-V-Villiers and L-L-L-Lor—"

"Indeed," Viscount Dewsbury interrupted

hastily. Nineteen years of age, he was the only one of Beth's remaining suitors who possessed any means, though the one with the least amount of address. He took her hand now and patted it in a patronizing manner. "Lady Elizabeth, there is no need for you to bother your pretty head remembering all of our names."

Beth had to bite her lip to smother a chuckle. "B-b-b-b-but I should th-th-th-thank you all f-f-f-f-or—"

"Precisely," the duke interrupted with a rather superior smirk. "Lady Elizabeth, I hope you have saved a dance for me?"

"I-I-I-I-I—"

A young matron in pink burst into view. "There you are!"

Beth gasped. "Beatrice!" She was instantly enveloped into a heavily perfumed hug. "When did you arrive in London!"

Tall and buxom and with the same honey-colored hair, Beatrice—now know as Mrs. Thistle-Bridgeton—was as well known for her jocular ways as for her rather pronounced nose. "I just arrived this evening. Your grandfather said I was to find you as soon as possible and make certain you came to no harm."

Beth smiled and began to answer, when she caught sight of her audience's rapt gaze. Oh yes. Her stutter. She managed a smile as she said, "Wh-wh-wh-wh-wh-why, Cousin B-B-B-B-Beatrice! It is so g-g-g-good to see you!"

Beatrice blinked. Once. Twice. Thrice.

Beth raised her brows meaningfully. "I-I-I have so m-m-m-m-much to tell you!"

Beatrice pasted a rather weak smile on her face. "Yes, you *do* have a lot to tell me, don't you?"

"Beatrice, h-h-have you met the D-D-D-D-Duke of St-St—"

"Oh yes!" Beatrice said hastily, sending Beth a sharp look. "I know the duke quite well." Beatrice hurried to add, "I know them all, thank you! Gentlemen, I must steal Elizabeth away. I haven't seen her in forever and we have so *much* to discuss!"

"Of course," the duke said, tucking his thumbs in his waistcoat and beaming idiotically. "Mrs. Thistle-Bridgeton, I do hope you bring Lady Elizabeth back ere long."

"Oh, you won't even know she's gone!" Beatrice took Beth's arm and laced it with her own, an amused quirk to her generous mouth. "We'll be back before Beth can say, 'Dilly'!"

Beth scarcely had time to wave a hand in farewell before she was whisked away by her determined cousin. Beatrice immediately hissed in Beth's ear, "What on earth are you doing?"

"Keeping the wolves at bay."

Beatrice choked on her laugh, pulling her cousin out of the crowd and into a small alcove designed for more private speech. "Lud, Beth! I am sorry I was late returning from Italy! The weather was—oh, never mind. What on earth made you decide to affect such an atrocious stutter?"

"Those lump skulls. I am bored to death!"

Beatrice chuckled. "Your grandfather will put a stop to this the instant he arrives."

"He won't be coming to town anytime soon. Beatrice, he is not well."

Beatrice's expression sobered. "I wondered if that was the case when he wrote to me, but then I thought perhaps he simply didn't wish to leave your stepmama."

Beth frowned. "Not leave Charlotte? Why would he not—"

"Or the house," Beatrice added hastily. "He loves Massingale House."

"So do I. As much as I've enjoyed my time in London, I would much rather be there."

"Has Lady Clearmont been so horrible?"

"Not at all! I hardly ever see her."

"How horrid! My mother-in-law—gossip-monger that she is—wrote to say you'd arrived and were rumored to possess a dowry unlike any other. I daresay you've had admirers in droves!"

"*Had* admirers in droves," Beth said, smiling. "I have frightened them all off but these last few. No matter how much money one might have, it is quite lowering to think one might have to face th-th-th-this over the br-br-br-br-breakfast table every m-m-m-m-morning for the rest of your l-l-l-l-life."

Beatrice laughed merrily. "I can barely stand it this minute! What made you think of such a devious plan?"

"Desperation. Grandfather thinks I should marry now, before he's—" Beth could not say the words.

Beatrice sobered instantly. "Beth, I am so sorry."

"So am I. I promised him I would have one season. After that, he has promised never again to mention my leaving him for London."

"I see. He hopes you'll meet someone?"

"Of course. I can't have anyone running to Grandfather with an offer for my hand, at least not a man he might countenance. If he found someone he thought would be suitable, he'd insist I marry despite his promise. I know he would."

"You *are* in a fix! I hope your plan works."

Beth shrugged. "If it ceases to work, I shall simply develop another bad habit. And then another and yet another until not even you will be able to stand my presence."

Beatrice laughed. "Harry is going to love hearing about this. May I tell him?"

"Yes, but no one else." Beth smiled at her cousin, a wistful light in her eyes. "How is Harry?"

Beatrice's cheeks stained pink, a pleased smile softening the effect of her protuberant nose. "Unfashionable as it is, I am mad about my own husband. And he, me. It has been that way since the beginning, and only gets worse each passing year."

"Maybe one day I will be so fortunate."

Beatrice gave her an odd look. "It will happen, Beth. When you least expect it."

"Perhaps. But for now, I am well protected by my st-st-st—"

"Enough!" Beatrice giggled. "Pray do not do that when we are alone. I shall have to strangle you otherwise. Ah, Beth! You are such a minx! Your stutter should keep any sane man from falling in love with you." Beatrice's eyes narrowed thoughtfully. "The question is, will it keep *you* from falling in love with one of *them*?"

"Me? I am far too pragmatic to ever—"

"May I have this dance?" came a deep masculine voice from behind Beth.

She started to answer, but caught sight of Beatrice's face. Her cousin stood, mouth open, eyes wide.

Beth turned her head . . . and found herself looking up into the face of the most incredibly handsome man. He was quite tall, his shoulders broad, but it was his face that sent a flush straight through her. Black hair spilled over his forehead, his jaw firm, his mouth masculine and yet sensual. His eyes called the most attention; they were the palest green, thickly lashed, and wickedly beautiful.

Her heart thudded, her palms grew damp, and her stomach tightened in the most irksome way. Her entire body felt leaden. What on earth was the matter with her? Had she eaten something ill for dinner that evening? Perchance a scallop, for they never failed to make her feel poorly.

Unaware his effect was being explained away by a shellfish, the man smiled, his eyes sparkling down at her with intimate humor. "I believe I have forgotten to introduce myself. Allow me." He bowed. "I am Viscount Westerville."

"Ah!" Beatrice said, breaking into movement as if she'd been shoved from behind. "Westerville! Rochester's ba—" Color flooded her cheeks. "I mean—"

"Yes," the viscount said smoothly. He bowed, his gaze still riveted on Beth.

Before she knew what he was about, he had captured her hand and brought it to his lips, pressing a kiss to her fingers. Heat shot up her arm and warmed her to her toes.

"Well, Lady Elizabeth?" he asked, his breath brushing her hand. "Shall we dance?"

Chapter 3

There are many recipes for boot blacking, some of which include such unlikely ingredients as bat's blood extract, and dust from a corpse. I use a more simple recipe; one part candle wax to two parts champagne. When heated to the perfect temperature and rubbed on the boot with vigor, it rarely fails to leave a gloss of unprecedented brightness. And one is, of course, spared the necessity of locating a suitably dusty corpse. There are times when simplicity makes a decision for you.

A Compleat Guide for
Being a Most Proper Butler
by Richard Robert Reeves

A mere half hour earlier the front door of the Smythe-Singleton's residence had been opened by the butler. Beltson would later tell the housekeeper that of all the guests who had traversed the hallway that evening, the man who entered—a viscount—was by far the most interesting. Dressed head to foot in unrelenting black, the visitor carried himself with a coolness and self-possession that made him instantly recognizable as a man of distinction and character.

Better yet was the brilliant emerald that burned in the man's cravat, a jewel offset by the lord's pale green eyes and black hair. The housekeeper had shivered when she'd heard of the viscount's coloring, for she said such a sight must have sent Mr. Beltson's hair on end. Did he not think perhaps 'twas the devil himself he was welcoming?

The butler didn't answer, for the housekeeper had a horrid habit of repeating every word he uttered, though there *had* been a moment when he'd first opened the door that had given him pause. The expression on the gentleman's face had been one of such unrelenting and grim anger that Mr. Beltson had actually taken a step back.

The look had been quickly replaced with a more urbane one, and the gentleman soon identified as a member of the ton, but a strong sense of unease remained with Mr. Beltson. He was inordinately glad that the newly minted Viscount Westerville had not intended the look for him.

Christian would have found the butler's thoughts rather appropriate. He was here for one thing and one thing only—to locate the Duke of Massingale's granddaughter. He would find this Lady Elizabeth, gain an introduction, and through her win entry into his enemy's house.

It was a simple plan, and in Christian's experience as a highwayman, the simple plans delivered the best prizes. It took him less than two minutes after entering the ball to find his quarry.

It was well known that Lady Elizabeth was long of tooth; there had been much speculation about her before her arrival in London. However, whatever the lady's age, her appearance must not be as spinsterish as he'd hoped; rumor had it that she was taking the town by storm.

He knew a little of her appearance already. The groom he'd hired to watch her every move had become almost poetic in his description of her face and form, which was to be expected. The man was posturing for the gold coin he was supposed to be earning. It was a damned pity Lady Elizabeth was attractive, because now not only was every gazetted fortune hunter panting over her dowry, but every romantic fool in town would be following her about, writing the most horrid poetry in her name.

It was annoying to have to court such a public figure, and it would have suited his purposes far more had she been plump, short, and sadly freckled.

Christian smoothed his cuffs as he made his way into the ballroom, pausing to ask the first male he encountered as to Lady Elizabeth's whereabouts. As Christian anticipated, the fool knew exactly where she was to be found.

Lady Elizabeth stood halfway between the refreshment table and the terrace doors, surprisingly unfettered by suitors. Christian's gaze narrowed on her as he drew closer. From behind, her form hinted at the loveliness Christian's bloody groom had suggested; a vision of golden hair and sensual curves gowned in blue silk and cream lace. Her figure was delicate and well-rounded; her hair piled upon her head in delicious thick, golden curls.

It was a pity such a beauty was so closely related to his enemy, as she would have been worth a chase on her own merits. But life was never fair.

As he neared, Lady Elizabeth laughed at something her companion said. He slowed a bit, his gaze narrowing as he attempted to read her gestures, her movements. From his years estimating who would be a good mark and who would not, Christian had developed the ability to ascertain a few things from the way people moved, the way they spoke, how they gestured.

Lady Elizabeth was not as demure as one might expect. There was something very sensual about her posture, the way she threw back her head when she laughed, the manner in which she flicked her hand as if impatient with life.

She was a woman who craved something *more*. He recognized that aspect of her character at once, and to his chagrin, something deep within him responded in kind.

Christian's gaze narrowed. She was not what he had expected at all. His spies had informed him that she was bookish, not given to any sort of lively pursuits other than riding about the estates and being her grandfather's sole companion. He'd originally thought she would be a shy, retiring sort of woman who had dutifully given up her youth to keep her elderly relative company. Such a self-deprecating martyr would be an easy woman to charm.

It had not occurred to Christian that she might also be beautiful, sensual, and vivacious.

Whatever she was, she was now within arm's length. He waited for a pause in the conversation, and then at first opportunity said in a low voice, "May I have this dance?"

Lady Elizabeth turned, her gown fluttering about her, her startled gaze lifted to his. It was then that it happened; a jolt of pure, animal attraction hit Christian so hard, his heart leaped in his chest.

He could only stare. As he'd been told, she was beautiful, but nothing had prepared him for the reality of that beauty, of the smoldering passion that lit her large, brown eyes, of the tempting curve of her plump lips, of the sensual line of her cheek and throat. She was passion and pureness, temptation and desire, acumen and sensuality, all wrapped into one. As if she knew his thoughts, her lips framed into an entrancingly rich pout, one he instantly wished to kiss away.

Christian had to force himself not to reach out and yank her to him right there in the center of the ballroom. It was then that the truth hit him: he'd met the one woman he could never touch. Never give in to. Never admit into his life or his heart. The mysterious Lady Elizabeth was the granddaughter of Christian's most hated enemy, and he was not about to forget, no matter how his traitorous body answered to her mere presence.

Bloody hell, what was this? Never, in years of secret assignations and heated flirting with seductive and wealthy ladies in plush carriages, had Christian experienced such an immediate reaction.

She must have felt something, too, for she blinked rapidly, but said nothing at all, her eyes wide, something flickering deep in her dark eyes. Recognition, perhaps.

And that was exactly what it was, an odd sort of recognition. Almost as if he'd met her before, though that was impossible. He'd have never forgotten such a woman, the rich gold of her hair, or the entrancing curve of her cheek. As he looked at her, his reaction increased and intensified until he was caught in a flash of pure, hot lust.

What in the hell was wrong with him? This was no usual lady of the ton to be wooed to bed and then forgotten. No, this was the granddaughter of his greatest enemy.

Perhaps that was why his emotions were so tightly woven. Yes, it had to be that. Relieved, he collected himself and bowed. "I believe I have forgotten to introduce myself. Allow me. I am Viscount Westerville."

"Ah!" Lady Elizabeth's companion said, suddenly coming to life. Though she was a bit horse-faced, her eyes nonetheless shone with intelligence. "Westerville! Rochester's ba—" Her cheeks flushed.

"Yes," he said, not the least put out that his parentage was apparently in some question. He had no secrets. Not about that, at least. Society suspected that his father had fabricated the marriage certificate and witness that had declared Christian and his brother the legal heirs. They were correct, though Christian was not about to inform anyone of that. His father had done nothing for his children; it seemed only fitting that the old bastard should at least attempt to make amends while on his deathbed.

But now was not the time to dwell on his childhood. Christian bowed to the lady before him, his gaze still caught by her winsome face. He took her gloved hand and brushed his lips over it, feeling the heat of her skin through the soft material. A heady fragrance broke over him as he did so. She smelled of lilac and rose; rich scents, sensual scents. His body tightened in reaction, and it took all his composure to be able to say with some equanimity, "Well, Lady Elizabeth? Shall we dance?"

Her fingers tightened over his instantly, almost as if she feared he might turn and leave. But then Lady Elizabeth paused, shook her head slightly, and pulled her hand free. "No, thank you."

He lifted his brows. "No? Are you certain?"

The lady's mouth curved into a faint smile and she said in a smooth, rich voice, "We have not been properly introduced. Therefore, I cannot dance with you."

Christian had the impression that though she smiled, she had somehow moved out of his reach, hiding herself behind a wall of resolution. He forced his own smile to remain in place, though it was the last thing he felt like doing.

The chit was hiding behind convention. That

was a challenge, indeed. He risked a glance at the lady's companion and found the woman regarding Lady Elizabeth with an astonished air, as if she could not quite believe the words she'd just heard.

Christian hid a smile. Perhaps the lady was not usually such a high stickler? Well, he could play at that game.

He crossed his arms over his chest and looked down at her, his brows lifted slightly. "No, my lady. We have not been properly introduced. We are, in fact, *illicit* strangers." He let his voice linger over the word, caressing with seductive intent.

She looked down, her long lashes resting on cheeks suddenly blooming with color.

"My lord," the chaperone said sharply, her fan fluttering so fast it appeared it might fly from her fingers, "it is traditional to wait for an introduction from a third party before asking a lady to dance."

"Yes, but I didn't think the lady was the type of woman to insist on such a thing."

That brought Elizabeth's eyes back to his face. "Just what type of woman do you think I am?"

"One that won't tolerate boredom."

That seemed to both please and irritate her at one and the same time. He was amused, watching the conflicting emotions warring with each other. Finally, she shook her head with a bit of regret. "My lord, you don't know me at all."

"Uhm, Beth?" her companion said, an oddly warning note in her voice.

Lady Elizabeth faced her companion. "Yes?"

The lady glanced from Elizabeth to Christian, then back. "You, ah . . . You have forgotten something."

Lady Elizabeth's brows drew together. "What?"

The chaperone did a most curious thing—she tapped her lips with a finger.

Lady Elizabeth frowned. "Wha— *oh!* That. I quite forgot." She bit her lip and sent Christian a quick glance before looking away.

Christian had to force himself not to reach out to run a finger over her bottom lip where her teeth were gently worrying the tender morsel. Damn, but the woman's mouth was made for passion. "Pardon me, my lady. What exactly did you forget? Perhaps I could be of assistance in locating whatever you've lost."

Lady Elizabeth's friend cleared her throat. "It's nothing, really. Lady Elizabeth is supposed to guard her voice carefully this evening in case she, ah, sings later"—the woman waved her hand vaguely—"or . . . something."

"Sings? Here? At the ball?"

An awkward silence met this.

Christian frowned even as he admired the fresh line of her cheek, the graceful curve of her neck. Just looking at her was a delight. A pity her grandfather was a villain.

His jaw tightened. *That* was what he needed to remember—the truth about the Duke of Massingale and how the man had sent Christian's mother to a horrid death in a damp cell. The thought of his mother alone and dying of the fever, stripped of her possessions and dignity, would keep at bay any attraction he might feel for the woman before him.

Elizabeth chose that moment to peep at him through her lashes. Humor glimmered in her gaze, as did something else . . . something sensual and yet innocent. A faint stirring of regret made Christian wonder if perhaps he was doing the right thing.

Bloody hell, what was he thinking? Of *course* he was doing the right thing—hadn't he planned this for years? Life had left him with no recourse. She was his entryway, the key to the mystery of his mother's death. But first he had to alter his plans. No longer was he seducing a secluded innocent, but instead a beautiful woman besieged by suitors.

He glanced around and wondered why none of them was present now. Whatever the reason, Christian knew they were there, biding their time. The woman before him was too lovely, and too wealthy, to be left alone. He would have to stand out from the hordes of her admirers. The best thing he could do was be different, intriguing, and, whenever possible, worth pursuing himself.

He tilted his head to one side, meeting her gaze directly. "Some crave the safety of boredom while others crave the bravery of adventure. Which are you, Lady Elizabeth? A retiring maid who longs for safety? Or a woman of chance and mystery?"

Beth bit her lip as the warm words floated over her, sending odd shivers across her. One would never call the man before her safe or boring. No, he was far more polished than the men she'd met so far, and definitely more intelligent. She was drawn to him, challenged by him in some way.

"Well?" he said softly, flashing a breathtakingly lopsided grin. "Which are you?"

Beth allowed herself to smile—a little. "My lord, what I am or am not is n-n-none of your concern."

His gaze flickered just a bit at her stutter and she cringed inwardly. It was sad, but she had no choice; thank heavens Beatrice had caught Beth's earlier error when she'd forgotten to use it.

If she wished her scheme to work, she could not falter, at least not this early in the game. She'd already managed to frighten off a number of suitors, but there were several more who needed to go, a few of them amazingly persistent.

Still . . . she flashed a glance at the man looking down at her and had to swallow a definite pinch of regret. She did not mind appearing incapable of speech with the dunderheads who'd so far offered to woo her, but she did not wish to be so encumbered in front of this man. She had things to say, quips to make, all sorts of witty comments that bubbled to her lips the second he uttered one of his caustic witticisms.

Beatrice must have caught Beth's regret, for she said quickly, "Beth, don't even think—" She snapped her feathered fan closed with a great display of firmness. "My lord, as Lady Elizabeth's chaperone, I fear I must cut this conversation until the proper introductions have been performed." With that, she gave the man a regal nod, took

Beth by the elbow, and hauled her toward the refreshment tables.

"Really, Beth!" Beatrice muttered. "You owe me for that little maneuver. Had I not troubled myself, you would have ruined your own scheme."

"I would not have," Beth protested, though her own voice rang hollowly in her ears. She glanced over her shoulder. The viscount was standing as they'd left him, one hand negligently on his hip, his eyes on her, a glimmer of humor touching his sensual mouth.

Hesitantly, Beth returned his smile.

His reaction was instantaneous; his entire face lit with an answering grin. Beth's breath caught at the warmth of it. What was it about this man that made him so different from every other man in the room? He was so . . . present. So powerful. Every inch of him emanated purpose, capability, and a barely contained passion. He was arrogant and impetuous, proud and unrepentant. She could read all of that and more in his expression, and she found herself fascinated as never before.

Beatrice pulled Beth to the other side of the refreshment table. "Safe at last!" Beatrice glanced back the way they'd come. "Good. Lady Cumberland is approaching him now and will soon have him locked in conversation. She's not one to let a handsome rake out of her sight once she's captured him, so we needn't fear he'll follow us."

Beth stood on tiptoe. Beatrice was right; Lady Cumberland was indeed talking to Westerville, her hand laid possessively on his arm. "What is she doing, leaning against him like that?"

"She leans against every man she talks to."

"I know. It's just that—oh! If her décolletage was any lower, she'd spill out." Beth scowled. "How can she display herself in such a way? I would never—"

"Good God," Beatrice said, her voice stunned. "You cannot be attracted to that man!"

Beth reluctantly tore her gaze from the viscount. "Attracted? Who said anything about attracted?"

"I can see it in your face. You had best leave that stone unturned. Westerville may be a viscount, but his position is very smoky, and it is said that he has not truly secured the fortune, either. In fact, there are rumors that he—" Beatrice pressed her mouth in a firm line. "Never mind."

"What rumors?"

"Nothing. It's nothing at all. I-I was just mumbling off the top of my head."

"You might as well tell me all you know now, for I'll wheedle it out of you before tomorrow, anyway. You never could keep a secret."

Beatrice sighed. "I know, I know! But only if you'll promise me you are not attracted to that man. Your grandfather would kill me."

"I am not attracted to Lord Westerville." It was more than attraction. It was a reckoning of some sort. "As for Grandfather, it is none of his concern what I do."

Beatrice sent Beth a flat stare.

Beth wished her cousin didn't know Grandfather quite so well. "Oh, very well. Grandfather *would* be concerned." Beth glanced back at the viscount and wondered if this was how Grandfather had felt upon seeing his future wife that first time.

The thought sent her heart thundering. She might be intrigued, but she was *not* in love, which was what Grandfather had been.

"What a coil," Beatrice said, shaking her head. "Beth, there is something between the two of you. Even I felt it, and I wasn't trying to feel anything, especially not *that*."

Beth glanced across the table toward the viscount. He'd bent down to listen to something Lady Cumberland had to say, her red curls a perfect foil for his black hair.

Beth's heart ached inexplicably. Perhaps what she felt was a simple physical reaction. She watched him a moment more, resentment rising. Shouldn't she at least investigate this odd feeling? Make certain it was nothing more than a physical attraction?

"Beth, please don't do anything rash."

Beth blinked at her cousin. "What makes you think I'm going to do anything at all?"

"I have known you since you were born and I can see from your expression that you've some scheme in mind. That's the same expression you wore that time you convinced me to stand watch so you could steal one of your grandfather's new geldings—"

"Borrow," Beth said, grinning a little. "We were going to return the horse, weren't we? Technically, that is not stealing."

"Grandfather didn't see it as 'borrowing.' Especially after that wild horse threw you. Lud, but

I just knew you were quite dead. You're lucky you didn't hit your head upon a rock. And your grandfather—" Beatrice shivered.

"He's always upset about something."

"My point exactly! I see enough of his irritation as it is. I have no wish to experience more." Beatrice met Beth's gaze. "Whatever you are thinking, I want your word you will forget about it this very instant."

Beth almost refused. But then she caught sight of the arrogant Comte Villiers bearing down on them. If she did not maintain her pretense, she could very well end up shackled to a man like the comte. The thought was sobering, to say the last.

She gave one last, regretful glance at the handsome viscount. From across the room, his gaze locked with hers over Lady Cumberland's head.

It was the hardest thing Beth had ever done, but she fought the very real impulse to just throw convention to the winds and walk toward him. Gathering her errant thoughts, she turned away, presenting him with her shoulder as she managed a smile for her cousin. "Very well. I promise to have nothing more to do with the viscount."

Beatrice shook her head, a comical expression of dismay on her face as she glanced at the viscount herself. "The problem is that I don't really blame you. He is quite handsome, and the fact that they say he's a—" Beatrice sent a quick glance at Beth, then looked away.

"A what?"

Beatrice sighed. "Oh, you are right; you would

get it out of me sooner or later anyway. Before he inherited his title, Westerville was a lost soul of some sort, wandering about. His mother died in gaol, accused of treason, and his father was the Earl of Rochester, though the man never claimed him. Even more shocking, upon his deathbed, the earl suddenly *remembered* that he'd really married Westerville's mother and produced two now-legitimate children."

"Surely no one believes such a story!"

"No one has been able to disprove it. The earl produced documents and a witness, even a priest who swears he performed the ceremony."

"No!"

"Oh yes! What's even more fascinating, though, is where the viscount spent the years when he was not a viscount." Beatrice's voice lowered to a delicious level. "They say he was a highwayman!"

"What?" Beth looked at Westerville. He was talking to yet another woman, this one a brunette with sapphires sparkling in her hair. He was bent low to catch her words over the music, his dark hair falling over his brow. Though he was quite easily the most fashionably dressed man in the room, there was still an air about him . . . something raw and untamed. She shivered. "I could see him as a highwayman."

Beatrice nodded. "So could I. They also say— oh, blast! There is the comte. Pray stutter to your utmost ability. I cannot bear to be near that man!"

Beth grimaced. "He is a pompous ass."

"And in dire need of a wealthy wife. Perhaps

you should find a twitch to go with your stutter."

"I would fall upon the floor in a fit if I thought it might do some good. The man is a menace."

The comte was upon them before Beatrice could respond. Beth spent the next several moments stuttering out answers and trying not to giggle at Beatrice's broad hints to the man that Beth's stutter was the very *least* of her problems.

During this time, it took quite a bit of Beth's self-possession not to look in the viscount's direction. She had to acknowledge that the man was a danger, but one easily avoided.

Finally, Lady Clearmont appeared from the card room, her reticule noticeably thinner as she shooed away the comte. Beth was more than ready to leave. She made arrangements to meet Beatrice the next morning and was soon in Lady Clearmont's carriage.

Soon enough, she and Lady Clearmont arrived at the Massingale London House, where Beth bid Her Ladyship a good night before making her way to her bedchamber. There she undressed with haste, brushed her hair, pulled on her night rail, slid between the cool sheets, and blew out the candles. Only then, in the total darkness, did Beth allow herself to contemplate in uninterrupted splendor the devastating effect of a pair of thickly lashed green eyes and a charmingly lopsided smile.

Chapter 4

With care, a good servant can be right in most things, a feat most masters and mistresses would find difficult to match.

A Compleat Guide for
Being a Most Proper Butler
by Richard Robert Reeves

*H*ours later, Christian returned home quite content with the evening's work. He'd been very aware of the lady's eyes on him throughout the evening. One thing he knew about human nature was that people coveted what other people admired. And so, after Lady Elizabeth's chaperone had swept her to safety, Christian made certain she witnessed him flirting with a number of other women. He didn't care who they were—tall or short, fat or thin, handsome or comely—none of them could hold a candle to Elizabeth, a fact he found far too disturbing.

He met Reeves in the entry upon his arrival. Christian allowed the butler to remove his coat. "Good evening, Reeves!"

"It is well after midnight, my lord. 'Good morning' would be more appropriate."

"It is almost three, to be exact. So good morning, 'tis."

Reeves handed the coat to a waiting footman and absently watched the man leave. As soon as the hallway was clear, Reeves turned back to Christian. "Will you retire at once, my lord? Or do you require some nourishment to assist you in recovering from your debauchery?"

Christian grinned. "I am not a bit hungry and I am far from sleepy. I believe I shall have a glass of port."

"You have a constitution of iron, my lord," the butler said in a dry voice.

"Thank you." He turned on his heel and entered the library. "Any word from Willie?"

"Yes, my lord. There is a note on your desk."

"Excellent." Christian crossed to the desk. He picked up the missive and ripped it open.

Reeves followed closely, watching in respectful silence while Christian read.

"Good!" Christian tossed the note on a side table. He caught Reeves's expression.

"I am sorry, my lord. I am just a bit astonished Master William can pen a letter."

"I taught him. Quite a useful fellow is Willie."

"I am certain, my lord."

"He arrives tomorrow and with something of

note." Christian nodded thoughtfully. "Our suspicions seem to have borne fruit."

Reeves walked to the fireplace where a fire was already laid out. He removed the tinderbox from the mantel, and within moments, flames licked the new wood, a faint heat permeating the room.

As soon as the flue had been properly adjusted, the butler crossed to the sideboard and poured a measure of port into a glass, then brought it to Christian.

Christian gratefully took the glass, sank into a chair by the fireplace, and took a long drink. The amber liquid burned pleasantly. "This is excellent stock. Almost as good as a shipment I once stole from an Italian count outside Bath."

"Please, my lord. Do not mention those times."

Christian flashed a grin. "I shall try not to."

"Thank you, my lord. Just where is this port that you, ah, *procured*?"

"I drank it."

Reeves looked offended. "By yourself?"

Christian considered this. "Well, yes. Most of it."

Reeves sighed. "There are times when you are very much like your father."

Christian's good humor fled. "I will thank you not to mention him. At least not until I've had time to put a bottle or two of this behind me."

The butler bowed and wisely made no further comment. Christian's jaw ached and he realized he was clenching his teeth. His father, the late Earl of Rochester, had never acknowledged either

Christian or his twin brother. Oh, he'd sent the requisite stipend to cover expenses, but that was all.

Worse, when Mother had been falsely imprisoned, Christian and his brother had written their father begging him to intervene; there had been no answer. Eventually, when they had been reduced to rags, their tutor had sold the two boys to a press gang. Tristan had assisted his younger twin brother in escaping, but had not been so fortunate himself. Tristan had ended up consigned to sea. Eventually, after enduring beatings and worse, he'd come to love his new life at sea, though not for many painful years.

Christian, meanwhile, had been left truly alone. Only ten and frightened beyond reason, he had slowly made his way to London. It had taken weeks and he'd nearly starved to death in the process, until he'd learned the trick to taking what he needed. But when he arrived at the prison, he discovered his mother had died only days before, a victim to a horrid fever caused by her squalid living conditions. Alone, living in the streets, Christian had been forced to fight every day in an effort to merely survive to the next.

Odd as it was, even in those desperate hours, every night he'd dreamed of Father arriving in time to save him, to save his brother, and especially to save Mother. Morning after morning, he'd awakened to find his dreams just that— dreams and nothing more.

Christian caught the butler's gaze now. "Never again compare me to my father. I will not be insulted in my own house."

Reeves sighed deeply. "I can understand why you would harbor ill feelings toward your father, but he did care for you and your brother, in his way."

"His way is too little, too late."

"Very true, my lord. Your father was not a responsible parent in many aspects. Nor was he as caring as he should have been. But you cannot hold him responsible for your mother's death. He was out of the country and was unaware of her predicament."

"Had he cared, he would have made certain she could reach him. That *we* could reach him."

"The late earl had many, many faults. I cannot defend him as a parent, for he failed so miserably. However, he *did* know what was due his title and name. I think you should learn the same. It will help you secure the fortune from the trustees."

"I have already met the trustees, and they were duly impressed with my elegant manner and tonnish ways," Christian said a bit bitterly. "They are a pack of fools, the lot of them, impressed with the fold of one's cravat over one's character. Providing I do not make a total cake of myself, they will approve the release of the fortune."

"I hope you are right, my lord. I fear your assessment of the trustees is painfully accurate. Your father's cronies were not, perhaps, the best choice to oversee the disbursement of his funds."

Yet another example of Father's innate selfishness, to foist such silly conditions upon his will. The titles were Tristan's and his to keep no matter what, but the fortunes were tied up upon the approval of the trustees.

It irked Christian to have to deal with such weak men. Not a one of them would have lived more than a day had they been forced to take care of themselves. Christian, on the other hand, had honed his abilities. He had also developed a hard shell where his heart had once been. In a way, his father had done him a favor by staying away. Life was a hard teacher, but a thorough one.

Christian supposed he should be thankful for Father's unexpected change of heart. At an advanced age, the late earl had married a young woman in the hopes of producing some heirs, but no issue was forthcoming. The thought of seeing his title and funds dispensed to distant relatives had been too much for the man's overly stiff pride, so he'd deftly fabricated documents and found a "witness" to attest to a supposedly secret marriage between him and Christian's mother. In this way, the earl had secured the family lineage through the children he'd so far successfully ignored—his illegitimate sons.

However, as both boys had been left unattended since the delicate age of ten, the earl feared that they did not possess the social skills necessary to maintain a place in society without garnering the ridicule of the ton. And that was something the earl would not countenance. So Reeves, the earl's most loyal servant, was sent with a packet full of money and instructions to civilize Christian and his brother.

Christian hated the trustees and despised being

forced to become a part of their hypocrisy. Unfortunately, he needed his father's fortune, and not just for himself. His brother, Tristan, was counting on him as well.

As the oldest son, Tristan had inherited Father's title but none of the trustees would have approved Tristan's choice of wife. By virtue of the circumstances of her first husband's death, Prudence had been involved in a horrid scandal that had precluded her from ever being considered an acceptable countess.

Thus, Tristan had handed the fortune on to Christian, secure in the belief that his brother would win it for them both. This added responsibility had put quite a crimp in Christian's plans. Now he was forced to play by societal rules.

Reeves seemed to catch Christian's thinking, for he smiled slightly. "Never have I seen a man more happy to give up a fortune than your brother."

"I promised to fund his home for injured sailors. I cannot let him down." Christian managed a faint smile. "It was the least I could do. I would have given him more had he allowed it."

"He was quite happy at the way things turned out." The butler paused a moment. "Perhaps you'll find a Lady Prudence of your own, my lord. That would be quite the thing indeed."

The last thing Christian wanted or needed was a wife. He'd lived an unencumbered life, drifting from inn to inn, taking what he needed to survive and no more. The moment things became complicated, he moved on. As soon as he was done here and had exacted his revenge, he would leave once more.

Perhaps he would ride to Scotland with his servant, Willie, to see the countryside there, swords drawn in the dark of night, blood quickening in excitement. Christian rubbed his fingers together where they itched for the smooth cool feel of his rapier.

Soon. Once he was finished here . . . He looked at his glass. "Thank you for the port, Reeves. It was just the thing."

"I took the liberty of having some of the late earl's carefully guarded stock brought here, for your pleasure. Your brother insisted on it."

Christian looked at his glass. His brother was even now residing in a snug cottage on the cliff overlooking the seas in Dover, his wife at his side. Christian had faced enough aching loneliness to appreciate the need for companionship.

But love? True love? As wretched as loneliness could be, it was nothing compared to the pain of betrayal. He'd seen with his own eyes what "love" did to a person—how it built hopes that were rarely, if ever, realized. Falling in love meant being weak, vulnerable to the whims of another. He'd watched his beautiful, confident, strong mother become frail and maudlin, watched her allow events to manipulate her until she was stripped of everything, thrown into jail, branded a traitor.

Christian took a slow sip of port. He would be damned if he ever let anyone get close enough to make him vulnerable.

Reeves looked at the clock as it chimed. "I fear it is getting late. Shall I have your bed turned down?"

"In a moment."

"Of course, my lord."

Christian took another drink. "Reeves, you are the best of all butlers."

"You sound as though you've experienced quite a few, my lord. May I ask how that is, considering that you once resided in an inn?"

Christian grinned, "Not all of the women in those coaches were content with a mere kiss. I daresay I've been in half the boudoirs in London."

Reeves looked pointedly at the ceiling.

"What is it?"

"Nothing, my lord. You said you did not wish me to state when you say things that remind me of your father, so—"

"Very well," Christian snapped. He shifted restlessly, rubbing his fingers together yet again.

"Yes, my lord." Reeves made his way to the sidebar again, this time returning with a small wooden box. He opened it to reveal several thin, rolled cigars. "My lord? I procured these this morning while at the market."

Christian selected a cigar, a fragrant scent wafting up as he rolled it between his fingers. "Thank you for reading my mind once again."

"That is not a very difficult feat when one realizes your mind possesses such magnificent thoughts as 'I need a drink,' 'A good cigar would be nice,' and 'I wonder if Lady Bertram is wearing that silk chemise trimmed with little flowers.'"

Christian slowly turned his gaze on the butler. "I beg your pardon? What was that last one?"

Reeves pursed his lips. "The last what, my lord?"

"The last statement you made."

"After 'A good cigar would be nice'?"

"Yes," Christian said grimly.

"Hm. Let me see. I believe I said, 'I wonder if Lady Bertram is wearing that silk chemise with the little flowers.'"

"How do you know about Lady Bertram?"

Reeves reached into his coat and produced a small, folded swath of silk. "Her Ladyship's chemise. It has her name monogrammed upon the hem. I found it beneath the seat of your carriage and had it washed. I thought perhaps you might wish to return it when, of course, Lord Bertram is once again out of town."

Christian took the chemise and tossed it onto the table beside him. "Thank you, Reeves," he said dryly. "I appreciate your efforts."

"It was nothing, my lord. May I ask if you succeeded in your efforts this evening?"

"Perfectly." Christian looked into his glass, noting the firelight sparkling on the amber liquid. "When I find the information I seek . . . it will be my finest hour."

"Yes, it does add a certain panache to one's life, does it not, seducing an innocent woman?"

Christian choked on the port.

Reeves stepped forward and delivered a solid thwack on Christian's back.

"Ouch!" Christian rubbed his back, glaring at Reeves.

Reeves picked up the decanter he'd left on the small table and calmly returned it to the sideboard. "I was merely attempting to clear your mind a bit, my lord."

"Clear my mind? Why would you think I need such a thing?"

Reeves raised his brows.

"I don't need your help." Christian held his cigar between his teeth, though he made no move to light it. "For the love of Zeus, Reeves, if you've something to say, just say it."

Reeves sniffed. "There is no need for such a tone, my lord."

Christian scowled.

"Do not worry, my lord. I shall keep my ruminations to myself, as befitting a man of my station. Far be it from me to infringe upon Your Lordship's existence with meaningless comments that you obviously do not wish to hear."

Christian cocked a brow at the butler. "Are you done?"

Reeves pursed his lips. "No."

"I didn't think so. What is it that has you in such a lather?"

The butler sighed heavily. "Very well, my lord. But only because you insist—"

Christian snorted.

"—it is simply this. I cannot decide which I dislike more, your plan to seduce a virgin or"—Reeves closed his eyes and turned away—"that waistcoat."

"What's wrong with my waistcoat? Black silk is— Hold one moment. I have no plans to seduce a virgin!"

"Ah, what a relief! I must have misheard you, then. In the coach on the way here, I thought you said you were going to attempt to ingratiate yourself with Lady Elizabeth, the Duke of Massingale's granddaughter. I am quite sorry, my lord. My hearing is not as good as it once—"

"I *am* going to ingratiate myself with Lady Elizabeth, as you so succinctly put it. But that does not qualify as a seduction."

Reeves appeared perplexed. "Is this the same Lady Elizabeth just entering society this season?"

"Yes, but do not think she's a chit of seventeen. She's twenty-five. Her uncle died the year she was to come out, and her entry into society was delayed."

Reeves met his gaze steadily.

Christian set down his glass. "Do not look at me like that. She is no green girl. In fact, she is the most self-assured woman I've yet to meet."

"Indeed?"

"Indeed. Not that it matters, because I have no intentions of actually seducing anyone." Not unless he had to. He glanced back at Reeves. "I am only going to pretend to be her suitor."

"What if Lady Elizabeth succumbs to your pretend blandishments?"

"She won't; she has a dragon-faced cousin standing guard. My lady's virtue is well protected. Even from me."

"I am glad the lady's grandfather understands the dangers involved in launching a delicate young lady in a town where there are so many"— Reeves's gaze flickered over Christian—"wolves."

Christian quirked a grin. "Are you calling me a wolf, Reeves?"

"I wouldn't dare, my lord. It would be presumptuous."

"That has never stopped you before." Christian eyed the butler for a long moment, and then sighed. "I suppose I should tell you my plan lest you think worse of me than you already do, if that is possible."

"Oh, it is possible," Reeves said, bringing the decanter to Christian's chair to refill the glass, "though highly unlikely."

"Thank you," Christian snapped.

"You're welcome, my lord. If you find honesty too taxing, I can, of course, continue to gather information through my usual means."

"Usual means?"

"Bits of information you drop, actions reported by the other servants who witness your movements, eavesdropping."

"*You* eavesdrop?"

"Not I, my lord," Reeves said, clearly offended. "The footmen."

Christian took the cigar out of his mouth. "The footmen eavesdrop."

"They all do, my lord. I even did it myself, when I was a footman, though that was years and years ago."

"Now that you're a butler, I suppose you leave such odious work to your underlings."

Reeves bowed. "You are indeed quick, my lord."

"Thank you," Christian said with a sardonic glint. He shook his head. "You are incorrigible. I do not know how my father stood to have you about."

"Oh, that was quite simple, my lord. I have a wretched memory. Your father would dismiss me quite frequently but, alas, I always forgot to pack. Within a day or two, he would be back in good fettle and glad to have me about. I do have a way with providing the little luxuries, you know. His Lordship found that very comforting."

Christian looked at the unlit cigar. "Is that what this is all about, the port and the cigar? An attempt to become irreplaceable?"

"Yes," Reeves said in an apologetic tone.

Christian had to laugh. "You are a complete hand, Reeves."

"Thank you, my lord. Coming from a onetime highwayman, that is quite a compliment indeed." Reeves cleared his throat. "Now, my lord. About your plan?"

"Ah yes." Christian stood and crossed to the desk. He opened the top drawer. "It is quite simple. As you already know, my mother died in Newgate prison."

"I am aware of that sad fact, my lord. Your brother explained what happened to the two of you when you were but ten—how your mother was thrown into gaol, accused of treason."

"Yes. For a while, Tristan and I were together, but then—" Memories of that day crept to the fore—of the cold hard earth that had broken his fall from the inn window. Of the sound of Tristan's cry as he'd attempted to fight his way to freedom and failed. Then, later, not knowing his brother's fate, of the drenched and freezing nights during the frantic trip to London to find Mother. And on reaching London—

Christian closed his eyes and refused to listen to the painful echoes of his past. Slowly, the memories faded. He took a deep breath and opened his eyes.

Reeves quietly regarded him from across the room. "I am sorry, my lord."

"It's nothing," Christian said shortly, embarrassed. He pulled an old box from the drawer and set it on the desk. "My brother and I were sold by our tutor, who had an addiction to gaming. Tristan sacrificed himself to give me time to escape. He was impressed into the navy."

"While you disappeared."

Christian managed a bitter smile. "I suppose that is what I did do in a way; I disappeared into the bowels of London."

"I do not know what happened during those years, but I am certain they could not have been pleasant."

"Pleasant?" Christian had to laugh at that. "You are indeed the master of understatement, Reeves."

"A necessary gift in my occupation, my lord, I am happy to see that whatever befell you as a child, you made it through with considerable aplomb."

Christian shrugged, as much to loosen the tightness in his shoulders as to agree with Reeves. "So I did. And now I plan to prove Mother's innocence. She was imprisoned as a traitor on charges that she'd had commerce with the French. The charges were later dismissed, but only after she'd already died, alone and locked away. Someone had to put forth those charges. Whoever that was, I believe they wished her dead and found a convenient way to do it without sullying their hands."

"May I ask how you plan on finding this person?"

"Of course." Christian opened the box. Inside lay an enameled snuffbox, a packet of letters tied with a pink ribbon, and a broken watch fob. "This is all my mother had left when she died."

Christian ran his fingers over the letter. "When I arrived in London after my brother's capture, I immediately traveled to Newgate. She was already dead, gaol fever having stolen her life two weeks before." If Christian placed a hand upon the box and closed his eyes, he could still feel his despair at that moment, taste the bitterness of death and defeat. "One of the gaolers remembered her well. He had this box and he sold it to me."

The box had been his for ten pence, a laughable sum now. But to a starving boy of ten, it might have well been a thousand pounds. Desperate for some part of Mother, he'd set out to get the money. It had taken all his effort, all his cunning, and a loss of his morals and innocence to procure the funds before the gaoler sold off the box and the treasures it contained.

"I feel certain," Reeves said into the quiet, "that your mother would be glad her possessions are now in your hands."

"She was in Newgate, Reeves. And no one would

help her. Not her supposed friends. Not her lover. Not even the man who sired me and Tristan." Christian threw up a hand. "I know, I know. My father—if you could indeed call him that—might have wished to help, but he had so removed himself from her life that he was not available."

Reeves nodded.

"However it happened, she was left alone. She sold her jewels to pay for a cell that was reasonably dry. When that was gone, she sold her clothing. Even her shoes. She was left in rags with nothing—" A wave of emotion swallowed him whole.

He knew from experience that he could do nothing but feel, accept, let the pain course through him. He took a deep breath and traced his fingers over the letters, over the ribbon she'd once tied herself, the small gesture soothing him somehow.

Reeves cleared his throat. "Are there clues to her predicament in her letters?"

Christian collected himself. "There is one letter from someone named Sinclair. It is a code name of some sort, for the wording is quite stilted. The letter is almost a confession. This Sinclair admits they provided false information to the Crown against Mother."

"Someone put her in gaol and then apologized?"

"It was not an apology. The tone of the missive is taunting. I suppose it was the ultimate irony for Mother; the letter is proof, but since the author disguised his hand, she could not use it to free herself."

"Then it is not much of a clue."

"Ah, but it is. That missive led me to the Duke of Massingale, Lady Elizabeth's grandfather."

"How so?"

"I took the letter to a friend of mine who specializes in missives."

Reeves frowned. "My lord?"

Christian chuckled. "My friend is a forger, one of the best."

"Ah."

"He used a powder to dust the surface, and we found a faint bleed from another letter. It was a franking mark. From the Duke of Massingale's own ring. The letter originated from Massingale House."

"I see. And what is the evidence from Master William?"

"I sent him to find the priest who attended Mother on her deathbed. Willie is on his way back. He says he has found something of import. That my suspicions of the duke are correct."

Reeves pursed his lips. "I suppose I cannot convince you to find another way into the duke's home other than using Lady Elizabeth?"

"No. The duke is a recluse. Lady Elizabeth is the only way." Christian closed the box and carefully replaced it in the drawer. "I do not yet have conclusive proof. I know that. But the more I sift through the layers, the more I find myself on Massingale's doorstep." Christian looked hard at the butler. "He had something to do with Mother's death. I just don't know the details."

"It is a very difficult and delicate matter, my lord."

"You don't know the half of it. But I will not cease digging until I uncover the entire truth. All of it." He traced the ragged edge of the box thoughtfully. So close to the truth, yet time and deceit hid it from sight. Christian would find a way to expose it. He owed it to Mother. Aware of the butler's considering gaze, Christian forced himself to smile. "I should retire now. Lady Elizabeth rides in the park every Thursday."

"You are watching her house?"

"Me and every other determined suitor. The lady is quite wealthy. I hadn't planned on her being launched into society." Christian shrugged. "But what good is a plan if one cannot adapt?"

"Yes, my lord. I can see where your ability to adapt has stood you in good stead throughout your life. However, I can't help but wonder . . . my lord, what if, during the process of your pretending to be a suitor, Lady Elizabeth develops feelings for you? Will you break off all contact?"

"Had you met her yesterday, you would know she is not likely to become mindlessly enamored of anyone, regardless of my intentions."

"I shall hope that is true, my lord," Reeves said. He made his way to the door. "I shall have your bedchamber readied, since you have such an early appointment in the morning." With a quiet bow, Reeves left.

Christian waited until the door had closed behind Reeves before he shut the drawer, running his fingers over the box one last time. His mother's betrayer was within his grasp. He could feel the power of vanquishing the man who had trampled Christian's life and left him and his family in the dust. Sighing, he turned away.

Christian trimmed the cigar and found the striking box. He leaned back in his chair and propped his feet on the table before him, contemplating the weeks to come. It seemed as if his entire life from the time he was ten had been planned for this one moment. This was one battle of wits he would enjoy, one contretemps he would throw himself into, body and soul.

He blew a gentle circle of smoke into the air, watching the ghostly ring climb and fade. It was late, but he was wide awake, his soul thrumming. It was the same excitement he felt while riding the heath, horse thundering beneath him, sword and pistol at his side, a juicy, fat nobleman in the carriage just ahead. Only this time, his weapons would be neither sword nor pistol, but his intelligence and the unknowing help of one very beautiful lady.

To Christian's surprise, he found himself smiling. Leaning his head back against the high back of the chair, he blew another smoke ring, this one larger. The silvered circle rose slowly and engulfed its twin, rising to the ceiling and lingering a moment against the dull mustard paint before disappearing into the air.

Christian nodded with satisfaction. He was ready. Now was the time—his time.

Let the fight begin.

Chapter 5

A gentleman will never put his needs before that of a lady. Unless, of course, the decision has to do with the procurement of his dinner. It is unfortunate, but all men are commoners when it comes to their beef.

A Compleat Guide for
Being a Most Proper Butler
by Richard Robert Reeves

"Just look at this one!" Beth twirled so that her skirts rustled out. She smiled over her shoulder at her maid. "I adore the new gowns!" She especially loved the many hues—soft blues and lacy whites, rich pinks and muted greens. They set off her coloring and made her feel as fresh as the spring air.

Annie sniffed. "Ye've enough clothes fer a trousseau, which ye don't want."

"I do want a trousseau. Just not yet."

"I can't imagine why ye wouldn't want to get married as soon as ye can," Annie said. "A good man is hard to find. I take 'em wherever I finds 'em."

"Which is why you've been married four times."

"Five, if ye count the Dane I met in Shreveport." Annie pursed her lips thoughtfully. "I don't always put him on the list, seeing as how he died the very next day."

Beth's lips quirked with amusement. She'd hired the dour Annie against her stepmama's wishes and had never regretted it. Charlotte had not liked that Annie was so forthright and, at times, quite depressing. The maid was also very free-speaking according to the common dictates of society, and she was certainly an oddity. Tall and gangly, with her square, mannish face encircled with rows and rows of improbably red curls, the woman was still a wonder with a needle and had a flair for putting Beth's long blond tresses into a variety of fashionable styles that was simply unequaled. All in all, she was a divine find as a lady's maid, no matter her manners.

"Annie, you are quite right not to count the Dane on your list of husbands. I would have left the scoundrel off, too. A man should be a husband at least a week if he wishes to receive credit for it."

"So I think, my lady." Annie handed Beth her bonnet and gloves, a suspicious look in her gimlet eyes. "Just who is the man ye're planning on meetin' in the park today?"

Beth became very busy pulling on her gloves. "I

don't know what you are talking about. Beatrice
and I are going for a ride in her new cabriolet.
That is all."

"Hm. Ye look a mite too excited to just be
jauntin' about in a new carriage." Annie stood back
and eyed Beth up and down and then nodded
fiercely, her red curls bobbing. "And ye put on yer
best ridin' gown, too. 'Tis a man. I'm certain of it."

"You can be certain if you wish, but you would
be wrong. I have no desire to meet any man in the
park today, or any other day." Which was a patent
falsehood; Beth had been thinking about the
dark-haired, green-eyed viscount all morning,
ever since she'd awakened to a rather disturbing
dream that had him bending over her, as if to kiss
her. Even now, if she closed her eyes, she could see
his handsome face moving toward hers, feel the
warmth of his breath, taste the excitement of being so close, so very close to him that—

"Ye can't tell me that look is fer a ride with yer
own cousin," Annie said with a smug nod. "'Tis
a man."

"It is not," Beth said pleasantly, looking Annie
right in the eye. "And I do not wish to hear otherwise."

Annie threw up her hands. "Very well, my
lady! Hsst it is, then. But take my word on it, if
Annie Brice don't know a woman on crusade, no
one does."

There were times having such a discerning
woman as a maid was a true annoyance, Beth decided. She pulled on her gloves and bonnet.

"Grandfather needs me too much right now for such silliness."

"That's not what he'd call it." Annie straightened the top of the dresser. "How is your grandfather?"

"Charlotte wrote and said he'd taken a turn for the worse this last week." Beth met Annie's gaze in the mirror. "I worry about him."

"Ye're wastin' yer time, my lady. The old duke is as tough as nails. He won't nab up his dusters until he's ready."

Beth had to smile. "I wish that was true."

"What's to say it isn't?" The maid picked up a reticule from the bed and held it out. "Off with ye now! No more mumblin' about what might or might not happen. 'Tis a powerful pretty day, full of nip in the air. Could be ye might meet a handsome lad in the park that catches yer fancy and makes yer grandfather happy as a lark. At least, ye might if ye weren't already on yer way to meet one now."

Beth took the reticule and pulled it over her wrist. "I won't deign to answer that. Please have the pink silk ready for the ball this evening. The hem is a little loose on one side."

"I'll have it done afore ye return," Annie said, opening the door and standing to one side. "Ye just go and enjoy yer jaunt in the park. *And* yer man."

Beth sailed by her maid. "I shall, Annie. Just for you." As she ran down the stairs, Beth wondered if Westerville would indeed be in the park. It was possible, as the day was uncommonly beautiful. Such weather brought people out in droves.

Her heart thudded a little faster at the thought.

The viscount interested her. Not as a potential mate, of course. He was definitely not the sort of man one settled down with. No, he was more the dangerous break-your-heart type. Beatrice had been right about that. Fortunately Beth had no desire to settle down just yet, and a pleasant flirtation would certainly be more fun than having to play the stuttering fool to a group of moneygrubbing and dull lords. The problem was, she could not do both—flirt with the viscount *and* frighten off her other suitors. Which meant that a flirtation simply could not happen.

Some of the brightness went out of the day. Beth found her feet slowing as she crossed the foyer to where a footman held open the door. Outside, she could see Beatrice and her groom beside a beautiful new cabriolet, but Beth could muster no excitement.

She suddenly hoped she wouldn't see the viscount in the park after all. Mustering a fading smile, she made her way to where Beatrice was waiting.

The door to Christian's bedchamber closed firmly. He opened his eyes and threw a hand over his face as the sun splintered through the crack in the curtain. Good God, what time was it, anyway? Squinting, he peered at the clock on the mantel, cursed loudly, and threw back the covers.

"Good morning," Reeves said from the wardrobe where he was placing some stiffly starched cravats. "Your robe is on the foot of the bed. I would appreciate it if you would wear *something*."

"I don't need my robe. Just give me my breeches."

Reeves sighed but handed the article of clothing to Christian.

Christian pulled them on. "You may look now."

"Thank you, my lord. Your valet, Walters, is unable to assist you this morning. He is suffering from a toothache."

Reeves opened the wardrobe door. "Shall you wear the black waistcoat, the black waistcoat, or the black waistcoat?"

"I like black."

"From the looks of things, I'd say you quite adore it, my lord. Passionately. With all of your soul. Your heart. Your every breath—"

"Give me my damned waistcoat!"

"Yes, my lord." Reeves pulled a waistcoat from the wardrobe and eyed it for a long moment. "I wonder if I have wronged you, my lord. Instead of an unfortunate and inexplicable passion for black, perhaps you sustained an unmentionable loss of some sort, say, of a favorite racehorse or a hound that did well at the hunt—and you feel the need to mourn it for the next fourteen years."

"Reeves—"

"Or are you perchance allergic to color staining dyes?"

Christian found himself grinning. "I've always favored black. It's a powerful color."

Reeves held up a black waistcoat and then placed it against yet another. "It is rather powerful. As are all mourning clothes."

"I wanted to arrive in London with some fanfare. It is important that I stand out."

"Ah. I see." Reeves placed one of the black waistcoats on the bed. "You would be a lump of coal among the jewels. A fat, black pigeon in the face of so many brilliant peacocks. A—"

"Bloody hell, were you this annoying with my father?"

"I fear I was more so, my lord. I was younger then and could go on and on and on—"

"Good. The old bastard deserved a difficult time."

"So many people believe." The butler handed a fresh shirt to Christian, then placed a heavily starched cravat on the bed. After Christian had donned the shirt, he took the cravat and carefully wound it about his neck, then tied it in an intricate pattern.

He examined himself in the mirror and dipped his chin just the slightest bit to adjust the cravat folds to perfection.

Reeves waited in respectful silence, then handed the waistcoat to Christian. "Black or not, your waistcoats are quite well made. That brocade is most wondrous."

Christian slipped on the waistcoat, sliding his fingers over the silky surface. "For a long time, I had so little. A bit of luxury does not seem amiss now."

"No, my lord. Now is indeed the time for you to spoil yourself." Reeve opened a pin box and held it out to Christian.

Christian selected a large ruby cravat pin and carefully placed it in the creation he'd tied at his throat.

"I don't believe I've seen that particular cravat design before," Reeves noted once this delicate operation was completed.

"It's one of my own," Christian said, admiring it himself. "I call it Vengeance."

"You will set a trend, my lord." Reeves smiled a bit. "It is odd to think how very different you are from your twin brother, not only in looks, but in attitude."

"Tristan does not care for fashion. He prefers to dress as if he was still on board ship."

"He is also quite satisfied not seeking vengeance for your mother's death."

"He is more focused on the future," Christian said with a shrug. "He was ever that way." Besides, Tristan had never understood Mother quite the way Christian had. Christian possessed not only her leaf green eyes and golden-hued skin, but also her appreciation for the finer things in life.

She had relished the silk sheets and heavy lace-trimmed coverlet that had decorated her bed. He could still remember how she'd run her fingers over the smooth surface of a fine piece of furniture, a look of deep pleasure on her face. She'd lived as fully as she could, enjoying every moment, every experience. He wanted to do that. Perhaps once this situation was settled, he would—

He frowned. Odd, but he'd never really thought of what he'd do once he'd brought his mother's murderer to justice. Perhaps because for so long, it had been such a far-off goal. Now . . . now it was but weeks away. A trill of determination squared his shoulders.

Reeves picked up the black coat from the bed. "Your father thought quite highly of your mother. I heard him say so on more than one occasion."

Christian met the valet's gaze in the mirror. "Don't try to make me think more of my father than I do."

Reeves held out the coat for Christian. "I wouldn't dare do such a thing. In fact, I do not blame you for being angry."

Christian shrugged into the coat. "I'm not angry. My mother and father are both gone. Anger would be a wasted emotion."

"I would still be angry, my lord. Very."

Christian regarded himself in the mirror. He was dressed head to foot in unrelenting black, with the exception of the snowy white cravat at his throat. Only the heat from the ruby at his throat and the vivid green of his own eyes marred the black and white picture.

He caught Reeves's gaze in the mirror.

The butler raised his brows. "Primping, my lord?"

"I've never had such a finely starched cravat. Do not tell me Walters did this."

"He took ill last night before he could complete the starching. I took it upon myself to finish the job." Reeves soberly studied Christian's appearance in the mirror and nodded. "I hate to admit it, but the black does seem to lend you a certain rakish air."

Christian grinned. "It's good to know that all those years on the High Toby weren't for nothing."

Reeves winced. "Please, my lord. I have asked that you do not mention your former profession, although . . . You do remember what you told me about killing people?"

"That I have never killed a single soul."

The butler heaved a relieved sigh. "I do love hearing you say that, my lord."

"You are quite safe with me, Reeves. Unless, of course, you continue to critique my choice of clothing. I am not responsible for my actions then."

Reeves smiled faintly. "When you smile like that, you look remarkably like the portrait of your mother, my lord."

"Her—" Christian looked at the valet. "There is a portrait of my mother?"

"At Rochester House, your father's chief residence. It now belongs to your brother, should you wish to see it."

Tristan would not part with it, and Christian did not blame him. "I wonder why Father had a portrait of a woman he refused to even so much as acknowledge?"

"He commissioned the portrait after her death. The artist used a miniature, though you would never know it to see the results." Reeves sighed. "I'm sorry, my lord. Your father was a bit tight."

"Tight?"

"Yes, my lord. Tight with both his funds and his heart, except when it came to things of fashion. A fact I think he came to regret."

"Too little, too late."

"Yes. In many things. Before he died, he said that of all the women he'd known, your mother was the loveliest both in body and spirit."

"She was lovely," Christian said harshly, "until she caught the ague in gaol and began to waste away."

"He always felt guilty he was not here to protect her."

Christian, putting on his riding boots, turned to look at the butler. "He was remorseful? You really believe that?"

"Very. He was out of the country when she was imprisoned. In Italy. He did not receive word about your mother until two entire months had passed. Because of the situation on the continent, it then took him a while to reach London."

Christian turned to face the butler. "Father came to London to save her?"

"As quickly as he could, though he arrived too late." Reeves quietly closed the wardrobe door. "It was at that time that he commissioned the portrait."

For a long moment, Christian stared down at his riding boots, a question trembling on his tongue. It was a question that had trembled on his tongue more than once, but he'd never had the courage to say it aloud. "Did he . . . did he try to find Tristan and me?"

"Your father paid a fortune to various unsavory individuals who swore they could locate you both. But no one found even a trace."

Christian tried to swallow, but couldn't. He'd so wanted to believe that his father had attempted to help him, to help his mother. So wanted to believe it . . . and yet, over the years, the belief had died. In its place was a hard seed of bitterness that refused to be dislodged. "Did Father believe Mother innocent of the charges?"

Reeves sighed. "I don't know what he thought, only what he was told. And he was told that she was guilty of the crime. That there was nothing he could have done even if he had made it to London in time."

"Who told him that rubbish?" Christian demanded.

"The king."

Christian gripped the bedpost with a white-knuckled hand. "The king?"

"Your father went to see him the second his ship docked. He didn't even stop to change, but rode straight to Whitecastle where the king was staying. Though the king was already abed, your father demanded an audience."

"He really did try to help her," Christian heard himself say in a voice filled with wonder.

"I don't think he ever forgave himself when he realized that their estrangement had placed her in so unprotected a position."

"He should have felt guilty."

"He did, however . . ." Reeves hesitated, then

said in a hurried voice, "My lord, whatever happened to your mother, it was heavily substantiated by some seemingly irrefutable evidence. The king was convinced of her guilt."

"The evidence was false. Willie will bring us the information we need so that we know what to look for. He's to arrive sometime today." Christian turned toward the door. "But for now, I must bid you adieu. Lady Elizabeth will be in Hyde Park this morning, if her footman is to be believed."

"Oh, footmen never lie," Reeves said in a dry voice.

Christian had to smile. "Not when they're well paid, they don't. How do I look, Reeves? Polished enough to become the lady's most determined suitor, after, of course, she becomes mine?"

"After she becomes yours?"

"Love is a game of chess, Reeves. Of the heart. I have studied every bit of information I have been able to glean, and Massingale's granddaughter is his one weakness, the only person he allows close to him."

"Is there not a daughter-in-law, as well?"

Christian frowned. "How do you know about her?"

"Servants' talk, my lord. Since you gifted me with information as to your plan, I have made some inquiries."

"Since last night?"

"*You* may have slept until ten, but *I* did not. I was up at dawn and went to the market. I spent several minutes inspecting the poultry, at which time I had a most interesting conversation with one Mrs. Kimble, who has the fortune of being the Duke of Massingale's housekeeper."

"Reeves! You—what did you discover?"

"The duke dotes on his granddaughter. She is apparently quite a favorite with the staff, too. I also discovered that the duke is not fond of his daughter-in-law and that his health is failing rapidly. In fact, there is some worry that he has not long to live."

Christian paused. He hadn't heard a word about the duke's health. Damn it, was it possible he'd spent his whole life dreaming of vengeance on the man who'd ruined his mother, only to be cheated by death?

He quirked a brow at Reeves. "Anything else?"

"Yes. It seems that Lord Massingale is concerned his daughter-in-law is interested in a man, one Lord Bennington, who is quite close to Lady Charlotte. The housekeeper seems to think the man is a menace of some sort, though I could not discover quite why."

Christian grimaced. It was ironic that he'd spent weeks and weeks infiltrating Massingale's estate and had gotten no closer than the stables while Reeves had merely taken a trip to the local market, cozied up to a housekeeper, and discovered as much information as Christian's month of hard work. "Old or ill, the duke is still responsible for my mother's death."

"Old or ill, he is *possibly* responsible for your mother's death," Reeves said gently. "You said yourself you had not yet collected enough evidence to prove your case."

"I will have it soon enough."

"Of course, my lord."

Damn it! Christian raked a hand through his hair. He hated being ungracious. Still . . . He shot a hard glance at Reeves. "If you find out anything else, you will tell me?"

"Yes, my lord. Without fail."

"Thank you. You are an exceptional man, Reeves."

"I try, my lord."

Christian took a last look at himself in the mirror, then turned toward the door. "I am off to the park, then." Within moments, he was striding down the hallway, the morning sun slanting across the polished floor. His entire body was focused on the upcoming dance he was to perform. He had to win his way into Lady Elizabeth's confidence. He had to. One part of him was rather excited about the prospect; but another reminded him rather forcefully of the fact that—had circumstances been different—he might well have pursued the intriguing Lady Elizabeth on her own merits alone.

He could not stop his active imagination from picturing the lush and lovely Elizabeth in his bed. Just the thought of her lithe form stretched naked across his sheets, her honey-streaked hair spreading around her, that expression of amusement and intelligence sparkling in her eyes . . . until, of course, her eyes darkened with passion from that surprisingly warm brown to heated black.

Or *would* her eyes darken with passion? Perhaps they'd light up.

He suddenly realized that the little bits of information he'd collected about the lady over the last few weeks had not given him a very accurate picture at all. He knew, for instance, that she preferred the quadrille to all other forms of dance. That she did not often ride in the park unless it was in a carriage. That she favored comedic plays rather than sober, sad ones. These were useful pieces of information, all discovered with cunning and guile. Still, he did not know what she wanted, what she feared, and perhaps—even more important—who she really was.

He paused in the hallway, the faintest hint of unease settling between his shoulder blades. For a long moment, he stood staring at the floor.

Then, a sudden resolute look in his face, he turned on his heel and went into the library to his desk. He uncapped the ink and dipped a pen, then wrote a single line on a bit of foolscap. That done, he shook it dry, returned the ink and pen, tucked the paper into his pocket, and left once again. In the hallway, he took his hat and gloves from the footman and walked out the front door to stand on the step, feeling as if he'd made a huge decision.

And he had. He was only doing what he had to. What the tragedy of his mother's death required. That was all.

Jaw tight, Christian made his way down the wide marble steps, his riding boots clicking briskly. Now was not the time to question his own motives. It was ridiculous the way he'd allowed Reeves to cast shadows on his carefully thought out plans. He knew damned well what he was doing and he didn't need his father's old butler giving him moral advice.

Things hadn't come to that low of a pass. Not yet, anyway.

Sighing, he took the reins of his favorite mount from a waiting groom and swung up into the saddle. "Let the siege begin," he said under his breath, pressing his thighs against the huge brute of a horse and letting the animal speed his way to the park.

Chapter 6

A good servant is always discreet, faithfully performs all duties, and never judges his employer's habits. Except, perhaps, the truly reprehensible ones.

A Compleat Guide for
Being a Most Proper Butler
by Richard Robert Reeves

As Christian cantered toward the park, he caught sight of Lady Elizabeth and her cousin, Mrs. Thistle-Bridgeton, the woman who'd been serving as chaperone the night before. It had taken very little effort to learn the cousin's name; now all Christian had to do was find a way past her to Elizabeth.

Impervious to his presence, they swept by in a rather showy carriage, the black lacquered sides catching the light almost as much as the matched blacks that pulled it.

The vehicle was enough to excite attention, every inch gleamed with newness. But the combination of the gorgeous horses and the shimmer of Beth's golden hair against the red velvet seat pulled the eye far quicker than mere money and position could account for. She was, quite simply, a stunningly beautiful woman.

It was a good thing he was protected from feeling more for her than was seemly. Her connection to her grandfather would forever keep her charms from working on his jaded palate. She was the key into her grandfather's world and nothing more, no matter what the troublesome Reeves might wish to imply.

Christian watched as she leaned forward to speak to her cousin. There was something innately graceful about Elizabeth. He wasn't sure if it was her gestures, the way she held her head, or the genuine charm of her person, but just watching her was a fascination in and of itself.

It really was a pity she was his enemy by birth. Still, he refused to feel poorly for admiring her beauty. How could he help it? Just seeing her there, reclining in the seat, dressed in a trim Russian-styled short coat, a white crown bonnet adorned with bluebells on her golden hair, he thought she looked like a wood nymph stolen from the forest.

His playful gelding shied in pretend horror from a flower cart that rumbled past. "Easy, Lucifer!" The beast snorted and pranced, arching his neck and blowing through his nose. Christian eased his heels into the animal's sides, keeping a firm hand on the reins. Lucifer recognized the touch of his master and quieted, though not before he gave one last defiant snort.

Christian turned his horse toward the park gates, following a short distance behind the cabriolet. The wind rose just as they passed through the gates and lifted a curl of Beth's golden hair about the edge of her bonnet. Christian's body tightened instantly. He could picture her as she'd been at the ball last night, her full lips pursed with interest, her eyes dark with unasked questions.

The wind lifted the tormented curl and pulled it along the edge of her bonnet, a golden banner. Christian thought of her hair, of her porcelain white skin and how it would look against his own darker coloring. His body tightened even more, his groin aching ever so slightly. Damn, but what he would give to see her in his bed, divested of her finery and trappings, nothing between them but unbridled passion.

Shaking his head a little at his own foolishness, Christian adjusted his seat in the saddle. Lucifer tossed his head and whickered as if laughing.

Christian leaned forward and said into the horse's ear, "I am not amused."

Beth's vehicle reached the outer loop of the path. Christian nudged Lucifer forward as a noticeable stirring of motion began at the side of the pathway. A small number of men—about five in all—who'd been rather listlessly sitting upon their mounts or leaning against their carriages, surged forward like ants scurrying from a kicked over anthill. They leaped upon their horses and climbed hurriedly into their carriages and then they merged, mingled, and dashed toward the cabriolet.

Christian frowned. He'd expected suitors, but . . . only five? A woman with Elizabeth's fortune alone could count on at least twenty suitors in the park on any given day.

It was odd in the extreme.

What made the situation even more curious was that the five men surrounding the cabriolet were all known to be seeking a woman of fortune. What was afoot? Besides fortune, Lady Elizabeth was beautiful and the daughter of a blasted duke, for heaven's sake! Surely there were men who would wish to court her based on those pronouncements rather than her dowry?

Christian glanced at Lady Elizabeth, but could detect no nuance in her person to show her feelings at being left in such thin company. By Zeus, he needed to find out what was occurring here.

Lady Elizabeth laughed at something her companion said, the sound drifting back with the wind to land delicately on Christian's ears. The curve of her pink lips seemed to beckon him forward, though he could not get near her on the narrow path due to the horses crowded about the cabriolet.

A flash of impatience flared, and suddenly, despite the fact that it complicated his plan, he found that he wished every man in sight to Hades. The reaction was so instantaneous, so thorough, that he drew up, frowning.

Somehow, perhaps because he needed her for his plans and had been listening to reports of her existence for the last six months, he'd begun to think of Elizabeth as . . . his. He stiffened in his seat. What the hell was he thinking? That sort of thing could lead to a far more serious relationship than he cared to claim. So why was he sitting here, battling a most uncomfortable and unfamiliar surge of bitterness? A feeling almost akin to jealousy?

Unconsciously, Christian tightened his grip on Lucifer.

The horse shied in reaction. Cursing a little, Christian fought to bring Lucifer under control, though he never stopped watching Beth. She'd seen the approaching suitors and was now leaning forward to say something to her coachman— perhaps urging him to move onward. But if that was her intent, it was too late; the pathway that wended about the park was blocked before she even made the first turn.

Damn them all to hell and back, the bounders. His only option now was to separate his quarry from her erstwhile fortune-seeking entourage. It was rather like trying to extricate a particularly juicy piece of meat from the jowls of a pack of salivating wolves.

Fortunately, Christian was more wolf than any of the others. Unlike the lily white pampered pets before him, he'd made his own way in the world, fought for his own food with sinew and stealth, teeth bared the entire way.

He turned Lucifer toward a side path and brought the restless horse through a low bracket of brush a short distance up the path. He caught sight of Elizabeth, her eyes meeting his for the space of a second. To his immense satisfaction, she reacted instantly. Her face brightened and her eyes flashed with pleased recognition, her lips parting as if to say his name.

But just as quickly, she rethought her reaction, for she bit her lip and looked away, her color high.

That decided it. "Come, Lucifer," he murmured. "We are summoned." Christian touched his heels to the sides of his mount. The gelding sprang forward as Christian guided him between the side of the cabriolet and the men who attempted to ride next to it.

No horse was a match for Lucifer. He sneered at the other mounts, snorting and baring his teeth. The other animals, as pampered and protected as their owners, took one look at the aggressive gelding and shied out of reach, away from the cabriolet.

Soon, Christian was in place beside the carriage. "Lady Elizabeth," he said, touching his whip to the brim of his hat, smiling down into her eyes. "You look"—he let his gaze drift over her—"lovely. A rose in a hothouse of daisies."

In Christian's experience, a normal maid—especially one so inexperienced—would have been immediately thrown into a flutter of unease and excitement. But Lady Elizabeth was made of sterner stuff.

Her brows rose ever so slightly, and she said in that slightly husky voice of hers, "I beg your pardon, but have we met? I don't believe I know you."

A smile danced in her eyes, a dimple quivered on one rounded cheek.

For an instant, Christian completely forgot his quest. He forgot he was in the park, on his horse. He forgot that there were other people about. He forgot everything but the smiling eyes of the woman before him.

He leaned forward. "My lady, it is my most fervent wish that you did know me. Well."

Her lips quirked in a delicious half smile. "Well, then. Perhaps that is something we can remedy, my—"

"Beth!" Her companion—Mrs. Thistle-Bridgeton—grasped Elizabeth's hand and said, "Careful!" in a warning tone very similar to the one she'd used the night before.

Elizabeth sent her cousin a reluctant glance, then winced as if remembering something unpleasant. "Oh yes," she said in an irritated tone. *"That."*

Christian did not allow the smile to slip from his face, but all his senses sharpened. What was this? He struggled to understand.

Beside Christian, the Duke of Standwich was trying desperately to keep his rather plump mare under control. The normally placid animal wildly eyed Lucifer and tugged her reins in a most unseemly manner. "My lord!" Standwich huffed, sawing unbecomingly at the reins. "Pray control your mount!"

Christian glanced down at Lucifer, who was prancing with glee beside the cabriolet but otherwise minding himself with fair decorum. "My mount *is* under control. Your mare is the one who is unruly."

Standwich's mouth thinned, even as he had to

pull his restive horse back onto the path. "Lady Bud never behaves in this manner—"

"I beg your pardon," Christian said, trying to suppress a grin and failing. "Did you call your horse 'Lady Bud'?"

Beside him, Elizabeth gave a short gurgle of laughter. Christian flashed a smile in her direction, their eyes meeting a moment.

Standwich's face reddened. "Yes! Yes, I did call her that. It is my mother's mare, if you must know. I only borrowed it because I thought it would behave prettily in a lady's presence." The duke sent a resentful glare at Lucifer. "Unlike *your* mount, which is not fit for public usage!"

Christian rubbed Lucifer's neck, which made the animal pick up his feet a bit higher. "I don't believe you have any right to question my horse. Nor I yours. If you wish to ride a prissy animal, that is none of my concern."

"Though my mare's name is Lady Bud," the duke said hotly, "she is not a weak animal. She's just called—oh, dash it! I am not explaining myself to *you*." He sniffed, his back so stiff it was a wonder he could still ride. "Besides, she's nothing like my usual mount. My horse is twice the animal of that brute you're on!"

"What's its name?"

The duke blinked. "Name? I don't—"

"What is the name of your horse?"

A deep flush rose in the duke's face. "That doesn't have anything to do with—"

"Afraid to tell me," Christian said with satisfaction. He glanced down at Beth and winked.

She colored, a quiver of laughter touching her lips.

The duke audibly ground his teeth. "I didn't name the horse myself! He was already two years old when I bought him and—"

"Perhaps his name is . . . *Sir* Lady Bud?"

"No! Of course not!"

Christian shrugged. "Fine. Don't tell us your mount's name. I daresay it is nothing unusual."

"It is too exotic! It's Bathsheba!"

"You named a horse Bathsheba?"

"I didn't name it, I tell you! Not that it matters. I find Bathsheba a lovely name."

"That's a horrid name for a horse. It's far too exotic and should be given, instead, to a creature capable of beauty and passion and desires." Christian turned to smile down at the lady. "Someone like Lady Elizabeth."

Elizabeth's cheeks pinkened though her companion was not so circumspect. She choked out a laugh. "La, Beth! You, as Bathsheba!"

The duke sputtered out a protest. "B'God, Westerville! Quite improper of you to say such things!"

"Nonsense," Christian said, leaning down so that only Beth could hear him. "Would you like to be rid of these fleas, my love? Or have you not yet finished amusing yourself at their expense?"

Beth's eyes met his with a warm look. "Fleas? Surely not."

The words were no sooner out of her mouth than her companion cleared her throat in a very telling manner. Lady Elizabeth glanced at her friend, then colored and gave a short nod.

Intriguing. Christian leaned down to speak yet again when Standwich's clumsy horse knocked against Lucifer.

Lucifer instantly whipped over to nip at the bumbling mare, which balked and tried to get away, bumping into the horses of two other determined gentlemen.

"Blast it, Standwich!" said one gentleman, glaring at the duke. "Take heed what you are about!"

His companion added with a heavy French accent, "Perhaps you should move to the back of the group if you cannot control your mount any better than that!"

Christian noted with amusement that several of the suitors had already given up and had fallen behind. There were but the three of them left, and he had procured the only spot where one could actually converse with the lady.

He leaned over to Lady Elizabeth from Lucifer's saddle. "If you will not call these lumps of manhood 'fleas,' then how about 'rats'? They are swarming in a pack, look as if they'd be delighted to nibble your toes given the chance, and several have rather frightening facial whiskers reminiscent of that species."

Elizabeth laughed, her eyes crinkling beneath the brim of her bonnet. She looked damnably fetching at that moment and incredibly feminine.

She opened her mouth to answer him when Mrs. Thistle-Bridgeton interrupted brightly, "They are more like little yapping dogs, don't you think, Beth?"

Lady Elizabeth's gaze narrowed annoyingly on her companion. There was a moment of silence, during which time her cousin sent her a warning look of such intensity that Christian raised his brows. Whatever warning Mrs. Thistle-Bridgeton communicated, it caused Beth to sigh. She sent Christian a rather apologetic look before saying, "S-s-s-so, my lord. How would you rid me of this pl-pl-plague?"

For an instant, Christian was too surprised to answer. Lady Elizabeth winced at his expression, her cheeks flushing a bit before she looked away. He didn't think he'd heard her speak in such a halting manner before, but perhaps he'd simply missed it; God knew her chaperone didn't seem to want her to speak at all.

Not surprisingly, Mrs. Thistle-Bridgeton broke the silence. "My cousin has some difficulty in forming words, as you can see."

Shoving his surprise aside, Christian shrugged. "There are times I am not as eloquent as I would like." He caught Lady Elizabeth's gaze and noted she didn't seem quite as distressed. He smiled, noting the gold and green that flecked her lovely brown eyes, a fact he'd missed last night in the dim light of the ballroom. "My lady, I would rid you of this rat infestation with alacrity. Of that, you can be assured."

Mrs. Thistle-Bridgeton nodded. "Beth, I suppose there is no harm in allowing the viscount to shoo away all of your suitors. We cannot run the carriage properly with so many people about. So long, of course"—and here the older lady pinned him with a determined smile—"he understands he is to leave as well."

Lady Elizabeth flicked a glance up at him. "Y-y-y-you are incorrigible."

Christian bowed. He could have sworn that the few brief sentences she'd spoken to him before had not been so encumbered. But perhaps it had been a simple case of the order of her words.

Whatever it was, he decided that he didn't really care if Lady Elizabeth's speech was halting, though it was possible that explained the mysterious lack of suitors. Truly the men in London were lily weak.

For Christian, it was damnably fascinating to watch her lush lips forming each word, stuttered or not. In fact, he realized with some surprise, her stutter made him want to kiss her all the more.

He grinned and touched the brim of his hat. "You, my lady, are too beautiful to sit in such a mundane manner, surrounded by such fools who think to amuse you with empty compliments."

Beth had to admit the viscount had taken an accurate measure of her suitors. They were indeed bothering her, the lot of them. Beatrice's new cabriolet was designed for a spanking pace, and because of the small squadron that had followed them down the path, they were forced to crawl along as if they were in a tiny cart pulled by fat ponies.

Westerville glinted an amused smile her way as if he could feel her frustration. She couldn't help but respond. It was odd, but though the man irritated her with his overconfidence, she found his presence both stimulating and reassuring in some way.

Westerville glanced at the few remaining suitors, all of whom seemed determined to ride abreast of the cabriolet. After a moment's consideration, he nodded as if making a decision, then leaned down. Pale green and rimmed by the thickest black lashes, his eyes were almost level with hers. "My lady," he said, his deep voice rumbling over her, "pray move to one side."

Beth raised her brows. "One side?"

Beatrice kicked her ankle.

Beth winced, then said in an oddly bored voice, "Wh-what I mean is, one s-s-s-side?"

Something flared in the viscount's eyes, an expression quickly shuttered by the fall of his lashes. Beth winced. Oh blast her stutter! She never seemed able to remember it when the man was around. Yet . . . when she'd finally remembered to use it, he hadn't been discouraged at all and had accepted her flawed speech without comment or even an outward wince. In many ways, he'd accepted it much better than the charlatans who continued to hound her.

In fact, she didn't think a single other gentleman had reacted so well. She stole a glance at him from under her lashes and caught him looking back at her, boldly and without pretense. There was a look in his eyes, one of enjoyment and . . . knowledge. As if he'd just discovered something about her and was relishing it. Goodness . . . did he *know*?

He winked, slowly and sensually, sending a

flutter of heat across her skin. Beth could only stare. Had he guessed at her subterfuge? Heaven knew that if he had, it was her own fault. She really should be upset. But instead . . . she winked back.

There was a stunned second's worth of a pause, just long enough for the viscount to blink once in astonishment, and then he tilted back his head and laughed—long and loud.

Beatrice looked from him to Beth and back. "What? What is it? Did I miss something?"

Beth bit her lip, trying to keep her own laughter from ringing out with Westerville's. Heaven help her, but the man was dangerous for a million and one reasons, not the least of which was his sense of humor that so closely mirrored her own. An intelligent, cautious woman would avoid the man.

But somehow, today, looking at him astride such a lovely horse, his green eyes shaded by the brim of his hat, his broad shoulders perfectly lined by an expertly cut riding coat, his finely carved mouth curved in a smile . . . What was one more day? she asked herself.

"So, will you slide over?" he asked, a rakish challenge in his gaze.

"She cannot," Beatrice said, leaning forward in a bristling mass of skirts and protectiveness.

Beth's smile did not waver. "Ah, but I can, too."

Had Annie seen her lady's smile, she would have been able to tell Beatrice to tread carefully. The maid knew that when Lady Elizabeth smiled that certain calm, determined smile, she'd made up her mind about something. And when Lady Elizabeth made up her mind about something, there was no changing it. But Annie was not here, and even had she been, it was highly unlikely Beatrice would have paid the maid the least heed.

Instead, Beatrice said with even more insistence, "No, Beth. You may *not* move aside. I will not allow it."

That did it. A smile firmly on her face, Beth gathered her skirts and slid over on the seat. Before Beth knew what the viscount was about, he had swung off the horse and, with a graceful vault, deposited himself neatly in the seat beside her, his horse never breaking stride.

"Well!" Beatrice said, her cheeks red. She glared at Beth.

Feeling a little guilty, Beth reached over and took her cousin's hand. "I am sorry. But you vexed me a bit."

Westerville handed his horse's reins over his shoulder to the outrider who held on to the back of the cabriolet. The man obediently looped the reins over a hook, and soon the beautiful gelding was trotting along behind the cabriolet.

Now, of course, Standwich was free to move closer to the cabriolet, but for naught. All he could do was ride beside Christian, who had his back toward the suitors.

"Well, my love?" Westerville said, leaning into the corner and trying to find room for his long legs inside the cabriolet's rather limited space. "Shall we take this smart carriage through its paces?"

Beatrice freed her hand from Beth's and sent an irritated glare toward the viscount. "My lord, please do not address Lady Elizabeth as 'my love.' It is vastly improper, as I am sure you are aware."

He slanted Beatrice a glance, a slow grin lifting the corner of his mouth in a way that seemed to light his green eyes from within. "Madam, I may not always act in a manner you think proper. But I can promise you this . . . I shall never bore either you or Lady Elizabeth. I don't think you can say the same of these paltry hangers-ons who are following us even now."

"Oh! The nerve!" Standwich protested miserably from his place beside the coach, well out of conversation range of everyone in the carriage.

"What did that man say?" demanded the Frenchman who rode at his side.

Christian looked at Beatrice. "Why don't you ask the coachman to give your carriage a good run? Didn't you say you wished to see how she'd go through her paces?"

Beatrice hesitated a second, her gaze meeting Beth's. Beth offered an encouraging nod of her head. Why shouldn't they enjoy a ride? After weeks of stultifying convention, it would be lovely to feel the wind in her hair.

As if he knew her thoughts, the viscount's leg moved ever so slightly to one side, touching hers through the skirts of her gown. It was a simple movement, with several layers of clothes between them, yet it sent a shock through her so sudden, so physical, that she had to grasp her hands in her lap as hard as she could to keep from reacting. The man was a menace to her peace of mind.

Beatrice saw none of this, for she was in deep discussion with the coachman. After a moment, she turned about in her seat with a decided flounce. Her eyes sparkled with indignation. "My own coachman tried to tell me he couldn't go any faster than what we were—ambling like old women in a farm cart! So I told him that Harry had bought this cabriolet for me to cut a dash in, and a dash I would cut."

"Good for you!" Beth said. She would have congratulated her cousin more, but the coachman chose that moment to let the leaders have their way, and soon they were flying down the path, traveling much faster than propriety allowed.

Beatrice grabbed the sides of the cabriolet as they swayed wildly down the path, one hand on her bonnet. The fresh air made her lift her face to the sun, and she laughed, glancing behind them. "Beth, your suitors appear quite put out!"

Beth turned to look back over her shoulder, but a curve in the path sent her sliding along the seat— and brought her firmly up against the viscount.

He looked down at her, a smile on his lips, his eyes alight with amusement. "Going somewhere?"

She pushed herself back to her side, grabbing her bonnet as a puff of wind threatened to rip it from her head. She began to say something, but the thought of stuttering at such a lovely moment was abhorrent, so instead she just smiled. That seemed to please him well enough, for he grinned back, his eyes bright beneath the brim of his hat.

It was a wonderful moment, Beth decided. Her bonnet ribbons flew behind her, slender banners of blue, the fresh wind ruffling her skirts and toying with her hair. Beatrice looked just as pleased even though the wind was hitting her full on and picking her hair apart, tossing her curls about her head until she looked like a medusa.

"Heavens!" Beatrice exclaimed as they rounded a corner at such a spanking pace. Her eyes shone, her face filled with mischief. "Wait until I tell Harry how I sprung 'em in the park! He'll have an apoplexy!"

They rode the rest of the way around the park, the viscount taking advantage of the sway of the carriage to lean against Beth whenever he could. She was achingly aware of him, and instead of watching the gorgeous array of flowers flying by, she found herself sneaking glances at him. Each and every time she did so, she discovered his gaze on her. She found herself admiring the masculine line of his mouth, the handsome set of his shoulders, the delicious contrast of his light eyes against his darker skin.

Beatrice and the viscount made desultory small talk, the viscount leading the way. Beth spoke but little, managing a minimal stutter, enough to keep Beatrice from kicking her ankles. It wasn't until fifteen minutes into the conversation that Beth realized something rather odd. The viscount was asking an inordinate amount of questions about her grandfather.

Warning bells sounded in the back of her mind. Why was the viscount so interested in Grandfather? There was no mistaking the intense focus that appeared on Westerville's face when

Beatrice answered his questions, as if her every word was of great import.

The carriage finally returned to where they'd begun, and slowed. Beth was glad to note that her suitors had dispersed; she had other things on her mind now.

"Well!" Beatrice said, a happy flush to her face as she attempted to stuff her rioted curls back beneath her bonnet. "That was certainly refreshing. I do hope your horse didn't get too fatigued."

"I am certain he enjoyed a little canter. He doesn't receive enough exercise in town." The viscount stood, opening the carriage door, and lightly stepped to the ground. He turned as he shut the door and tipped his hat. "Mrs. Thistle-Bridgeton. Lady Elizabeth. Thank you for allowing me to join you."

"You are qu-qu-quite welcome," Beth said, a sinking in her heart. She could not deny the viscount's charm. Yet neither could she pretend he was like her other suitors. There was something amiss about his pursuit. Something . . . suspicious. Why *had* he asked so many questions about Grandfather?

Westerville took the reins for his horse from the waiting groom, but before he mounted, he lifted Beth's hand from where it had been resting on the edge of the carriage window and pressed her fingers to his mouth. Tingles traced up her arm and settled in her breasts. Her fingers curled closed, and he released her, then stepped back to swing up onto his horse.

Once there, he smiled down at her, his green eyes aglow beneath the brim of his hat. "Good day, Mrs. Thistle-Bridgeton. Lady Elizabeth. I hope we meet again."

Beatrice sighed. "It was a lovely ride! Thank you for your company."

Beth, meanwhile, didn't say anything.

This didn't seem to bother the viscount at all. He merely smiled in her direction, turned his horse, and rode off.

Beatrice watched as he rode away, saying in a rather grudging voice, "I vow, but that is a handsome man." Beth raised her brows and Beatrice colored. "Well," she temporized, "he is handsome, and thoroughly ineligible."

Beth shook her head. "You are such a goose. All a man has to do is smile at you and off you go, melting into a puddle at his feet."

"I know. Harry says he despairs of ever going on holiday without me for I'm likely to fall in love with the new footman before he returns."

"You would never leave Harry."

"I know," Beatrice agreed, though she still watched the viscount's receding figure with admiration.

Beth opened her gloved hand to smooth her skirt where the wind had ruffled it. As she did so, a small scrap of paper fluttered out and fell to her feet.

Beatrice was still busy tucking her curls back beneath her hat, so she failed to see Beth bend over and pick up the small folded paper.

She carefully unfolded it. In bold, sweeping letters, it read, *Meet me at the British Museum tomorrow at ten. If you dare.*

Beth turned to look at the viscount, who was even now cantering away. He rode so confidently, a dark figure on a horse that far outshone any of the others in the park. Both the rider and the horse drew the eye, and more than one lady looked rather longingly after the retreating figure.

Beth's fingers tightened over the reticule she held in her lap. He was just so . . . delicious. Yes, strange as it sounded, the man was plain delicious, like a raspberry ice or a bonbon from the confectioner's shop. Odd, but she'd never really thought of a man in quite those terms. She slid a glance at Beatrice and caught her cousin staring after Westerville as if she'd like to taste him that very minute. "Beatrice!"

Beatrice flushed guiltily. "Just because I am married does not mean I do not appreciate a handsome man when I see one. Especially one with eyes like that and such a smile. Oh Beth, there is something almost angelic about him."

"Angelic? I was about to suggest he was Satan's own!"

"There is bit of a devil to him as well, make no doubt. But then he will smile and . . ." Beatrice sighed, fanning herself slightly as she did so. "All of this makes him even more dangerous, which is why I am going to find out all I can."

"About what?"

"About him, of course! I know a little, but not enough. As handsome as he is and as thoroughly

as he's been chased since he arrived in London, I
daresay there are hundreds of women who've
managed to worm some sort of information out
of him. I shall begin with the dowagers and work
my way to the fallen women and just gossip, gossip, gossip with the lot of them until someone
tells me something."

"That is quite a sacrifice, I am sure."

Beatrice patted Beth's hand. "Anything for you,
dear."

"I'm certain."

"I have no doubt that there are any number of
skeletons in that man's closet. He fairly radiates
danger and sultry intent and . . ." Beatrice shivered. "I vow, but I need to go home and see Harry
this very minute. Meanwhile"—she fixed a suddenly solemn gaze on Beth—"I want your promise not to see Westerville again. Not until I've
made some inquiries into his character. Perhaps—
just perhaps, mind you—I've been wrong. I mean,
all I really know about him is that his parentage
isn't what it should be. Other than that . . ." She
shrugged. "The rest is probably just rumor."

Beth looked forward. "What rumor?"

"Well . . ." Beatrice glanced around, as if someone might overhear her in her own cabriolet, before leaning forward to say in a loud whisper,
"He was not born into his title, you know. Some
people say the viscount was once a highwayman.
Others say he was involved in things much more
dangerous, smuggling on the coast or the dia-
mond trade in Africa. Whatever it was, I daresay it
was a matter of economy. A bastard son with no

father . . . well, it couldn't have been easy. Now, of course, he's so wealthy it almost hurts! Lady Chiltendon said he was as wealthy as the prince, maybe more so." Beatrice sighed. "It's a pity his lineage is in question. Your grandfather would never countenance such a match."

Beth looked down at her hand where the viscount had pressed his lips. The skin still tingled, her arm slightly numb as if she'd been holding it over her head too long. Rich, was he? Then he was not pursuing her for her dowry. An odd relief flooded through her at that; she hadn't even realized until that moment how much the thought had bothered her.

So why *was* he pursuing her? She frowned down at her closed fist, the paper tightly held between her fingers. For some reason, she was struck with the memory of his expression when he'd asked about Grandfather. Of all the men she'd met in the last few weeks, none of them had questioned her about that. Not a single one. Which made the viscount's questions all the more odd.

"Beth? Did you hear me?"

"I beg your pardon, but I am afraid I was woolgathering."

Beatrice leaned forward, concern etched in her gaze. "Do you promise not to see him until I can discover more? I wouldn't ask you if I didn't think him so attractive but . . . He even has me looking forward to meeting him again!" Beatrice made such a comical face that Beth laughed.

"He's dangerous." Beth pulled open her reticule and pushed the paper into it, then tied it closed. "Quite frankly, I think the less I see of the viscount—at least until we discover more about him—the better it will be for us all."

Beatrice heaved a relieved sigh. "Thank you! I know it's difficult to understand, but better to find out the ugly truth now rather than later, when it might be a bit more painful. You are an heiress, after all, and perhaps the rumors of his wealth are unfounded."

"You don't believe that."

"No," Beatrice confessed. "Frankly, there are some things that puzzle me about the viscount. A lot of things."

Forcing a smile, Beth turned the subject to Beatrice's new cabriolet and how well it had run. Beatrice couldn't resist such a topic, and she was soon expounding on how dear Harry was to give her such a luxurious present and how she wished she could think of something to give him in return.

Beth listened with half an ear, her mind still wrapped up in the viscount. She'd give Beatrice a week to discover the viscount's intentions and then, if she found nothing, Beth would set out on her own.

She'd always loved a good mystery, one of the reasons she read so much, and if the viscount had something to hide, she'd find it.

As Grandfather liked to say, there wasn't much one couldn't do, if one but put one's mind to it.

Chapter 7

When preparing a gentleman's clothing, it is important to ascertain the event. One dresses quite differently for a hunt than one does for a ball.

A Compleat Guide for
Being a Most Proper Butler
by Richard Robert Reeves

The trouble with sleeping was that one had no control over one's dreams, a rather bleary-eyed Beth decided the next morning. It was not really a horrid problem in and of itself. It was just that it made waking so disappointing, like discovering that instead of duck in mint sauce for supper, there was only thick, cold porridge.

She sat now at her dresser, pulling a heavy silver brush through her hair and absently gazing at herself in the mirror. She should not meet Lord Westerville in secret, and certainly not without a chaperone. Still . . . it was the British Museum and not some locale of debauchery like a gaming hell or . . . or . . . or . . .

She pursed her lips thoughtfully. What other debauchery locales were there besides gaming hells? There were houses of ill repute, to be certain—places where women of unsavory character might reside. And then there were . . . What else was there? Well, it didn't matter, really. Westerville had to know perfectly well that such clandestine behavior could have consequences. Serious consequences. Consequences like being forced to marry.

Beth curled her nose at her reflection in the mirror. That would certainly be a horrid way to wed, at the end of a sword as in a bad play. Of course, being married to a man like Westerville . . . A tiny shiver went down her spine. That might be something altogether different.

She turned her head and began to brush her hair over her other shoulder. It was so long it almost touched her lap, the honey blond and lighter strands curling a little at the ends. Meeting Westerville would be a very risky, very intrepid, very foolish endeavor indeed.

Her gaze found the clock on the dresser, and she noted that it was not yet nine. Plenty of time to go, if she was going to, which she wasn't.

Or was she? Somehow, even though she knew the potential pitfalls, she couldn't make herself give up the faintest hope that . . . well, that she might actually do it.

The truth was that she wanted to see him

again. And not where a million prying eyes could evaluate their every move. She wanted him to herself, to see if perhaps he felt the same tremors of excitement that she did. But especially to discover why he was so interested in Grandfather. Something odd was at work there; she could almost taste it. For Grandfather's sake, if not her own, she needed to discover what was afoot with the handsome viscount. It was entirely possible the man had nefarious plans, for his past was certainly shadowy enough to suggest such a thing.

She paused, the silver brush held motionless at her temple as she recalled her dreams from last night. Unsettling dreams. Vague dreams. Dreams of Westerville and his mouth on hers. What was it about the man? He was certainly handsome, devastatingly so. With his pale green eyes and black hair, he was the epitome of devilish good looks that could make a woman imagine herself wildly in love.

But Beth was not like that. Her pragmatic nature did not lend itself to such romantic goings-on. Indeed, though she appreciated the viscount's disturbing handsomeness, it was something else that drew her hither. It was the challenge. The excitement. The forbidden air of his very masculine—

"My lady?"

Beth started, whirling around to see Annie standing almost behind her. Beth pressed a hand to her thudding heart. "Goodness! You frightened me!"

"I don't know why when I've been natterin' at ye

all the way from the dressin' room. Are ye feelin' well?"

"Well?"

Annie glanced at Beth's hand where she held the brush motionless at her temple.

Beth replaced the brush on the dresser. "I am quite well, thank you. I was just thinking about something."

"Right deeply, from the looks of it," Annie said, her brows lowered. "Ye're already dressed, too."

Beth smiled a little at the hint of censure in Annie's voice. "I can dress myself, you know."

"The question is not whether ye can, but whether ye should." Annie looked her up. Then down. "I was right yesterday; 'tis a man," she said in a voice that brooked no argument.

Beth looked down at her walking gown of blue muslin. "How can you tell? I mean," she amended hastily, "of course it's not a man, but why would you think such a thing?"

"Because just last week ye said the neckline on that gown was too low. And now, here ye are, a-wearin' it. It's a man."

Beth made an exasperated noise. "I don't know what you are talking about."

Annie picked up the brush. "Would ye like me to put up yer hair fer whatever man it is that ye're after?"

"I am not *after* any man." At least, not to dally with. She just wished to discover the viscount's motives. The more she thought of it, the more she realized that the viscount had not sought her out solely to pay her compliments. Which was a sad thing, really. Had he seriously been interested in her, she might have rethought her plans. But that was neither here nor there—he had other motives; she was certain of it.

Though she was sadly flattered by his attention, she was not naive enough to think he'd fallen senseless at her feet because of her blond tresses or any other such nonsense.

No, the man was after something, and if it wasn't her fortune, what was it? She frowned. Upon catching Annie's considering gaze in the mirror, Beth sniffed. "I am not after any man. If you must know, I am embarking on a Mission of Truth."

Annie twisted Beth's hair into a neat knot at the base of her neck, and then pinned it all in place with a blue silk rose to one side. "If ye're not after a man, then there's at least a man involved in yer efforts, whatever they may be."

The maid stepped back to admire her handiwork. " 'Tis not so horrid, bein' after a man. I've been after one or two meself. My second husband, Clyde Darrow, was a right shy fellow. I had to almost toss myself at his head before he would so much as look at me." Annie patted her red curls. "But when he did finally notice me, he never stopped."

"Sounds like true love."

"Oh, 'twasn't love at all. 'Twas more lust with a little fondness tossed in. Still, I was powerful sad when he died." Annie paused and looked at the ceiling as if trying to remember the details. "Killed by the ague, he was."

"I thought he fell off the roof trying to fix a loose tile."

"That was me first husband, Peter Pool."

"Ah. Sorry."

"Don't think on it. I get them confused meself. No, Clyde caught the ague after a cockfight in Stafford-Upon-Wey. Would ye believe the fool wagered on a bird named Bad Luck?" Annie scowled. " 'Tis like throwin' yerself under the wheels of a carriage, spittin' at fate in such a rash manner."

"Did you love him?"

"No. Not at first. I grew to be fond of him, of course. But no more."

"Then why did you wish to marry him?"

Annie looked surprised. "I was a widow, weren't I? There he was, unwed and makin' a good living with no one to cook his supper nor warm his bed. And we was quite fond of one another, too."

"And was that enough? Just . . . fondness?"

"Depends on what else ye might have in common," Annie said with a wicked twinkle.

"I always thought love was crucial for a marriage to be successful. At least, that's what Grandfather has always told me."

"And yer father? What did he say?"

"I was young when he died. All I really remember about him was that he was quite busy trying to read every book in Grandfather's library and . . . well, he wasn't well the last several years of his life." He hadn't been happy, either, though he'd tried not to let it show. And Charlotte . . . Beth remembered how often her stepmama appeared at the dinner table with eyes reddened from crying. It seemed as if Charlotte was always unhappy about something, though Beth wondered if perhaps there had been a rift of some sort between her father and stepmama. It would explain a lot of things, now that she thought about it.

She'd even once asked Grandfather about it. He'd replied that Father had been deeply in love with Beth's mother and he shouldn't have been so quick to think he could replace her, especially with a nitwit like Charlotte. Beth had winced to hear such a sharp opinion, but she privately thought it was probably quite true. Father had succumbed to loneliness and married someone unsuited to life in Massingale House.

"Love or no," Annie said stoutly, "there's plenty to be said for marriage."

"Like what?"

"It gives a name to yer children."

"I know, I know. That part I understand. But why should anyone wish to marry other than that?"

Annie put the brush back on the table with a definite snap. "Ye don't know why people should marry? Why, because 'tis the way God meant 'em to be!"

"Without love?"

"Love can come or love cannot come. So long as 'tis a good man and ye're a good woman, ye'll be happy enough."

Beth didn't think she liked that answer. "Happy enough" was not how she wished to spend the rest of her life. Of course, she didn't really know what she wanted to do with the rest of her life ... but "happy enough" wasn't it.

Annie sniffed. "I've married plenty and only been in love once, meself. With my third husband, Oliver MacOwen, Now *that* was love."

"The one who died while herding pigs and they ate him?"

"No, no. 'Twas the other way around. The pigs didn't eat him; Oliver ate bad sausage and that's what did him in. 'Tis no way to die, let me tell ye."

"I can't imagine it would be." Beth wondered what it would be like to be married to Viscount Westerville. Certainly they'd have passion, for she felt definite waves of it every time he was near. She was fairly certain he felt it, too. But what else would they have? Perhaps a shared sense of humor; she'd caught a bit of that yesterday afternoon. But *that* was all.

Yet another reason to spend one more paltry hour with the man, she decided. Just to prove that he was not the sort of man one should marry. She had to smile a little at her faulty reasoning; if there was one thing she already knew, it was that the dark and dangerous Viscount Westerville was not the sort of man one should marry. He was, however, unusually interested in Grandfather.

The clock chimed the quarter hour and Beth looked at the clock. If she went, she was taking a chance with her reputation. If she didn't go, she would never discover why Westerville's interest in Grandfather was for good or ill.

Beth glanced at the maid. "Annie, I believe I shall visit the museum today."

"The museum? Again? Ye just went a week ago!"

"There's a new display."

Annie shook her head. "I don't see what ye find interestin' about looking at things that once't belonged to a bunch of dead people, but I suppose ye enjoy it well enough."

"I love the museum."

"Off with ye then," Annie said, straightening the bottles and brushes on the dressing table. "And don't forget to smile." She curled her top lip and tapped on her front tooth. "Men like a woman with a good set of nippers."

"I never said I was going to meet a man. I *am* going to the museum though." Beth stood. "But since we are talking about it, how do you know you are in love?"

Annie snorted, opening the wardrobe door and removing a mint green pelisse. "Law, my lady! That's as easy as they come. If ye find yerself thinkin' perhaps ye have the ague, but ye've no fever, then ye're in love."

"It feels like the ague?" Beth pulled the pelisse over her gown and buttoned it up. "Every time?"

"More oft than naught."

Goodness. What a horrid thing. "No wonder people run from it." Beth opened the door. "I shall return soon. Please have the blue and cream silk visiting gown ready. I'm to see Lady Chudrowe this afternoon."

"Yes, my lady."

Beth left her room, her mind racing. She would meet the viscount only this one time, and then— never again. Surely one more meeting would not put her in too great a danger of being seduced.

She took the stairs quickly and dashed through the foyer to where the carriage awaited. The day was gray and overcast, a heavy wind lifting her gown and swirling it about her ankles. Beth shivered a little and pulled her pelisse closer.

"My lady?" the groom asked as he opened the door to the carriage.

"The British Museum."

"Of course, madam." Within moments, the carriage was rocking its way through the heavily traveled roads of London. They reached the British Museum quite a bit earlier than ten. The coachman looked uncertain when he saw no one there to meet her. Beth had to inform him rather haughtily that her party was already inside and that naturally none of them was waiting for her on the steps as it was about to rain.

That satisfied him and soon the carriage was gone. Beth ran up the wide marble steps of the British Museum and made her way across the marble portico.

Her half boots clicked smartly as she pushed open the huge, heavy doors and walked inside. An attendant raced up to take her pelisse, but Beth shook her head. It was quite cold inside the museum, and she had no intention of shivering her way through the next half hour. Besides, the coat added yet another layer of protection, and she needed all she could get.

Beth paid for a subscription ticket, took the guidebook from the attendant, and made her way into the entryway toward several wooden and glass cases. Inside each was a variety of colorful and intricate Chinese silk fans being admired by several onlookers.

Pretending an interest she did not feel, Beth paused at the display. Inwardly she was trembling, wondering when the viscount would arrive and what he would say. Of their own accord, the memories of her dreams began to flash through her mind, vivid and startling.

Her body immediately began to respond; her skin prickled, her breasts tightened, a restless feeling spread from her stomach to her knees.

"Oh, just stop it!" she told herself. She caught the startled gaze of a matron who was standing near.

A hot blush rose in Beth's cheeks. If she was not careful, the entire world would think her mad. "I said, ah, 'How startling!'"

The matron blinked.

Beth pointed to one of the fans in the case. "The red fan. It is quite startling." She enunciated every syllable very distinctly.

An expression of relief crossed the woman's face. "I thought you'd said something about shopping." The woman's cheeks creased as she grinned good-naturedly. "I never miss a comment about shopping unless I can help it."

Beth chuckled. "Nor I! I am sorry to have disturbed your viewing."

The woman shrugged. "Not at all. I just—" Her eyes widened as she focused on something past Beth's shoulder. Her mouth sagged open, and she didn't move until her companion—an older man who looked sorely displeased when he realized what the woman was staring at—harrumphed loudly, took her by the arm, and pulled her to the other side of the room.

It was Westerville. It had to be. Blast it, why did she have to be attracted to a man who looked so like a fallen angel that women could not help but stare? It was most annoying. The sad truth was that she was mad. Mad to come here, mad to think she could get any sort of information from a man she barely knew.

She should just leave. That is what a sane woman would do. Leave and never look back. She could write a nice note from the safety of her own home and be done with the whole thing. Of course, she'd never discover his intentions toward Grandfather. She didn't think he'd respond kindly to such high-handed treatment, and it would definitely make her persona non grata in his eyes.

Oddly, the thought of never seeing him again made her feel strange. Not lost, really—she didn't know the man that well. But wistful, as if she'd found something special, and then misplaced it.

A prickle up her back told her he was approaching. She quickly pretended to be absorbed in her guidebook. As she stood there, head bent over the book, a faint sliver of heat tumbled over her skin and between her shoulders.

Her entire body tightened with response. She had to remember herself and, worse, remember to stutter, at least a bit. She wet her lips, straightening her shoulders and trying to ignore the crazed beating of her heart.

It was ridiculous to have such a reaction to a mere presence. Ridiculous and a complete waste of time.

A hand closed over her elbow, and heat flared up her arm, making her breasts tingle, her lashes flutter over her eyes.

"There you are." The deep, melodious voice dipped lower, nearer. "I have been looking for you."

Beth sucked in her breath and tried desperately to gather herself. "H-have you?" She tugged her arm gently, trying to pull free.

He released her elbow, but slowly, allowing it to slide from his long fingers, his touch lingering. "I did not know if you would come."

Gathering herself, she turned and smiled brightly up at him, trying not to look him directly in the eyes. "Of course I c-c-came. I could not resist a ch-ch-challenge, and you know it."

He grinned, his lips quirked in amusement. He looked much as she'd thought he would, except for one thing. He was slightly unkempt—his eyes unusually bright, his hair mussed, a faint shadow to his face as if he'd just—

He was still wearing his evening clothes.

"You . . . you haven't been home since last night!"

His teeth flashed, startlingly white. "Observant lass, aren't you?" Dissipation etched deep lines in his face, making his eyes appear more deep set than usual.

The jackanapes didn't even have the decency to pretend to be embarrassed. Beth plopped her hands on her hips, righteous indignation flooding away her previous trepidation. "My lord—"

"Christian."

"My lord," she repeated stubbornly, "I don't know why I agreed to meet you here."

"I do."

She paused at the sound of certainty in his voice. "Why?"

"Because you are curious."

"Yes," she said. "Yes, I am." She met his gaze directly. "Why are you interested in my grandfather?"

There was a long, heavy pause, then the viscount leaned one shoulder against the wall and slid his hands deep into his pockets.

Beth thought he would argue with her, or at least downplay his interest from the day before. She was ready for prevarication, deception, and subterfuge.

She wasn't ready for him to look directly at her mouth and say, "You have quite an unusual stutter."

She ground her teeth, her hand fisting about the hapless guidebook. She'd forgotten that silly stutter once again, blast it. "Un-un-unusual? H-h-h-how so?"

Christian watched his now-flushed companion with amusement. "It's odd; it comes and goes at the most opportune times."

Elizabeth's fists clenched at her sides, her mouth pressed into a straight line. He could tell she was struggling with irritation at her own forgetfulness and discomfort at his direct questioning. He hadn't planned on taxing her so, even though he'd decided yesterday that her stutter was a scheme of

some sort, probably a simple attempt to free herself from the clutches of those fools he'd seen pes-
tering her in the park.

Frankly, he'd have done far worse to be rid of
the lot of them.

But when she'd looked directly at him and
asked why he was interested in her grandfather,
his good intentions flew out the window. He
hadn't meant his questioning to be so obvious. But
perhaps he hadn't been. Perhaps he had just been
dealing with a very, very astute young woman.

He stepped forward, his arm brushing hers.
"Please feel free to stammer away. I find it quite
attractive."

Her irritation disappeared behind a flash of
surprise. "Attractive?"

"Very." He took her hand and placed it within
the crook of his arm and led her out of the display
room and down a side corridor. He paused at the
door to the first room and glanced in, but found it
far too crowded. He took the crushed guidebook
from her hand and paged through it. "Are you interested in Etruscan art?"

"What? I—no. I don't think so."

"Good. Neither am I. Furthermore, I doubt anyone here is interested in it, either." He slid the
book into his pocket and drew her down the hallway, toward the last door.

"Where are we going?"

"You will see." He reached the door and looked
inside, then gave a satisfied nod. "Ah. Just as I
thought. It is perfect."

She halted on the doorway, pulling her hand

free from his clasp as she looked about the exhibit room. "No one is here."

"Did you wish someone to be?" Christian leaned against the wall and crossed his arms over his chest, admiring the way the soft light from the window caught the light in her curls. "Someone other than me?"

She bit her lip and looked at the door, then back to him. He could almost see the war being fought behind her brown eyes. She was curious about him, of that he was certain. But she was also cautious.

She sighed. "I should have known this would turn out like this. I should not have come without a chaperone."

"Why?" he asked, amused. "Are you afraid I will attempt to seduce you?"

To his surprise, his comment did not embarrass her. Indeed, she sent him an exasperated glance before saying in a chilled voice, "With you, I am never certain of anything. You are always . . . hinting."

"Hinting?"

"Yes," she said severely. "About things. Things like—like us. Do not pretend you don't know it, for I am quite certain you do."

Christian laughed a little at that. He'd spent the entire night in a gaming hell just south of here. He'd gambled and flirted and drunk his fill, trying all the while not to think of this meeting. He'd been grossly unsuccessful. The blue ink on the gaming cards had reminded him of Elizabeth's bonnet ribbons, the warm brown ale had carried the same

light as her expressive eyes, the widow who'd tried
to tempt him into going upstairs with her had—for
all her obvious beguilements and wiles—been
plain and unexciting compared to Elizabeth. All in
all, his "escape" had turned into an endless cycle of
memories.

She was damnably entrancing, and he regretted
having to use her. His admiration of her was real,
though. Too real. So real, in fact, that last night
when he'd returned home after having a late supper at White's, he had been unable to sleep, but
had tossed and turned in his bed. Every time
Christian closed his eyes, he saw Elizabeth's face,
peeping up at him, that damnably certain smile
on her lips, her brown eyes warm and inviting.

It was quite unlike Christian to lose sleep over
anything. Not since he'd been a child had silly
emotions kept him awake all night. But thanks to
Reeves and his constant harping about "seducing
innocents," sleep had proven elusive indeed. After
an hour of uncomfortable reflection Christian'd
gotten back up, dressed once again, and left the
house. Free from the whispers of his bedchamber,
he'd made his way to the nearest gaming hell
where he'd spent the time 'til dawn tossing his
coins on the table and drinking just enough to
keep his thoughts dulled and unsharpened.

Now, awake but heated by the brandy he'd con-
sumed, Christian pushed himself from the wall
and moved until he stood directly before Elizabeth. It always startled him to realize how small
she was; the top of her head barely reached his
shoulder. For some reason, she always seemed

taller. Elizabeth raised her brows, but did not pull back.

Christian lifted a finger to the lace at the shoulder of her gown and traced the outline of the fleur-de-lis embroidered on her pelisse. "I have been thinking about that entrancing stutter of yours. I quite believe it to be a ruse to chase off those mongrels that were sniffing at your skirts in the park."

An arrested expression froze on her face before she flushed deeply. "I don't stutter all of the time."

"Oh, pray don't explain it away. I enjoy your stutter."

"How can you say that?"

He grinned. "Because I love the way your lips pucker at the sounds. Your stutter is an act of seduction. An invitation to seal your troubled lips with a kiss."

"If you think a stutter is an invitation to a kiss, then it's a good thing I did not belch, else you might have thought that an invitation to my bed."

He threw back his head and laughed, long and loud. "I do not think you capable of either." His fingers lifted to her chin, and he held her face tilted to his. "In fact, I'd wager my entire fortune you no more stutter than I."

"Who are you to—" She snapped her mouth closed, a frown on her brow. Her eyes glared into his for a full moment before she sighed sharply and waved a hand. "Oh blast it all! You are right, of course. I do not stutter. I just did not want some fool offering for me. Grandfather might—" She stopped, her gaze narrowing.

"Your grandfather might what?"

"Nothing."

Before, Christian had always thought brown eyes were merely soft and feminine, but hardly exciting. But on Elizabeth, they became something more—wildly determined, warm and unyielding, sparkling with anger, and altogether exciting.

He chuckled, rather pleased. "So the lovely Lady Elizabeth is frightening off her suitors one st-t-t-tuttered word at a time."

"Lord Westerville, what I do or do not do is none of your concern."

"I beg to differ," he said softly. He brushed the back of his hand over the soft skin of her cheek. "What you do is of the utmost concern to me."

And it was. This woman held the key to everything—to his past, certainly, and perhaps even his future. In some ways, because of that connection, Elizabeth was bound to him more closely than any woman he'd ever known.

Something of his thoughts must have shown on his face, for her eyes narrowed and she leaned away ever so slightly. "Why are you looking at me that way?"

He captured one of her curls as it fell over her ear. Silky soft, her thick blond hair begged to be released from the pins. "What you do is important to me because you are who you are."

She jerked her head back, pulling the silky soft curl from his fingers even as her eyes blazed up into his. "Who I am? You mean the granddaughter of the Duke of Massingale. Westerville, it is time you explained your interest in my grandfather."

Christian managed a casual shrug. "I was just being polite in asking about your closest relative."

"I don't believe that." Her gaze never wavered, and the faint smile on her lips did not reach her eyes. "Yesterday, every time Grandfather's name was mentioned, you lit up like a newly clipped candle."

Damn it! She was quick-witted. Almost too much so. What could he say now?

Her mouth tightened. "I know you are not pursuing me for some silly, passion-filled notion. You are not the type for such romantic drivel and neither am I."

She was right. If it had been any other woman than Elizabeth, he'd have simply declared himself deeply in love; most women wanted to hear such drivel and would believe it no matter how improbable.

But he somehow thought Elizabeth was made of sterner stuff. She would not accept a romantic declaration, which was a pity for he'd had just enough wine to make such a thing desirable. And being close to her was increasing the heady effects of the libations he'd used to drown out his sleepless night. That left him with the truth, and he had no intention of imparting that.

He bowed, smiling faintly. "Whatever I do, I will *not* bore either of us with romantic drivel, as you so correctly term it."

"Thank you," she said, turning and walking toward the closest display case. It held a number of small stone figures, which she peered at with feigned interest, her smile set in a way that made him uneasy. After a moment, she turned to look at him. "I am going to discover why you want to know about my grandfather, one way or another."

He could not mistake the sincerity of her words. "Indeed."

"Yes," she said firmly, then turned back to the display.

He came to stand beside her, leaning on the case with one arm and noting that the nape of her neck was exposed as she bent over the display. "How do you plan on discovering my secrets—*if* I have any?"

She glanced up at him, her lashes casting shadows over her cheeks. "Logic. You are obviously a man of sophisticated tastes. I do not think you would normally dally with a woman who is so obviously being placed out for marriage."

He raised his brows. "You?"

"Don't pretend you don't understand. My grandfather was not hesitant in letting the world know I was on the market and his heir as well." She leaned her elbow on the case and faced him so that they were now standing mirror image.

"Let me explain what bothers me thus far," she said smoothly. "First, you are sending out the unmistakable message you are pursuing me."

He moved forward ever so slightly. She had the lushest lips. Plump and pink and turned up ever so slightly at the corners, even when she was in repose. "Go on."

"Second, you are not interested in me in a romantic fashion. You, my lord, are not that sort."

Her hair, too, was such a sensual shade. He

smiled, remembering the feel of it beneath his fingertips. "Elizabeth, I find you attractive. I will not deny that."

"Yes, but I am an unattached, marriageable female. Under other circumstances, you would run from an acquaintance with me."

Damn, but she had measured him well. Still, it would not do to encourage her. "Perhaps." His gaze drifted over her. "Perhaps not."

"And third," she replied in a firm voice, "You don't seem all that interested in my dowry, either."

"You are right. I have my own funds, my love. I have no need of yours." He shrugged. "My father did me the favor of dying without legitimate issue. My brother and I benefited greatly from it."

Her brows drew down. "Without legitimate issue? But your brother inherited the title, did he not?"

"Yes. And I inherited the title of viscount, but only because my father forged a church registry saying he'd married Mother years ago."

Elizabeth's eyes widened. "Forged? Are you joking with me, Westerville?"

"Would I joke about being illegitimate?" He shook his head. "I am a bastard, though a wealthy, titled one. My father, the late Earl of Rochester, attempted to legitimize me, poorly done as it was. All the world knows. Not that it matters."

"I cannot believe you would so freely admit to such. Surely there are other relatives who might come forward if what you say is true. Relatives who might want both the title and the fortune."

"They'd have to battle their way through a swarm of trustees, many of whom wear very large buttons, have exaggerated shirt points, and possess far too many little yappy dogs." Christian feigned a shiver. "Personally, I would rather eat raw snails."

Her lips quivered. "A swarm of Bartholomew Babies, I take it?"

"Complete fribbles, the lot of them." He returned her smile. "My father did not care if he was a good father, but he was bound and determined to always be first in fashion."

"That's a pity."

Christian shrugged. "When he needed a group of trustworthy advisers to administer his estate and assist his lost sons, who other than the very men who'd critiqued his cravat for years on end?"

She tilted her head to one side, her gaze thoughtful. "You sound a bit bitter."

"Me? Bitter?" Christian waved a hand. "Rochester's obsession with fashion was more important than his responsibility as a parent. With that, I have no problem; what little I know of him, I don't believe he would have been very good at it, anyway. But that he allowed my mother to die in a prison, falsely accused—" Christian snapped his lips closed. "I find it difficult to either forget or forgive that."

"So would I."

"Lest you think my father completely worthless, let me state that his stewardship was unparalleled. Under his touch, the estates flourished in a way few other men could have done."

"My grandfather is the same way."

Christian gave a mirthless smile. "And there ends their similarities; they are both good stewards. I have been going through the estate records left by my father; it astounds me the amount of time he put forth to bring the family fortune to what it is."

"You sound as if you admire him a little."

"That would be too kind of a word. Let us just say that I respect his ability to get things done. There is much to be learned from a man's successes, no matter who he is."

"This is all very interesting, Westerville," Beth said, sending him a surprisingly level look. "But that is neither here nor there. What is it you *really* want from me? What is it about Grandfather that interests you so?"

Christian's gaze touched the curve of Beth's lashes and the proud line of her cheek, the delicately audacious chin, to the swell of her breasts beneath her gown. In all his years of riding the High Toby and trysting with the women whose jewels he stole, he had never met a woman like this.

She was neither jaded nor spoiled, but simply herself. There was a freshness about this woman, the feeling of a bed newly made with just-washed sheets still warm from the iron. It was the feeling of coming home and leaving for some great adventure, combined into one.

He reached up and cupped her cheek, sliding his thumb over her warm skin. "I will admit to one thing and one thing only, and that is that you are beautiful."

Her fingers closed over his wrist, halting his wandering hand just short of her hair. "And you, Westerville, are not answering my question."

Christian almost allowed his frustration to show. He could not answer her question without giving himself away, and his avoidance of it only made her wonder all the more.

It was a damnable quandary, one to which he had no easy answer. So, left with no choice, he did the only thing he could do—he kissed her.

Chapter 8

I recently read a story in the papers about a servant who, in a fit of pique, poisoned his master. It is, alas, a too frequent tale and the ultimate sign of poor training. If you ever catch your hand wavering over the arsenic bottle, please put down the roast mutton, return to your quarters, pack your bags, and find another post immediately. There are better ways to correct a joyless situation.

A Compleat Guide for
Being a Most Proper Butler
by Richard Robert Reeves

$\mathcal{B}$eth didn't have time to think. The kiss was so unexpected that she was responding before she even realized it. She couldn't help herself. She was instantly enveloped in him—in the feel of Westerville's hands as they slipped about her and pulled her to him, the heat of his body pressed to hers, the taste of him as he parted her lips with an insistent urging. Shivers wracked her head to toe.

The kiss deepened as his hands roamed over her back, pulling her closer, molding her to him. Something stirred inside her as she arched against him, her arms tightening about his neck.

Sensations rippled through Beth in a tangle of unthinking passion. Her body craved this, yearned for it, begged for it.

He turned slightly, pressing her against the exhibit case, the frame cool against her back, even through her pelisse. Beth was barely aware of that fact, scarcely felt his hands as he slid them down her sides, to her hips. Warmth radiated from each place he touched, and her knees felt oddly weak.

Good God, he was kissing her. *He was kissing her.*

Reason returned with a rush. This was not the way she'd planned this meeting to go. She placed her hands on Westerville's chest and broke the kiss instantly, turning to one side, her breath rushing past her lips.

She could not believe she'd allowed the kiss to happen. She pressed her hands to her eyes, her entire body trembling. It was madness. A rich, raucous riotous sort of madness, the type of which Beth had never before experienced. Standing there in the circle of Westerville's arms, struggling to catch her breath, her lips still moist and tingling from his kisses, she felt . . . wonderful. Absolutely and inexplicably wonderful.

Christian looked down at Beth's bent head. It had taken every ounce of his strength to break the delicious kiss. His hands remained where they were, simply because he could not move away. She was as intoxicating and succulent as a freshly picked berry, the oddest mixture of innocence and sensuality he had ever met. Despite his intentions otherwise, he had to admit that he was honestly attracted to her. And not because of the opportunity to discover the truth about the man responsible for his mother's wrongful imprisonment. No, it was more than that. Elizabeth was beautiful, unconsciously sensual, intelligent, and oh-so-willing to control every situation, which made him more and more determined to remain in charge himself—he could not easily walk away from such a tempting combination.

Right now, his hands still on her waist, she was achingly near. Yet he did not pull her closer. She stood, head bent, hands over her eyes as if she were trying to eradicate the last few minutes. He could feel the tremble of her body beneath his fingertips, see the rapid rise and fall of her chest. She struggled with as many emotions as he.

The thought pleased him. She was not immune to him, at least. In fact, judging by her passionate response to his kiss, she was as affected by him as he was by her. He waited for her to move, to say something, but she did nothing but keep her eyes covered. But . . . His smile slipped. Good God, she wasn't crying, was she?

Never, of all the kisses he'd given and received, had any of them ended in tears. But then he'd never had anything to do with a woman who was so obviously an innocent. He bent a little, trying to see behind her hands, but couldn't.

Bloody hell, he hadn't wished to upset her. All he'd really wanted to do was keep her from asking questions he wasn't ready to answer.

This would not do. Not at all. A voice sounded in the hallway, a man intoning a lecture on the intricacies of ancient Etruscan art.

Christian cursed silently. He steeled himself and lifted a hand to Elizabeth's chin, then raised her face to his. She dropped her hands to her sides and met his gaze.

She wasn't crying. She was, in fact, smiling. A soft, tremulous smile that not only sent a flood of relief through him, but made him pull her a bit closer.

But this was not to be for the fair Lady Elizabeth. She immediately stepped out of his embrace. "No," she said in a rather breathless voice. "Don't!"

He shoved his hands into his pockets, fighting the urge to reach for her once more. "You needn't worry. I am not a man to force myself upon a woman, no matter how beautiful she may be."

"I didn't think you were," she said. "I am not maligning your character, but questioning my own judgment. None of this should have happened. I should not have met you this morning, I just thought—" She shook her head. "I was wrong."

"Didn't you enjoy the kiss?"

Her gaze flew to his. "Yes. I did. However, that doesn't mean it was the right thing to do." A resolute look entered her eyes, her smile grew a touch more fixed. "We should not be alone again."

"Never?"

"Never," she said, that damnable half smile on

her lips, her eyes shining with an odd determination.

Christian began to feel the slightest bit uneasy. "Elizabeth, I did not wish to upset you. I find you attractive and I—"

She held up a hand. "We've played enough games today, don't you think? Thank you for your invitation to visit the museum. I shall never think of Etruscan art in quite the same way."

He had to smile a little at that even though he had the oddest feeling that he'd just lost something. Something infinitely valuable. "Elizabeth, we should talk—"

"I really must go."

He took a step forward. "Surely you can stay another ten minutes. We have yet to enjoy the Roman friezes."

The faint smile on her lips never changed, though her cheeks bloomed with fresh color. "Enjoyment is not the question." She tightened her reticule where it swung from her wrist. "I asked you about your interest in my grandfather and you answered with a kiss, which was highly inappropriate."

"It was just an impulse. I could not help myself."

"I don't believe you. That kiss was nothing more than an attempt to avoid my question. It proved I was correct in my suspicions." Her clear brown gaze found his. "You have an interest in my grandfather that I must assume to be against his well-being. Otherwise, had you a benign reason, you would have explained yourself and been done with it."

Christian's hands curled into fists. Damn it! This was not the way this meeting was to have gone. "I am only seeking the truth."

"About?" She waited, brows lifted.

Christian forced a smile, struggling with a very real impulse to just tell her. But he couldn't just blurt out that he suspected her grandfather of dire actions that had led to Mother's death. It was becoming painfully clear that she held her grandfather in considerable esteem. And if that was so, she would take any information he might let slip and run straight to Massingale House, throw the bolt, and tell her grandfather everything.

Christian was not willing to lose the element of surprise; it was one of his few weapons.

Her gaze narrowed. "I want the truth, Westerville. Our attraction is not all there is to your pursuit and I know it."

"You enjoyed our kiss."

"I did." She pulled on her gloves, carefully adjusting each finger so that they fit perfectly. "Which is why I shall take care never to see you alone again. Ever."

"Elizabeth, there is no—"

"Good day, Lord Westerville. It is obvious you will not confess your intentions. I wish things had ended differently, but they have not. Just rest assured of this—I shall discover what you are about and I will do what I can to stop you."

Christian scowled, all of his earlier pleasure gone. "Are you threatening me?"

"Oh no, my lord. That is no threat, but a promise." With those clipped words, that damnable smile still perfectly poised on her lips, she turned on her heel and walked out the door.

Christian started after her, but loud booming voices in the corridor just outside the doorway halted him cold.

Blast it all to hell, this had not gone the way he'd wished it. Not at all. He turned back into the display room, slumped against the wall, and raked a hand through his hair. She was the key to the Massingale estate, and in one short interview she had all but called his hand.

What was he going to do now?

The door to the Rochester London House opened as Christian walked up the front steps.

"There you are, my lord," Reeves said, taking Christian's coat and handing it to a hovering footman, "When you didn't return last night, we began to wonder if you'd forgotten the way home. I was just about to dispatch a search party."

"If you ever send one, please arm them with a bottle of my best brandy," Christian said, walking to the library. "It is the only way I would allow them to persuade me to come home."

"I shall remember that," Reeves replied evenly, following Christian into the library. "Master William arrived."

Christian stopped. "Where is he?"

"In the kitchen, eating his weight in cabbage soup. He rode all night, but refuses to sleep. I suggested a change of clothing might not be amiss, but he won't do a thing until he has spoken to you."

"Send him to me."

"I already took that liberty, my lord."

The door opened and a footman entered with a tray. "Ah!" Reeves said with evident pleasure. "Your tea."

"I didn't ask for tea."

The butler took the tray and shooed the man from the room, then set the tray beside Christian. "I know you did not ask for tea, my lord, but I thought it might revive you after such a long evening. Seducing innocent virgins is such a tiring venture."

Christian lifted a brow. "Are we back to that?"

"Am I mistaken? Or did you not meet with Lady Elizabeth?"

"Perhaps."

"I see. I shall assume that you behaved as a proper gentleman should."

Christian glared at the butler. "I don't like tea."

Reeves paused in pouring a cup. "No tea, my lord?"

"*No.*"

"A pity. I'd hoped it might wake you a bit. Master William seemed quite full of news and you will need to be at your sharpest." Reeves held out the steaming cup.

Reluctantly, Christian took the tea and, after sniffing it suspiciously, took a small sip. He grimaced. "Is there sugar?"

"Of course, my lord."

Christian placed the cup back on the table. "Three teaspoons."

Reeves paused.

Christian did not give the butler time to speak. "Yes, damn it! I said three."

"In one cup?"

"Either you put the sugar in my tea, or I will not drink it."

With a vaguely dissatisfied air, Reeves added sugar to the cup.

"That was but two. Add another."

Reeves sighed, but complied. "A man given to excesses, aren't you, my lord?"

"Whenever I can, Reeves. Whenever I can." Christian took another cautious sip. It was much better this time, robust and sweet and almost good.

A light knock sounded and a footman opened the door to announce Willie's arrival. The Scotsman appeared, a huge, lumbering figure wrapped in a long black coat and wearing thick black leather boots. His red hair was pulled back and braided, his face covered with a few days' growth of beard. He appeared tired, but elated.

Christian's hopes flickered.

Willie lifted a foot to step onto the carpet.

"Halt!" Reeves commanded.

Willie put his mud-spattered boot back down and glared at the butler. "What're ye wanting now, ye old nabler?"

Reeves took a small towel from the tea tray and crossed to where Willie stood. Reeves laid the towel on the carpet, one step inside the room. "Pray stand here, Master William. And do not move from that spot."

"I am not going to stand on no tea towel!"

"Then you may tell the housekeeper why all of the carpets must be cleaned again. She will have an apoplexy."

The Scotsman scowled, but there was no denying the mud on his feet. He stepped onto the small towel with the most obvious reluctance.

His huge feet touched each side of the tiny cloth, and it appeared for a moment that balancing in such a small area might cause him a problem. But by the judicious effects of crossing his arms over his huge barrel chest and rocking back on his heels, he managed to remain on the towel. " 'Tis like visitin' me grandmither," the Scotsman growled. "She's forever placin' blankets over the chairs so no one will mar them 'til it looks as if she lives in a ghostie house."

Christian lifted a brow. "What did you find? Did you locate the bishop?"

Willie's face cleared, a glow shining in his blue eyes. "I have a letter from him."

Christian leaned forward.

"Aye. I didna get to speak to him meself as he was ill as a jackrabbit's hind leg. He's not expected to live the week. I had to give his daughter the questions ye wished to ask. She says he answered them all here." Willie pulled open his leather vest and pulled a small packet from an inner pocket.

Reeves took the letter and brought it to Christian.

Christian looked at the neatly pressed sheet of paper, the edges crisply folded. Here it was. The answer to his questions.

With hands that shook slightly, he opened the letter.

My dear Lord Westerville,

I cannot tell you how blessed I am to receive your inquiry about your mother, Mary Margaret. I knew her when she was a young girl and her family attended the church where I was doing my prelate studies. She was one of the most generous and giving people I have ever met, which is why when I learned many years later than she was in gaol, I visited her. I knew her imprisonment had to be an error. To this day, I still believe that.

I was only able to see her a few times before her death. You ask if I witnessed anything unusual or odd, and I must say yes. Several things come to mind, now that I think of it. The last time I went to see your mother, there was a coach outside with a crest of purple and gold—

Christian looked at Reeves. "What are the colors of the Massingale crest?"

Reeves pursed his lips. "I believe it is purple and cream, although . . ." He frowned. "There might be some gold, as well."

"Aye," Willie agreed. "I've followed that carriage oft enough to know."

Christian nodded and returned to the letter.

—though I cannot be certain. I regret to say that I never saw the person in that carriage as I had several others to visit before your mother. By the time I reached her cell, the visitor and coach had left. Your mother was ill by this time, and there was

*a certain nervous apprehension to her movements,
and that saddened me greatly.*

*I asked your mother what was wrong, but
being fevered and at times incoherent, she did not
answer me directly. I did what I could to make her
more comfortable and covered her with an extra
blanket I had brought, but she kept removing it,
claiming she needed to get up. That she'd paid
her enemy with her last remaining valuable—her
famous sapphire necklace. For that, your mother
thought whoever had provided the evidence
against her would withdraw it.*

*But something had gone amiss with this plan,
for though she'd delivered the necklace, the charges
were still in place. Your mother asked if I would
deliver one last letter for her. She handed me a
missive, and I tucked it into my pocket and spent
a few more minutes with her. As I left the cell, she
clutched my arm and begged that I find you and
your brother. She spoke of you both often, and
you were her main concern.*

Christian realized he was holding the letter so
tightly, he'd crumpled the edge of it. He relaxed his
hold and smoothed the letter a bit, his mind
whirling over the words. His mother had asked
about him and Tristan often. And wished them
found.

Of course, by that time, he and Tristan had been
forced to move from their house because of the
creditors, but Mother wouldn't have known that.

Christian continued reading.

Later, on my way out of the prison, I looked at the missive. I was quite surprised to discover that it was addressed to the Duke of Massingale's residence, to someone addressed as "Sinclair." I delivered the letter as your mother requested and was rather surprised when the butler did not seem to find this odd sort of address amiss. He took the letter, thanked me, and escorted me out the door. A day later, your mother died.

I wish I had more information to impart, but I do not. You ask for some proof; all I can say is this—find the necklace and you will discover who wished your mother ill. Your mother was a good and godly woman and I am sure she found her way at the end, as I am sure you will.

God bless you, my son,
Father Joshua Durham

Christian set down the letter. Sinclair. There it was again, that name. Was it a code name for the duke? Christian sucked in a deep breath.

"My lord?" Reeves's voice broke through the silence.

Christian struggled to the surface to answer. Mother had not been completely alone at the end. Father Durham had found her and had done what he could for her. Until that moment, Christian hadn't realized what a burden that had been.

Reeves's voice cut through the fog in Christian's mind. "What His Lordship needs is more tea."

"Humph," Willie said. "Brandy is more like."

Christian folded the letter and placed it on the table beside him. "No more tea. Or brandy."

Reeves bowed. "May I ask if the letter contained what you thought it would?"

"Yes," Christian said, staring down at the folded missive. "Somewhere in the duke's house is a necklace belonging to my mother. If I can find that, then I will have proof he was involved in my mother's false incarceration."

Willie scratched his ear. "What sort of necklace is this?"

Christian glanced at the letter, his heart sinking. "I don't know. The bishop said it was famous, though."

"Ah, the sapphire necklace." Reeves nodded.

Christian looked at Reeves. "You know it?"

"Your father gave your mother a sapphire necklace the day you and your brother were born. It was quite spectacular, as it was set in a very elaborate silver setting. I've never seen one like it."

"Do you think you could draw a picture of it? I must know what it looks like."

"I can do one better. I can show it to you as it is featured in the portrait of your mother which is hanging at your father's country estate. It is but a two-hour ride from here."

It was ironic that the portrait his father had commissioned would assist Christian in finding who betrayed his mother. In some ways, it was as if his father was helping him from beyond the grave. Christian shook off the thought; he didn't believe in things he couldn't see. He never would.

He looked at Reeves. "Excellent! We will leave within the hour and then return this evening. And then—" Christian nodded to himself "—then I must find a way into the duke's household. Now, more than ever."

"Can't ye just go callin' and visit 'im?" Willie offered helpfully.

"He doesn't receive anyone. That's why his granddaughter is so important to this project. Only she and her stepmother have access to him, and the stepmother is almost as reclusive as the duke. She goes nowhere without the escort of a certain Lord Bennington."

"Well, then," Willie said affably. "Ye'll have to go through the granddaughter then."

"I was attempting to do just that, but . . . now things aren't so simple." Christian rubbed his chin. He supposed he *could* do this without Elizabeth's help, but it would be so much easier *with* her.

He frowned, wondering if perhaps he was simply looking for reasons to be with her again. Their meeting this morning had whet his appetite for her company, even though she'd made it plain she'd no longer meet with him alone. It would be difficult to find a way to have private speech with her, but it could be done. The problem was whether he could get close enough to her, gain her trust enough to garner an invitation to visit Massingale House, especially as he'd already managed to raise her suspicions. He thought of her fixed smile as she'd left him at the museum and he sighed. "I do not know if I will be able to gain Lady Elizabeth's confidence or not."

"And why is that?" Reeves said, suspicion in his voice. "What happened in your meeting with Lady Elizabeth, my lord?"

Christian shrugged. "At the moment, she will not have anything to do with me."

"How do you know this?"

"She realized I was interested in meeting her grandfather and not in her alone and she—" Christian made a slicing motion with his hand.

"Goodness!" Reeves said, a pleased expression on his face. "What a very astute young lady."

"Women," Willie said with disgust. "Trouble, the lot of 'em."

Christian stood as a sudden realization struck. Perhaps he did know a way to gain Elizabeth's co-operation. "I am not done with her yet. Lady Elizabeth will assist me, one way or the other."

"What is 'the other'?" Reeves asked.

"The lovely Lady Elizabeth has great cause to fear me as I know a secret about her." Christian smiled for the first time that hour. "Did you know that her voice is as pure and musical and lilting as a summer brook?"

"If that is her secret, then I can see why she would fear you," Reeves said in a dry tone.

"Ah, but she has no wish for that information to leak out. She has been affecting a stutter while in public. It is her protection against a swarm of importuning suitors."

"If Lady Elizabeth has already challenged you as to your designs, it might be a better plan to simply tell her the truth and enlist her aid."

"Gor!" Willie exclaimed. "I thought ye was on our side."

"I am," Reeves said smoothly. "But there are times when the truth is the best policy."

Christian shook his head. "You want me to tell Lady Elizabeth that I think her beloved grandfather is responsible for my mother's death?"

"Yes, my lord. I believe she will help you search for the evidence merely to prove you wrong."

"If I get desperate, I will remember your suggestion." Christian refolded the bishop's letter. "In the meantime, I have a few other ideas. Willie, off the carpet. Clean up and rest. I may need you soon. Reeves, order warmed water sent to my room. I want a bath, and then we'll be off to see that portrait. I need to know what that necklace looks like so there can be no mistake."

"Very well, my lord," Reeves said, watching Willie hop off his towel rather like a very large and ungainly toad, mud and dirt smearing the towel and the area around it. "I can see we shall all have a very busy afternoon ahead of us."

Chapter 9

When a task is not going the way you wish, leave it for another time and instead work on something else for a short while. You can return to the task later, when your mind is fresher. There are few difficulties which patience and hard work cannot overcome.

A Compleat Guide for
Being a Most Proper Butler
by Richard Robert Reeves

Beatrice set down her cup of tea, the click of cup to saucer quite loud. "What I just told you is completely untrue."

Beth blinked.

"You did not hear a single word I said, did you?" Beatrice said in an accusing tone.

Beth hadn't. She'd been thinking about her meeting yesterday with Westerville. Since that meeting, she'd had the uneasy suspicion that though she'd won the battle, she still had an entire war to fight.

She'd been absolutely right to tell the man she'd never see him again as it was painfully obvious his real desire was to get closer to her grandfather. The problem was, that did not lessen her interest in the man one bit. If anything, it had sharpened it.

She sighed loudly. "Beatrice, I am sorry. I am a sad woolgatherer. Grandfather is forever scolding me for that."

Beatrice slathered butter on a piece of toast with more force than form. "I don't care if you ignore me before we've had tea, but anytime thereafter, I expect your complete attention. Especially when I'm talking about something important."

Harry lowered the morning paper just enough to peer over the top. "You were talking about bonnets."

Beatrice's face colored. "Bonnets are important!"

He raised his brows. "Why?"

She opened her mouth. Then closed it, her brow furrowed in thought. Suddenly, she gave a little hop in her chair. "Bonnets are important because without them we all might have horrid freckles!"

Beth chuckled, but all Harry said was "Humph!" He was a handsome man, but with none of his wife's gadfly tendencies. He was quite happy to stay at home with a thick tome, or visit his club, or attend any one of the dozen or so of the scientific societies he so loved. They were a very disparate couple, Beth thought wistfully, but still quite in love with each other. It did her heart good to see them together.

Even now, Beatrice leaned across the table and pulled down one corner of Harry's paper, amused outrage on her pouting lips. "Harry, if you have something to say, then say it and do not make those rude humphing noises behind your paper."

His blue eyes, exaggerated in size by the wire-rimmed spectacles perched on his nose, twinkled a bit at this direct sally. He obligingly put the paper down. "My love, it is not fair for you to tell Beth you expect her complete attention when you ramble on for so long about a bonnet. I couldn't have borne such a weighty conversation, either."

Beatrice sent a frowning glare at her husband before turning to Beth. "I asked if you wished to see that adorable bonnet I saw in Bond Street yesterday, the one with the blue flowers and silver bells? It is gorgeous and would look absolutely lovely with your coloring. I just thought that if you wanted to see it, we could—"

"There!" Harry laughed. "Rambling. Thank you for proving my point."

Beatrice flounced. "Beth, do you see what I have to live with? The harshness I must endure? The criticism I am subjected to? I am so put upon I scarce know whether I should stay or go."

Harry chuckled, lifting his paper back in place. "You will do what you will do, my love."

"I am quite distraught. There is only *one* thing that will cheer me up."

"Beth," Harry said from behind his paper, "pray escort my poor, forlorn wife to Bond Street. She will perish does she not spend some of my hard-won funds this very instant."

"With pleasure!" Beth said, standing. "I will get my reticule."

"Excellent!" Beatrice said, smiling at her cousin. "I shall order the carriage and then tell Harry what a horrid husband he has become. We can meet in the hall in ten minutes."

Beth bid Harry goodbye and made her way to her room, where she quickly changed gowns, and then collected her reticule and a pelisse with green stripes that perfectly matched the color of the leaves embroidered on her slippers. She paused in the foyer to admire her morning gown of white muslin. It was adorned on one shoulder with pink and green flowers. A wide green ribbon delineated the seam just below her breasts, while her skirts flowed over her hips and to the floor. The neckline of the gown was deceptively simple, rounded with tiny cap sleeves that fit her to perfection.

"Admiring your gown?"

Beth turned to find Beatrice standing a little behind her, a knowing look in her blue eyes. "What?" Beth said, her cheeks heated. "This gown? It's nothing special—"

"Oh, don't even start that with me. Have you forgotten who I am? I can only wonder who you might be hoping to meet in Bond Street. Westerville, perhaps?"

"I don't care what Westerville thinks of this, or any other gown."

"Of course you don't. By the way, I found out some very interesting tidbits about our friend."

"That's nice," Beth said, trying not to meet Beatrice's gaze. Beth knew she shouldn't ask any questions. The less she knew about the viscount, the better.

"Don't you want to know what I discovered?"

"No. Not really." Beth removed her gloves from her reticule and pulled them on. "Shall we leave? I must see this bonnet you're so in love with."

Beatrice's brows rose. "Beth, you must want to know about the viscount."

"Well, I don't. Now, may we go shopping? I need to find a pair of slippers to go with that new silk ball gown Grandfather sent last week."

Beatrice looked Beth up and down. "Hm. I see what it is. You are upset. With Westerville."

"I am not."

"You are, too. Why else would you not want to hear the gossip about Viscount Westerville unless you were angry with him? Which means, of course, that you've seen him since we last talked."

"Ah!" Beth said with relief at the sound of a carriage pulling up. "There is your cabriolet. Are you ready?"

"Beth, I want to know what happened. Has he said something to you? Been rude or suggested something improper? Did he—" Beatrice's eyes widened. "He *kissed* you, didn't he?"

"No!" Beth said, very aware of the stoic footmen who stood flanking the hallway. She grabbed her cousin's hand and pulled her to the front door. "Come! We can finish this conversation in the cabriolet."

"Oh yes we will," Beatrice said, not a bit abashed. She tucked Beth's arm in hers and led the way to the waiting carriage.

They were barely settled and on their way when

Beatrice faced Beth. "*Now*. Tell me everything. Why are you upset with Westerville?"

Blast it, would Beatrice never leave this alone? Beth gritted her teeth. "I told you before that I am not upset with him, I only—oh bother. Just tell me what you found out about the viscount."

Beatrice sighed. "You are a woman of secrets. I wonder why I never knew this before." She slid a bit closer in the seat and leaned toward Beth. "When I started inquiring about our friend, I was given the oddest looks, but no one would really say anything! Oh, there were the usual rumors, that he'd taken up with Mrs. Edlesworth, which is not to be wondered at, for I vow, every man newly come to London seems to do the same thing. She's had more traffic through her doors than London Bridge. They should just declare the woman a national monument and put a plaque on her door that reads, 'Here is the house of Louisa Edlesworth, London's most notorious female!' I would pay money to see such a thing and I think other women would, too, if—"

"Beatrice."

Beatrice blinked. "What?"

"What did you find out about the viscount other than he dallied with Louisa Edlesworth?"

Beatrice clasped her hands together excitedly. "Well! There are the oddest rumors floating about that have to do with the viscount—"

"Yes, yes. You said people were whispering that he was a highwayman. I don't believe that myself, but—"

"Oh, they are saying all sorts of things! Apparently he was nowhere to be found for several years. Rumors are rife that he was doing something"—Beatrice lowered her voice—"illegal."

"It would not surprise me."

"Or me!" Beatrice gave a delicious shiver. "There is something dangerous about that man. Lady Chudrowe was wild with envy when I told her he'd ridden with us in my new cabriolet." Beatrice sighed happily. "And Lady Thimpkinson was positively *green* when she discovered I—"

"Beatrice, I am certain you are widely admired. What else did you find out about Westerville?"

"Well, some would have it he runs a widespread smuggling operation off the French coast. Others whisper he was the kept lover of an Italian countess—"

"Those all sound preposterous to me," Beth said in a lofty tone, though to be honest, she could see any of those dashing professions fitting the viscount. He seemed to have no fear of danger, and heaven knew he enjoyed taking chances.

She frowned. She knew how he *seemed* but not how he really *was*. The man was a mass of secrets. In fact, all she really knew was that he could turn her bones to jelly with one well-placed kiss. Well, she knew a little more than that. She knew, for instance, that he had an interest in Grandfather for some inexplicable reason. That he had a warm and witty sense of humor. That his eyes crinkled in the most beguiling way when he smiled. That his lips were firm and—

"Beth? There you go again! I have said not less

than three important things in the last minute and you haven't heard a one."

"I'm sorry," Beth said, instantly contrite. "What did you say?"

"Lady Jersey says Westerville asked if he could meet her privately to discuss his mother."

"His mother?"

"Yes. I don't know the entire story, of course, but Lady Jersey thinks he's on some sort of quest to find out about his past."

Beth found herself looking down at her gloved hands, which were clasped in her lap, the fingers neatly interlocked. Westerville had said something about searching for the truth. But what truth?

The truth about his mother, perhaps?

Beatrice pursed her lips. "I think I like the story of the Italian countess best, though I can quite see him as a highwayman. He does wear black well."

"As do all the best highwaymen," Beth said in a dry voice. "Beatrice, did you find anything else out? Anything certain?"

"Well . . . he dresses well and dances divinely. Lady Hemplewaite declares she's in love with him, and Miss Lucinda Garner has already told her father—who is nothing more than a fat cit—that she will marry Westerville and no one else."

For some reason, the mention of so many admirers quite put Beth out of humor. "Yes, yes. The list of his admirers is endless. Lady Hemplewaite and Mrs. Edlesworth and Miss Sofia Longbridge and Julia Carslowe and—"

"The Carslowe chit? The one with big front teeth? I didn't know—"

"Beatrice, the point is that it would be simpler to list those women who do *not* admire him rather than those who do."

Beatrice pursed her lips. "I can only think of one. You."

"If you knew him as I do, you wouldn't think him so dashing, either."

Beatrice's brows rose. "Beth, just how well *do* you know him?"

Beth toyed with the ribbons on her reticule. "I *may* have spoken to him after our cabriolet ride."

"I knew it!"

"It wasn't anything serious. I ran into him at the British Museum."

"When?"

"Yesterday."

Beatrice's eyes narrowed. "By yourself?"

"No! Of course not. There were many people there. I was standing at one of the front cases, talking to a woman about a fan that was on display, and suddenly, he was there."

"I see. Did you speak for long?"

Beth hoped her cheeks were not as red as they felt. "Not long, no. He . . . he knows I do not stutter."

"Thank goodness for that!" Beatrice exclaimed.

Beth frowned. "That is not a good thing."

"It is for me," Beatrice said frankly. "The sooner you get rid of that stutter, the better. It is most vexing for those of us who must listen to you."

"As soon as there are no more suitors, I shall do just that."

"I know, I know. And I do not blame you for taking up a stutter in the first place. Being placed upon the marriage mart is a fine idea for a chit of seventeen; you are too mature to be cursed with such an effort. What your grandfather should have done was simply sponsor some quiet house parties at Massingale House. House parties are all the rage nowadays. Perhaps I should mention that to him the next time I see him. I am certain he would—"

"No. Beatrice, please. Massingale House is my home and I love it because it is peaceful. It would not be so if it was infested with obnoxious suitors who might trod upon my flower gardens, spill their wine on my carpets, and never give me a moment's peace."

Beatrice looked at her oddly. "Beth, do you never wish to marry?"

"Of course I do. Only . . . it must be someone *interesting.*"

"And none of your suitors are interesting? What about the viscount? You seemed quite taken with him. In fact, I was worried you'd do something rash, like meet him in private or begin a correspondence with him, both actions that could get you into severe trouble with your grandfather. Of course," Beatrice sent a sly glance at Beth, "your grandfather might well find the viscount a good match for you."

"You said it's rumored he was a highwayman!"

"He *was* a highwayman. Or a smuggler, depending on who you ask. Now it seems he has

joined the cream of society and everyone is enamored of him. Beth, I was astounded at how many
people are inviting him about."

"I am not surprised. The man thinks he's a
charmer."

"He does have excellent manners. I did hear
that one of the stipulations of his fortune is that he
cannot be involved in a scandal. Of course, now
that I've thought about it a bit, I can see where he
might have been desperate before coming into his
inheritance. There is no telling what I might have
become had I been left alone at the age of ten."

Beth raised her brows. "Left alone?"

"His mother was imprisoned, charged with
treason. It was later disproven, but he was left to
fend for himself. He and his brother, Tristan, who
is now the new Earl of Rochester."

Beth bit her lip, thinking of Westerville's expression when he'd spoken of his past. There was
something dark there. Something infinitely sad.
She wondered if she'd dismissed him too quickly.
Perhaps what he'd needed was understanding.

But no. She couldn't allow pity to rule her emotions. She had been right to decide to avoid him; it
had been an act of self-preservation on her part. He
was too handsome and too appealing for her to just
allow him to walk in and out of her life, especially
since she knew he wasn't pursuing her for her own
sake at all. His motives were unclear, but they had
very little to do with her. Of that, she was certain.

Which was still quite puzzling. Perhaps Beth
should ask Grandfather what *he* knew about the
viscount and his family. That might be the best

thing. She caught Beatrice's stare and lifted her chin. "I must say, you have certainly changed your opinion of the viscount."

"Not really. I think he is dangerous. But a man who is dangerous and *ineligible* is a different horse than one who is dangerous and *eligible*. There is no harm in being seen with Westerville, though I certainly wouldn't advise anything more."

The cabriolet pulled up to the modiste's on Bond Street, where a large window displayed an amazing assortment of bonnets. Beatrice collected her reticule and smoothed her gown. "By the way, we have an important decision to make. Tomorrow night there are two entertainments scheduled, which is quite unacceptable as they are both touted as the events of the season."

"They always are."

"Yes, usually by a friend of the person holding the event. Anyway, we must decide which we want to attend—the Crossforth Ball or the Devonshire Musicale. They are too far across town to attend both."

"The Crossforth Ball, please. The Devonshire set has never been a favorite of mine. The new duchess is positively horrid."

"I cannot abide her, myself. The entire lot of them is thick with politics, too, yet another reason to miss their musicale." The coachman opened the door, and Beatrice gathered her skirts and stepped lightly out into the sunshine. "Very well then, the Crossforth Ball it will be."

Beth allowed the footman to assist her from the carriage. The sun warmed her instantly even as a cooling breeze ruffled the hem of her skirt. It was a lovely day.

Beatrice tucked Beth's hand into the crook of her elbow. "There it is!" Beatrice pulled Beth down the street to a large window filled with hats of all kinds and sizes. "Here is the adorable bonnet I saw yesterday! Beth, it's just the thing for you."

Beth pretended an interest in the straw formed bonnet before her. It was quite pretty, even to her distracted gaze, trimmed with a blue and silver ribbon and adorned with flowers and tiny little bells. She had to admit Beatrice was quite right— the bonnet was adorable.

But even as she looked at it, her mind roiled around the information Beatrice had given her. All those women interested in Westerville. It stood to reason, of course. He had wealth, title, and was certainly pleasant to look upon. Had those women any idea how talented he was at kissing—Beth didn't want to even think about how the viscount would be pursued then.

She wasn't sure how long she was standing there, staring blindly into the display window before she became aware that her gaze was not focused on the bonnets or hats, but rather on the reflections in the glass. She and Beatrice stood, the wind ruffling their gowns. But it was the figure over Beth's shoulder that captured her attention.

Beth whirled around to face Westerville.

He was standing directly behind her, dressed in his usual black, a damnable half smile on his face. He captured Beth's hand, bowed over it, and placed a kiss on her gloved fingers. Beth's body reacted instantly, a shiver tracing through her. She snatched her hand back and without thinking, hid it behind her.

He laughed softly at the childish gesture and, color high, Beth forced herself to put her hands back at her sides.

The sound of the viscount's laughter turned Beatrice's attention away from the display window. "Viscount Westerville! What brings you out today?"

He bowed, tipping his hat in a rakish manner, his green eyes shimmering under his hat brim. "I am shopping, Mrs. Thistle-Bridgeton."

"So are we!"

His eyes found Beth's and she saw that he was tempted to tease her, which would never do. Beatrice would miss nothing of this encounter, both because she wished to brag upon the meeting to all her friends, but also because she was still a bit wary about how Beth felt about the mysterious viscount.

Right now, Beth could have set her cousin's mind at ease—all she wanted was to get far away from the viscount, and soon. She wished with all her heart she was immune to the man, but the truth was, she was far from it. Every time he was near, her stomach tightened, her lips tingled in memory of their kiss, and her fingertips itched to touch him.

His gaze met hers, and she thought she detected the slightest bit of mockery in them, though all he said was, "I wish to buy something for a friend of mine. A *female* friend."

"Oh!" Beatrice brightened immediately. "We can help you with that."

Beth had to grit her teeth to keep her smile in place. Beatrice was already imagining how much in demand she'd be if tomorrow morning she could tell one and all that she'd helped the dashing viscount choose a gift for his lady love. She'd be invited to every private party, every special event at Vauxhall, every balcony box at the theater.

Well, Beth would put a stop to that. "Lord Westerville, I wish you luck in your purchase, but my cousin and I have many errands to do and we really must be going."

Beatrice frowned. "No, we don't. Harry doesn't expect us back for hours, and the only reason we came here was so that you could try on that bonnet I told you abut."

"Bonnet?" the viscount asked, slanting a look at Beth. "Perhaps I can help. I am considered something of an expert in assisting women with their raiment."

Beatrice gasped, but then laughed. "I daresay you are."

Beth did not find this nearly as amusing as her cousin. "Come, Beatrice. The viscount has many things to do and—"

"Yes, I do," he agreed smoothly. "I have many, many things to do. Like look inside this very shop for a bonnet." He smiled down at Beatrice and held out his arm. "It so happens that I was looking for a specific bonnet for a female acquaintance of mine. A friend of the family, you might call her."

"How fortunate!" Beatrice said, all smiles and

blushes as she took the viscount's arm, glancing around as if hoping someone of importance might see her thus occupied. Seeing no one, she said to Beth, "Perhaps Westerville will give us his opinion of this hat for you, while we are here."

Beth had to force her stiff lips to smile. There was really little else she could do without appearing rude. With just enough reluctance to let Westerville know how she felt, she followed Beatrice into the store. Westerville stepped inside the door and released Beatrice and closed the door the second Beth whisked inside.

While Beatrice went in search of someone to assist them, the viscount stood beside Beth, a bit too closely for her peace of mind.

Of course, anything this side of London Bridge was too close, so perhaps it was too much to expect him to keep a healthy distance.

A young lady bustled forward, Beatrice following as they went to the window to remove the admired bonnet. While the two were thus engaged, Beth hissed under her breath to Westerville, "You, my lord, are incorrigible!"

He looked at her with such an innocent expression that for an instant, her lips quivered irrepressibly. He must have caught her spontaneous amusement, for his innocent air slipped behind a grin. "I don't know what you are talking about, my dear. I am just shopping."

"For a woman?"

"Yes. An *elderly* woman."

This startled her a bit. She glanced toward Beatrice to make certain she was still well out of hearing, before whispering back at the viscount, "Lady Jersey, perhaps?"

His brows shot up. "Lady Jersey would not appreciate being described as 'elderly.'"

Beatrice came over at that exact moment with the bonnet held aloft like a prize, "Here, Beth! Do try this on! I would buy it for myself, but the colors are horrid with my eyes."

Beth raised her brows. "The bonnet is trimmed in blue."

Beatrice colored. "So?"

"Your eyes are blue. It would look wonderful on you."

"But it is perfect for *you*—Westerville! You are here. You must tell Beth it's the most beautiful hat you've ever seen and that she looks positively ravishing in it!"

Westerville nodded, his green eyes sliding over Beth as he bowed. "It will be my pleasure."

Beth hid a grimace. But she had no choice; she took the bonnet from Beatrice and walked to the mirror to put it on, far too aware of the viscount's presence for her own peace of mind. It was so awkward, doing things while he was about. Her hands and arms felt wrongly jointed, as if they'd suddenly grown larger than they should be.

Still, she forced herself to stop before the mirror and place the hat on her head. She tied a bow to one side of her chin, then turned. "Well?"

Westerville crossed his arms, tilting his head to one side as he carefully looked her over. Though his attention was supposed to be on her hat, his gaze wandered literally everywhere. Beth shifted her feet, her face heating. "Westerville, if you do not have an opinion—"

"I have an opinion. That bonnet . . ." He leaned back and tapped a finger against his lips. For all his serious expression, his eyes laughed at her. "I believe I like it quite well. It makes you appear younger."

Beth narrowed her gaze. "It is obvious you know *nothing* about bonnets."

"Beth!" Beatrice bustled up. "I am certain Lord Westerville knows all about women's bonnets." She blinked. "I mean, I do not mean that he knows *all* about them, but—"

"I know more than the average man," Westerville finished helpfully.

She beamed. "Exactly! Therefore, Beth, you should let him render his opinion. For my part, I think it is ravishing! Even more on you than in the window, which is not usually how things happen for me. I don't know if it's the color or the shape of the brim, but it suits you monstrously well."

Westerville nodded. "Mrs. Thistle-Bridgeton, you are an arbiter of taste. You have created a picture of loveliness that will stay with me for days to come."

Beth saw the exact moment her cousin melted. It was obvious in the way she giggled a bit when he bowed in her direction. And no wonder—in one short statement he had validated Beatrice's sense of fashion with an almost pithy quote. And a quote it would become when Beatrice repeated it far and wide.

The viscount sent a glance toward Beth from under his long lashes. "Lady Elizabeth, what do *you* think of that charming bonnet?"

She untied the ribbon and took it off. "I don't know; I am not a woman given to sudden decisions." She handed the bonnet to the disappointed assistant who hovered nearby. "I shall think on it a few more days, and if I find myself longing for it, I shall return."

His gaze narrowed. "And if you don't?"

"If I find it unworthy of my time and effort, then I shall leave it in the window for some other women of less discriminating tastes."

Beatrice gasped. "Someone else is bound to see it and snap it up and then where will you be?"

"Yes," Westerville said, his lips curved in a knowing smile, "then where will you be?"

"Precisely as I am now," Beth said, turning to the door. "Perfectly happy *without* the bonnet." With that, Beth turned and made her way back to the street. Westerville and Beatrice caught up with her there.

Beatrice looked regretfully at the display window where the assistant was placing the hat back on a stand. "You are going to regret that decision. At least let me purchase it for you now and if, later on, you decide you don't wish for the hat, you can give it to your stepmama."

"Charlotte would like that," Beth said, "though the color is too strong for her. She needs more muted blues."

"I suppose you are right," Beatrice said with a disheartened sigh.

"The bonnet is better left in the window where it can be admired." Beth slanted a gaze toward Westerville. "I think it rather enjoys that."

"Who doesn't?" The viscount looked at her from beneath his lashes. "Even you enjoy being admired."

Beth sniffed.

"Oh, I know when you enjoy something, my lady." He leaned a little closer and said under his breath, "I can taste it on your lips."

Beth gasped.

"I beg your pardon," Beatrice said eagerly, trying to lean closer. "What did you say?" She looked at Beth. "What did he say? I couldn't hear."

"Nothing," Beth said, her face heated. She shot a resentful look at the viscount. "Westerville merely sneezed."

His brows rose, an amused twitch to his lips. "Indeed. I fear I am allergic to beautiful women. Walking between the two of you is almost overpowering."

Before Beth's disbelieving gaze, Beatrice broke into a decided simper. Beth sent an annoyed glare at the viscount.

There was a devilish gleam to his eyes that sent Beth's heart pounding into her ears as she remembered their kiss from the day before. She wished she could forget that blasted moment. Of course, wishing to forget something and actually forgetting it were two different things, something she was just coming to realize.

"What is it?" Beatrice asked, looking from one of them to the other. "That was no sneeze. What *did* you say, Westerville? Beth is positively pink."

He adjusted his hat a bit. "Nothing, Mrs. Thistle-Bridgeton. Nothing at all. Ladies, it was a pleasure seeing you. Will you be at the Crossforth Ball tomorrow evening?"

"No—" Beth said at the same time Beatrice blurted out, "Yes."

For an instant, the two cousins glared at each other.

Westerville laughed. "I shall hope to see you there, then. Good day, ladies." He tipped his hat, then turned and began sauntering down the street, whistling as he went.

Beth watched him go, her hands fisted at her sides. Of all the arrogant, insufferable, rude—

"I thought we *were* going to the Crossforth Ball," Beatrice hissed, though her gaze was still on the viscount. He'd paused by a shop window filled with watches and snuffboxes and was even now being eyed by every passing damsel.

"We were," Beth said. "But not now. Now we will go to the Devonshire Musicale."

Beatrice sighed. "I do wish you'd make up your mind."

"I have," Beth said, catching the viscount's eyes on her once again. He smiled, this time a slow and lazy grin that crinkled his eyes and made him look almost carefree.

Beth didn't respond. She turned on her heel, pulling Beatrice with her. "Shall we look for a pelisse? I don't have a thing to wear with my new morning gown."

Beatrice was distracted soon enough. As they

entered a modiste's shop a little way down, Beth glanced back to where the viscount had been. There was no sign of him; he must have entered the store.

That was fine, she decided, for she did not need to see him again. Tomorrow she'd go to the Devonshire Musicale and not think about the viscount even once, no matter the cost. She would discover the viscount's plan soon enough, but in her own time and manner. It would not do to see him any more than was necessary, as every meeting seemed to increase the tension between them. Besides, the Crossforth Ball would be hugely attended, and every eye would be fastened on the viscount.

Beth would find a place and time of her own choosing and then woe betide the man. She'd show no mercy, none at all.

Chapter 10

Running a household is rather like running a good military campaign. One should plan well, prepare well, and put all of one's heart into every effort. It is only through these principles that you shall win every engagement.

A Compleat Guide for
Being a Most Proper Butler
by Richard Robert Reeves

"Oh no," Beatrice muttered. "I think she's going to sing again."

Beth opened the program and ran her finger down the long list, wincing when she reached the center. "Miss Temple has not one, but two more songs."

"I shall die," Beatrice groaned. She glanced to her side where Harry sat, legs crossed at the ankle, arms folded across his chest, chin sunk into his cravat as he slept peacefully, his spectacles perched rather precariously on his nose.

She lifted her elbow as if to jab him in the ribs, but stopped just short of it. She sighed and turned to Beth. "I can't do it. He looks so peaceful."

"He *did* come with us though he didn't wish to," Beth pointed out. "I think he deserves a nap."

"We all do," Beatrice said with some asperity. "Unfortunately not all of us are blessed with the constitution that allows one to sleep through such hideous caterwauling."

Beth bit her lip. "Miss Temple isn't that horrid. She's only a little off-key and then only during the high notes."

"That last song was made up entirely of high notes and I have the goose bumps to prove it! If I have to listen to any more hideous noise, I shall die. Beth, we made an error coming here!" Beatrice twisted in her chair. "People are leaving in droves. Can't we just—"

"No. I am not attending the Crossforth Ball. It is fine with me if you and Harry wish to attend it, for I would be perfectly happy just to go home." An evening of unalleviated peace and quiet seemed just the thing. Not that she'd get much quiet, for London never really went to sleep. She sighed a bit, missing Massingale House and Grandfather in equal amounts.

The last letter she'd received from Grandfather had been as terse as Charlotte's letter had been long. Beth could tell that Grandfather's temper was wearing thin and Charlotte was taking the brunt of it. It was a pity they didn't get along. Thank goodness Lord Bennington was there to take Charlotte out a bit; it would do her a world of good. "I believe I'll go home now and write Grand-father. I haven't sent him a letter in a while."

"You sent him one two days ago. I watched you post it." Beatrice grimaced as Miss Temple smoothed her gown, preparing herself for another round. "We will stay. Besides, if we were to leave, I'd have to wake Harry, and he gets grouchy if he doesn't get at least an hour's nap."

They suffered through two more musical en-deavors by the enthusiastic Miss Temple. Her final note—quavering and shatteringly off-key—pealed through the room, bouncing off the glassware and shimmering like a bloody haze through the minds of the audience.

Harry was finally startled awake. He jumped to his feet, his spectacles flying, and tried to find his balance. It took him a moment and he stood, arms flapping, his eyes wide, his mouth agape. Beatrice grabbed his sleeve and yanked him back into his seat, though not before several people around them broke into laughter at the expression of pure fright on his flushed face.

"Harry!" Beatrice hissed as everyone clapped wanly, but politely, for the now-leaving Miss Temple.

"Good God! What in the hell was that noise?"

The man in front of them turned in his seat. "That's what I've been asking myself this half hour and then some."

"Huntley!" the woman at his side chided, look-ing somewhat embarrassed. "Pray keep your voice down."

"Keep my voice down? I wasn't the one screeching like a hung cat!" The man stood. "Mary, I love you dearly, but I am not staying for another minute of this atrocity. I am going home." He turned and walked to the door, his lady sending a harried look at Beatrice before she gathered her things and rushed to join him.

Harry stood. "Huntley—whoever he is—is a genius. Beatrice, I am going home. Gather your things." He started for the door, but found his wife planted in front of him.

"We cannot leave Beth here alone."

Harry looked back at Beth, his sleepy blue eyes hopeful. "Had your fill of music for the night, m'dear?"

"More than enough." Beth found her reticule at her feet and stood, smiling a little as she did so. "I don't know what it is, but I am a bit homesick tonight."

"Oh Beth!" Beatrice exclaimed. "I am so sorry! Have we not been staying busy enough?"

"Oh, it's not that. I just miss Grandfather and the house. My roses will have bloomed and I am not there to make certain they are trimmed correctly, and Grandfather does not eat well unless someone makes him. But"—Beth straightened her shoulders—"I will be home soon enough. I promised him this one season, but that is all he shall get."

"I would never be happy buried away like that," Beatrice said with a rueful smile. "You were always happy there."

"I wish you could make Grandfather understand that!"

They made their way to the door and had just reached it when a commotion rose in the hallway. Before she even saw him, Beth knew who was arriving—Westerville.

It was indeed the viscount, but he was not alone. With him was a tall, well-formed, rather horse-faced woman. The two were instantly surrounded as they entered.

"That's Sally Jersey with Lord Westerville!" Beatrice said. "I vow but that lady never lets a handsome man get by, does she?"

"It appears not," Beth said, more determined than ever to leave.

Harry stopped in the aisle. "There are too many people trying to get in now, damn it. The aisle is completely blocked. I suppose everyone who was leaving changed their mind once they saw Westerville and Lady Jersey enter."

Beatrice nodded. "Westerville is quite the fashion setter." She looked back over her shoulder and grimaced. "Oh no. The next performance is about to begin. We cannot be standing in the aisle when that happens. We shall just have to stay for the next few minutes, I suppose, until the next break in the program."

Harry cursed under his breath, but even he was forced to agree; there were far too many people in the way now. Sighing, he turned back to where they'd been sitting before and reclaimed their seats. Beth took her place beside Beatrice as Harry stretched out, preparing once again to sleep despite

Beatrice's entreaties that he instead enjoy the music. Harry merely patted her hand before giving a prodigious yawn. Within moments, he was back fast asleep.

Beth meanwhile, forced herself to face forward, away from where she knew Christian must be. She could feel his presence like the aura of a thunderstorm. Her skin prickled, her neck tingled with the same awareness. It took all her control not to turn in her seat and look behind her to see where the handsome viscount and his party decided to sit. Fortunately for her, the women in front of her were not so circumspect. They twisted and turned, peeking over their shoulders and looking somewhere directly behind Beth.

It was horrid, having to sit so still. Horrid and yet rather exciting. For the oddest reason, she felt not only irritation, but anticipation, too. He would seek her out, she knew. As soon as the next musical effort finished and they rose to depart, he would put himself in their way and—

A warm hand came to rest on her shoulder, sending a flash of heat through her. A deep, intimate voice sounded in her ear, "I believe you dropped something."

Beth looked down at her lap. Her hands were clenched in perfect fists. It took a moment of concentration to unlock them and turn around.

Westerville was but a few inches from her, his green eyes so close, she could see tiny flecks of gold in the centers. He smiled at her and slid a folded program of the evening's events against her bare arm. "This was on the floor next to your chair. It must be yours."

Beth took it unthinkingly. "I-I—" Good God, she didn't know what to say.

He chuckled a little, his teeth white. "You don't need to stutter around me. I find your mouth divinely lovely, no matter what you do with it."

Beth tried to glare, but failed. All she could do was stare. His eyes were so beautiful, so compelling.

Westerville's smile deepened and her gaze was drawn to his handsomely carved mouth. She remembered in painfully vivid detail how his kiss had felt and tasted. How his lips had covered hers, how he'd gently opened her mouth and teased her with his tongue.

Her breath caught at the thought. She could no more talk than she could think. Memories rushed through her, hot and furious.

"Westerville? What on earth are you doing to Lady Elizabeth?" The amused, sophisticated voice poured over Beth like ice water, breaking the spell and making her realize how silly she must have looked. She forced her gaze away from Westerville and turned it to his companion. "Lady Jersey. How nice to see you."

"And you, my dear," Sally Jersey answered. A wealthy woman in her own right, she was happily married to Lord Jersey, whose mother was the prince regent's "special friend." Because of her connection to the royal house, and her wealth as well, Lady Jersey had built herself a place in society that was unequaled. This was proven when she became one of the patronesses of Almack's, that most famous of all marriage marts, where no single man of fortune was safe from the devouring eyes of fund-hungry mothers and their desperate daughters.

Needless to say, Beth was not fond of Almack's, for not only did they play nothing but country dances and the occasional quadrille, but they served lamentably stale cake and indifferent ratafia, neither of which found favor with Beth.

She nodded now to Lady Jersey. "My lady, how are you this evening?"

"Oh la! I am exhausted. I asked Lord Westerville to escort me to the Crossforth Ball and what does he do but walk once through the ballroom and then insist we drive here! I vow, but I am vexed, especially as I had it from two people in the foyer that the entertainment here is sadly lacking in quality."

Beth winced as Lady Jersey's voice carried loudly through the room. It was a common joke of the day that Lady Jersey should be called "Silence" to commemorate both her propensity for gossip and her less than peaceful tone. It was a nickname she quite relished. No speck of rumor was too small for her to repeat at the top of her rather spectacular voice.

Beatrice had turned by now and positively beamed when she saw whom Beth was speaking to. "Lady Jersey!" Beatrice said in an excited voice, "How lovely to see you!"

"Mrs. Thistle-Bridgeton," Lady Jersey responded, eyeing Harry where he slept. "I see you managed to drag your husband out of the house.

Did you have the servants carry him in like that, or is he tired from applauding so furiously?"

Beatrice laughed. "It may have been a somewhat lackluster evening, but perhaps it will get better now. The next piece is said to be quite acceptable."

Before she could say more, a pianoforte trilled and the music began. Beth and Beatrice turned back around in their chairs. Beatrice leaned close and whispered, "Lady Jersey is an excellent contact for you, my dear. She knows every eligible man in the ton."

"And yet she came with Westerville. How can one explain the vagaries of human nature?" Beth muttered.

Beatrice looked surprised, but the loudness of the music prevented her from replying. The music was indeed better than the previous offerings, and had circumstances been different, Beth might well have enjoyed the performance. As it was, she was painfully aware of the man sitting directly behind her. He, for his part, made certain she did not forget he was there. He slid his feet forward so that the tips of his shoes were evident on either side of her chair, and occasionally jiggled her seat while shifting in his own.

It was a relief when the music finally finished. Beth clapped even more loudly than the others, and was the first one on her feet, collecting her things and quietly urging Beatrice to hurry and wake Harry. But before Beth knew what was happening, Sally leaned over the seat.

"My dear Mrs. Thistle-Bridgeton, would you be so kind as to walk with me to the refreshment table? I am positively dying from thirst, and my escort has rudely refused to bring me a glass."

Westerville grinned. "I did no such thing."

Sally's smile was just as wide and for an instant, Beth caught a glimpse of the charm that had made "Silence" a favorite with the ton. "Your lack of enthusiasm was all the rejection I needed." Her gaze flickered to Beth. "Lady Elizabeth, I leave Lord Westerville in your care while your cousin walks with me to find the lemonade. Pray keep a close eye on him, for he is far too handsome to be left alone for any length of time."

Beth didn't know what to say to this rather heavy-handed attempt at matchmaking. She looked appealingly at Beatrice, but her cousin was too busy eagerly making her way to the end of the chairs to meet Lady Jersey that she quite missed Beth's silent request for assistance.

Moments later, Beth watched in irritation as the two women slowly strolled to the table at the far side of the room.

"That was remarkably easy," said a deep voice at Beth's ear.

She turned on Westerville. "You planned that."

"I only accepted Sally's invitation to escort her for the evening. The rest was her doing."

Beth's gaze narrowed. "She is helping you?"

"I don't know if I'd call it that." He lifted his brows, no trace of a smile on his face. "Is she?"

"No." Beth glanced at Harry, who was still deep asleep, his arms crossed, his chin sunk to his chest. She was alone with a man she had no qualms in thinking a wolf. "Well, you may stay here if you like, but I must excuse myself. I've torn my flounce and it must be repaired." She turned toward the doorway, but he forestalled her with a single word.

"Afraid?"

She turned her head to look at him. "Yes."

With that, she left. He would not be alone for long; too many women were avidly watching his every move. Beth told herself she did not care, though she knew the thought was a lie.

Once outside the door, she made her way upstairs to where the women gathered. The chamber set aside for the ladies was so crowded, Beth couldn't think. She just wanted a quiet place to wait until the next musical performance began. That would preclude any conversation with Westerville and it would be safe to return to her seat.

Beth glanced around and found a doorway to her right that was partially open. Inside, she could see walls lined with bookshelves, a billiard table gracing the middle of the room.

She glanced about. No one was paying her the least heed, so she slipped into the room and closed the door.

Once there, she heaved a deep sigh of relief. The room smelled of leather and brandy and carried the faintest hint of a cigar. Obviously this was a haven for the men of the household, but for now, it would serve Beth as the same. Being so near Westerville was many things, but restful was not one of them.

Feeling better at the solitude, she idly walked to

the table and ran her fingers over the green felt surface. Tomorrow, she'd go home to Massingale House and visit Grandfather. She'd been away far too long and a visit would not be amiss.

Beth picked up a small white ball and hefted it absently in her hand.

"Do you play?"

She whirled toward the now-open door. Her heart pounded furiously as she faced Christian, dark and dangerous, a perilously handsome figure in black. "Good God, Westerville! Must you do that?"

A faint smile touched the corner of his mouth. The sapphire that burned in the white of his cravat was the only color in his entire ensemble other than his eyes. "Must I do what?" he asked, coming farther into the room. "Ask you questions?"

"I don't mind you asking questions, but I must protest the way you sneak up on people." She pressed a hand to her thumping heart, which was still pounding an unsteady rhythm in her chest.

His gaze followed her gesture, his eyes lingering in appreciation at the neck of her gown. "I was not sneaking. Although I could, if you found it amusing—"

She dropped her hand from her chest. "Oh! Everything I say to you, you turn into some sort of innuendo. You are insufferable."

He chuckled. "And you, my sweet, are too easily startled. I admit I did not knock, but then the door was open."

"The door was closed and I know it. I didn't hear the latch, so you must have been very careful."

He pretended to consider the door, which he'd not only opened, but silently closed, as well. "Perhaps the latch is broken."

"Pish. There is nothing wrong with that latch and you know it."

He grinned, his teeth flashing whitely. "Perhaps. All I know is that the hinges are well oiled."

"I could tell." Beth eyed the scoundrel narrowly, aware that if she wished to maintain her decorum, she'd have to calm her already jangled nerves. The bounder had been in the room mere minutes, and already her palms were damp, her heart lurching along like a drunk. Thank goodness he was all the way across the room, by the door, and she was here, protected by the expanse of mahogany and green felt. Yes, that was quite good indeed.

As if aware of her thoughts, Christian shoved himself from the door frame and walked to the table, regarding her from the other side of it. Immediately the room grew smaller, somehow more intimate. His eyes still meeting hers, he reached across the table . . . and picked up a black billiard ball.

Beth's fingers closed over the smooth wooden edge of the billiard table. "This will not do," she said, wincing when her voice cracked just the slightest bit. "Pray open the door."

"Why? Do you wish others to hear what we have to say?"

"I wish to maintain my reputation, my lord. There could be repercussions if you do not open that door, repercussions neither of us will like."

His eyes sparkled. "How do you know what I would like?"

That was an interesting question indeed. Beth regarded him a long moment. "We've already established that you are not pursuing me out of romantic interest, but simply because you wish to discover some sort of information about my grandfather. Whatever it is you wish to know, I cannot imagine it is worth giving up your freedom. If we are caught alone together, that is exactly what the cost will be for us both."

He tossed the ball into the air, catching it with one hand. "What if I have decided to tell you the truth about why I have been asking about your Grandfather? What then?"

Her gaze narrowed. "Have you?"

He tossed the ball again. It arced and landed in his palm with a firm smack. "Perhaps."

"Are you playing with me, Westerville?"

"Not yet," he said quietly.

She frowned. "You came here with Lady Jersey. She is quite a fascinating woman."

"Yes, she is," he drawled. His eyes flickered over Beth, lingering on her eyes, her mouth, her gown. "But she is not one hair's breadth as fascinating as you."

Beth had to fight a very unladylike urge to grin. "I am sure she is an admirable person and quite lovely, as well."

"She is an amusing companion, no more. I hold her husband in too much esteem for her to be else."

"That is very honorable of you," Beth said, a touch of sarcasm deepening her voice.

"I call it necessity. Sally is a woman who would devour as soon as love. I would rather not be with a woman who so confused the two."

"I don't know about Lady Jersey's propensities in that direction."

"She does not matter, my love. I did not come to the musicale to see Sally Jersey." He set the ball on the table, then crossed his arms over his chest, leaning against the mahogany edge with one thigh. "I came to see you and no one else."

She really shouldn't have been pleased at this news, but she was. Very pleased.

"I knew you were here the moment I arrived because I saw your coach. It has your family crest emblazoned across it."

She made a face. "It is horridly gaudy, isn't it? Grandfather says—" She stopped when she noted how his gaze had sharpened. Disappointment lent a bitter tone to her voice. "We are back to that again, aren't we? You wish me to speak about Grandfather. Why, Westerville? Why are you so interested in him?"

Christian heard the almost plaintive note in her voice. He'd had such plans for this evening. He'd compliment her, tease her, perhaps win a few smiles. He'd wanted to woo her, and then . . . when she wasn't thinking about it, ease her into talking about her grandfather. But now, looking at her across the billiard table, her honest gaze locked on him— "Damn it all."

Her brows rose. "I beg your pardon."

Frustrated, yet with no way to show it, he reached over and with a deft twist of his wrist, sent the black ball spinning across the table. "Reeves was right, blast him."

She looked thoroughly confused now. "Reeves?"

"My butler. I inherited him from my father."

"Ah." She thought about this a moment. "And what did he say that was so right?"

"That I should not involve an innocent in my schemes."

She stiffened, her gaze even more wary than before. "How does he know I'm an innocent?"

Christian slowly raised his brows.

A delicious pink flooded her cheeks. "I am, of course. I just wondered why he knew—or at least thought he knew—although he couldn't, of course—"

"You are adorable." He leaned against the table, placing his hands on the mahogany edge, smiling gently at her, his frustration slipping away.

She bit her lip, unconsciously wringing her hands.

"Elizabeth, my love. I am going to do what I should have done since the beginning. What I must do because you are far too intelligent to let me get away with subterfuge. I am going to tell you everything and hope you will help me."

"This has to do with my grandfather."

"It has everything to do with your grandfather."

She regarded him for a long minute. He could see the thoughts raging behind her eyes.

Finally, she straightened. She met his gaze and nodded. "I am listening. Tell me what you want."

Christian took a deep breath. Everything hung on this moment; if he could gain Beth's help . . . that was all he needed. "It is a long story, but I want you to know everything. This is about my mother."

"Ah." She nodded. "I thought it might be."

He looked at her. "You know about my mother?"

She shook her head, her cheeks pink. "No, not really. I mean, I don't know much. I just heard—" She bit her lip.

"When I was ten years of age, my mother was imprisoned for treason. Someone provided the Crown with evidence that she had commerce with France while we were at war. She was innocent, a woman who had harmed no one and yet—" He winced at the harshness of his own voice. "I am sorry. I cannot tell you how much it hurts to know she was subjected to such a horrid ending when all she did was trust too well."

Beth's gaze never left his. "I understand. Please go on."

"Someone provided that 'evidence' to the king. Someone who wished her ill."

"And you think my grandfather knows who did that."

Christian didn't answer. He absently reached out to pick up another billiard ball, this one white. Smooth and cool, it rested perfectly in the palm of his hand. "Not quite."

"Surely you can't think—" she breathed, her face suddenly pale. "You think Grandfather was the one who provided the false evidence."

"I have reason."

"No," she said, her voice deadly calm. "It was not him. He would never do such a thing. Never."

"I can prove what I say."

"How?"

He glanced at the closed door. "We cannot talk here for long and it's complicated. Will you meet me somewhere else? I will tell you everything I know."

"And then?"

"And then it is up to you. I want your help, Elizabeth. But with you or without you, I will find what I am seeking."

"What are you looking for?"

"There is a necklace that was once my mother's. It is a very special necklace. Just before she died, she discovered who had betrayed her. They offered to admit their deceit if she'd send them the necklace as an inducement."

"Did they?"

He placed the ball back on the table. "No. They kept the necklace and she . . . she died."

Elizabeth pressed her hand to her forehead, her gaze clouded. "You think Grandfather has that necklace."

"Yes."

"Well, I don't," she said loudly.

He raised his brows. "Elizabeth, it's not a pretty picture. But at least I am telling you the truth, why I wished to know more about your grandfather."

She bit her lip, her brows lowered. "I don't wish to return to the musicale just yet. I-I must think," She rubbed her temples. "I cannot believe such a thing of my grandfather."

"I have evidence that someone from your household betrayed my mother. It can be no one else."

"No! You must be wrong." She turned in a jerky movement, her elbow accidentally hitting the rack that held the billiard sticks. With a noisy clatter, they fell to the floor.

"Oh!" she said, her hands clenched in irritation.

"Leave them," Christian said, moving to pick them up. He began replacing the sticks in the carved wooden rack. "I did not want to tell you this, but I need your help."

"*My* help?"

"The necklace must be in Massingale House; I am certain of it."

"I have never seen my grandfather with such a necklace."

"Then you have nothing to fear. If he does not have it, then perhaps someone else does."

She looked at him, her brown eyes steady and unwavering. "What if you do find this necklace? What then?"

His jaw tightened. "Then your grandfather is guilty."

A long silence met this.

"Westerville, I don't know what to say. What to think. I just know Grandfather would never harm another person. I know it."

"I can show you what information I have collected so far and we can begin from there." He leaned forward, his gaze earnest. "Beth, will you meet with me again, let me explain why I think it was your grandfather? Why I think someone in Massingale House is to blame for my mother's death?"

"Someone at Massingale House? How do you know it wasn't one of the servants? Or Charlotte?"

"None of the servants would have visited my mother in gaol in a carriage emblazoned with the Massingale crest."

She winced. "I see. And Charlotte?"

Christian pursed his lips, his brows lowered. "I had dismissed her because she does not seem capable. Do you think I am wrong?"

Beth's shoulders slumped. "No. She can barely manage to deal with Grandfather. She spends more of her time in her room or with Lord Bennington."

Christian nodded. "Well? Will you meet with me again and see the information I have collected?"

"I suppose I must."

"And if I convince you that my suspicions are founded?"

She was silent a long moment. Finally she nodded as if she'd made a decision. "Then I will see to it that you are invited to the house so you can search."

That surprised him. "Yes?"

"Of course," she said coolly. "I will do what I must to prove Grandfather's innocence. I know he didn't do this, so why should I fear what you might find?"

"You trust him deeply."

"So would you, if you knew him. Grandfather cannot abide someone who tells falsehoods. I can't imagine—" She bit her lip and looked down, unconsciously running her fingers over the mahogany edge of the billiard table.

Christian watched her for a while. She didn't look upset so much as she looked thoughtful. He wished he knew of a way to explain himself better, but there was none. His fingers tightened about the billiard stick. He hadn't meant to tell her any of this, but somehow, in looking into her honest gaze, he'd suddenly known he could do no less.

The silence stretched, loud and uncomfortable. The desire grew to break the invisible wall that had sprung between them.

Before he could think of a way, she lifted her head and looked at him. "You should know that Grandfather is not well."

Christian tried to dredge up some pity, but could not. "I know he is quite old."

"Yes, though his mind is as sharp as they come." Elizabeth bit her lip. "Westerville, if I do not help you, what will you do?"

"I will find some other way to search for the evidence I need."

"If you do it by force, someone will get hurt."

"Someone already has. My mother died in that gaol. She deserves the truth and so do I."

Elizabeth shook her head. "I knew you would say that. Just know this; there is a cost for my help."

"Such as?"

"From now on, you will involve me fully in all aspects of your search."

"Wait a moment—"

"You will do nothing—not write a note, make a call, visit someone with information—without letting me know about it and, whenever possible, taking me with you."

"Anything else?" Christian asked grimly, setting the billiard stick to one side.

"No. Not if you wish entry into Massingale House."

Christian rubbed his fingers together, his mind working furiously. He had no wish to include Beth in all his plans. It was not only inconvenient, but it could also be dangerous. "What if I say no?"

"Then not only will I not help you, but I will go straight to Grandfather and divulge all you've told me." Her gaze pinned his. "You will never, ever find a way into Massingale House if you don't agree."

"Damn you." The words were out before he knew it.

She flushed, and he immediately regretted his temper. "I'm sorry," he said. "You seem to think I'm out to harm your grandfather for no reason. I have no wish to hurt anyone other than the person responsible for my mother's death."

She looked at him for a long moment, then nodded. "I suppose I would do the same, if it had been my mother. At least we understand one another in that respect."

"Then we are partners," Christian said with a smile.

"Uneasy partners."

"Oh, it will get easier. We have but to become used to one another." His gaze fell on the billiard table. "Have you ever played?"

"What?"

"Billiards. Have you ever played?"

"Oh. There is a table at my grandfather's, but I have not touched it in months."

"Let us play then."

She appeared aghast. "Now?"

"Why not? If we are to begin on an adventure together, surely it would behoove us to learn a bit more about one another. What better way than a game of billiards?"

"Westerville, you just told me you suspect my grandfather of sending false evidence to the Crown about your mother, evidence that put her in gaol where she eventually died. That does not make me want to play billiards."

"Nothing can be answered at this moment, so you might as well enjoy a game of billiards with me." He placed a hand on her shoulder and turned her toward the table. He was now directly behind her, the curve of her bottom beguilingly near. His legs brushed her skirts. "First lesson— how to control the stick."

Christian reached around her and placed the pole in her hands, arranging her fingers to clasp it correctly. His body pressed intimately to the back of hers.

Beth had to fight a shiver as his warmth began to seep through her thin skirts. Her mind was awhirl with the accusations he'd made. The only reason she hadn't raised her voice and called him a liar was his own calm, deadly sure demeanor. Wrong he might be, but he truly believed what he said. It was sobering and just the tiniest bit frightening.

She knew why he'd suggested the lesson in billiards; the silence had been just as difficult for her. But still, her heart was not in it. "My lord, I don't really feel like playing right now—"

"Shush," he said, one arm reaching around her to grasp the billiard pole. His hand closed over hers on the stick, his fingers warm against her bare skin. "It is an honor to assist such a lovely woman." His voice brushed over her and sent a thousand trembles across her skin.

Beth bit her lip as she stared blankly at his hand where it encircled hers. Large and well formed, it completely engulfed hers. She moved her fingers the slightest bit and was rewarded when he rubbed her hand with his own.

"I-I—" Beth swallowed. "Your skin is rough, my lord." She glanced back over her shoulder, up into his eyes. "They are not the hands of a gentleman."

She hadn't meant it as an insult. Indeed, she rather liked the feeling of skin that had experienced life and accomplished untold deeds to be bared against her own.

But his eyes flared at her words, his lips thinning ominously, his hand tightening almost painfully over hers. "I have the hands fate has given me." With that he slid his hands off hers and below them on the stick.

That was all the explanation he proffered. All the explanation she was going to get. But somehow, she knew she'd wounded him and in a way that went far deeper than it seemed. Impulsively, she lifted the stick, bringing up his hand. She then placed her cheek against his fingers. Beth closed her eyes and willed away the pain she heard in his voice, saw in his eyes.

For the longest moment, Christian just stared at her, too bemused to react.

He'd been with many women. Had shared laughter and talk among pillows and candles. He'd made love to them for hours on end and listened to their stories—sad and happy both. And yet no moment in all of those moments had he ever felt as close to a woman as he did here, now, fully dressed, and—so far—following the dictates of polite society.

It was the oddest, most painfully dear sensation he'd ever felt. All he could do was look down at her as she pressed her soft, warm cheek to the back of his hand, her fingers delicately latched on to the billiard stick below his.

She sighed, her breath sweet on his skin, then lifted her head, her rich brown eyes even darker now, filled with a mysterious emotion. "I am sorry. I did not mean to imply anything negative. I just meant that—"

"It's nothing. Nothing at all," he said, trying hard to get his bearings. What was he supposed to be doing here? Oh yes. He'd come to seduce her, to entrance her into giving up her secrets. Instead, he'd blurted out the truth and allowed her to set the terms of a partnership. And now he was losing complete control of his entire plan.

Shaking his head, he moved the stick until it pointed to the table. "Are you ready to play billiards? It is a confounded game, but addictive."

Disappointment flickered through her eyes, but

she nodded, "Of course. I've played it before, though not often."

"I will show you a few tricks." He leaned forward slightly, his legs pressing against the backs of hers. It was funny, but she always seemed so much taller than she was. Her head barely reached his chin, the sweet fragrance of jasmine and lavender tickling his nose and making him want to bury his face in her thick, honey-colored curls.

In fact, as he leaned forward, he could just brush his cheek against her hair and—

Good God! What the hell was wrong with him? Christian grasped his wandering imagination and firmly put it back in place. He had things to do here other than seduce a maid for his own pleasure, damn it. If they were to work together and untangle the mystery of his mother, then the last thing he needed to do was make her feel uneasy in his presence.

"Westerville?"

Her voice was soft, diffident even. He took a deep breath, inhaling her scent and capturing it for his own. "Yes?"

A twinkle lurked in her brown eyes. "Shall we make a wager? Ten pounds, perhaps."

"On what?"

She pointed to the billiard table. "On this shot. It looks easy enough."

He glanced down. "Though it may look like it, that is not an easy shot."

"All I have to do is make the ball go over there"—she used the stick to indicate a spot on the far side of the table—"and then roll over here." She pointed to the leather netting that covered a corner pocket, her warmly curved rump rubbing against him as she did so.

It took Christian a moment to collect himself before he replied, "You can't make that shot."

She turned her head to smile up at him. "I think I can. Shall we wager? It will make the effort worthwhile."

He had to smile at her innocence. "It's far more difficult than it looks, but . . . if you insist—"

She bent, eyed the table, and then clicked the end of the pole into the ball.

It banked, spun, and danced into the corner pocket so neatly, he knew it could not be luck.

Beth turned then to face him, peeping up at him through her lashes, a devilish grin in her eyes. "You owe me ten pounds."

He'd been taken. Robbed like a newly born babe left in the woods for the wolves to ravage. For a moment, he couldn't believe it, couldn't accept it. Suddenly, he was back in the streets, a lost and frightened urchin of ten, fighting for every piece of moldy bread he managed to steal. He'd learned then about mockery and the coldness of human nature; he knew the devastating feeling of trusting someone, only to awake in the morning, what little you possessed gone.

He had fought tooth and nail to be the victor and not the victim. The thin veil of civility he'd been wearing for so long ripped into a thousand shreds. Suddenly, he wanted more. More than a smile. More than a kiss.

He pressed against her, pushing her back, against the edge of the table.

Her eyes widened. "Westerville, what—"

Christian kissed her. Not gently as before. This kiss was fueled by passion and need. By the fact that he'd opened himself to her and she had, in return, mocked his attempts. The kiss was harsh and passionate, a fiery outburst against the forces that had pressed his life into this vise of longing and lust.

Through a haze of red heat, he became aware of Elizabeth pressing back against him, clutching him with the same need and desperation. Her response rippled through him, fanning his passions to new heights, devouring his resistance and pressing him forward.

Her hands clutched at his coat. He splayed his hands over her back, then lower, holding her to him, pressing his erect manhood against her. Her breathing sounded harsh in his ear, matching his own. He lifted her, setting her on the edge of the billiard table, his thighs spreading hers.

She gasped against his ear and he bent his mouth to her neck where he traced a heated path down the sensitive line of her throat. Her head fell back and her knees rose the slightest bit. He pressed himself against her, his hand threading into her hair. It was savage, harsh. She was his, damn it. And always had been.

He could feel her thudding heart, the heat of her skin through the thin silk gown she wore. He wondered what she'd look like without the gown. He immediately had a picture of her reclining on his bed, his pillows piled beneath her, her thick, blond hair curling across the mattress like a river of honey.

Her skin would gleam whiter than the sheets, her eyes dark with passion as he brought her to the brink of desire over and over and over.

Waves of heated lust rippled through him. And he traced a hand along her thigh, admiring the plumpness of her. She was a *lush* woman, this one. Delicious and ripe. Christian didn't think he'd ever stop reveling in such richness. Such wanton passion.

He lifted his head long enough to look into her eyes, now smoky dark with passion. "This is why we were brought together." He rubbed himself against her, pressing forward. "This is what we were made for."

Beth gasped at the onslaught of heated desire that raced through her, robbing her legs of stiffness, imbuing her body with an insufferable heat. She should resist him. She knew it. But somehow, she could not. All she wanted was to feel him, experience the wildness he brought into her life, taste the freedom that rested always on his lips.

She pulled his mouth to hers, throwing herself into the kiss with a wild abandon that grew by the moment. At first, he'd been the one to press their contact, but within seconds, she was leaning toward him, pressing her hips to him, her hands sliding over him, restlessly tugging, pulling, moving. She didn't know what exactly she wanted except that the kiss had ignited a fire. She wanted more even though she wasn't quite sure what that "more" was.

For his part, Christian was overwhelmed. She exploded beneath his ministrations, seeming to grow more powerful, more womanly with each touch of his lips and hands. It was intoxicating, maddening, and furiously sensual.

Christian knew he had to stop. But couldn't. He was afire for her, burning inside and out for the taste of her. He moaned against her lips, sliding his hands around to cup her gently against him, letting her feel his erection against the soft planes of her stomach.

It was a bold move, one destined to make a timid wench turn and run. But Beth was not timid. Instead of recoiling, she moaned against his mouth and instinctively rocked her hips back and forth against his hardness.

Christian's breath caught in his throat. By Zeus, but she was magnificent! He could barely contain his excitement, his desire.

Her hands tugged furiously at his waist, drawing him closer and closer still, unwittingly fanning his passion with her own. Her skirts ruched up, her legs locked about him. All he had to do was reach down, untie his breeches, release his manhood, and she would be his. He reached down to tug on the tie—

The door opened. "Good God! Unhand her, now!"

Christian pulled Elizabeth off the table, wrapping his arms about her and hiding her face, the cloud of lust that had fogged his brain instantly dispelled. Standing in the doorway, eyes wide, stood Beth's cousin with her husband at her side. Both of their faces mirrored shock and horror.

But it was the face that peered over their shoulders that made Christian grit his teeth. It was that of Sally Jersey, the ton's worst gossip. She looked furious rather than horrified.

A tight, cruel grin touched her wide mouth. "Well, Westerville! Had I known you enjoyed billiards so, I would have offered to let you use the table at my house!"

Chapter 11

Life is sometimes a cruel trickster. If ever you face a seemingly hopeless situation, calm your mind and busy your hands. You will be surprised how many potential answers will find their way to you under such circumstances.

A Compleat Guide for
Being a Most Proper Butler
by Richard Robert Reeves

Christian walked into his house to find the front hallway empty. He shoved out of his coat and tossed it on a chair, stalking to his library. "Reeves!" he yelled at the top of his voice.

A stately trod was heard almost immediately. Reeves appeared just as Christian reached his library. The butler followed him into the room. "My lord, we were not expecting you for hours yet! Has there been some mishap?"

Christian splashed a liberal amount of port into a glass and tossed it back. Then he poured another.

Reeves's brows rose. "Well," he finally said into the silence. "If it is that bad, perhaps you had best tell me what has occurred."

Christian shot the butler a dark look. "I don't wish to talk about it."

"I see. So you called me in to watch you partake." The butler composed himself, hands folded before him, an expression of extreme interest on his face. "Pray continue."

Christian slammed his glass onto the table. "This is not a laughing matter. I did as you forewarned. I-I ruined her, Reeves."

The butler raised his brows. "Lady Elizabeth?"

Christian nodded. "We were at the Devonshire Musicale and—" He slumped in his chair.

Reeves went to the sideboard and found a decanter. He brought it to Christian and refilled the glass, then placed the decanter at his elbow. "Here, my lord. Try this."

Christian took a long pull of his drink—then promptly coughed, choking furiously.

Reeves thunked his back.

"Ow!" Christian glared at the butler. "Must you do that so hard?"

"Yes."

Christian pointed to his abandoned glass. "What the hell did you pour in there?"

"Ratafia."

"Rataf— Bloody hell, are you trying to kill me?" Ratafia was a thick liquor that was overly sweet and shudderingly nauseating.

"No, my lord. I merely thought it unwise for you to visit the Duke of Massingale and request his granddaughter's hand in marriage while intoxicated." Reeves replaced the stopper on the decanter and carried it back to the sideboard. "His Lordship would not appreciate such a display."

Christian scowled. "I am not going to offer for Lady Elizabeth's hand."

"No?" Reeves's gaze met his steadily. "What do you think the trustees will think of such behavior?"

Christian raked a hand through his hair. Damn the trustees. Reeves was right yet again, blast the irritating butler to hell and back. Christian had no choice, none at all. Within a day, maybe less, the Duke of Massingale would descend upon the Rochester London House and demand satisfaction, raising all sorts of racket. The entire town would know the story soon enough, anyway, unless Christian had misread the irritation in Lady Jersey's eyes.

"Damn, damn, damn." Christian covered his eyes with his hands. Why had he allowed his lust to rage out of control? To his chagrin, he found that even with his hands over his eyes and a good dose of port in his stomach, he could still see Beth's expression as her cousin burst in on them in the billiard room.

What had he been thinking? He hadn't been, truth be known. Not a bit. He'd been led on by his urges, something he hadn't allowed to happen since he'd been a youth.

He'd already won his battle in so many ways. Reeves had been right—telling the lady the truth had opened doors, not closed them. And what had he done but let his lusty thoughts overwhelm him? Of course, when one was with a woman like Elizabeth—so lush and damned intelligent—it took more self-control than he possessed to keep his distance. She beckoned him with every sway of her rounded hips, teased him with every sharp comment and glance. It was more than a man could bear.

Christian scowled. "Reeves, I absolutely *detest* it when you are right."

"Yes, my lord. It is a great burden to me, as well. However, I am certain that once you think things through you will realize it is not a matter for despair. Lady Elizabeth is a lovely woman. Most men would be delighted to form such a connection."

"I don't wish to marry," Christian said stubbornly. "And if I did, she would not want such a thing, herself."

"Why not? You are quite handsome, polite under most circumstances, and bathe more than any man I've known."

"Thank you," Christian said dryly. "Unfortunately, I also believe her beloved grandfather a liar and murderer."

"And she knows this?"

"She does now. I told her everything and asked her to assist me in finding the evidence."

"What did she reply?"

"She agreed, though her purpose is to prove her grandfather's innocence. Still . . . I had finally gained my entry into Massingale House, and now I would that I had anything but."

Reeves pursed his lips. "It is a very complicated situation."

Christian gave a mirthless laugh. "Beth loves her grandfather dearly. I see it in her eyes every time she talks about him." He looked down at his hand where it lay fisted on his knee. "She will not wish to be aligned with a man who feels thusly about her grandfather."

Reeves paused, his blue eyes intent. "That concerns you."

Christian didn't hesitate. "Yes. Yes, it does, though I do not know why."

An odd wave of loneliness swept over him, pulling down his shoulders. He wished his mother were alive; somehow he rather thought she'd have loved Beth. He frowned at the directions his thoughts were taking. Good God, but he was maudlin. "Enough of this."

He stood and paced a short distance, then back. God, what a mess. What a horrid, awful mess. But there was nothing for it. He stopped before Reeves. "I shall go to see the duke this evening."

"It will take a little over an hour to reach his home."

Christian looked at Reeves.

The butler smiled and shrugged. "I made inquiries for the day you might wish to make the trip."

"I will ride Lucifer. It will not take long then."

"Yes, my lord. What will you say to the duke? You have ruined his granddaughter. He is not likely to welcome you with open arms."

"He will rail, I've no doubt. But then he will accept my suit; her reputation is now in shatters." Christian thought of Sally Jersey's delighted expression. Word was even now spreading throughout London. He, more than most, knew the price society could impose on those who had fallen from favor. He would not allow Elizabeth to suffer the ignominy of being shunned as his mother had been. "I will marry her as soon as possible."

"But what if you determine that your suspicions about her grandfather are true? She may never forgive you."

"Damn it, Reeves! Do you think I don't know that? I have no choice in the matter and neither does she. If I do not bring my mother's betrayer to justice, I will never forgive myself."

Reeves pursed his lips. "My lord, may I make a suggestion?"

"Not after pouring ratafia into my glass."

The butler smiled. He crossed to the sideboard, collected a fresh glass and a decanter of port, and set them on the table by Christian. "Allow me to make amends."

Christian gratefully poured himself another glass of port, though only a little. He sighed as the liquid slid down his throat.

"My lord, I suggest you use the same strategy with Massingale that you used with his granddaughter. When you go to ask for her hand in marriage, admit your attraction for her."

"I have never admitted to you that I find her attractive."

"You didn't have to. It was quite obvious in your voice. That was why I kept warning you of using innocents in your plan."

Christian rubbed a hand over face. "I wish I'd

realized how strong that attraction was. I've never felt— Reeves, it is the most amazing thing."

The butler nodded. "Love sometimes surprises us."

Christian cut an amazed glance at the butler. "Love?" he snapped. "I didn't say anything about love!"

"No, my lord. You didn't. I believe that was my contribution."

"I don't need contributions like that."

"Yes, my lord," Reeves said obediently. "The duke will be angry with you for what has occurred with his granddaughter, but if you honestly admit your attraction to her, he will have to understand. I daresay he thinks as highly of Lady Elizabeth as she thinks of him."

Christian sighed. "You are right. Damn it! This was not how I'd planned this."

"No, my lord. You are far too intelligent to come up with such a hurly-burly plan."

"Thank you," Christian allowed a smile to touch his lips, though he knew it was bitter and hard. "This situation is temporary. Once I have proof of her grandfather's perfidy, Lady Elizabeth and I will part ways."

Reeves's frown deepened. "My lord?"

Christian met Reeves's gaze, a strange desperation filling his heart. "She will wish it no other way. Of that, I am certain."

Harry walked back and forth in front of the fireplace, his hands clasped behind his back. Every third trip or so, he'd stop, look at Beth, close his eyes as if to dispel her image, then glumly turn back to his pacing.

It was horrid. Each time he looked at her, Beth wished the ground beneath her chair would open and swallow her whole, but no such luck was to be had.

Sad as Harry's reaction was, it was not nearly as bad as Beatrice's. Upon finding Beth and Westerville locked in an embrace on the billiard table at the Devonshire Musicale, Beatrice had promptly gasped, screamed, and then fallen into a senseless heap at Lady Jersey's feet.

Nothing could have been more ruinous. Beatrice's scream drew attention and brought even more people to peek over their shoulders where Beth was frantically attempting to put herself to rights while Westerville glared at their audience with a white fury that even now sent a shiver through her.

He'd been horridly silent except when Harry had, in a rather stiff voice, requested Lady Jersey's silence. The viscount had interrupted the request with a short, derisive laugh that had quite set up Her Ladyship's hackles. It had been a very poor move for there was no hiding the malice that shone from Sally Jersey's eyes at his dismissal.

The next hour had passed in a blur. Westerville had refused to acknowledge Harry's demands for satisfaction, made a bow to Beth, told her that he would visit her soon, and then taken his leave. Slowly, the crowd had dispersed, including the horrid Lady Jersey. After taking a rather red-faced leave of their host and hostess, Beth, Beatrice, and Harry had finally returned home.

Once there, they had retired to the sitting room, and there they'd been ever since, turning the horrible event over and over, wishing for a solution. None was forthcoming. Beth must face Grandfather and tell him the truth.

As bad as the night had been, today was going to be an even longer day. Beth did not know whether to laugh or cry, but she feared at any moment she might do both.

From where she lay on the settee, Beatrice moaned loudly, her smelling salts clutched in one hand. "I cannot believe this. I simply cannot believe this."

Beth rubbed her head where it had begun to ache. She couldn't believe it, either. She'd known she had to avoid the viscount. She'd known it and yet, somehow, she'd failed to do it. If she was honest with herself, she'd admit that there was a deeply sensual connection between herself and Westerville. She didn't really know how to describe it . . . only that it existed.

Still, that did not explain what had happened in the billiard room. Beth rubbed her temples wearily. What had happened was a mixture of passion, attraction, and—strangely enough—anger. It had been a heady, thoroughly irresistible mix.

Beatrice moaned. "I cannot believe this. All is ruined."

"No," Harry said, pacing wildly. "There must be something that can be done. I cannot allow that all is lost."

"It's lost, Harry," Beatrice said, sniffing loudly, and waving her handkerchief as she spoke. "Lost, lost, lost! The second he hears what has happened, my great uncle will descend upon the house and— oh, I don't know what he will do!" Tears threatened. "But he will be so angry with me for failing to take care of Beth!"

"He will not be angry with you at all," Beth said quietly. "Nor you, Harry. He knows I am no milk and bread miss to be taken at a glance. What I did, I did myself, and no one else will pay for it."

Beatrice's lips quivered. "The duke will blame me for—"

"He will not! I will see to it that he knows this is entirely my fault."

"No," Harry said grimly. "It is Westerville's fault and so your grandfather will say."

"I am not a child to be led astray. I knew exactly what I was doing." She'd been lost in a blaze of passion unlike anything she'd ever dreamed or read of. But had she wished it, she could have stopped the entire incident. Westerville was many things, but he had never forced her in any way. He may have been annoyingly *present* and perhaps a *little* demanding—deliciously so, in fact— but nothing more.

She sighed. "I shall speak to Grandfather and—"

"No!" Beatrice said, swinging her feet to the floor and slumping wearily against the cushions on the settee. "Let Harry deal with it. He will travel to Massingale House as soon as he's had breakfast and will let the duke know what's occurred."

Harry stopped his pacing, turning to Beth. "Yes. I will tell the duke how that—that—that person tricked you into—"

Beth stood. "*No.* You will *not* tell Grandfather that because it would be untrue. I knew *exactly* what I was doing."

Harry's expression softened. "Beth, my dear, Westerville is an experienced seducer. You don't know how these things work, but trust me on this, he is not what you think him."

"I know enough to realize that what you are saying isn't true. This was not Westerville's fault at all. I just—"

"Beth!" Beatrice exploded, throwing herself to her feet. "How can you stand there and defend that man? Especially after the way he simply left? Without a word! Not even—an apology or—" Beatrice pressed her hands to her cheeks. "Do not look at me that way, Beth. I know what I am talking about. An honorable man would have been here first light, ready to make things right. But where is he, I ask you?"

"I don't—"

"I'll tell you where he is," Beatrice said, her jaw hard. "He is out somewhere seducing yet another woman. There aren't enough women in the world for men like him."

Beth's hands curled into fists. But before she could answer, the door opened and the butler stepped in. "Sir. Madam. Miss." He paused dramatically. "The Duke of Massingale and Viscount Westerville."

Beth whirled to face the door. Beatrice clutched her hands to her heart, while Harry muttered an impatient oath and started forward.

A large, gold-knobbed cane in one hand, Grandfather hobbled painfully into the room. He did not spare Beth so much as a glance, though he had plenty of time to glare at Beatrice and Harry. Beth's heart squeezed painfully, though she refused to let the tears rise.

Westerville followed Grandfather. Dressed in a riding habit of unrelenting black, his face tense, he looked as dark and dangerous as ever. He was dangerous, Beth thought miserably.

His gaze swept the room, finding Beth almost immediately. She tried to read his expression, but could not. Beth didn't know what to think. Unlike the others, she knew Westerville had a special reason to wish to see Grandfather, and now, because of her foolishness, she'd given him the perfect excuse.

Her eyes narrowed, a horrid thought rising. Was this what he had planned all along? Perhaps Harry was right. Perhaps Westerville had purposefully seduced her to gain access to Grandfather. Her jaw tightened with each thought.

Grandfather walked straight to the large chair by the fire and sank into it, wincing as he did so. "Damned leg." He flared a hot glance at Harry. "Well? Don't just stand there. Get me some brandy."

Harry started toward the small table in the corner of the room, then stopped. "Brandy?"

"Damn it, yes! And be quick about it."

"But . . . it's not even seven in the morning!"

Grandfather glared. "What? You don't drink in this house until eight? Sissies, the lot of you!"

Harry sent a startled glance at Beatrice, who managed a weak shrug. "Very well, then," Harry said, a note of uncertainty still in his voice. "I suppose a glass wouldn't hurt."

"Of course it wouldn't hurt! Didn't hurt me an hour ago when I had two glasses, did it? Won't hurt me now." He glared at Westerville. "Demmed if I didn't need more, though, having to deal with such a frolic."

Grandfather's gimlet gaze now rested on Beth. Something passed over his face, a flicker of . . . was it uncertainty? Whatever it was, it was gone in a second and in its place was his usual, irascible expression. "There you are. Making a mess of things, are you?"

Beth took a steadying breath. "Grandfather, I was going to come and see you this morning—"

"Not before I was," Harry said somewhat desperately. He handed the duke a glass of brandy. "My lord, something has occurred. Something dreadful. I feel—it is unacceptable what has happened, for I took your granddaughter under my roof and thought to protect her and—"

"Well, well. Can't be everywhere at once, can you?" Grandfather said in an unexpectedly mild tone. "Demmed good brandy, Thistle-Bridgeton. Better than mine."

A stunned silence met this. Harry looked at Beatrice, who shrugged helplessly. "My lord," Harry tried again. "I was coming to see you after breakfast—"

"After breakfast, eh? Well, you're a mite too late for that. You should have known Westerville here wouldn't wait for you to come and sweep off his porch. He did it himself. Came to me last night, in fact, and told me the whole."

Beth's mouth dropped open. "*All* of it?"

Grandfather's bright eyes pinned her for a moment. "Aye. How he set out to seduce you and almost did so. Won't pretend I was happy with the whole thing, for I'm not. Westerville acted like a damned scoundrel."

The viscount gave Grandfather a mocking smile, then bowed. "I have tendered my apology. My behavior was unacceptable."

Grandfather snorted, sending Westerville a hard look from beneath his craggy brows. "That's not the half of it. You're lucky you're young, wealthy, and titled. If you weren't, I'd have shot you last night."

Westerville's mouth tightened slightly, but he merely bowed again, and said nothing more.

Beth's cheeks heated. "Grandfather, did . . . did the viscount tell you *why* he did this?"

Westerville answered. "I set out to seduce you because I could not help myself." His gaze flickered over her. "You are a beautiful woman, my dear, and I am, alas, but human."

The fool. Beth glared at him.

Grandfather set his empty glass on the table. "Looks like her mother, she does."

Westerville had not told Grandfather everything then. He was playing a deep game, there was no doubt about it. One she wanted no part of. But what could she do? Announce that he had seduced her for no other reason than he was looking for evidence of a long-ago crime and needed access to Massingale House? That would solve nothing. If she knew anything about Westerville, it was that he was persistent to the point of death.

If she protested, he would simply overrule her, and now that he had Grandfather so firmly on his side . . . No, now was not the time. If she pressed this, there was a very real likelihood Grandfather might force her to marry the viscount. She would wait until she had him alone, and then she would make him see reason. For now, with so many people about, her hands were tied.

But if she seethed at the circumstances, it could honestly be said that Westerville smoldered. Every line of his body was tight with barely suppressed anger, and she knew it had gone sorely against his principles to confess to Grandfather what had occurred. Beth eyed him uneasily. He stood beside the door they'd come in, his arms crossed over his chest, rocked back on his heels. His black hair fell over his brow, his green eyes bright as if ready for a challenge.

He smiled at Harry, a cold, insulting smile. "I beat you to the punch, did I? You should have gone to see the duke last night, as I did."

Harry started forward, hands fisted.

Grandfather held out his cane, hooking Harry's leg.

"My lord! Unhand me!"

"No, damn you!" Grandfather snapped. "There's to be no fisticuffs, not while I'm here!"

Harry controlled himself with an effort. "My lord, you don't know the character of this man!"

"I know him well enough." Grandfather looked at Westerville with a critical eye. "Won't say as I like this upstart, for I don't. But I will say this; he has more sand than most of the fluff heads who wear titles today. And more eloquence, too."

"My lord!" Harry said, his face red. "There are rumors—I must tell you—you need to know it is said that this man was once a common high-wayman!"

"*That,*" Westerville said, "is a lie. While it is true I was once a highwayman, I have never been common."

Grandfather barked a laugh. "There! See why he's at least stomachable as a grandson-in-law? The man already told me that story last night. Told me about every despicable thing he ever did. Bored me to death, but I suppose it was for the best."

Beatrice pressed a hand to her heart, her wide gaze on Westerville. "You mean . . . it's true? You were—I cannot believe it!"

He bowed, a sardonic twist to his lips. "Gentleman James, my lady."

Harry's lips thinned. "Damned braggart."

"Oh, he is a braggart, that I will give you," Grandfather agreed. His gaze rested on Beth, and for the first time, she saw the determination shining in his eyes. "He is also my granddaughter's fiancé."

Fiancé? Beth blinked. Beatrice gave a faint scream. Harry stared. And through it all, Westerville just stood, smiling at the lot of them.

Chapter 12

It is a servant's greatest pleasure to take pride in his master's appearance and actions. Or so I have been told.

A Compleat Guide for
Being a Most Proper Butler
by Richard Robert Reeves

Three days later, Jameson motioned for the footman to lower the tea tray for inspection. The butler critically eyed the small silver pot filled with fragrant, steaming tea. A matching service of cream and sugar sat in the center, delineated by a single silver teaspoon engraved with twining roses.

A delicate china cup, painted with blue and yellow flowers, had been placed beguilingly empty to one side, while on the other sat a small china plate covered with a tempting array of tea biscuits.

The butler looked at the tray a long moment,

then added a napkin of the whitest linen and one, single rose. Satisfied all was as it should be, he nodded. "Follow me."

He led the way to the garden. The sun peeked merrily through the trees. The wind stirred the tiniest bit, cooling the air to a perfect temperature.

He went down the main path, then through a small gate to one side, and passed under an arbor. There, at the end of the path, on a low marble bench, sat Lady Elizabeth.

Jameson paused when he saw her, for she looked like a picture—sitting in her white gown, the skirts ruffling in the wind, her blond hair framed by the dark green hedgerow behind her. There was no mistaking the downturn of her mouth, an unusual sight that sent his old heart plummeting.

For the last three days, the entire household had been under a cloud. Just this morning, the upper maid had burst into tears for no reason and one of the grooms—a stout fellow who had been in the master's employment for years and years and never caused a single flicker of harm—had forced a fight on one of the stable hands and ended up with a broken nose.

"The mistress is a lovely woman," the footman said softly. "Pity about—"

Jameson sent him a searing glare.

The man fell silent and red-faced.

"This way, Master Charles. *If*, of course, you are through gossiping."

Chastised, the footman nodded miserably. Jameson turned and led the way to the end of the path. "My lady?"

Beth looked up, raising her brows at the sight of the tea tray. "Oh! Why, thank you, but . . . I did not request tea."

"No, my lady. I took it upon myself to bring it. I thought perhaps you would enjoy the sunshine a bit longer."

Her face softened. "You are too kind."

"My lady, we are just glad to have you home." Jameson ordered the footman to place the tea on a nearby bench and then shooed the man away. The butler made a few minute adjustments to the tray. "The tea is quite hot, my lady."

She smiled, though it did not reach her eyes. "Unlike Grandfather, I will not hold you responsible if it's either too hot or too cold."

"Thank you, my lady. That is a great relief."

Usually this dry sort of sally would have brought a smile. Today, she barely dredged up an acknowledging nod before sinking back into silence.

Jameson had to swallow a sigh. Lady Elizabeth had not been herself since she'd returned from London, engaged and disgraced. It was horrifying to think that being in town might have such an effect on such a level-headed young lady. It had been suggested that Her Ladyship had been importuned by a rakehell. Indeed, Jameson himself had witnessed the young man's arrival late at night, and heard the subsequent verbal thrashing the duke had delivered.

Jameson shuddered thinking about it, though the young man had fared fairly well, emerging from the library pale, his eyes flashing with suppressed fury, but his pride unbowed.

It was a pity things had come to such a pass; everyone had hoped Lady Elizabeth might meet a nice, quiet gentleman and fall in love. Jameson was beginning to wonder, judging from Her Ladyship's face, if perhaps stronger feelings were indeed involved.

Of course, it was not his place to suggest such things. So instead, he confined himself to pouring Her Ladyship a cup of tea and fixing it just as she loved it—with cream and a liberal dosing of sugar.

Though Jameson would not admit as much, he was worried. Things at Massingale House were not as they should be. His Lordship had been unusually quiet and spent a considerable amount of time sitting at the window of his library, staring out at the garden. Lady Charlotte was staying in her room even more than usual, seeming more restless and distracted than before. But the worst was Lady Elizabeth; she had lost her smile, which was something Jameson had never thought to see.

The butler waited a moment more, busying himself by dusting the surrounding stone benches with his handkerchief. He wished he could find the words to let Lady Elizabeth know that he and the rest of the servants were with her in spirit. But no spate of brilliance descended upon him and so, with nothing more than a kind smile and a heavy heart, he left, hoping the tea might revive her a little.

Beth didn't hear him go. She was too lost in thought, struggling with the outcome of what she'd come to think of as her Greatest Folly.

Upon making his announcement that Beth was now engaged to be wed, Grandfather had decided it was time she came home—home to Massingale House. Beth was relieved to return, though it irked when Westerville made no objection to this decision. He merely bowed over her hand and said he would see her soon.

"Soon" was now three days hence, and she hadn't received so much as a single note from the scoundrel. Blast him, this was the invitation he'd been waiting for, to visit Massingale House. To be honest, Beth had expected Westerville on her doorstep the very next morning.

But the day passed without notice. Then another. And another. She was beginning to wonder if something was amiss.

She lifted her hand to a rose that waved in the breeze by the bench. The velvet petal warmed her fingers. The heavy rose scent lifted on the breeze, and she leaned back against the bench and tried to calm her agitated thoughts. It had all happened so fast. Even now she could not quite accept things. If Grandfather had his way, she would already be married. Just this morning, over breakfast, Grandfather had astounded her and Charlotte with the announcement that a modiste would be arriving soon to begin work on Beth's wedding gown.

Beth had protested, of course. She felt as if she were a ball rolling downhill, out of control of either her direction or her fate.

She sighed, leaning back. Whatever Westerville had said to Grandfather, it had left the older man with a tinge of respect. Not much, of course; no nonfamily member ever merited more than that, as was evidenced by Charlotte. But still . . . all things considered, even that little bit of grudging admiration was astonishing.

A rustle sounded over Beth's shoulder. She turned to find Lord Bennington standing awkwardly just inside the arbor. Beth had to force herself to smile.

He bowed and gave her a ponderous smile. "Lady Elizabeth. I am sorry to intrude. I thought Lady Charlotte might be here."

"No. I don't think she's risen yet."

Bennington looked at his watch, a displeased frown marring his expression. "It's well after one. Wasn't she to see the doctor this morning?"

"Yes, but she sent word last night that she hadn't been sleeping well and that she would see him next week, instead."

Bennington's displeasure was an almost palpable thing. Beth wondered once again at the man's depth of feeling for her stepmama.

"Charlotte should see the doctor when he comes." He fell silent once again, fidgeting with the gloves he held in his hands. Suddenly, he burst out, "Lady Charlotte seems well, doesn't she?"

Beth hid a smile. What Bennington lacked in eloquence, he made up for in ill-at-ease speech. "Yes, indeed. She has been much better since you began escorting her about."

To her surprise, he flushed a deep red. "I think so, too. In fact, I asked your grandfather if—" Bennington glanced at Beth from under his brows, then clamped his mouth closed. "I'm sorry. I shouldn't burden you with my thoughts."

"It's quite all right. We are almost family as it is."

He stepped forward eagerly. "Yes! I feel the same way! In fact, I would be remiss if I did not tell you—I mean, offer you—Lady Elizabeth, I heard from Charlotte about what happened in London."

Beth's cheeks heated. "How kind of her to inform you."

Bennington shook his head. "She did not mean it unkindly. She was distressed for your sake. She thinks very highly of you, you know, and she has no love for the viscount. In fact, she's always—" Bennington stopped. "What I mean to say is that she cares for you."

"I know. I am sorry; I did not mean to overreact."

"It is quite understandable. I know your grandfather arranged this marriage for you. I do not pretend to know the viscount, but if for some reason you ever need a sanctuary, I hope you will let me know. I have a maiden aunt who lives in Brighton. Your grandfather would never know you were there, yet you'd be safe and well taken care of."

Beth's heart swelled. "I don't know what to say. I . . . Thank you, Lord Bennington. That is most kind. I will keep your offer in mind if things become untenable."

A slow, almost pleased smile touched Bennington's face. "I hope you will, Lady Elizabeth. Your father was quite special to me, and so, too, is your stepmother. Charlotte has always been—" He caught Beth's gaze and winced, his former stiffness returning. "I am sorry. I should go inside and see if Charlotte is up yet. She is expecting me."

"Of course." Beth tilted her head to one side. Was that a carriage rounding the back of the house? How odd. No one used the back drive, unless . . . She straightened a bit.

Lord Bennington bowed. "I shall have Jameson find her for me. Thank you, Lady Elizabeth. I will leave you to your tea."

A low whicker of a horse, followed by the jangle of a harness, made Beth start. It *was* a carriage! It took all her composure to bow calmly to Bennington. "Thank you, my lord. Perhaps you should take Charlotte for a ride today? The fresh air might revive her."

He brightened. "That is an excellent idea! Thank you, Lady Elizabeth. I hope you have a pleasant afternoon." He bowed with a touch less of his usual formality, turned, and made his way back to the house.

Beth watched him go, though her mind was still focused on the sounds of the carriage.

"Did you miss me?" came a low, deep voice directly behind her.

Beth jumped. Hand over her thudding heart, she whirled around to find Christian standing in the garden, his lips curved into a sardonic smile.

"Goodness, Westerville! *Must* you do that?"

"Didn't you hear the carriage?"

"Yes, but only a second ago. You could not have made it from there to this bench in such a short time."

"I didn't. I had the coachman put me down by the side gate."

"Ah." She clasped her hands nervously in front of her. It was at that moment that she realized how much she'd wanted to see him. "I was beginning to wonder if I was to be abandoned before I even reached the altar."

Christian's gaze narrowed, something warm flashing in his eyes. "I am many things, but a promise breaker is not one of them."

For some reason, Beth suddenly felt as if she had too many hands. Her gaze fell on the tea tray still sitting on the bench and she made her way to it. "Would you like some tea? I can call for another cup."

"No, thank you. I can't abide the stuff."

"Then I shall have some." She refilled her cup, looking over her shoulder at the viscount as she stirred the sugar and cream. "We are in a fine fix."

He smiled, his teeth flashing whitely. "So we are."

"I must ask if this was part of your plan? To trick me into an engagement so I could not keep you from Massingale House?"

She hadn't meant to ask the question so baldly, but it was out before she knew it.

His smile disappeared. "I had no intentions of compromising you. It just happened. Besides, you had already agreed to help me." He shrugged. "Why would I need anything more than that?"

Beth paused with the teacup almost to her lips. He was right; she *had* already agreed to help him. Relief flooded through her and she found herself smiling for the first time in days.

He grinned back. "You hadn't thought of that."

"No. Somehow I kept thinking you *meant* to seduce me."

"I did. But not for that reason. Beth, you are a damnably attractive woman. I shouldn't have done what I did, but no man on earth could blame me."

Beth didn't know what to say. She forced herself to take a sip of tea before answering him. "Yes, well, we are still in this horrid predicament. Grandfather is determined we should marry."

"As he should." Westerville said, leaning against a tree, arms crossed over his chest. "You are ruined."

She shrugged and took another sip of tea. The warmth of the drink calmed her nerves somewhat. "I don't feel ruined."

His expression darkened. "You have no idea what being an outcast can do to you. To your soul."

She shrugged. "It means people will talk."

"They will not only talk, they will laugh. They will forget to invite you to various places. And then they will forget you altogether."

She paused and then replaced the cup in the saucer with a gentle click. "Like your mother."

"Yes."

Beth nodded, her expression thoughtful. After a moment, she lifted the cup. The sight of her lips brushing the edge of the delicate china hit Christian like a brick. Every time he was in her vicinity, he lost sight of everything else. Which was why he'd taken three days to visit. He'd thought the time would have cooled the ardor she stirred in his blood, but he'd been wrong. Dead wrong.

She lowered her cup and glanced up at him. She was sitting on a wide pale gray marble bench, a billow of silk skirts, gold hair, and lovely brown eyes. Christian sensed that beneath her calm air was a lingering shock over what had occurred and it pained him.

Christian raked a hand through his hair and leaned back against the tree. By Zeus, how had he let things get to this pass? It was untenable. He'd just meant to rattle her into assisting him. He'd never meant to compromise her.

He suddenly realized that somewhere along the way, his goals had changed. At the beginning of this venture, he'd been more than willing to use her to get to her grandfather. Now . . . now, he would take only what he had to take. He had no desire to hurt Elizabeth. In fact, what he really wanted was—

He cut the thought where it sat. Damn his arrogance. Lady Elizabeth was not for him. She was for someone kinder, gentler, someone who would cherish her and protect her. He was not the man for her.

He met Beth's concerned gaze and forced a smile to his own lips. "This is certainly awkward."

"That is an understatement." The teacup trembled a bit in her hands and she quickly set it to one side.

"How is your grandfather?"

"Angry," she said, then smiled wryly. "And pleased. All at the same time."

Christian frowned. "Angry? Does he abuse you?"

She met his gaze, her color returning in a flush. "No! How can you suggest such a thing?"

"I don't know him that well and . . . Well, I want to be certain you're fine."

"My grandfather would never hurt me. He would never hurt *anyone*."

"I have very little experience with grandfathers or fathers even, for that matter. What little I know of mine makes me quite glad he never bothered to present himself into my life."

Her brows drew down a bit. "Your father was the Earl of Rochester. I saw him once, at a play." She tilted her head to one side. "You don't look like him at all."

"My brother, Tristan, does."

"I've heard that about the new earl."

"He has even less fondness for Father than I." Christian grinned. "Tris hates being called Rochester, so I do it every chance I get."

Her lips quivered. "That does not surprise me. You've a devilish streak."

On impulse, Christian pushed himself from the tree and came to sit beside her. "Beth, I am sorry this came to pass. It was not what I wanted."

She took a steadying breath. "Nor I. But it is what we have. Westerville, do you think—"

"Christian." He reached over and took her hand in his and turned it over, noting the lack of calluses. Her fingers were long and delicate, the tips pink and well shaped. He traced his thumb over her palm, fascinated with the softness of her skin. "We might as well dispense with the formalities now. Besides, I think I would like hearing my name on your lips."

Her cheeks flushed, but she said with some composure, "Very well, Christian. Do you think we could find a believable way to explain our presence in that billiard room? Perhaps if we told Grandfather—"

"No. We could not. And you know that. Besides, no matter what we might believe, society has other ideas of what occurred, thanks to Lady Jersey."

"Why did you have to go to the musicale with that dreadful creature?"

"She's not so dreadful. Just talkative. Besides, I wished to go to the musicale to see you and I didn't have an invitation."

Beth blinked, her long lashes sweeping over her eyes, then up. "You came with Sally Jersey just to see me?"

Christian rubbed the back of Beth's hand over his cheek. "Yes."

"Did Lady Jersey know that?"

"She figured it out fairly quickly. At first she was amused, but I think later on, she felt somewhat slighted." Christian shrugged. "Pity."

Beth laughed softly, her white teeth showing just beneath the edge of her lip. Christian had to fight the urge to lean over and kiss her.

To cover the impulse, he instead kissed her fingers.

She smiled. "You are wasting your time. I cannot be charmed."

"No?" He wondered what had made her so . . . bright. She radiated warmth and humor. He forced himself to look away, his gaze resting on the house before him.

She followed his gaze. "Ah, yes. You wish to search it, don't you?"

"Yes." He turned back to her. "But not now."

"I suppose that would look suspicious."

"Indeed. I have waited twenty years for this; a few more days or weeks won't matter." He glanced at the house. "I can see your butler peering from a window."

"Jameson." She leaned forward, trying to see. "He is rather protective."

"Have you always lived here?"

"Yes. My father and I moved here to be with Grandfather after my mother died."

"Do you remember her?"

"No. I was quite young."

He rubbed his thumb over her wrist. "Were you close to your father?"

"Not really. He was very intelligent and forever puttering about with a book. When he was working on a translation, he would forget to talk for days on end." She smiled. "Grandfather despaired of him ever taking an interest in the estates, which is a pity, for now there is no one to do it."

He traced a line along her thumb to her wrist, then back. "What about you?"

She made a face. "Grandfather is very definite in his concept of acceptable roles for women."

"What a fool."

To her surprise, Beth could see that he meant it. She looked down at her hand, held so warmly in Christian's. A tremble of heat seemed to radiate out from that spot, warming her as it traveled up her arm, over her shoulder, and to her breasts. Beneath the light silk of her chemise, she could feel her breasts swelling, her nipples tightening. It was a very unnerving thing, this pull she felt toward Christian. It was very . . . physical.

She swallowed a sigh. How she wished her mother was still alive to explain such things to her, although . . . was that the sort of thing one confided to one's mother? Certainly Beth could not imagine saying anything to Grandfather. As for Charlotte, they had never been that close.

Beth gently withdrew her hand from Christian's and managed a stiff smile. She would need all her wits if she wished to find a way out of this engagement. "Christian, I have been thinking."

His eyes glinted, but all he did was raise his brows.

"Since neither of us wish to be married, we must think of a way to soothe Grandfather's irritation."

Christian looked amused. "I suppose I could put an end to my existence. That would please him a good deal."

"Nonsense. He is not an impractical man. He has to know that would just lead to more scandal."

Christian's lips twitched. "That would be horrid, wouldn't it?"

Beth had to fight the urge to smile herself. "Horrid, indeed."

"I suppose I shall not put a period to my own life then."

"We will save that as our Avenue of Last Recourse."

"Thank you," he said dryly.

"Meanwhile, we must do something to calm Grandfather. Not much, but enough that he doesn't rush to put the announcement in the paper. If I can find some way to convince him not to post the banns just yet, then it will give us some time to convince him we should not wed."

"Beth, society will not let him simply change his mind. You are ruined."

"I don't care about that. I never wished to go into society, anyway. Besides, when Grandfather dies, I shall inherit all of his money. If there is one thing I know about society it is that they will always forgive one if one is but wealthy enough."

"You wouldn't be happy with a husband won solely on the size of your fortune."

"Look, Westerville," she said with a sudden show of asperity. "I don't want a husband at all. I don't know why anyone would need one. Anything a husband could provide, I could find here, on my own."

Christian raised his brows, humor sparkling in his eyes.

Beth flushed. "Almost anything, I mean."

Christian chuckled.

"Oh, stop that!" She took a deep breath and turned in her seat until she was facing him. "Christian, listen to me. I have decided we must do what we can to stop this marriage. Are you with me, or not?"

Chapter 13

It is interesting how every master differs, and not just in height and weight. Some are good natured, some are not. Some are tight with their gold, others spend it like water. Some are appreciative of their servants, others eat cold mutton and wear over-starched shirts. Ah, yes, the differences are far and wide.

A Compleat Guide for
Being a Most Proper Butler
by Richard Robert Reeves

Christian opened his mouth to respond, but couldn't. Of course he had no wish to marry, especially not the granddaughter of the man responsible for his mother's death. Still, looking down at Beth as she sat on the bench, surrounded by flowers, her silk gown a perfect foil for her honey-colored hair and brown eyes, he was struck with the most amazing thought—why *shouldn't* he marry her? Life with Beth would be one of excitement and challenge. She was beautiful and charming. And there was an instant rapport between them that he'd never before experienced.

Startled at the thought, he forced himself to smile. "I am not sure I follow your meaning."

"I have an idea to save us both from this predicament, but it will take your cooperation. Do I have it?"

"What is your idea?"

"We must see this engagement as nothing more than a minor setback. All we have to do is accept Grandfather's orders, but just *pretend* we're willing to marry. Then, before any serious plans have been made or the banns posted, I will cry off." Her smile faded. "Of course, that will make me look sadly frivolous."

He laughed softly. "My love, you *are* frivolous. I have yet to see you wear the same pair of shoes twice."

Her cheeks heated. "I don't own that many!"

Christian chuckled. "Don't eat me! They are lovely shoes, all of them." He leaned forward a little, his shoulder rubbing against her and sending a thick heat into the air about them. "I especially love the blue satin heels with gold trim. One day, I may have you wear those for me—"

Beth managed a smile. "I would be honored."

"—with nothing else on."

For a moment, she could only stare up at him. "With nothing else on? That's—that's—that's—"

"Sensual? Exciting? Stimulating? Exhilar—"

"Obscene."

"Nonsense. It's perfectly acceptable." He leaned back, stretching his arm behind her, his shoulder temptingly near. Hell, he was engaged to her, was he not? Why *shouldn't* he put his arm about her?

"This is not a proper conversation."

"Nonsense," he said again, laying his arm across her shoulders, enjoying the way her scent rose about her, as fresh and fragrant as the flowers. "We are now engaged to be married, my love. This is all perfectly acceptable."

She took his hand and lifted it over her head and placed it on his own lap. "You, sir, are taking advantage of a very distressful situation."

"I am merely enjoying a happy happenstance, is all. Shouldn't I do that? See the bright side of things?"

"There is no bright side of this. We must find a way to convince Grandfather not to post the banns. Otherwise—" Beth clamped her mouth together, unwilling to continue with that line of thought. "We must try this."

He looked at her for a long moment, his eyes shadowed, hidden. She wondered what he was thinking, what sober thoughts held him.

Finally, he shrugged. "Very well. We will see if your plan works."

"It will be easy. We will simply put him off about the date—I shall argue that I need a better gown or that lilies won't be in bloom and then, when the scandal has faded, you and I shall have a huge row and finish this charade. We will never have to speak again."

He didn't answer.

"Was— I mean, Christian. What do you think? Is that not a plausible plan?"

"It is certainly desperate," he said in an emotionless voice. "But I suppose I do not blame you. Being married under such circumstances is not what anyone would wish."

Her chest tightened. "No. It is not. I just thought . . . this way, we escape the marriage, but you will have the opportunity to search the house. Everyone will expect you to visit me. Grandfather stays in the library and cannot walk upstairs without assistance. And Charlotte stays in her room. So we should be able to look without interference. The only problem will be the servants."

Christian's gaze met hers. "You have thought of everything, haven't you?" he said.

"I tried to," she replied.

He nodded, offering no comment, though he seemed far from pleased.

Beth bit her lip. She truly wished to assist him. Once they ascertained the necklace was not at Massingale House, Beth wondered if she could help Christian in looking for it elsewhere. There had to be some clues he was missing, some evidence he had misinterpreted for him to think the culprit was Grandfather.

"Westerville, what do you say? Are you willing to help me convince Grandfather to wait on the barns?"

"It's Christian to you, my love." His gaze heated, though he smiled. "I am glad you agreed to do the crying off. When a man does it, he is considered a cad. When a woman does the crying off, she is considered to have come to her senses and made an escape from a Bad Situation."

Her lips quivered just a bit and Christian was encouraged to add, "I do not know why that is so, but I've seen it time and again."

The smile didn't come all the way to fruition, but some of the tension left her expression. "I'm sorry. I don't mean to be so weak-livered."

"You? Weak?" He waved a hand. "Perish the thought."

"Yes, well . . . you seem to be taking this in much better part than I."

"Perhaps I am just better at hiding my fear. No matter who you are, it's daunting to realize how close we are to being marched will ye nill ye to the altar."

She looked at him for a long, level moment. He took the opportunity to admire the sweep of her lashes; thick and dark brown, they complemented her fair coloring no small amount.

"My lord, I do not think anyone could ever make you do something you don't want to do, especially something as important as marriage."

"No one could make you, either, unless you allow them. To be honest, when I spoke to your grandfather, he did not seem all that certain of his ability to make you follow his wishes."

She smiled a little. "I could refuse him and he knows it. Still, it would be a battle of no small order."

"Two stubborn people, locked horn to horn. I daresay it would be a sight worth seeing."

A chuckle burst from her lips, her eyes crinkling charmingly. "It would not be worth seeing at all. He would bluster and thunk his cane on the floor, all red in the face, while I glared and snapped at him like an angry turtle."

He had to laugh at that picture.

She leaned back on her hands, the sun filtering through the leaves of the tree, a look of sudden realization warming her expression. "You are right, though. Grandfather cannot make me wed. I just want to ease out of it without having to fight with him. He—he is not well."

Christian nodded. He'd thought the same when he'd first met the man. "This whole episode was a bit of a shock to you and me. The thought of marriage makes me queasy. In fact, I am feeling a bit ill right now."

Her eyes glimmered with humor. "You are not."

"I vow it. I am ill to my stomach at the thought of marrying you." He grinned. "Very."

She gave a prim sniff. "I do not blame you one bit; you would hate being married to me."

"Oh? Why is that?"

"I am short tempered in the mornings before I've had my tea."

"So am I."

"I sneeze every time I step out into the garden."

"How horrid."

"I am not very good at lawn tennis, either."

He raised his brows. "Anything else?"

This time, her gaze locked with his. "I would not accept carousing in a husband."

"I would not carouse were I a husband."

"Never?" Disbelief dripped from her tones.

"Never. Which is why I'm not married and have no intention of doing so."

She pursed her lips. "That is a big statement."

"It is a deeply felt one. Tell me honestly; have you ever seen a marriage worth emulating?"

"My parents. I don't remember much, but even my grandfather says they were deeply in love. After Mother died, Father just . . . stopped."

"He remarried, didn't he?"

"Yes. Years later, to Charlotte." She gave a rueful smile. "It was difficult giving up the position of Only Female in Residence. I fear I was a little spoiled and made it difficult on her at first."

"That is about the same time my mother was incarcerated."

Beth's eyes darkened. "That had to have been much more difficult. I am sorry, Christian."

He shook his head. "We were talking about you. Is your stepmother good to you?"

"Yes. She and I aren't close, of course. We're too different to become true friends. But we brush along well enough. Grandfather says Father never cared for Charlotte as he did for Mother." A troubled look entered Beth's eyes. "I've always thought that was why Charlotte—" She caught Christian's gaze and blushed. "Never mind. You don't want to know about that."

But he did. He wanted to know everything there was to know about this woman. It was odd, but the more he saw of her, the more he wanted to find out all of her little foibles, her likes and dislikes, what colors she loved, which flowers she adored . . . he wanted to know all of it as if that would help him capture some small essence of her. Something he could take with him when he finally had to leave.

The pressure in his chest deepened. She was so sweet, so remarkable. Yet she didn't even know it.

Something inside him loosened, then broke. A surge of emotions sent Christian forward. He leaned down and gently placed his lips to hers. She willingly accepted it, her face turning up to meet his. It was a remarkably chaste kiss considering some of their other kisses. But it was sensual all the same.

For Beth, it was something more. A promise of a sort. The sealing of a companionship that had started far before they'd ever met.

His lips were firm and warm against hers, his scent rising to fill her with a longing for . . . something. Something new. Something exciting.

Lately, she'd lived a life of dreams. She'd been dressed and pressed, riding in the best carriages and attending the best soirées and balls. But somehow, that wasn't living. Going through the motions of polite society was about acting, not being. And for once in her life, she wanted something more. She wanted to just *be*.

The viscount's kiss was that something more. She was no longer just watching others. Instead, she felt alive in a way she never had. Her entire body pulsed with awareness, her mind whirled with passions and thoughts so rapid they pressed her onward. Before she knew what she was about, she'd thrown herself into the kiss, twining her arms about Christian's neck and pressing herself against him. She wanted more of this, more of him.

A deep groan sounded in his throat and then his hand found the back of her neck, his warm fingers pulling her forward. He deepened the kiss, opening his mouth ever so slightly, his lips warm and deliciously firm over hers.

Heated sensations burned through her. Beth shivered when Christian raked his tongue over her teeth. Her body tightened and tingled, hot and cold warring for release.

His hand slid from her neck to her shoulder, then down her back, trailing waves of passion. There was something about this man with his wild handsomeness and the wounded look deep in his eyes that made her crave his touch as a starving man craved food.

Suddenly he released her and then rose from the bench, turning on his heel and stalking down the path a short way.

Beth was left half reclining on the bench, her hair unbound, her heart thundering in her chest.

Two things dawned on her in rapid succession. First, she had not wished Christian to stop. Second, even now, without the distraction of his warm mouth on hers, she couldn't think of a single reason *to* stop. They were engaged, weren't they? Surely such exchanges as this were normal between engaged couples?

He flicked a look at her, his brow lowering as he took in her mussed hair. "You may need a comb."

Beth smoothed her hair with hands that shook slightly. "I look as if I've been kissed, which I have been. And if I cannot be kissed by my fiancé, then who should kiss me?"

He didn't smile. Instead, he passed a hand over his face and sighed. "Beth, we cannot keep doing this. I cannot stop it every time."

"I know." She bit her lip. "Christian, I am sorry. I just thought that since we were engaged—"

"It's not real!" His voice rang harshly through the garden.

She stiffened, color high in her cheeks. "I know."

A deep silence filled the garden. Somewhere in the distance, a bird trilled, then silence once again.

Finally, Christian sighed. "I am sorry. I didn't come here to argue with you or—" He shook his head. "I came to give you something." He reached into his coat and pulled out a packet. He brought it to her. "This is the information I told you about. I put a letter with it, describing the importance of each piece. I want you to understand why I must search the house. Why I think your grandfather is guilty of a great crime."

She took the packet, the foolscrap cool and crisp. She rubbed her fingers over the ribbon that bound them all together.

"I need that packet back." Christian nodded at the letters. "In a way, the letters are all I have of my mother."

Beth nodded. "I will take care of them, I promise."

"Thank you. Now, I must go."

"Don't you want to go inside?" Beth stood and

placed the letters into a pocket in the folds of her gown. "Grandfather has been looking for you."

"Unless I mistake my guess, he has seen me. He has been staring out that large window on the far end ever since I arrived."

Beth smiled. "It's a good thing the arbor hides us from view."

"Indeed. Beth, I . . . thank you for reading the missives and hearing what I have to say. That means a lot."

"I agreed to help you find your mother's betrayer. We will keep our deal from the billiard room."

For a long moment, he did not speak. When he finally did, his words were thick with emotion. "Thank you. I must go." He turned to leave.

"But Grandfather—"

"I will speak with him tomorrow," Christian said over his shoulder, walking even more quickly now. All too soon, he disappeared down the path. She heard the slap of his boots on the pathway, then the distant click of the side gate followed by the unmistakable sound of a carriage being sprung as he raced off.

Beth sank back on the bench, her thoughts whirling. Her gaze fell on the now-empty teacup. At some point, it had been knocked off the bench and lay on its side in a thick patch of grass. She picked it up and placed the delicate china back on the tray.

Tomorrow, he'd said. That would have to be soon enough. She reached into her pocket and took out the packet. Slowly, she undid the ribbon.

Christian stepped down from his carriage, deep in thought. Every time he got physically close to Beth, she drew him to her in other, less definable ways.

But what really bothered him was the way she spoke to him, as if they were . . . equals. Companions. *Partners.*

He paused on the top step, realizing that the carriage was still sitting at the curb. He frowned at the coachman. "You may take the carriage to the stables. I will not need it again today."

The footman exchanged a startled glance with the coachman. They looked so shocked that a wave of irritation tightened Christian's jaw. Good God, did everyone around him think him a complete and utter wastrel?

The footman cleared his throat. "My lord, are you certain you don't wish us to just wait? 'Tis fairly early and you might wish to go out again and—"

"Take the carriage to the stables. I am done for the night."

"But . . .'tis only four in the afternoon, my lord!"

"I have a damned watch!"

The footman jumped back a step and began bowing profusely. "Yes, my lord! I'm sorry, my lord! I just didn't think—"

Reeves opened the door. He looked from the flustered footman to Christian's stern visage and carefully stepped back out of the way. "Welcome home, Lord Westerville. I thought I heard voices."

Christian entered his house and took off his

gloves and hat. "I was having a discussion about my evening habits."

"Of course," Reeves said soothingly. He glanced down the steps at the coachman and footman who stood stock-still on the walk below. "His Lordship will call if he needs you." With that, he shut the door with a sharp snap and turned to Christian. "I shall inform the cook you will be home for the rest of the evening. He will be shocked as well, but perhaps he can find something worthy for your dinner."

"Thank you," Christian snapped, turning toward the library.

The butler murmured some instructions to a footman, then followed. "Since you will be staying home this evening, would you like a fire lit in the dining room?"

"Whatever you wish." Christian sat in a chair by the window and stared sightlessly at the carriages and horses riding by.

Reeves watched him a moment, then busied himself adding to the fire. After a few moments, he said, "Did you find Her Ladyship at home?"

"Yes. In the garden, to be precise."

"And the duke?"

"I didn't see him. As I was rounding the bend of the drive, I saw Lady Elizabeth among her roses, so I met her there." She'd looked damnably attractive, sitting among the greenery, too. He rubbed a hand over his face, wondering why things seemed more complicated now. They weren't, really. They were, in fact, better. She'd agreed to call off the wedding before it happened and had offered to assist him still in looking for the necklace. Surely that was cause for celebration?

Instead, he felt like the biggest heel on earth.

"My lord, you appear almost glum." Reeves came to stand beside Christian. "I must assume your meeting with Her Ladyship went poorly."

"No. It went fine. Better than fine, I just—" Christian leaned forward, elbows on his knees. "Reeves, you were right. I should never have used Lady Elizabeth to reach her grandfather. It was dishonorable of me."

No answer was made.

"I made a horrible error, one I cannot fix. And now we are to marry, although she is working on a way to break off the engagement."

"Is she indeed, my lord?"

"Yes. I cannot allow her to do that, of course. She would be ruined. Of course, she would be ruined anyway, marrying me. I am not fit for marriage. I . . . cannot." Christian rested his head in his hands and waited. After a while, he lifted his head and asked, "Did you hear me?"

"Yes, my lord. You said I was right and you were wrong and that if you could undo it, you would."

Christian frowned. "I didn't say that, exactly."

"Perhaps it was just my imagination. I sometimes daydream, you know."

"Well . . . I *would* undo it, you know. But I cannot. I just wanted you to know that from now on, I will heed your advice more."

Reeves's gaze dropped to Christian's waistcoat. "Indeed, my lord?"

"Except in matters of dress."

Reeves sighed. "I knew there would be a caveat, my lord. There always is."

Despite everything, Christian had to smile, though it was not a large one. "I will tell you one more thing, too."

"I await with bated breath, my lord," Reeves said dryly.

"You were right about Lady Elizabeth, too. She is quite special."

"Indeed, my lord. One has but to see her to know that. Innocence is a difficult trait to hide."

Innocence. Christian considered this a moment. She was innocent, indeed. But she was also intelligent, sensual, and generous. He thought it was perhaps that last aspect of her character that engaged him the most; she effortlessly gave of herself—her thoughts, her abilities, her heart.

But innocent? That did not quite describe the quality that gave her that soft glow. It was more the quality of goodness.

For a man who'd once lived in the cold and dirty alleyways and back streets of London and knew hardship as a way of life, someone who had sold his soul so many times, he had long since given up hope of getting it back, Beth's generous spirit was almost overwhelming. And yet . . . he craved it. Craved her.

Christian caught Reeves's questioning gaze. "She is one of the most beautiful women I've ever known."

"I would have to agree," Reeves said reflectively. "Lady Elizabeth is quite beautiful, perhaps the most beautiful of all the women I've had the pleasure of meeting."

"Have you met many?"

"Your father was a very well-known and well-liked man. He never lacked for female companionship."

Some of the humor left Christian. "Then they must not have known him."

"Precisely, my lord. And once they did, they left."

Christian frowned. "Like my mother?"

Reeves bowed.

"Really? I always thought he had left her."

"He begged her to return but she would not. And frankly, I do not blame her. He was innately selfish. I do not think he could change, even if he wished to." Reeves paused. "I have often thought that the facility to change, to adapt for the better, was a trait to be valued. It is what makes us redeemable."

Christian considered this. "Perhaps I have been inflexible, though I still believe Beth's grandfather to blame for Mother's death. The evidence— I think Beth will have to agree once she reads all of it."

Christian stirred restlessly, wishing he could see her again now. He glanced at the clock and frowned. It was early yet. He rubbed his fingers together, realizing that he found being "respectable" onerous. God, how he missed riding the heath, the flash of a sword in the moonlight, the shrill cries of the outriders.

There was nothing more exciting than that. Or

was there? He had an instant vision of Beth this afternoon, sitting in her garden, the soft breeze stirring her hair, the scent of lilies and roses all about. What was she doing now? he wondered. He pictured her in the garden, reading the missives he'd left with her. Would she be shocked to find that her grandfather was, in fact, responsible for a crime?

He frowned. He hoped she was not too upset at the thought. Because of Beth and her unique way of experiencing life, he was beginning to think his own existence a little lacking.

Something stirred in his breast, something warm and expanding. Something a little like love.

By Zeus, where in the hell had that thought come from? Christian shook his head to dislodge the ridiculous idea.

"My lord?" Reeves appeared concerned. "Are you well? Does your head pain you?"

"No, no. I am fine. I just had a stupid thought, is all."

"Ah. And what was that thought, my lord? I take it that it did not have anything to do with wearing that black waistcoat?"

"It had nothing to do with clothing."

"A pity," Reeves said with a long-suffering sigh. "If you were not thinking of clothing, then your thought must have had something to do with Lady Elizabeth."

"Reeves, I am not going to tell you anything."

"Yes, my lord." Reeves walked toward the door. "Though it is a pity . . ."

"What's a pity?"

"That you will miss so much sleep. Unsettled thoughts will fester in the night air and leave one tossing and turning. I have seen it many times." With that cheery thought, Reeves opened the door. "I shall be just outside if you decide you wish to discuss the matter further."

Christian glared at the closed door but did not move to call Reeves back in. The butler was probably right and there would be little sleep tonight. But Christian was not going to share such a preposterous idea, one born, no doubt, from the difficult situation he and Beth found themselves in.

He needed to focus on finding that damnable necklace, and then he could extricate himself from Beth's life and they would all be the better for it. Tomorrow, when he saw her, he would be all business. Never again would he succumb to the temptation of a kiss.

Chapter 14

If you find your employer out of sorts, do not immediately leap to the conclusion that his mutton was burned or there was too much starch in his cravat. It is a foolish man who apologizes without reason.

A Compleat Guide for
Being a Most Proper Butler
by Richard Robert Reeves

"What are you doing?"

Beth glanced from the library window to Grandfather, who stood inside the door, leaning heavily on his cane. "As you can see, I am looking out the window."

"Waiting on that jackanapes, aren't you?"

That was just like Grandfather to call the man he'd forced to declare himself to her, a jackanapes. Beth shook her head wryly. "If you are referring to my fiancé, yes."

"Fiancé, humph!" He glared at her from under his bushy brows as he went to sit in his favorite chair by the fire. He sat heavily, wincing as he did so, then pulled his shawl from the arm of the chair and spread it over his lap.

Beth went to help him, making certain his feet were covered.

He glanced up at her. "So? How do you like having a fiancé?"

"Does it matter?" She took the chair opposite his. "Grandfather, let me remind you that *you* were the one who wished me wed."

"Yes, but *you* were the one who made such a cake of yourself that I had no choice but to insist on it," he returned sourly. "You didn't leave either of us a choice."

"A fact you turned to your advantage. You wished me married well before the scandal."

"It was fortunate, though I wish you had taken better care of the family name." Real anger flared in his gaze.

A pang of remorse pinched Beth. "I'm sorry about that. You are right."

"Yes, I am. The family name has been damaged already, what with—" His thin lips snapped together. "Never mind that. As you say, it worked out well enough, I suppose."

"I suppose Westerville will do," Beth said, keeping her voice as neutral as she could. "It's not as if there were a hundred suitors knocking down my door."

His brows lowered even further. "Never could

figure that out. Fine-looking gel like you, no nonsense to her, neat as a pin, and with a fat dowry; I don't understand what went wrong."

Beth looked down at her slippers. "Who knows? Men are very difficult to figure out."

"No, we're not," Grandfather said, stamping his cane on the floor. "Men are very simple creatures, the lot of us. There's no reason you didn't take."

Beth bit her lip. "Well . . . actually, there is a reason."

"What?"

"I, ah . . . well, I didn't really wish any of the men I met to importune you with offers and such." Beth fidgeted with the fringe on a pillow under her elbow.

"Go on," Grandfather said grimly, his white brows lowered.

"So I thought that I could help with that."

"What did you do?"

"I stuttered."

"You did *what*?"

"I stuttered. L-l-like th-th-th—"

He threw up a blue-veined hand. "No!"

She hung her head, peeping up at him, a smile trembling on her lips. "Yes."

Grandfather dropped his hand into his lap. "You stuttered. And they all ran off like—"

"The fools that they were? Yes."

He shook his head, though an amused gleam lit his eye. "You are incorrigible. I hope Westerville knows what a handful you are."

Beth wisely didn't answer. The truth was, of all the men she'd met in London, only Westerville had been the least bit interesting. What was it about him? He was certainly handsome, but it was more than that. It was the way he looked at her as if infuriated and fascinated at the same time. The way he was so steadfast about finding his mother's betrayer.

Beth slipped a hand into her pocket. There rested the packet of letters. She'd read them yesterday in the garden, then twice more in her room before retiring for the night. Hours later, she'd found herself in bed, awake, her mind still mulling over the words, picturing the plight of the woman who'd written most of the letters, could hear the echo of deep, residing pity in the missive from the bishop. It was a convincing and emotional collection; she could see why Christian was so convinced that her grandfather was involved.

Yet there were still things that didn't quite ring true. Why would Grandfather wish Christian's mother such ill? There was nothing in the evidence to suggest a tie of any sort. Furthermore, Grandfather had an extraordinary amount of funds and he was not fond of jewelry; he wore nothing more than a signet ring, in fact. Why would he wish to procure a necklace?

Something was missing from this story. Yet Beth had to admit that Christian's suspicions weren't entirely unfounded; though the evidence was not damning, it was certainly significant. She might not agree with his hasty conclusions, but she had to admire his unwavering commitment to his goals.

And then there was the way he made her feel . . . She'd spent a good half hour this morning questioning Annie on this rather alarming aspect of being near Westerville. Annie seemed to think Beth a woman to be envied.

Was she? Beth wondered. Was she to be envied?

"Beth?"

She looked up to find Grandfather regarding her. "Yes?"

"Why don't you want to marry?"

"I don't think I ever really said I—"

"Don't tell me that! I know what you think and you don't wish to marry, not even Westerville." He leaned forward. "Why not?"

"Because . . ." She bit her lip. To be honest, somewhere deep in her heart, part of her wondered the same thing. What would it be like to be married to Christian? To wake up with him? Eat breakfast with him? Share the newspaper and gossip? She looked around the library, trying to picture him here.

Strangely, she could. He would enjoy talking politics with Grandfather, she just knew it. And he'd already admitted an interest in managing the land—he'd even admired his father's abilities for that. She sighed. "I don't want to marry because I don't wish to make a mistake." She caught Grandfather's gaze. "Like father and Charlotte. I don't remember much, but he was never happy with her."

Grandfather winced. "Your father regretted that marriage from the day it happened."

"Then why did he marry her?"

"He was lonely. And he thought it would be good for you, although one only has to look at the woman to know she hasn't a mothering bone in her body."

Beth sighed. "I want a relationship, but then again . . . I don't."

To her surprise, Grandfather cackled. "That's quite normal, my girl. Quite normal indeed. There are no guarantees in this life. You have to take what you can get and enjoy it while you have it. That's what your father didn't do." Grandfather's face darkened. "After your mother's death, he locked himself away, translating this and that and ignoring life. I don't ever want that to happen to you."

"He loved literature."

"He should have loved life. And you. You were the best thing that ever happened to him, and he was too busy moaning over the loss of your mother to realize it. Then, when something did wake him up and make him feel alive, it was too late. He'd already settled for—" He stopped and clamped his lips shut.

Beth frowned. "Grandfather, what are you—"

The door opened and Jameson entered. "Pardon me, my lord, but it is eleven."

Grandfather tossed aside the shawl. "Time for my nap." He took his cane and hobbled toward the butler. "Beth, you should get some sleep, too. You might need it if that fiancé of yours ever makes an appearance. You're looking a bit haggard lately."

"I'll have to ask Charlotte for some of her medicine. I'm getting as distracted as she is."

"Hardly. You could go for two weeks without sleep and still outwit that ninnyhammer."

"Grandfather! You are so unkind to Charlotte. To everyone, in fact. Even Lord Bennington—"

"Is an even bigger fool! He takes advantage of Charlotte and she lets him."

"I don't know why you think that. Bennington has never been anything but kind to her."

"You don't know either of them the way I do," Grandfather snapped.

Beth sighed. It would do no good to upset Grandfather. She stood. "I suppose I should go upstairs, too. Perhaps a nap would be just the thing. By the way, if Westerville comes today, will you please attempt to be nice to him, at least?"

"I am nice to him! Told him he had to marry you, didn't I?"

"I would hardly call that 'nice.' If you wish me to get married, it seems you could show a little respect when I speak about my fiancé."

"I show respect."

"You did everything but spit at my feet when I said his name."

Grandfather's blue eyes twinkled reluctantly. "Well? I didn't spit, did I? That's something, isn't it?"

Beth had to smile a little. "I want your promise you will be polite. It's important to me."

Grandfather's gaze sharpened. "Oh! It's like that, is it?"

Her face heated. "I don't know what you're talking about."

He cackled, pleased with something as he hobbled to where Jameson stood patiently holding the door. "No, my dear. You probably don't. But you will!" With that cryptic statement, he disappeared with the butler to the hallway.

Annie leaned against the windowpane, her cheek smooshed almost flat as she tried to peer out the corner of the window.

"Can you see anything?" Beth asked for the hundredth time, tying a ribbon in her hair.

"No. Not a bloomin' thing." Annie sighed and straightened. "Ye'd think yer man would have come to see ye already."

"He came yesterday, while I was in the garden."

"Hooee, ye didn't tell me that!"

"I don't have to tell you everything. He is coming again today."

"It's gettin' late, isn't it?"

"He keeps London hours still, I daresay." Plus, she'd sent him a note this morning not to come until well after eleven. That was when Grandfather took his daily nap. That way, she could be assured of at least a little privacy before Grandfather joined them.

"London hours," huffed Annie. "London this and London that. I wouldn't give ye ten pence fer the whole town."

"Didn't you like it there, Annie?"

"Not a bit, my lady. I was never so glad as when

I came home to me own room and trundle bed."
Annie shook her head. "There's a sight more men
there, I have to admit that. But they don't be of the
quality I'd recommend."

Beth fidgeted with the silver-handled brush on
the dresser. "Annie, you once told me you knew
you were in love when you felt like you had the
ague, but didn't. Well . . . what if I don't feel like I
have the ague exactly, but I feel . . . trembly inside."

"Oh yes, my lady! Trembly will do it, too. Ye have
to feel different and sometimes sort of scared-like."

"Ah!"

"Aye. Sort of prickly-like. And a little itchy in
places I won't be mentioning."

Beth blinked. "Itchy?"

"Some might call it a quiet yearnin'. But me, I
call it 'itchy.' "

That was certainly interesting . . . and far more
information than Beth had wished. "I see. Well. I
will remember that." She thought for a few minutes. Christian would be here soon. And he did
indeed make her a little "itchy," if she understood
Annie's term correctly.

She looked up at Annie. "I need you to do
something for me, if you please."

"Aye?"

"After His Lordship comes to call, could you
get the footmen out of the front hallway?"

Annie beamed. "Planning a tryst, are ye? Well,
seein' as how ye're engaged to the fellow, I don't
see why not. A little rumpus never hurt no one."

Beth started to correct the maid, then thought
better of it. "Yes, well. Thank you, Annie."

"Aw, 'tis naught." Annie smooshed her cheek back to the glass. "I think . . . aye, there he be!" The maid straightened, smiling widely. "My, he looks right well, dressed like a prince."

"I shall go downstairs immediately."

"Wait there, my lady! Ye don't want to appear too interested."

"But—"

"Trust me on this. It does 'em good to be kept waiting. Makes them crazed to see ye."

"Crazed is right, but not in a good way. Besides, I want to get there before Grandfather knows he's here."

"Your grandfather's napping. It will be at least a half hour before he's up and about."

"Exactly my point. *Only* half an hour. Don't forget to call the footmen away. At least for a few minutes." With that, Beth left the room. She was just coming down the steps when Jameson answered the front door and escorted Christian to the foyer.

He saw her at the same moment, and there was an awkward pause. Beth wondered if just the sight of him would always affect her so, making her knees weak, her chest ache. She collected herself and managed a credible curtsy before turning to the butler, who was even now holding Westerville's hat and gloves.

"Jameson, I will take His Lordship into the front sitting room. There is no need quite yet to inform Grandfather that Westerville is here."

Christian's brows rose, his green eyes dark with a question.

Beth smiled at him, shaking her head just a little. Jameson bowed. "Shall I bring tea?"

"No, thank you," Beth said, placing her hand in the crook of Christian's arm and leading him to the sitting room.

The butler spoke briefly with one of the footmen in the front hallway, then made his way down the hall to the servants' quarters.

The second the butler was out of hearing, Christian looked down at Beth. "Well, my love? Are you stealing me away for some illicit purpose? I feel as if I'm slipped into a married woman's boudoir, only to discover that her husband is still home."

Beth raised her brows. "A married woman's boudoir?"

His smile faded a bit. "Perhaps that was a poor example."

"Perhaps it was," she said stiffly, wondering at the pound of instant emotion she'd experienced at his suggestion.

He grimaced. "I didn't think how that would sound. I only meant—"

"It's nothing," she said in a clipped tone. She reached into her pocket and drew out the letters he'd given her from the day before. "Here." She held them out. "These are yours."

He took them, though his eyes never left her face. "Well?"

Beth hesitated. There was such an intensity to his expression that she knew he'd been anxiously waiting for this moment. "You are right when you say someone at Massingale House is responsible for the ill brought on your mother. I just cannot accept that it was Grandfather."

"Who could it have been?"

"Father was already gone by the time your mother was arrested."

"I know. Do you think Charlotte capable of such intrigue?"

"No. She is not strong enough and I cannot see her being so heartless. I do not know who was the villain. I only know there is a connection between Massingale House and your mother's false imprisonment and I will help you find out what I can." A noise drew her gaze to the door.

"Beth, I—"

"Shhh!" Beth hissed. She tiptoed to the open door and looked out. The two footmen stood in stoic silence.

"What is it?" Christian whispered directly behind Beth, his breath warm and unexpected on her cheek.

She had to rein in a shiver, but she managed to whisper back, "Wait!"

There was no sound until, from a distant door, Beth heard Annie's voice. It grew louder until Beth could tell her maid was speaking to Jane, one of the downstairs maids, the one Grandfather was forever calling "that horrid flirt."

Sure enough, as soon as Annie and Jane were within range of the front hallway, they began calling out a greeting to the footmen.

Christian watched with Beth from around the edge of the doorway as the two maids flirted with the footmen, asking them to come and help with their laundry baskets.

"It will never work," Christian whispered. "They will not leave their posts."

"You don't know the power of Annie." Sure enough, moments later, Annie and one of the footmen disappeared down the hallway, Jane and her beau following after.

Beth grabbed Christian's hand. "We haven't much time!"

"Time? For what?"

She tugged him along, leaving the sitting room and making their way to Grandfather's library. Beth opened the door, pushed Christian inside, then followed, glancing over her shoulder.

As soon as the door closed, Beth turned on her heel to face Christian, crossed her arms over her chest, and managed a smile. "Well?"

He looked around, realization dawning. "This is your grandfather's library."

"Yes. If he has hidden anything, it would be in here."

He caught sight of the desk and began to move toward it, but then stopped. Instead, he walked toward Beth, bent, and placed a gentle, sensual kiss upon her lips. "Thank you," he said simply.

Her whole body burned and she began to realize what Annie meant by an "itch." "You had better hurry. He is sleeping. He normally naps for an hour, but you never know."

He nodded curtly, began to say something else, then changed his mind. "Come."

She looked around. "Shall I begin looking through the bookshelves for a false book or a hidden cupboard?"

He glanced at her, amusement curving his lips. "Beth, this is not a novel. If your grandfather has anything to hide, it will be where he keeps his usual things."

"Oh," she said. It would have been nice to have found a secret chamber, or at least a hidden safe.

Christian laughed softly. "Stop looking so disappointed. This is my quest. Not yours. I don't wish you to do anything that might put you in a bad position with your grandfather."

"Like sneak you into his library when he's taking a nap?"

Christian paused. "You are taking a chance for me, aren't you?"

"No. I am taking a chance *on* you. That is much riskier."

"I will not disappoint you, Beth." He crossed to the desk and ran his hands over the surface. He sat in the large leather chair. "That necklace has to be somewhere."

"How do you know that whoever took it didn't sell it?"

"It was a spectacular piece. I made inquiries and it has not shown up in any private collection." Christian found the knob of the top drawer and pulled. It slid out the tiniest bit, then stopped, the lock thunking at the pressure, "Damn."

Beth had begun running her hands over the bookshelves, looking for irregularities. She looked over at him at that. "What is it?"

"It's locked."

"Of course it is."

"Why 'of course'?"

Her brows lowered. "Because Grandfather always keeps the desk locked."

Bloody hell. Christian tugged at the drawer again. It didn't budge. He cursed, then glared at Beth. "Doesn't that strike you as strange? That he keeps his desk locked in such a fashion?"

"No," she said baldly. "Don't *you* lock *your* desk?"

He paused. He did, of course. There were servants about, some of whom he never saw, like the sweep boy and the underfootmen who beat the rugs every month. Christian only knew about them because once or twice, he'd come to the library unannounced and found those individuals there. "I suppose I do keep my desk locked," he said grudgingly.

"No man of sense would do otherwise." She crossed her arms over her breasts, her shoulder against the bookshelf. "This is why you should not investigate your theory by yourself. You need someone impartial to assist you."

He cocked a brow in her direction.

"You, my Lord Westerville, have lost your ability to judge people and things."

"I have not."

"I think you have," she replied with unabashed good humor. "You want to believe my grandfather did this horrid thing so much that you are interpreting everything you find to prove it true."

He reached for the second drawer and found it locked as well. He rattled it for a moment and then pushed back from the desk and sent Beth a dark glare. "I have not confronted your grandfather, have I?"

She pursed her lips; her eyes settled on him with consideration. "Not yet. But as soon as you find something—anything—no matter how thin—to implicate him, you will not only leap to a conclusion of total and absolute guilt, you will fly to it."

"I promise that my judgment is not so obscured."

She raised her brows but said nothing, that damned seductive half smile on her lips. Christian leaned back in the chair. There was more than one way to skin a cat and definitely more than one way to shatter the false confidence of an attractive woman. "I suppose you think you are better at reasoning than I am."

"In this instance, yes."

He let his gaze roam over her, settling first on her full breasts, then her rounded hips.

"Westerville, stop that!"

"Stop what?" he asked as innocently as he could.

"Turning everything we do into a seduction. I am here mainly to protect my grandfather. One or two little heated looks from you is not going to change that fact one bit."

Christian thought he rather liked the way she said she was there *mainly* to protect her grandfather. He grinned at her now, a strange tightness in his chest. "I was not giving you a heated look."

"What do you call it then?"

"I was merely appreciating your, ah . . . finer points."

"Yes, well, I could do the same for you except—"

"Except what?"

"They are all under the desk."

There was a moment of splitting silence, then Beth laughed. And not just a little laugh, either, but a loud peal that trickled delicious and cool over his ears.

He half stood and waved for her to be quiet, realizing with some shock that his face was heated. "Quiet! They will hear you!"

She clapped a hand over her mouth, though her eyes still gleamed brightly. After she'd regained control of herself, she said, "Let them hear me. Unlike you, I am allowed in this library. My grandfather would not think it amiss for me to be here at all."

He returned to the desk. "You snuck me in here. I'd hate for all of your hard work and cunning to be lost for nothing,".

"It would be sad," she agreed, her lovely lips curving into a grin. "But perhaps worth it, too."

He shook his head, amused despite himself. "I never know about you. One minute, you are all prim and proper and the next—" He had to grin himself. "I believe I like that about you."

"Don't like it too much. I don't usually say such outrageous things."

"No, but I daresay you think them."

Her cheeky grin answered that. "See how horrid I would be at playing society hostess? I am much better served being left in the library with my own amusing thoughts." Her lips quivered. "I do wish you could have seen your face. I wonder if anyone ever shocks you."

They didn't, of course. That had been his place in the world as a highwayman—to shock and surprise. Yet somehow, it seemed right that this woman, with her extreme intelligence, unusual penchant for boldness, and untailored manners and complete disregard for her own attractiveness, kept him always guessing who she was and why.

His chest tightened as he looked at her. She was his . . . and yet she wasn't. Life had never been kind to the Llevanth family. He turned his attention back to the desk, his chest aching even more.

He rattled the drawers again, but nothing happened.

"There is a key somewhere."

He glanced up at her through his lashes. "I'm sure there is."

"No, I mean there is one on the desk." She was still leaning against the bookcase, her arms over her chest. Gone was the humor from a moment before. Instead, she was regarding him thoughtfully, as if measuring him.

He rattled the drawer again, then began to look for a letter opener.

She stepped forward, pushing herself from the bookcase with a graceful move. "Westerville, would you be interested in a wager?"

A wager. With Beth. It was a playful gesture, one that defined this woman more than any. One

that made his lips curve upward of their own accord. She was a joy, this woman. A provocative,
challenging female who deserved far more than
fate had allotted her. Once he'd proven her grandfather's duplicity and their relationship was at an
end, this would be all that they'd have . . . memories of moments like this. "My love, what are the
terms of this wager?"

Her gaze narrowed. "I am not your love."

"You are at this moment."

She harrumphed, sniffed, then said, "The wager is this: every time you jump to conclusions
regarding any evidence found, I win a point.
Like when you suggested it was unusual to lock
a desk. In reality, it is quite a normal thing
to do."

"I do not always make such hasty judgments."

"You do when you speak of my grandfather.
You've convicted him already and every bit of evidence you find, you interpret against him."

"It is not that way," he growled.

"If not, then you will win the wager. As it
stands, every time you make such a rash judgment, I win a point. And every time you find *real*
evidence indicating my grandfather is guilty, then
you will win a point."

That seemed fair. As much as he hated to admit
it, she was right about his reaction at finding the
desk locked. He wondered how much of his
thinking about his mother's death had been faulty.
What if all of it had? What if her grandfather was
indeed innocent?

Christian nodded. "Very well. It is a wager. What are the terms? Or do I get to name them? If I do"—he let his gaze drift over her—"you can guess what I shall require should I win."

Her cheeks flushed, but she met his gaze gamely enough. "What is that?"

"You. In my bed."

Beth's mouth fell open. But she quickly recovered and said with a reluctant twinkle, "I suppose it would be softer than a billiard table."

He laughed, and it dawned on him that this was what he was going to miss the most—all the possibility that was Beth and he. The future moments like this, of laughing and loving. Of sharing and touching.

All of it was naught but a dream. God, but he hated this whole thing. If Christian found her grandfather guilty, what would he do then? He was honor-bound to seek vengeance, to make the man who killed his mother pay with his own life. "No. No wager. Forget it," he heard himself say, turning his attention back to the desk.

"No," she said, her voice breathless. "I agree to your terms."

"You don't need to."

Her gaze met his. "I want to." Silence met this. He clearly read the desire in her eyes, and it sent a shocking trill through him. Within seconds his body was hard and ready. "Beth. You don't have to do anything—"

"I am not a child. I know what I want. I want to make this wager." A smile touched her mouth. "Besides, what makes you so certain you will win?"

She had to know what she was doing to him. She had to. He took a deep breath. "Very well. What are your terms, then, since you know mine?"

"If I am proven right and you are indeed interpreting things toward your own theory, then you will buy me a lovely ruby necklace. We will call it a wedding gift."

"We aren't getting married."

She smiled, her full lips parting to reveal her white teeth. "That does not mean you cannot purchase a nice present for me. If you'd like, we can even call it an un-wedding present."

"That would definitely make it more palatable." Though he was beginning to wonder about that, too . . .

"It would make it more palatable for me, as well," Beth said with such insouciance that he winced. "In fact, as soon as you buy it for me, I will break off our engagement."

He almost laughed. There was something so taking about her when she flashed that mischievous look his way.

Beth walked to the desk, reached under the lamp, and picked up a letter opener. She handed it across the desk to Christian. "Open the drawers, please."

His smile burst forth. "Done," he said softly.

"Done," she answered.

They stayed where they were, staring at each other. A heavy prickle of heat traced across her body, tightening across her breasts and settling in her stomach and lower.

In that instant, Beth was awash in the memory of Christian over her, around her; of the feel of the green felt table beneath her. A heated shiver wracked through her and she forced herself to breathe slowly so he wouldn't notice how flustered she'd become.

Christian slowly turned his attention back to the desk. He inserted the tip of the letter opener into the lock, and twisted it. With a loud click, the lock popped open. His heart pounded in his throat. He carefully pulled open the drawer. Inside was an assortment of papers and leather pouches.

He rifled through them, examining each piece as quickly as he could.

Beth stood with her head tilted toward the door. There was still no sound from outside, though she had to assume the footmen had returned.

A muffled curse from Christian made her turn her head. "Well?"

"Nothing."

"Excellent!" she answered.

He slid the letter opener into the next keyhole. One after the other, he opened drawer after drawer. Each time, he found nothing.

The last drawer finally opened, the one on the very bottom. Beth glanced back at the desk, but she could see only the top of Christian's head. He began to dig through the contents, suddenly giving a muffled curse.

He stood, something in his hand, a stunned expression on his face. He cupped the object and ran a hand over it with an almost loving gesture.

Finally, he looked up and met Beth's gaze. "I believe I win this point."

Beth's heart thudded to a halt before bounding back to life. He couldn't have found something that implicated Grandfather. He couldn't have. She would not believe it. She walked to stand beside him.

In his hand was a small miniature. It was of a woman with thick black hair and the most beautiful green eyes . . . "Your mother," Beth breathed, running her fingers over the surface. "You look just like her. But how . . . why would Grandfather have a miniature of your mother?"

"I don't know," Christian said grimly. He caught Beth's gaze. "Do you believe me now? Your grandfather has something to do with her death. I am certain of it."

She wanted to answer him, but her throat was too tight. How could it be? Was it truly possible? Beth could not believe it. "Grandfather would never—"

A noise arose in the hallway. Jameson was giving orders, and in the background came the sound of a cane tapping heavily on the ground, coming closer with each step, a querulous voice raised in protest over the chilled air.

Beth grasped Christian's coat. "It's Grandfather! He's awakened from his nap!"

Chapter 15

A proper butler must always knock before entering any room. To forget to do so could result in a variety of mishaps, many of which are unsuited for the printed word.

A Compleat Guide for
Being a Most Proper Butler
by Richard Robert Reeves

$\mathcal{G}$randfather's cane tapped closer to the door, his irascible voice cracking with irritation as he ordered one of the footmen to do something about a rug in the hallway.

Christian grabbed Beth's wrist. "Under the desk."

"What?" She looked at the desk, then at her gown. "I don't want to—"

His hold tightened. "Get under the desk *now*."

Before Beth knew what had happened, Christian had pulled her behind the desk. The library door creaked open as Christian ducked beneath the opening and then tucked Beth in neatly beside him.

Christian slipped an arm about Beth and settled her close. It was surprisingly spacious under the desk, as the drawers were all rather small. But it was still a tight fit, especially as Christian's shoulders were so wide.

Beth wiggled a bit, trying to settle, her elbow unwittingly coming to a halt in Christian's ribs.

She heard his startled grunt and froze, holding her breath.

Grandfather paused, then muttered, "Damned pipes. Paid a fortune for those things and what do they do but grunt and groan like an old woman."

Beth met Christian's gaze and had to press a hand to her mouth to keep from chuckling aloud.

Grandfather's cane tapped closer, then closer still. "Jameson!" he called, so close to the desk that Beth jumped a little.

"Jameson!" Grandfather called again.

This time, the butler answered. "Yes, my lord?"

"Bring me a rum toddy."

Beth glared at the bottom of the desk. Grandfather was not supposed to drink rum as it made his leg ache. Thank goodness Jameson knew not to—

"Yes, my lord," the butler said. "Shall I put it in a teacup so that Lady Elizabeth doesn't see?"

Christian clapped his hand over Beth's mouth as she gasped.

She shoved his hands aside and glared.

"Yes," Grandfather said ungraciously. "And this time, make sure it has enough rum that I can taste it. I don't want that swill you gave me last time. Made me throw my damned cup. I have to pay for those, you know!"

"Yes, my lord." Jameson's voice was fading, as if he was walking toward the door. "My lord, Viscount Westerville arrived."

"About damned time!"

"Yes, my lord. He is with Lady Elizabeth in the sitting room. Shall I bring your 'tea' there?"

"In the sitting room, eh? How long have they been in there?"

"Twenty minutes, I'd say."

"Good. See to it they aren't disturbed."

Beth's mouth dropped open.

Grandfather cackled. "Might do 'em some good, spending a bit of time together!"

"Yes, my lord. Oh. And, my lord, Lady Charlotte was asking when you would be up."

"What does she want?" Grandfather said, his voice instantly waspish and impatient.

"I don't know, my lord. She seemed quite upset. I suggested she might wish to speak to Lady Elizabeth but she refused."

"Wonderful," Grandfather said, his tone glum. "Whatever it is, I hope she doesn't start crying. Never could abide a woman who tears up over every little thing. Don't know what in the hell my son was thinking, bringing a woman like that into the family."

"I shall fetch your drink," Jameson said in his impassive tone. "Will there be anything else?"

"No, no! Just the toddy."

"Yes, my lord." The door closed behind the butler

and Beth listened, her heat beating anxiously as Grandfather's cane thumped to the desk—straight to where she and Christian were hiding.

She met Christian's gaze with a wild look.

He tucked her closer to him, his eyes level with hers. "If he finds us," he whispered, his voice tickling her ear, a glint of amusement in his eyes, "we will tell him we were lost in passion, much as we were on the billiard table."

Beth could almost picture Grandfather's expression on hearing such a thing. She had to bite her lip to keep from laughing a little. She was relieved when Grandfather picked up the morning paper from the desktop and then thumped his way back across the room, the thick carpet muffling the thud of his cane. His favorite chair creaked as he settled into it, followed by the crackle of the paper being opened.

The door opened again.

"My lord?" It was Charlotte.

"Bloody hell, can't a man have some time to himself?" Grandfather snapped.

"I must talk to you. It's important."

There was a moment's silence, during which time Beth imagined Grandfather glaring at her stepmama. "Are you taking your medicine?"

Beth shook her head. It was always the same with Grandfather; he worried more about Charlotte's medicine than about his own health.

"Yes, yes. Of course. It's not me. It's about Bennington."

"Bennington?"

To Beth's surprise, Grandfather's voice took on a more serious note.

"What does he want this time?"

"You see why I am upset! He is so controlling, so—"

"That, my girl, is a pie of your own making. So now you'll eat it and stop crying about it."

"He—"

"No. Not another word."

"But he is asking about Elizabeth!"

"What about her?"

"Bennington spent some time with her in the garden the other day. I-I saw them from my window. I asked him what they'd talked about, but he was almost secretive. My lord, I think she has been asking questions, especially now that she is with Westerville. I have to wonder what you were thinking to allow that man, of all those in London, to be with her!"

"She was ruined," Grandfather snapped. "And he ruined her. What else could I do."

"I don't know. I only fear she will ask questions and—you don't wish her to know, do you?"

There was a moment of silence. Beth looked at Christian, her heart sinking. What on earth was Charlotte talking about?

"We will deal with Beth when the time comes."

"My lord, you don't understand, she is—"

"Charlotte! I won't hear another word!" His voice cracked with rage.

"But . . ." Charlotte's voice quivered. "I am afraid."

"Go to your room. I will have Jameson bring some of your medicine."

"But I—"

"Now!" Grandfather thundered.

With a muffled cry, Charlotte ran from the room.

She must have passed Jameson, for the butler's voice was the next thing they heard. "My lord?"

"Has Lady Charlotte seen the doctor?"

"She was asleep when he called last time."

"That is not to happen again, do you hear me? Send for the fool now and tell him he is to see Lady Charlotte this very afternoon. And tell him to be damned sure she's taking her medicine!"

"Yes, my lord. Shall I put your toddy here, by your chair?"

"No. You can put it right in my hand. I intend on drinking it now, and then I shall visit my granddaughter."

"Yes, my lord."

There was a short silence as the butler did as he'd been instructed, followed by a slurping sound from Granddaughter.

Beth bit her lip. Was it possible that Charlotte knew Grandfather's secret? Was that why he was always so bitter about her, why he insisted she take her medicine?

She glanced at Christian and could tell from his expression that he was thinking the same thing.

"Ah!" Grandfather said. "Much better. Thank you, Jameson. You have a way with a toddy."

"Thank you, my lord. Will there be anything

else? Shall I inform Lady Elizabeth you wish to see her now?"

Another noisy slurp was heard. "No, no. Give them some more time to talk. I daresay they've much to settle between them."

"Yes, my lord. Please ring if you need another 'tea.' " The butler's measured tread shuffled across the carpet, then withdrew, the door closing behind him.

Beth's shoulder was pressed to Christian's chest, his heart beating a steady rhythm. She turned her head just the slightest bit and found him looking at her, his eyes darker than usual.

They were so close, tucked away where they could not be found. Safe and yet . . . not. The tension of being found heightened her senses. Beth shivered, intensely aware of the heat of his thigh pressed against the back of hers.

In the novels she loved, the women always swooned any time someone kissed them. None of the books ever talked about how lovely it was to be held. How warm a man's rough skin could feel beneath one's fingertips. How strong a desire one could feel, or how arousing it was to sit in a man's lap and feel his reaction.

All the heroines in her novels seemed forever frightened, yet she wasn't, not in the least bit. Oh, her breath was coming fast and her body was tight with excitement, but she was not in the least fearful.

She was, in fact, rather . . . comfortable. As if she belonged here. Excited *and* comfortable. How come none of the heroines ever mentioned that particular aspect of being held in a man's arms?

The newspaper rustled across the room. "Damned Tories." As this was followed by a blissful "ah" as Grandfather slurped his rum toddy, it was obvious Grandfather's hated Tories were behaving themselves today.

Beth would have a word or two with Jameson when this was all over. Meanwhile, she might as well enjoy where she was. There would not be many more times she would be so near Christian. Fewer than she wished to think.

She lifted her fingers and trailed them over Christian's face, the faint roughness tingling beneath her fingers. He caught her hand and pressed it to his mouth, his warm lips firm against her skin.

Grandfather's paper rattled again.

Christian glanced at Beth through his long lashes. "Should I release you?" he whispered.

"No," she answered.

His lips twitched and she had the oddest impulse to kiss him.

Instead, she leaned her head against his shoulder, feeling a lump in his coat pocket. Ah yes, the miniature. Beth frowned. Why would Grandfather have a miniature of Christian's mother locked in his desk?

She traced her fingers over the circle that outlined the tiny painting. Etched on ivory, it was a delicate and lovely piece and not something someone would toss aside.

Her gaze met Christian's. As if he was reading her thoughts, he leaned down and whispered, "Because he feels guilty."

Beth still couldn't accept it. There had to be an explanation. She leaned forward and pressed her lips near Christian's ear. "I wish Grandfather had kept a journal. Then we'd know what it means for certain."

Christian shook his head and whispered in return. "He is too intelligent to do such a thing."

Beth nodded. They were silent a moment more, the sense of closeness binding them. Beth tried to breathe deeply to inhale his scent. He was so close, his hips against hers, his arms about her. If she leaned forward just the smallest bit, her breasts would have been pressed against his chest. She wondered if she could feel his heartbeat if she did.

Suddenly, she wanted to lean forward. Wanted to collect the warmth of his hips against hers. Wanted to feel his heartbeat and mingle it with hers. When this was over, when she'd settled the issue of Grandfather's innocence, Christian would be gone. The thought tightened her chest.

She must have shown some quiver of emotion, for Christian's arm came to rest around her shoulders. Beth tilted her head back, her eyes meeting his.

Something flared and sparked. Slowly, ever so slowly, as if he was afraid of scaring her, he lowered his mouth to hers.

As he did so, his thigh pressed against her knee, forcing it down. A low heat began to build in her as his tongue slipped along her lower lip, tantalizing her with promises of other fascinating things.

It was absurdly sensual, kissing in total silence.

She couldn't moan, couldn't speak, couldn't allow her breath to quicken. She fought for control even as she savored the temptation to lose it.

His hand slid down her arm to her shoulder, then softly cupped her breast. His thumb rolled over her nipple, teasing it to a peak through her gown and chemise. Beth had to fight a deep moan, her thighs parting slightly as she turned more toward him, pressing against him in their small, dark space.

She'd never been kissed like this. Never been so sensually touched and handled. She found that her body flared with delight, softened and pressed against him. She wanted him, desired him, loved him.

She froze. She loved him. Oh God, when had that happened? And why? She tried to figure it out, but his hands found both of her breasts and she forgot everything as she arched into him. Her nipples hardened, heat flaring in her stomach. She wanted him, wanted this. And somehow, knowing that she loved him made her want to press against him all the more.

She ran her hands over his shoulders, up his neck, to the raspy sides of his cheeks. She pulled his mouth to hers and gave him a deep, longing kiss.

His hands clutched at her convulsively, holding her brutally tight.

A loud snore erupted from Grandfather, the noise breaking the spell that held Christian and Beth in its thrall.

Christian sent an annoyed glare at the back of the desk in the general direction of where Grandfather slept. Then he took Beth's hand in his own. "We should leave while we have the chance."

"Now? But—"

"Follow me," he mouthed, quietly climbing out, pulling her along by the hand.

They came out from behind the desk to find Grandfather asleep in his chair, a splash of sunlight limning his white hair into a halo. Christian put his fingers to his lips, then tiptoed across the room to the door. Quietly, he opened the door and slipped out, pulling Beth behind him.

They found the footmen and Jameson staring at them with astonishment.

Oh no! Christian opened his mouth, but Beth tugged her wrist from his grip and quickly stepped forward. She smiled calmly at the butler, hoping he didn't know she was sorely out of breath. "Jameson?"

He straightened immediately. "Yes, my lady?"

"I just found my grandfather sleeping in his chair, an empty glass of rum in his hand."

The butler's ears reddened. "Did you, my lady? How . . . how horrid."

"I want you to find whoever is responsible. That is not acceptable."

"Y-yes, my lady. I, ah, shall do so immediately."

Beth turned and led the way to the sitting room. "Lord Westerville? Would you join me for a moment before you leave?"

Christian followed her, amused at her haughty demeanor and still burning with the desire to touch her. She had driven him to distraction under the desk, and following her now, watching her sexy sway as she marched to the sitting room, was stirring his masculinity to new heights.

He wanted this woman. Not just once. But over and over. Yet the weight of the miniature in his pocket told him that his time with her was limited. She would never look at him the same once she discovered the truth about her Grandfather. This could be their one chance.

The moment they reached the sitting room, he knew he had to have her. She closed the door, then turned, her back against the oak panel, a look of such heated longing that he hesitated no more. He was against her in an instant, pressing her back against the door and giving her the kiss he'd been holding since they'd left the library. His hands roamed, molding her hips, sliding down her flat stomach. God, but she felt so good. So right. He could not stop touching her.

Beth moaned against him, her arms tight about his neck as she unconsciously moved her hips against his. It was almost more than he could take. He had to have her. If this was to be their last day together, their last taste of passion before they were split apart, then so be it. At least it would be one worth remembering.

He broke the kiss long enough to sink to his knees before her. Her hands rested on his shoulder, her eyes dark with passion and curiosity.

He bent to his knees before her and lifted her gown, running his hands up her leg over her silk stockings.

"So lovely," he murmured, cupping her calf, his fingers brushing over the back of her knee.

Tremors of sensation rippled through Beth.

She gasped as his hand slid higher still. He was pushing up her gown, bunching it about her thighs and lifting it farther. Some innate sense of modesty fought for breath, sent her trembling hands to the edges of her gown. She had to fight the impulse to tug her gown back into place, to hide from the passion inside her. The passion he was fanning to new heights.

He looked up at her, his eyes shimmering with heat, his black hair over his brow. He was achingly handsome and all hers. Hers for just this moment. All too soon, they would find their answers, whatever they were, and he would be gone.

Her throat tightened; her chest ached. Her fingers closed over the edge of her gown . . . and she lifted it higher, up her thighs to her hips. The coolness of the air chilled her through her thin silk pantaloons, sending waves of tantalizing shivers across her skin.

Beth threw her head back and closed her eyes, letting her gesture speak for itself.

She could hear his breathing as he placed his hands on her hips beneath her gown. She was almost reclining against the door now, her back flat on the panel, her legs slightly apart, her gown lifted to her hips as he knelt before her.

Suddenly he was touching her over her pantaloons in the most intimate place, kissing her through the thin silk.

"Christian!" she gasped, her hips lifting of their own accord. His warm mouth continued, his tongue lashing at her through the material.

She writhed, her hands crushing the muslin gown, her breath harsh in her throat. It felt so sensual, so decadent.

Beth pressed forward, her hand finding the silk roughness of his hair as she pressed him forward, closer to her. Closer to her still.

A wave of passion broke across her and she gasped, her hips thrusting forward. Christian grabbed her hips and held her to him, driving her mad with a prolonged sensation as the feeling came and grew and flooded her through and through.

When it was done, she was panting and weak-kneed, her eyes rich with passion.

He stood and untied his breeches with one hand. Then, without warning, he lifted her, pushing her gown up about her waist. Before she knew what he was about, his arm snaked around her and he pressed her against the door. Clutching at his broad shoulder, she clasped her legs about him and she drew him forward.

His erection pressed against her, and she caught her lip between her teeth, shivering slightly at the firmness of him, a flicker of uncertainty attempting to invade the sensuality of the moment. But his mouth descended on hers and there was no more time for thinking. Passion overrode her fears. She tightened her legs and pressed herself down upon him, settling over his fullness a slow inch at a time.

Christian's expression became strained, his hands tightening about her waist. Beth had never felt so many sensations at the same time. She thought she might go mad any minute from the delight that flooded her.

There was a slight pressure and then, with a suddenness that caused her to cry out, he slid into her, deep and true. Beth gasped and threw back her head; she ran her hands up his chest, over his shoulders, frantically trying to pull him closer.

Christian's breathing grew harsher, his breath stirring her hair at the temple. His hands tightened about her waist and he lifted her.

He moaned as she slid up. He held her there a moment, their breathing mingling. She stole a glance at his face. It was twisted with a mixture of pain and pleasure, his brow furrowed.

Some primal instinct gave her the strength to tighten her legs and she slid herself back down on him, enveloping him until he closed his eyes as if in pain and gasped her name.

The sight sent a flood of power through her. She was doing this to him, making him pant hungrily, making him desire her and no one else.

Together, they began to move. Each stroke, the motions flowed more smoothly, more powerfully. Heat began to build in Beth's stomach and lower.

She was inanely aware of the most minute details; the feel of the cool wood of the door against her back, the heated pressure of his hands on her waist, the touch of his bared skin against her inner thighs.

The heat flared into a flame. Beth gasped with wonder as he lifted her over and over, filling her and then denying her with each move. Her thighs grew damp, her breathing ragged. It was as if a hot coal had been planted deep within her and she could not get enough of the warmth, cling to it though she might.

Each stroke pressed her toward the heat, tantalizing and making her crazed with desire. Each withdrawal sent her back to the edge of madness and beyond.

Suddenly, her body clenched about him. She cried out his name, tightening her thighs around him, arching her back as pleasure flooded through her.

Christian never released her, nor did he stop thrusting into her. As her heart subsided to a more normal beat, she could hear his own breathing growing more labored, his actions more strained.

"Do you like that?" she whispered into his ear, her heart racing once again.

"God, Beth," he managed to say through clenched teeth, his skin damp, his heart almost audible in the room. "Do it . . . again."

She pushed herself up, clinging to his shoulders, then slid downward, upon his shaft.

Some imp of madness possessed her. She allowed him to lift her up again, but the second he did so, she clamped her legs tightly and threw herself down upon him as hard as she could.

This time Christian did more than gasp. He cried out, clasping her to him. She felt him inside her, heat flooding her as he curled his body into hers and he filled her with his passion.

Trembling and clinging to each other, they stayed where they were. Moments passed, yet they were unaware of them.

His breathing slowly, slowly returned to normal. Christian leaned forward, pressing her back against the door. He still supported her with both hands, though his forehead was now resting against hers, his heart thudding hard against her fingertips.

They clung to each other for long moments after that, too exhausted to move. Christian was leaning on his elbows against the door, his head bent against Beth's, his skin damp where it touched hers.

Slowly, she unhooked her ankles where she'd crossed them at his waist and slid her legs to the ground. They immediately collapsed, but he caught her to him, laughing softly as he did so.

He swung her into his arms, kissing her neck, her cheek, her hair as he carried her to the settee. He sat and settled her in his lap, tugging her skirts into place with one hand, even as he held her tight with the other.

Christian pressed his lips to her forehead. He didn't think he'd ever seen a more beautiful sight. Her face was tilted toward his, her eyes closed so that her lashes were crescents on her high cheeks.

Her skin was smooth, flushed with passion, a faint sheen of perspiration moistening her skin. He bent forward and traced his lips over her cheek, welcoming the faint hint of heated salt.

She was so sensual, so vibrant. She smelled of life and lust, of laughter and the promise of something more. He sighed deeply and rubbed against the silk of her hair.

She opened her eyes and smiled. It was a luxurious smile, that of a woman who had been deeply and thoroughly pleasured. Her arms tightened about his neck and she leaned up and pressed her lips to his cheek. "Thank you," she whispered against his skin. "I shall take that memory with me when we are done."

His heart froze on his chest. *When we are done.* The words brought the reality of their situation back to him with a roaring crash.

He became aware of the weight of the miniature in his pocket, where it hung heavy and cold. He shivered and closed his eyes. He should ask to see the duke today. Now that Christian had the portrait, he was prepared to confront his enemy. It wasn't the necklace, of course, but it had served one very important purpose—it had convinced Beth that Christian's suspicions were valid. The duke might lie to Christian, but he would be hard pressed to lie to his own beloved granddaughter.

Christian rubbed his cheek against Beth's hair. They sat silently, holding each other as if fearful to let go. The truth was, he *was* afraid. He'd come to care for Beth, and the thought of losing her, of being alone yet again—he buried his face in the corner of her neck and closed his eyes, fighting a wave of emotion so powerful it threatened to engulf him.

He didn't want to lose her yet. They would face the truth tomorrow. Then, less muddled by passion, Christian would be able to do what he'd vowed to do so long ago.

Tomorrow he would return and, with Beth,

speak with the duke. Armed with the miniature, he would force the old man to tell the truth. And then . . . Christian pressed a kiss to Beth's forehead and held her tighter. For now, he wouldn't— no, he couldn't—think beyond this moment.

How had this become so complicated? he wondered, feeling more disconsolate than ever before. How?

But inside his heart, he knew the truth. Somehow, Beth had slipped behind the barriers he'd so carefully erected about his heart.

Damn Reeves for being right yet again.

Chapter 16

No matter what station you hold in life, there will always be things that will surprise you. Whether you choose to be outraged or delighted is up to you.

A Compleat Guide for
Being a Most Proper Butler
by Richard Robert Reeves

"Christian?"

He gave a deep sigh, and beneath her ear Beth could feel the rush of his breath. He placed his cheek against her hair.

"Yes?"

"Grandfather will wake soon."

Again the sigh. "I know."

But his arms did not loosen.

She closed her eyes and inhaled him, soaking in his warmth, luxuriating in his nearness. This time seemed so fragile. She wished they could stay like this forever, cocooned from the outside world. But it was not to be.

She sighed and opened her eyes. She could just see the outline of Christian's chin where he rested his cheek against her. "Christian?"

He opened his eyes and looked down at her, a smile appearing when he caught her gaze. "Yes?"

"We must talk."

His arms tightened.

"About Grandfather."

"I know." He leaned back against the settee, and loosened his hold a bit.

Beth sat upright. Her body still hummed, a glow warming her, head to toe. It was sad to have to discuss something painful right now, when she felt so close to him, so intimate. But it had to be. Grandfather could wake and come into the room at any moment.

"I must rise." She went to stand, but Christian's arm remained firmly in place.

"No." He pulled her closer, sinking his face into the warmth of her neck. "I want you here. At least for now."

"I want to be here, too. But Grandfather might come in at any time and find us."

"What will he do to us? Force us to marry?"

Oh. Yes. She grinned. "I never thought of that." She sighed happily and settled back against him. "I suppose we can talk from here. As much as I hate to admit it, there is something afoot here. I do not like that I'm losing our wager."

His humor faded and he looked at her with a

very serious expression. "Beth, there is no wager. Your grandfather is the man I have been seeking."

"No," Beth said thoughtfully. "All you found was a miniature of your mother in his desk. That is evidence that he knew her, not that he is responsible for giving false proof and sending her to gaol."

"It is enough for me. Added to the statement from the priest who attended my mother in gaol and her own letters . . . That is a formidable amount of information."

"It still doesn't point to any one person in particular. Christian, you are making conclusions with very little proof. That gives me a point in our wager."

His jaw hardened. "You are wrong. And soon, you will see that you are."

She traced a line down his jaw, kissing his chin. "May I see the miniature again? I didn't have a chance to admire it properly."

He fished it out of his pocket, his expression grim.

Beth's fingers closed over the cool, ivory edges. She looked at the portrait for a long time. "She was lovely."

"More than you know."

"It's a wonderful portrait. You look just like her."

"Thank you."

"But what I can't see is where this miniature says—beyond all doubt—that my grandfather betrayed your mother." She peered closely, then flipped it over and examined the back. "I don't see it written on here anywhere. And even if it was, unless we knew who had written it and why, it wouldn't be valid."

His hand closed over hers, curling her fingers around the miniature. "Beth, name one good reason why your grandfather would have a miniature of my mother. Just one."

The edges of the small portrait were rounded and smooth beneath her fingers. She bit her lip, her mind racing. "He could have known her when she was a child and been fond of her. Or perhaps he—he found it in an antique store and it appealed to him. Or he bought it at an auction and—"

His arms tightened. "That is nothing but conjecture and you know it."

"So is your theory about this portrait." She reached up and cupped Christian's face, running her thumb over his firm chin. "We have to ask him. It is the only way to find out what happened, how he knows your mother."

"I planned on it. Tomorrow."

"Why not today?"

Christian's arms tightened about her. "I have things to do before I am ready for that. I will return first thing in the morning and we will ask him then."

She smiled and nodded, though in truth, it didn't make her happy at all. They were about to accuse Grandfather of something horrible. Yet there was no other way. "Very well, then. We will meet with him tomorrow."

"Excellent. Since that is settled, perhaps I can importune you to spend a little time with me today."

"Oh! Do you have another clue for us to pursue?"

"No. This doesn't have anything to do with my mother. I just thought it would be nice if we could go for a ride. Just you and me."

Beth raised her brows. "Just us? But . . . why?"

To her surprise, his cheeks reddened a bit. "Can't I ask my fiancée out for a ride without being quizzed as if I'd requested a rum toddy at eleven-thirty in the morning?"

Beth laughed. "Yes! Of course you can. I was just—I didn't realize what you meant." Oddly pleased, she looked down at her crumpled gown. "I will need to change."

He kissed her nose. "Of course. And so will I. Shall I return at six?"

"That would be lovely."

Christian nodded, savoring her smile even as his emotions roiled. He had wished for this confrontation—had dreamed of facing his mother's betrayer his entire life. But not now. Despite himself, uncertainty began to creep through him. Not about the duke. Christian was certain he'd found his man. But damn it, why couldn't they have found the sapphire necklace? The one bit of incontrovertible proof there was.

But even that would have caused heartache. He pulled Beth close once more and rubbed his cheek to the silk of her hair. In a moment, he would let her go. He would return home and wait for this evening. Then, tomorrow, he would force her grandfather to confess his duplicity. After that . . . He gritted his teeth. Using every ounce of strength he possessed, he gently set Beth aside and stood, fastening his breeches and straightening his clothes.

She made no move to follow suit, but sat watching him, her dark eyes lingering on his every move, her gown and hair adorably mussed.

"I must go." He managed a brief smile, though his heart ached as if someone had sliced it with a knife.

"I know." She picked up a pillow and hugged it to her. "I will see you at six."

He winked at her, and was halfway to the door when her voice reached him.

"Christian?"

He paused, his hands fisted now at his sides.

"What will you do if you discover it was indeed Grandfather?"

Christian could not look at her. Instead, he opened his hand and looked at the miniature. It was still warm from Beth's clasp; the silky feel of her hair still lingered on his fingertips. But as much as he loved Beth, he owed his mother this. "I cannot answer that."

"I see." Her voice was husky with emotion. "Then . . . what about us, Christian?"

The words sliced through him. He grimaced, clenching his jaw.

Slowly, he curled his fingers back into a fist and straightened. "I will see you this evening."

With that, he let himself out of the room and walked away. From where she sat on the couch, Beth hugged the pillow tighter, staring at the door with unseeing eyes that were now bright with tears.

Beth cut a rose and laid it in the basket on her arm. As the afternoon wore on, clouds had roiled in, the wind blowing harshly, tossing her skirts and tugging at her basket. The wind pulled at her hair, too, and the curls Annie had so carefully pinned were in dire danger of coming loose. Beth lifted her face to the wind and let it tumble over her.

She wished Christian would hurry; she wanted to discuss the miniature with him some more, suggest some other places in the house to look for clues. Find *something* to avert the meeting between Christian and Grandfather. Though she knew it had to occur, she couldn't help but feel that she needed that one bit of missing evidence that might right this mess and make it all just go away.

That was what she wanted. She thought of when she'd asked Christian what would happen if his suspicions were correct. There had been a cold, almost hopeless tone to his voice. As for what would happen to her and Christian . . .

She closed her eyes and let the wind buffet against her, clearing the cobwebs from her mind.

What would Grandfather do when Christian taxed him with the miniature? Would he confess? Did he have anything to confess to? Or would it ignite a scene of another kind?

Beth rubbed a hand over her eyes. Each and every time she came back with the same thing— Christian was right. Grandfather had *something* to do with his mother's incarceration.

And yet . . . she could not reconcile herself to the fact he was wholly responsible. A dull ache pressed against her forehead, her thoughts as black as the clouds gathering overhead. In addition to thinking about Grandfather, Beth hadn't been able to stop remembering her time with Christian. There was something between them—a raw passion that transcended everything else.

She loved him. Deeply. Richly. With all her heart. It was funny, but she'd always thought such a passion would be giddy and earth-shattering. Instead it was steady and deep, a thick certainty upon which one could stand. She loved him but . . . did *he* love *her*? There were times when she thought she'd caught a flash of warmth in his eyes that went far beyond mere friendship. But what else could it be?

It was all so confusing, so frustrating. There was Christian and his quest, Grandfather and his secrets, and—

"Beth?"

Beth turned to find Charlotte standing on the terrace, arms crossed to ward off the wind. "What are you doing out in this weather? It's about to storm."

"I know." Beth bent and cut one more flower, then placed the knife and the rose in her basket. She had about two dozen; enough for a nice centerpiece for the mahogany dining table.

Thunder rumbled overhead, the wind rustling restlessly. Beth gathered her skirts and joined Charlotte on the terrace. They went inside together.

Charlotte bent to smell a rose. "Those are lovely."

"I thought we might make an arrangement for the table." Beth set down the basket and removed her gardening gloves.

She laid them in the basket over the knife and went to the mirror over the fireplace to right her hair. "Oh dear! I look like Medusa."

"Oh, I don't think it's so bad," Charlotte said, tilting her head to one side and smiling nervously. "All you need is a hairpin here and a hairpin there and it will be good as new."

Outside, thunder cracked, rattling the windows. Charlotte jumped, her hand rising to her throat.

"That was a bit abrupt," Beth said. Her stepmama seemed even more nervous than usual. "You never liked storms. I remember you used to be terrified."

Charlotte absently rubbed her arms as she looked out the window at the rapidly darkening sky. "I have always hated them. Your father used to get very impatient with me for that. He loved storms."

"Yes, and would stand out on the terrace and get soaking wet sometimes. I always wondered how he kept from getting struck by lightning."

Charlotte nodded absently.

Beth smoothed her hair where the wind had tousled it, her mind going back through the conversation she'd heard while under the desk with Christian. Charlotte knew whatever it was Grandfather was hiding. But why would Grandfather have confessed anything to Charlotte? He thought her a nitwit and worse.

Charlotte had to have stumbled upon the information by accident. It was the only explanation. It would explain why Grandfather was forever worrying she was not taking her medicine—because he feared she might tell something she'd discovered.

Beth began to feel ill. There was so much she didn't know. So many secrets that seemed to be lurking. With all her heart, she did not want to believe that Christian was right.

Thunder crashed, lightning blinded Beth for a moment. Charlotte cried out and covered her eyes.

Beth went to Charlotte and put an arm about her thin shoulders. The older woman's skin was hot to the touch. Beth frowned. "Come. Sit down. I'll call for some tea and—"

"No," Charlotte said, her chin firm, though she trembled head to toe. "It is time I was not afraid."

Beth smiled. "Good for you! You will see that there is nothing to hurt you here. Shall I get you some ratafia? Perhaps that would be better."

"Yes. I would like that."

Beth went to pour her stepmother a glass of ratafia. She carried it to Charlotte, waiting until her stepmama had taken a few sips and was steadier. "Charlotte, may I ask you something?"

Eyes still on the dark sky outside, Charlotte nodded absently.

"Did you know my fiancé's mother?"

Charlotte's eyes widened just as a huge strike of lightning flashed. In the blinding light, Beth saw Charlotte's white and terrified face.

Beth instinctively took her stepmother's arm, but Charlotte jerked free, dropping the glass as she backed to the doorway. "Stay away from me!"

Beth blinked. "Charlotte! I just asked if you knew—"

"No! Just stop it!" Charlotte pressed a hand to her mouth. "You cannot say that woman's name. Bennington says—" She pressed her fingers over her mouth. "I won't do it."

Bennington? Beth hadn't thought of him, but he had been quite a close friend of Father's. The rather somber lord also could have used the Massingale coach. It was not unlikely, for the lord frequently used it if he rode to the house and the weather turned abrupt, as it was now. Beth's heart quickened. Was this it? Was Bennington the missing link between Christian's mother and Massingale House?

Beth placed a calming hand on Charlotte's arm. "What does Bennington say, Charlotte? What does he have to do with . . . the lady I mentioned?"

"Nothing. He and your grandfather, they don't like to hear of her. Every time I say her name, they yell at me and make me take more medicine." Charlotte shook her head, tears glistening in her eyes. "I am not going to do that anymore, Beth. The medicine isn't good for me. It makes me sleep and sleep and I cannot think and all sorts of things."

"Charlotte! That is horrible. Why do you take it, then?"

"Your grandfather says I cannot live here unless I do. That I will have to go somewhere else, all alone. Beth, I loved your father, though he may not have loved me. I am closer to him here and— and I *need* that." Charlotte clutched at Beth's arm. "Do you understand? Please say you do and don't tell your grandfather that we talked about this. He would send me away and I could not bear it."

Feeling ill, Beth quietly asked, "Is that what Grandfather told you, Charlotte? That he would send you away if you mentioned . . . *her* name?"

Charlotte nodded, her eyes wide. "I dare not disobey him. No matter what happens, he will think it is my fault. That's why he wants me to take the laudanum." A sly look entered Charlotte's eyes, surprising Beth. "Sometimes I take it and sometimes"—she leaned forward to whisper—"I don't!"

Beth eyed Charlotte uneasily. "Did you take it today?"

Charlotte smiled, looking absurdly pretty and youthful. "Of course." She tilted her head to one side, her blond ringlets falling back from her cheek. "You don't know it all yet, do you? I thought you did, but you don't."

"All I know is that Christian's mother was wrongly imprisoned and she died there. Charlotte, did Grandfather put her there? Did he put her in prison?"

Charlotte stared, her eyes wide. Slowly she nodded. "Yes."

The word was a whisper. Light and frothy, it hung between them.

The room whirled about Beth, and somehow, she found herself sitting on the settee, blood rushing behind her eyes, her heart pounding raggedly. Christian was right! He had been right all along. "I-I can't imagine Grandfather doing such a thing."

"Perhaps you don't know him as well as you think."

"I know him better than anyone."

"No, you know the kind part of him better than anyone. There is a side of him . . . Even your father was not comfortable with him."

A low rumble of thunder made Beth look toward the windows. "The storm is moving out," she said absently, her mind whirling with this new information.

Charlotte nodded, her gaze locked on Beth. "It is a pity you found out, but I suppose it was bound to happen."

"I suppose so. Christian is coming here this evening. We are going to ask Grandfather for the truth tomorrow morning. We were looking for a necklace his mother—"

"No!" Charlotte clutched Beth's arm. "You can't do that! He will lock you both away or worse!"

Beth shook off Charlotte's hands. "Nonsense. Even if Grandfather did this, I know he would not hurt me."

"You don't know him!" Charlotte's brow furrowed. She bit her lip, her eyes flickering here and there. Suddenly, she nodded. "I know what you need." Charlotte looked around as if to make certain they were not heard, and then she leaned forward and whispered, "The necklace, the one you were speaking of. I know where it is."

Beth sucked in a deep breath. "I need to see it."

"Then we shall go. It is not far from here. We can walk. Lord Bennington hid it for your grandfather, away from the house so it would not be found."

"What has Bennington to do with—"

Charlotte took Beth's elbow and pulled her to the door. "I will explain as we go."

Beth resisted. "Charlotte, I can't. Christian will be here soon and—"

"You will be back before he returns." She took Beth's hand and pressed it between hers. "Please?"

Beth saw the tears in the woman's eyes. Poor Charlotte had been guarding this information for so long. Beth squeezed Charlotte's hand and glanced at the clock.

Christian would be here in half an hour. She would have the necklace by then. She would meet him at the door and hand him the final piece of proof he'd been looking for—the evidence that would condemn Grandfather forever in Christian's eyes.

Beth's heart ached. What would Christian do then? What would any of them do?

"You want to marry Westerville, don't you?"

The simple question gave Beth pause. "Yes," she finally said, her voice so soft, Charlotte had to lean forward to catch it.

"Then you must solve this riddle, else the viscount's life might also be at risk. The only reason the duke would countenance such a match is to keep Westerville where he could be watched."

"No! Charlotte, Grandfather is not—"

Charlotte sighed and dropped Beth's hand. "You do not believe me. I will go and fetch the necklace myself, then. But you have to promise to protect me from your grandfather. When he is really angry . . ." Charlotte shuddered.

Beth bit her lip. She could not allow Charlotte to go alone; Charlotte never went anywhere alone unless Lord Bennington—Beth paused. Was *that* why Bennington always escorted Charlotte? Because he was in Grandfather's confidence and they did not trust her to be out in the world, where she might talk?

Everything suddenly seemed so sinister. Beth's mind simply could not countenance the fact that Grandfather could possibly be anything other than who he'd always been.

Charlotte went to the door. "I shall leave now and—"

"No." Beth stepped forward. "I shall go with you. But we should leave out the terrace doors so the house servants don't realize we've gone."

Charlotte managed a tremulous smile. "I shall fetch our pelisses from our rooms."

Beth caught her hands. "Be careful. I-I have an uneasy feeling about this."

Charlotte nodded. "I have had an uneasy feeling for over twenty years." She squeezed Beth's hands, and slipped out the door.

Beth looked outside at the rain-filled clouds. Huge thunderheads loomed over the countryside, casting a dark pall over her beautiful garden. A tingle of foreboding traced through her. Perhaps there were other bits of evidence with the missing necklace. Something that would exonerate Grandfather. Beth squared her shoulders. She would do this. Do it for Christian *and* Grandfather. Only the truth would help them now.

Bracing herself, she went out the terrace door and looked out, pausing beside the basket of flowers. She fingered the roses, her expression thoughtful. If only things were as simple as the flowers.

Moments later, Charlotte returned, wearing a pelisse and carrying another. Beth was by the far window, but she turned when her stepmama entered. "The rain has not begun yet."

"Good!" Charlotte held out a gray pelisse. "It's an old one of mine. Annie was in your room and I didn't dare let her see me."

Beth took the pelisse and drew it on.

"Are you ready?" Charlotte said, opening the terrace door.

Beth nodded. Within moments, they were making their way through the garden and out the back gate, Charlotte almost skipping in her excitement, Beth walking heavily, her heart as dark as the sky overhead.

A half hour later, Christian rode Lucifer up the long, winding drive to Massingale House. Rain threatened overhead.

He glanced up at the sky as a rumble of thunder rolled across the sky. "Not yet," he murmured. "I would that you'd wait until dinner."

Though it was silly to address the clouds, they heeded him and didn't deliver a drop. Christian reached Massingale House at ten 'til six and tossed his reins to the waiting groom, then ran lightly up the stairs. He could not wait to see Beth. It was odd how one could long for something and yet dread the brevity of it at one and the same time.

Jameson met him in the foyer and took his coat, hat, and gloves. "My lord. We didn't expect to see you again today."

"Lady Elizabeth is to ride with me. Is she ready?"

"I shall send a footman to her room now." The butler glanced at the nearest liveried man, who bowed and immediately left. That seen to, the butler turned back to Christian. "Would you like to await Her Ladyship in the sitting room?"

"Of course."

Jameson went to lead Christian to the sitting room.

A thump came from behind them. "Ah! Westerville!" called the duke's aged voice from the door of the library. He stood leaning on his cane, his blue eyes shrewdly regarding Christian. "Thought I heard your voice. Come! Join me for some brandy."

Without waiting for an answer, the duke turned and limped back into the library.

Christian stifled a sigh. He didn't want to do anything but see Beth. But there was little he could do about an invitation—if one could call it that—from the duke. Christian followed the old man into the library.

The duke settled into his chair by the fireplace. "Jameson, two glasses of brandy, please."

"Yes, my lord." The butler went to pour the brandy.

"Well, Westerville. We've not had the opportunity to talk, have we? Perhaps now is the time."

Christian's jaw ached, it was set so tight. But he could do no more than nod.

"Your brandy, my lord." Jameson handed a glass to the duke, then turned to Christian. "And yours, my lord."

Christian took the glass just as the door opened and the footman reappeared.

"Ah!" Jameson said. "Master Charles! Did you inform Lady Elizabeth of her guest?"

"No, sir. Lady Elizabeth is not in her room."

Christian frowned. "I didn't see her in the garden when I rode up."

The duke eyed Christian. "Did she know you were coming?"

"Yes, my lord. I told her so this morning."

Jameson's face creased with a frown. "She is usually early."

The footman opened his mouth, hesitated, then said, "Her Ladyship's maid is somewhat upset. Says Lady Elizabeth asked for her riding gown to be laid out, but she never came to put it on."

The duke's frown grew. "Damn it! Where the hell is she?"

The footman shrugged helplessly. "I don't know, my lord, though one of the grooms said Lord Bennington's horse is in the stables. However, he is nowhere to be found."

"Bennington?" the duke repeated. "Where the devil is *he*?"

Something was not right. Every instinct that had been honed in Christian's time on the High

Toby came to the fore. "Find Lady Elizabeth," he ordered, setting his glass on a side table. "Have every room searched. She must be found."

The footman spun on his heel and was gone, but Jameson darted a questioning glance at the duke.

"What's this?" Massingale demanded, straightening his chair, his face red. "Westerville, who the hell do you think you are, ordering my servants about as if you were king?"

Christian leaned over. "Do *you* know where she is? And is she safe?"

Massingale frowned. "Safe? Why wouldn't she be . . ." He paused, his face paling ever so slightly. He whipped his gaze to Jameson. "What are you doing in here? Didn't you hear the viscount? Go and find Lady Elizabeth at once. Also find Lady Charlotte while you are at it. I want to know where they both are."

"Yes, my lord." Jameson bowed. "I will report back within a few moments."

"Do that."

She will be found; she must be. Christian could not allow it otherwise. He raked an impatient hand through his hair, his chest aching as if an iron band tightened about him. She was probably out walking, thinking of the complicated issues confronting them. He winced at the thought of her being upset.

He'd promised Beth to wait until she was present to confront her grandfather. But wouldn't that just cause them all more pain? It would be better to speak with the old man now, while Beth was not present to hear the painful truth.

Christian put his hand in his pocket. Inside was his mother's keepsake box that contained her letters. He withdrew the box and laid it on the small table beside the duke's brandy.

For a moment, there was only the ticking of a clock. The duke slowly reached over and picked up the box, then opened it. He looked carefully at the contents, his fingers trembling especially when he touched the letters.

He lifted his gaze to Christian. "Where did you get these?"

"From my mother's gaoler."

Massingale closed the box, setting it back on the table. "I'm glad you have something of hers."

Christian reached into his other pocket and withdrew the letter from the bishop, as well as the small miniature. He placed those on top of his mother's box.

Massingale glared. "You've been in my desk!"

"Yes, I have. Why do you have a miniature of my mother?"

The duke's expression darkened, appearing almost sullen. "I didn't. The miniature belonged to my son. He had it in his hand when he died. He had a raging fever and didn't know any of us the last few days." The duke picked up the miniature and gazed at it, suddenly appearing very feeble. "But he remembered her. Every time his gaze fell on this, he'd call for her."

"How did he meet my mother?"

The duke abruptly set the miniature back on the table. "This is a complicated tale." He looked at the letters and said testily, "Westerville, what exactly is all of this?"

Christian picked up the letter from the bishop. "You might want to read this letter."

The duke took the paper. The room was silent as the duke read the letter, except for the crack of the fire and the distant rumble of thunder.

Finally, the duke sighed and returned the letter to the table. He shot an unhappy glare at Christian. "I didn't want to have this conversation, though I knew it would eventually be coming."

Christian noted how the old man shivered slightly. To give himself something to do so he wouldn't go mad thinking about where Beth might be, Christian went to stir the fire, a gust of warmth heating the room.

"Thank you," the duke said unexpectedly. "It's a pain growing older, not being able to do for yourself." He sighed. "I suppose you wish to know about your mother."

"Yes."

The duke slanted a look up at Christian. "Your mother was beautiful, you know. Breathtakingly so. More than that, she was intelligent and had a lovely laugh. I only met her once, but I will never forget her laugh."

Christian nodded.

"My son met her more often than I, of course. I was busy with the estates. He never cared for them. He was bookish. So was your mother. They met at the lending library and became friends."

"Friends?"

"Nothing more than that—just friends, much to my son's chagrin." The duke shook his head. "For so many years after his beloved wife's death, he showed no interest in any woman. Eventually, he decided he would never love again and he married Charlotte. I think the fool thought she might make a good mother for Beth. Either way, they were not happy though they managed to live together fairly peaceably until . . ."

"He met my mother."

"She would have nothing to do with him as he was married. He ceased all contact with her, but he was never the same after that. He withdrew more and more. Charlotte was desperate for his attention. I truly believe she—"

"My lord?" Jameson stood in the open doorway, his face drawn with concern. "Lady Elizabeth is not in the house."

"Did you look in the garden?"

"We have searched the garden and the cellars. She is nowhere to be found."

Christian took a step forward. "Where can she be?"

"Nor," Jameson said in a voice heavy with meaning, "can we find Lady Charlotte."

Christian relaxed. "Then Beth is with Charlotte."

Beth's grandfather struggled to his feet. "Yes," he said harshly. "She is with Charlotte. We must go after them!"

Christian frowned. "But why—" A chilled thought settled in his brain, freezing him in place for a moment. Suddenly, he saw it all. "It was Charlotte. She also knew my mother."

"She ingratiated herself into your mother's company after she discovered where my son's true passion was. Charlotte can be very charming. She wrote her letters, pretended to be your mother's best friend."

"She is 'Sinclair.'"

"Her grandmother's name, one of the old Sinclairs." The duke was already limping toward the door, his cane in hand. "We must hurry. She is not to be trusted—" His foot caught at the edge of the rug and he fell forward.

Christian caught him before the old man could truly fall. The duke's hands clutched at Christian's coat and the old man's eyes met his. Tears welled in them. "You must catch up to them. Charlotte—she is not well."

"Not well?"

"She is not well. Ask Bennington. He knows all about her, though it has not stopped him from making a cake of himself. He loves her though she is mad."

Christian's heart tumbled. "Mad?"

"Completely."

Christian turned to Jameson. "Are any of the carriages gone?"

"No, my lord. And all of the horses are still stabled."

"Then send out the men, all of them! Have them scour the grounds. They can't be far."

He led the duke to a chair, then turned to go.

The duke caught his arm. "You need to know what she is like. What she is capable of. Charlotte was the one who was corresponding with the

French. She'd been doing it for some time, simply to gain extra funds to maintain herself. She took her own letters and copied them, forging your mother's handwriting. Then she delivered them to the king, pretending she'd found them while assisting your mother with some invitations to a dinner party. Since it was widely known Charlotte was close to your mother, no one questioned a word of the story."

"You knew this?"

The duke's eyes filled with tears. "I knew what had happened the day after they arrested your mother."

Christian's heart hardened. "Why did you not tell someone the truth?"

"You must understand. If I had exposed Charlotte, our family name would have been sullied. I wrote instead to your father, told him what had happened. He had the position and wealth to save her." Anguish passed over the duke's face. "I didn't realize he was out of the country until it was too late. She was already ill. I-I went to visit her, but even I could see—" The duke shook his head. "There was no reason to sully our family name as her time on earth was to be so short."

Christian swallowed a swell of bitter emotion. "We will discuss this later. I must find Beth."

The duke collected himself with an effort. "Yes, yes! If Charlotte decides Beth will harm her position, embarrass her in any way, which asking about your mother would—"

"Where could they be?"

"I don't know! They didn't take the carriage, so it

must be near. Charlotte wanders all over the place, too." The duke brightened. "The ruin! There's an old ruin by the lake. Charlotte is forever there. You go through the garden and over the back drive. You can see it from there—"

The duke stopped talking, for there was no one else in the room but him; Christian was already running through the house, his boots thudding as he found his way to the back terrace doors.

Chapter 17

Let me tell you this one thing—never come between a man and his dog, a man and his supper, or a man and the woman he thinks can walk upon water. You will come to a foul ending if you do any of these.

A Compleat Guide for
Being a Most Proper Butler
by Richard Robert Reeves

Beth paused at the edge of the clearing. The old ruins stood to one side, stately and vine-ridden against the side of the lake. Many people built their own ruins, trying to emulate fallen Greek temples and the like, but Massingale House boasted a real ruin, one of Roman design, and just as intriguing.

"I haven't been here in months," Beth said as they neared the ruin.

Charlotte led the way, lifting her skirts from the tall grass. "Hurry!" she called over her shoulder.

"It is going to rain. I don't wish to be caught in it."

Beth followed, almost running. She wished Charlotte would not go quite so fast, but she supposed that with the weather hanging over their heads in such a threatening manner, it was a good thing. It was long past the time for the truth to be revealed, come what may. She steeled herself and increased her pace.

Charlotte veered to one side as they came closer to the ruin. "It's in here." She disappeared around the corner of the building.

Beth followed, coming to a halt a second later. "Charlotte!"

"Down here." Charlotte's voice drifted up from the wine cellar that had been dug to one side of the ancient portico.

Beth went down the stone steps to the heavy door, a thick musty odor rising to meet her. The door was much smaller than a normal one, and she had to duck a little as she went.

Charlotte was there, in the back of the room, kneeling before a dusty shelf and feeling about for something.

"I have never been in this place."

"The gardeners once used it to store their extra things, but since your grandfather built the new hothouse, they never come here." Charlotte glanced back over her shoulder. "I love Massingale House. I believe I have been in every nook and cranny."

"I love it, too," Beth replied, stung a little by the implied criticism. "But I am not addicted to crawling into such small places as this."

"Ah!" Charlotte pulled forth a small, leather-wrapped bundle. "Here it is!" She held it out to Beth.

Beth took the bundle and fell to her knees. Inside the leather pouch came the unmistakable jangle of metal and jewels. Slowly, she opened the pouch and gasped. A sapphire and silver filigreed necklace lay in her hands. Even in the small light coming from the partially open door, it was obvious that the piece was of master workmanship. The silver chain was intricately formed, generous pearls threaded between some of the most breathtaking sapphires she'd ever seen. But the most beautiful thing about the necklace was the large teardrop sapphire that hung from the center. "Oh Charlotte, it's beautiful. How on earth did you end up with this—"

A scraping sound shattered her sentence. The room was plunged into black.

Beth leaped to her feet, the necklace forgotten as she frantically tried to make her way to the door. She ran into a broken crate, her shins smarting painfully before her hands found the door frame. *Charlotte!*

From the other side of the door came the unmistakable sound of laughter.

Beth placed her hands to the door and shoved with all her might, but the door did not move. *"Charlotte!"*

"Don't even try! It is closed forever!" Charlotte said, her voice unusually crisp and clear.

Beth stepped back, trying to breathe, think, *do*. "Charlotte! The door—"

"Is locked. I will only be here a few moments and then I shall return to Massingale House and tell everyone you went for a walk beyond the grounds and that you were plainly distraught. After I leave, no one will find you. You will die here, alone and away from everyone you love. Even Westerville, though he will forget you soon enough."

Beth pressed a hand over her mouth. "Charlotte, you cannot mean that."

"Oh, but I do." Charlotte gave a laugh that was not quite steady. "Beth, you want to turn your grandfather against me, to remind him of my mistakes, mistakes I paid for already, so many years ago—"

"Mistakes?" Beth leaned against the heavy wooden door, pushing with all her might. Christian would come looking for her. She knew he would. If she could just keep Charlotte talking, it would draw him to this place.

Her heart sank. It was thin reasoning. But it was all she had. She thought furiously. "Charlotte . . . you were the one who turned false evidence against Christian's mother."

"I put that witch where she needed to be! I had her locked away forever where men wouldn't fall for her sick beauty. Yes, that was me. You did not know her, but she was evil, always entrancing men and then leaving them."

Beth pressed her forehead to the smooth, cool door. "Wait? Father *cared* for her?"

"He was mad for her! But she would have nothing to do with him. Nothing! Before she came along, he loved me. Or was beginning to; I could tell. When he grew ill, he needed me. I thought he'd finally realized we were meant to be together. Instead, the more ill he became, the more he called for her. It was as if I didn't even exist." Charlotte's voice cracked on the last word.

Beth winced. That was just like her father, she thought. He'd always been so wrapped up in himself, in his own world. "You discovered how he felt about Christian's mother and you forged the false evidence."

"Oh, it was not that simple. I had to find a way into her life, be seen as her best friend. Everyone thought we were inseparable. She called me Sinclair, which is my family name, and I called her Titania, after the fairy queen. She thought that a compliment, but it was not."

"Why did you bother with all of that?"

"To learn her handwriting. I had to change the letters to make them look like hers. Also, if I was her best friend, who would think I was lying when I was sadly forced to turn over evidence I'd 'found' in her desk?"

Beth turned her back to the door and squinted into the cellar. She had to think. She didn't recall a window, but . . . was there a vent of some sort? A small one, even? She began to walk around the room blindly, running her hands up and down the walls. "You were very clever, Charlotte," she called loudly. "Cleverer than I thought you could be."

"No one ever pays me the least heed. Usually I like it that way, though I do not like it when your grandfather thinks me stupid. That makes me mad."

"It would make me mad, too. How did he find out about everything?" Beth tripped over something in the dark, her leg banging painfully against a sharp edge. She reached down, blindly feeling for the object. It was a cask. Hope lifted and she turned it on its side, grunting a bit as she did so. Perhaps she could stand on it and—

A thud sounded as something hit the door.

Beth paused. "What's that?"

"I thought perhaps I should cover this door. Just in case someone comes looking for you."

"They will hear me scream."

"Not unless they stand right where I am, leaning against the wood." Another thud hit the door.

Beth gritted her teeth and stood on the cask, groping along the high part of the wall for an opening of some sort, swiping aside cobwebs and centuries of dust. Where was the opening? Where was—Ah! Her fingers brushed a small indentation in the wall.

It was a small opening, barely large enough for her fingers to fit through. It was small, but perhaps it would be enough. "Charlotte? How does grandfather know your secrets?"

There was a pause in noise outside. "What?" Another thud hit the door.

"I asked how Grandfather discovered your secrets?"

"Lord Bennington. He found out what happened and told everything to your grandfather. Between them, they decided the best thing to do in order to stifle any possible scandal was to lock me away."

Bennington knew? Beth couldn't see the staid lord keeping company with a woman he thought guilt of such duplicity. She ran her hands along the thin slit in the wall that was way over her head, her fingers barely brushing it. It was filled with decades of muck, mold and debris. Some of it rained down on her as she tried to dig it open, but she ducked her head and kept her hands busy. If she could get it open enough, perhaps she could tear some of her skirt and hang it from the window to draw attention. It was a pale plan, but all she had.

Meanwhile, she had to keep Charlotte busy. "Charlotte, how did Bennington discover what had happened?"

"He found some of the practice letters I'd forged. It was horrible, that night. Especially after he forced me to tell your grandfather everything."

Outside the door, noise continued. "What are you doing out there?"

"You'll see," Charlotte answered in far too calm a tone.

Beth bit her lip. Even standing on tiptoe, she was too short to really clean out the slit. She needed a tool of some sort. She climbed off the cask and sank to her knees, then began blindly stretching out, looking for something she could use. Her fingers sifted through straw and dirt. Finally her fingers closed over a wooden peg that probably had once been hammered into the wall to hang herbs. It wasn't much, but it would have to do.

"What are you doing in there?" Charlotte asked suspiciously.

"Wondering why my father did not value you as he ought. That is criminal."

"It is more than that," Charlotte said, clearly miffed. "I was the perfect wife for him. I was young and able to have a child and I loved him so much."

"That was his loss."

Another thud against the door rang through the room. "He didn't love me."

"He was very sick."

Beth pressed her hands together, trying to make them stop shaking. *I have to do this. I cannot let Charlotte win again. For myself. For Christian. For Father.* With superhuman effort, Beth dashed the tears from her eyes, picked up the stick, and began digging at the opening with renewed effort.

"Charlotte? What are you doing?"

Beth paused. It was Lord Bennington! She ran to the door and pounded her fist, but all it did was bruise her flesh on the hard wood. "Bennington! Help me! Charlotte has trapped me in here and I cannot—"

"Charlotte! What have you—"

"She knew about what I did to Westerville's mother."

There was a long silence.

"Bennington!" Beth shouted again. "Please help me!"

A muted sigh was heard. "Charlotte, I cannot allow you to do this."

"If I don't, she will tell the world of her suspicions and I will end up in gaol. Is that what you want? Me in gaol?"

"No, no. Of course not. But to do this—Charlotte, I cannot allow—"

There was a dull thwack and then a tremendous weight thudded against the door. Bennington's voice was not heard again.

Beth turned away, a hand on her stomach where it roiled. God give her strength, but she didn't know what to do. She dropped back to her knees. A signal. That's what she needed. Her fingers closed over the stick she'd found. If she could light this and stick it out the window, there was a chance someone from the house might see the smoke.

Beth's heart leaped. But just as quickly as she felt the spring of hope, a new fear entered. Smoke was seeping into the room already, but from *under* the door.

Charlotte had caught the door on fire. The small vent was pulling the smoke now, filling the room with the fetid thickness.

"Beth, I am going to leave now! At least you won't die alone. Bennington is here to keep you company."

Beth could barely make out Charlotte's voice. It came as if from a long way away. Beth covered her mouth with the edge of her damp skirt, her eyes burning. She was not going to die of hunger after all.

Eyes filling with tears, Beth looked around her. What was she going to do now? *Christian, hurry!*

* * *

Christian ran down the terrace steps and tore through the garden. His gaze was drawn to the bench where he'd once kissed Beth. *Do not look. Do not slow down.* He reached the small gate in the back and threw it open.

Charlotte stood in the opening. Her gown was soaked, bits of leaves and bark clung to her. A slightly dazed look was on her face, a streak of black down one cheek.

He grabbed her by the shoulders. "Where is she?"

"Someone took her! We were walking down the road and—"

He shook her roughly. "Damn you to hell! You will tell me where she is or I'll—"

From over her shoulder, he saw it. A thin trickle of smoke. It climbed up the sky and disappeared into the gray clouded air.

Christian pulled Charlotte close and spoke through clenched teeth. "If she is harmed, you will be next and by God, no force on earth will save you then."

He threw her from him and raced on, covering the ground in great strides, branches whipping at him, cutting his cheeks and neck, though he felt nothing. All he knew was that Beth was within reach.

He stopped when he reached the ruin. The thin line of smoke had thickened now, great puffs billowing up to fill the sky.

"Bloody hell!" He ran to the back of the ruin and came to a halt. Before him was a steep incline rimmed by a set of stone stairs—a cellar of some sort. Down the stairs was a pile of brush higher than his head. The brush smoldered and crackled, fire licking higher and higher.

"Beth!" he called.

No answer came. He tried to fight his way closer, but the now-thick smoke began to curl at him. Coughing, he took off his coat and turned, running to the lake. He soaked it, then ran back to the cellar. Wrapping his arm in the coat, he began knocking the large pieces of burning wood from the door.

"My lord?"

He turned to find Jameson and the footman, Charles, their faces flushed from running.

"More water! Now!"

Jameson nodded, turning to run toward the lake, peeling off his coat as he went; Charles followed behind him. Christian's coat was drying now, the heat from the burning wood searing his hands.

"Beth!" he called desperately, his arms aching with the effort.

As if from far away, he thought he heard an answer. He paused, then yelled again, but no other answer was forthcoming. Christian clenched his teeth and looped his coat over a burning log and tugged it, yanking it from the pile and out of the way. As he did so, he noticed a boot at the bottom of the stack of wood. His heart sank. It was a man's boot. *Bennington*.

Christian grabbed the foot and tugged. Two

smaller branches rolled out of the fire, showering the grass with ashes and sparks. Bennington lay pale and unmoving, a deep gash on his forehead, blood covering his coat.

Damn it all! Christian hurriedly unwound his cravat and tied it about the man's head, then rushed back to the burning pile. The door itself was now burning; he could see it through the remaining brush. The smoke soaked his lungs and burned his eyes, but he kept going. He had to reach her. He loved her more than anything. More than life. More than vengeance. *"Beth!"*

This time, an answer echoed, choked and desperate. No sweeter sound had ever been heard. *"Christian!"*

Jameson returned. "Here!" He thrust his deliciously cold and wet coat into Christian's burned hands. Christian wrapped the coat over his face and picked up a large piece of wood that was not burning. "See to Bennington. He is badly injured."

The butler nodded and left.

Christian turned to the burning pile of wood. He hefted the log to his shoulder and, using it, rammed the door.

The footman, Charles, was beside him in an instant, covered by his own dripping coat.

"Together!" Christian ordered.

They positioned themselves with the limb as a battering ram. The fire licked about them, the smoke obscuring everything.

They coughed and choked, but did not let go of the log.

"Now!" Christian yelled.

The log smashed into the door. With a resounding splintering, it broke neatly in two, a billow of smoke emerging to completely engulf Charles.

Christian pulled the wet coat closer as Charles staggered off, searching for fresh air. Into the black hole, Christian went. For an instant, he could see nothing in the smoke-filled room. Then, on the floor, he caught a glimmer of white. Beth lay, arms outstretched, as if she'd tried to reach the door, but couldn't.

His heart thudded. He stooped and picked her up, pausing only to wrap the wet coat over her head, then, shoulder first, he raced out of the building.

The duke's carriage pulled up. The groom dismounted, and with him, the duke.

Jameson was at Christian's side. "Place her on the ground, my lord!"

Christian did so, barely able to remain upright himself. He coughed and choked, bending over as smoke-tears rolled down his face.

"Come, my boy!" the duke said, pulling him to one side. "Jameson can—"

"No!" Christian said, finally catching his breath. He pulled himself to where Beth lay and collapsed beside her. Lifting on one elbow, he looked down into her face.

Her breathing was labored. Jameson was wiping her face with a wet cloth. Christian took the cloth from the butler and gently rubbed it over her chin and forehead.

Dirt streaked one cheek. Her gown was ripped

and filthy beyond measure. But never had Christian seen anything so beautiful. "Beth—" The word sent him into a fit of coughing.

Finally, when he could breathe again, he lifted back on his arm and looked down at Beth. She lay so still. So quiet. He traced a finger over her cheek where a welt was rising. "Beth. Please—" He could not continue, though not because of his coughing. This time, a wealth of tears clogged his throat. He would not let her die. He would *not.*

He reached for her, lifting her into his arms, into his lap. He placed his cheek to hers. "Beth," he whispered. For the first time since he'd been a boy of ten, left to fend for himself after his mother's death, Christian Llevanth prayed. *"Please, God!"*

Beth coughed, her entire body curling up. Christian tightened his hold, smoothing back her hair as blessed fresh air revived Beth.

Her eyes opened, red-rimmed and watery and completely beautiful. She coughed even more and he lifted her a bit to help her fight the spasms. "Just relax," he murmured. "It's the smoke. You are just getting it out of your lungs."

She nodded, coughing even more and gasping now and then, her eyes clenched closed.

He held her to him, speaking foolish words, little endearments, and silly chastisements. He loved her so much . . . more than life itself.

Finally, she managed to draw an even breath. Her eyes opened again, traveling across his face. And she smiled. "I knew you would come."

He hugged her, burying his face in her hair.

"Are you done?" The duke's cranky voice rose over the crackle of the fire.

Christian lifted his head to meet the duke's gaze. Though the old man's words had been harsh, there were very real tears in his eyes. "No, my lord. I am afraid I am never going to be done holding your granddaughter. Not now. Not next year. Nor the year after that." He looked down at her and lifted a hand to her cheek. "She is everything to me."

"Christian!" Beth caught at his wrists. "Your hands!"

He looked at the blisters and burns. "A little scratch, my love."

"A little—" She struggled to sit up, but he refused to allow it. "Christian! The necklace! It is in the shed and—"

"Forget about it."

"But—"

"Beth, I don't care."

She blinked at him, uncertainty in her gaze.

He lifted the wet cloth to her cheek to brush away another streak of soot.

She caught his wrist again. "Christian, you must get some salve for your hands! They must hurt dreadfully."

"I have all the salve I need, right here." He wrapped himself about her once more and held her close. "Beth, when I saw you lying on the ground, I thought—"

She pushed him away. "Christian, I have to tell you. Charlotte is the one who—"

"I know."

"We must stop her!"

"Don't worry about Charlotte," Grandfather said. "She was attempting to take Bennington's horse. I had an undergroom lock her in the tack room on orders of a flogging if he dared allow her to escape."

"Lord Bennington!" Christian exclaimed. He looked at Jameson.

The butler wiped his hands on a piece of ripped cloth, blood staining the material. "I believe the bleeding is stopped. I sent Charles for the doctor." Jameson glanced at the duke. "My lord, I fear the constable will also have to be notified. There will be an inquiry."

Grandfather winced. "Surely we can just—"

"Massingale," Christian said quietly. "There *will* be an inquiry."

The duke scowled, the old man's gaze slipping to find his granddaughter, lying so quietly in Christian's arms. Something in the old duke's gaze softened and, after a long moment, he nodded slowly. "It is time for everything to be brought into the open. I will welcome an inquiry."

"What will happen to Charlotte?" Beth asked, turning to look at her grandfather.

"If we are permitted, I will ask that she be sent away where she cannot hurt anyone again." The duke's expression crumbled. "Beth, I'm so sorry— it's my damnable pride. I wanted to protect our name. In the end, I didn't protect anyone."

"We all fight pride," Christian said. "I fear very little else has been driving me." He brushed a tear from Beth's cheek. "I am sorry about Lord Bennington."

"He is fortunate to be alive. He was a fool to think Charlotte would ever be well enough to return his regard."

Beth sighed. "He really did love her, didn't he?"

"Too well," Grandfather said.

Christian brushed the hair back from her forehead. "Beth, I am sorry."

Her brown eyes fixed on him. "For what?"

"I have been a fool. I thought the most important thing in my life was finding who was responsible for my mother's death. Now, I realize what is really important is you."

Her breath caught in her throat. Beth blinked up into the face of the man she loved more than life itself. "You love me."

"Desperately. Madly. To distraction and back. And when we are wed, I will love you even more."

"But . . . your mother—"

He sighed. "I know what happened to my mother. Sadly, it does not change her fate. But what I do know changes mine. I am through with the past. *You* are my future. You and the love we share and the children we will have. That is all I want now. All I'll ever want."

Beth couldn't say a word. She simply reached up and drew him to her, gulping a sob into the crook of his neck as she held him tightly.

Behind them, Grandfather sniffed loudly.

"They make a lovely couple, my lord," Jameson said, fishing in his pocket for a clean handkerchief. He found one and handed it to the duke.

"Indeed they do," the duke said, blowing his

nose rather loudly. "They will be even lovelier once they're properly married!"

Beth caught her breath and peeped up at Christian, wiping her eyes with a ragged sleeve. "I need a bath."

He chuckled. "You smell of smoke, as do I."

The duke turned, leaning heavily on his cane. "Jameson, open the carriage door. We shall return to the house."

Beth smiled up at Christian. "Shall we adjourn to the house to get some ointment for your hands and a bath, my love?"

His eyes lit. "A bath?"

Grandfather snorted. "Someone send to London for a special license! *Now.*" He allowed the butler to assist him into the coach and sent everyone scurrying to find a blanket for Lady Elizabeth.

"Indeed," Christian said. "I would like to marry tomorrow morning, if possible."

Beth blinked. "Tomorrow morning?"

"Is that too soon? How about tomorrow afternoon, then? I shall send to London and have Reeves bring the necessary clothing." He twinkled down at her. "I really must introduce you to Reeves."

She paused. "Your butler?"

"The one and only." Christian stood, then reached down and lifted his lady love in his arms, silencing her protests with a hard kiss. "My father sent him out to civilize the lost sons he'd neglected, but damn me if all I've seen him do is marry us off."

"Oh dear, how dreadful!"

Christian smiled down into Beth's eyes as he carried her to the waiting carriage. "If this is dreadful, then I want more of it." He gently set her on the seat of the carriage. "Much, much more!"

Epilogue

Ah, the joys of wash day! When all the dirt and horror of the previous week is set to rights, all with a tub of water and the fresh scent of soap!

A Compleat Guide for
Being a Most Proper Butler
by Richard Robert Reeves

"You requested more brandy, my lord?"

Christian turned from the desk. "Yes. The decanter is dry."

Reeves brought a new decanter and set it on the table. "That is my fault, my lord. You don't empty it as often as you used to and I am off schedule."

Christian laced his hands behind his head and leaned back in his chair. "Well, Reeves. It has been an adventure, has it not?"

"Quite, my lord. Are you satisfied with the outcome of events?"

Christian grinned. "I am wed to the most beautiful of women. What could I regret?"

"What will happen to Lady Charlotte now?"

"She has been assigned to Bedlam. The duke is paying a fortune to keep her in comfort there, but she is secure. She will harm no others."

"I am sorry your adventure was such a painful experience."

"Me, too. But sometimes one must travel the rough road to reach one's ultimate destination. I found my mother's killer and brought her to justice of a sort. But more importantly, I learned that my future—and Beth—are more important than any past I might have had."

"Certainly, my lord," Reeves said. "That is a very important lesson, indeed." He picked up the old decanter and placed it on the tray. "Will there be anything else?"

Christian sighed. "You aren't going to say anything, are you?"

"My lord?"

Christian stood and held his arms out to his sides. "My clothes."

Reeves looked Christian up and down. "Something is wrong, my lord."

"Wrong?"

"You aren't wearing black."

Christian grinned. He had donned a brightly white cravat and shirt. His waistcoat was of deep red damask. "Do you like it? I am wearing it for my meeting with the trustees. They are to sign over the fortune today."

"You look dapper, my lord. I must immediately congratulate the viscountess on her excellent taste in waistcoats. You are indeed a fortunate man. Not only is she a lovely woman, with an amiable disposition and an exceptional share of intelligence, but she dresses you far better than you ever dressed yourself."

Christian sighed. "Must you do that? Steal all the glory from my days?"

"Not for long, my lord," Reeves said, smiling. "I regret to inform you that I must be leaving soon."

Christian's smile faded. "But . . . why?"

"Between starching your cravats and assisting you in discovering the errors of your ways, I have been writing a book."

"A book? On what?"

"How to be a proper butler."

Christian sighed. "I was just a research project to you, wasn't I?"

Reeves's lips twitched. "I shall dedicate the book to you and your brother, my lord. I must say, I have never served two more worthy men."

"Thank you. I am certain my brother will thank you even more than I."

"Why don't you ask him yourself, my lord?"

Christian paused. "Tristan? He's—"

"The earl and countess are in the sitting room. I saw their carriage as I was bringing you the decanter."

Christian was halfway out the door.

"My lord?" Reeves called after him. "Your coat—"

But Christian didn't slow down a step. He raced down the steps and burst into the sitting room. Tristan stood leaning against the mantelpiece, a cane in one hand. Tall and broad shouldered, as blond as Christian was dark, Tristan's face bore the imprint of the sea upon his tanned face.

His lovely wife, Prudence, sat beside Beth on a settee.

Beth stood as Christian came to a halt in the middle of the room. "There you are!" she said, coming toward him. "I was just meeting your brother and his countess!"

Christian slipped his arm about Beth. Dressed in a lovely gown of wine red silk, her blonde hair luminescent in the sunlight streaming from the window, the sight of her warmed him head to toe. "I didn't know we had visitors."

"Which must be why you arrived half dressed," his brother said. His deep voice, used to shouting orders from the deck of a ship over the roar of the ocean, rumbled noisily. "I never thought I'd see the day when I'd outdress you, but here it is."

Christian grinned. "Here it is! What brings you here, you old hellion?"

Tristan drew himself up to his full height. He was far broader across the shoulders than Christian, of a heavier frame. "Chris, Prudence and I came to visit for two reasons."

A delightful color brushed Prudence's cheeks. "Mainly we came to meet your new bride."

"Yes," Tristan said, pride glowing on his face. "We also came to inform you that you are about to gain a new title. That of 'uncle.'"

"An uncle?" Christian looked from his brother, to his sister-in-law. "But . . . how?"

Prudence laughed, Beth chiming in.

Tristan shook his head ruefully. "I will explain it to you later."

"No, no! I didn't mean that! I just—when did this happen? How long have you known?"

"We just discovered it," Prudence said. She sent a loving glance at her husband. "I hope it is the first of many."

Tristan reached over and took her hand in his, pressing a kiss to the back of it. "We shall have an entire ship full, should it please you, my love."

"One crew member at a time, please," Prudence said archly, her soft brown eyes twinkling up at her husband.

Christian released Beth long enough to cross to his brother and envelop the scoundrel in a hearty hug. "What a wonderful thing!"

Tristan hugged him back, pounding his back solidly. "You have been married a week or two now. When will you and your lovely viscountess grace us with the same news?"

Children? Christian turned to look at Beth. "One day, perhaps. But for now, I want my wife all to myself."

Beth's eyes twinkled at him. "You shall have me, my love."

Tristan returned to the settee where Prudence sat, and settled beside her, capturing her hand and pressing a kiss to her fingers. "Christian, I am happy to report that the House for Retired Sailors has grown." He looked at Beth. "Your husband is something of a philanthropist."

"Yes, he is," Prudence said, smiling sweetly. "There are over seventy men housed there now."

"It would not be possible without you, Christian," Tristan said.

Christian shrugged. "All I do is send a bank draft every quarter. You and Prudence do all of the work."

Beth slipped an arm about Christian's waist, leaning against him. "I had no idea you were a philanthropist, my love."

"Lord Westerville." Everyone turned to find Reeves standing in the doorway, a coat in his hand. "You forgot a part of your raiment."

"Oh no," Beth said. "You have wounded Reeves's sensibilities."

"Yes, my lady. My sensibilities are indeed wounded." Reeves came forward and assisted Christian into the coat. He gave the coat a final smoothing across one shoulder, stood back, then nodded. "Excellent. I feel better already. My lady, you have had a very positive influence over Lord Westerville. He has left the morbid world of Only Black behind and now embraces other colors of the spectrum."

Beth peeped up at Christian, a flash of a dimple tempting him to drop a kiss on her forehead. "I hope he is ready for my influence for many more years," she murmured.

Christian held her closer. "You influence my every breath, my love. And always will."

"Enough of that!" Tristan draped an arm around his wife. "Reeves, you have performed magic."

Reeves smiled at both couples. "The old earl would have been pleased."

Christian tilted Beth's face to his. Ever so gently, he placed a kiss on her soft lips. Magic was what it was; the best kind of magic—true love.

Why Do Women Love Inappropriate Men?

You know who you are, but perhaps you won't admit to it. You're the wild child drawn to the quiet, bookish guy reading *The Economist*; or maybe you're the reserved society lady who secretly loves nothing better than a ride on a Harley clutching a leather clad biker; or perhaps you're human and he's a vampire . . . But any way you look at it, there's no greater thrill or challenge for you than being with someone you know you shouldn't.

Well you're not the only one . . .

In these four upcoming Avon Romance Superleaders, the old adage that opposites attract never rang more true. Enjoy!

Coming May 2006

♥

THE
Care and Feeding
OF
UNMARRIED MEN

♥   ♥

By Christie Ridgway

Palm Springs's "Party Girl" Eve Caruso has finally met her match. "The Preacher," aka Nash Cargill, is in town to protect his starlet sister from a stalker, only to realize that he'd rather "stalk" Eve! But can this granddaughter of a notorious mobster be tamed?

♥

The rain was pouring down on the Palm Springs desert in biblical proportions the night he stalked into the spa's small bar. He was a big man, tall, brawny, the harsh planes of his face unsoftened by his wet, dark hair. Clint Eastwood minus forty years and plus forty pounds of pure muscle. Water dripped from the hem of his ankle-length black slicker to puddle on the polished marble floor beside his reptilian-skinned cowboy boots.

She flashed on one of the lessons her father had drilled into her. *A girl as beautiful as you and with a name like yours should always be on guard for the snake in Paradise.*

And as the stranger took another step forward, Eve Caruso heard a distinctive hiss.

The sound had come from her, though, the hiss of a quick, indrawn breath, because the big man put every one of her instincts on alert. But she'd also been taught at the school of Never Showing Fear, so she pressed her damp palms against the thighs of her tight white jeans, then scooted around the bar.

"Can I help you?" she asked, positioning her body between him and the lone figure seated on the eighth and last stool.

The stranger's gaze flicked to Eve.

She'd attended a casual dinner party earlier that evening—escorted by her trusty tape recorder so she wouldn't forget a detail of the meal or the guest list, which would appear in her society column—and hadn't bothered to change before taking on the late shift in the Kona Kai's tiny lounge. Her jeans were topped with a honey-beige silk T-shirt she'd belted at her hips. Around her neck was a tangle of turquoise-and-silver necklaces, some of which she'd owned since junior high. Her cowboy boots were turquoise too, and hand-tooled. Due to pressing financial concerns, she'd recently considered selling them on eBay—and maybe she still would, she thought, as his gaze fell to the pointy tips and her toes flexed into involuntary fetal curls.

He took in her flashy boots, then moved on to her long legs, her demi-bra-ed breasts, her shoulder-blade-length blonde hair and blue eyes. She'd been assessed by a thousand men, assessed, admired, desired, and since she was twelve-and-a-half years old, she'd been unfazed by all of them. Her looks were her gift, her luck, her tool, and tonight, a useful distraction in keeping the dark man from noticing the less showy but more famous face of the younger woman siting by herself at the bar.

Even placed a hand on an empty stool and gestured with the other behind her back. *Get out, get away,* she signaled, all the while keeping her gaze on the stranger and letting a slow smile break over her face. "What would you like?" she asked, softly releasing the words one by one into the silence, like lingerie dropping onto plush carpeting.

"Sorry, darlin', I'm not here for you," he said, then he and his Southern drawl brushed past her, leaving only the scent of rain and rejection in their wake.

Eve froze in—shock? dismay? fear? *"I'm not here for you."*

What the hell was up with that?

Coming June 2006

♥

Her Officer and Gentleman

♥   **By Karen Hawkins**   ♥

Christian Llevanth isn't you average highwayman—he's inherited a title and a fortune. But
he's unable to enjoy his newfound status as he
continues to seek revenge and close in on the
Duke of Massingale, the man Christian believes
murdered his mother—if only he wasn't so
drawn to the duke's beguiling granddaughter
Lady Elizabeth.

♥

"I have no wish to fall in love," Beth declared.

"Which is exactly why you are so vulnerable
to it."

"Nonsense. That will never happen to me. Beatrice, you seem to forget that I am far too pragmatic—"

"May I have this dance?" came a deep voice
from behind Beth.

She started to answer, but caught sight of Beatrice's face. Her cousin stood, mouth open, eyes
wide.

Beth turned her head . . . and found herself
looking up into the face of the most incredibly

handsome man she'd ever seen. He was a full head taller than her, his shoulders broad, but it was his face that caused her to flush head to toe. Black hair spilled over his forehead, his jaw firm, his mouth masculine and yet sensual. His eyes called the most attention; they were the palest green, thickly lashed, and decidely masculine.

Her heart thudded, her palms grew damp, and her stomach tightened in the most irksome way. Her entire body felt leaden. What on earth was the matter with her? Had she eaten something ill for dinner that evening? Perchance a scallop, for they never failed to make her feel poorly.

Unaware his effect was being explained away on a shellfish, he smiled, his eyes sparkling down at her with wicked humor. "I believe I have forgotten to introduce myself. Allow me." He bowed. "I am Viscount Westerville."

"Ah!" Beatrice said, breaking into movement as if she'd been shoved from behind. "Westerville! One of Rochester's—ah—"

"Yes," the viscount said smoothly. He bowed, his gaze still riveted on Beth.

Before she knew what he was about, he had captured her limp hand and brought it to his lips, pressing a kiss to her fingers, his eyes sparkling at her intimately.

"Well, Lady Elizabeth?" he asked, his breath warm on her hand. "Shall we dance?"

Coming July 2006

♥

A Bite to Remember

By Lynsay Sands

♥　　　　　　　　　　　♥

When Vincent Argeneau's production of *Dracula: The Musical* closes, he suspects sabotage and calls in private detective Jackie Morissey. He quickly sees that she's more than just a tempting neck, but unfortunately, Jackie doesn't have a thing for vampires . . . that is, until she meets Vincent.

♥

*V*incent Argeneau forced one eyelid upward and peered around the dark room where he slept. He saw his office, managing to make out the shape of his desk by the light coming from the hallway. Oh yes, he'd fallen asleep on the couch in his office waiting for Bastien to call him back.

"Vincent?"

"Yeah?" He sat up and glanced around for the owner of that voice, then realized it was coming through his answering machine on the desk. Giving his head a shake, he got to his feet and stumbled across the room, snatching up the cordless phone as he dropped into his desk chair. "Bastien?"

"Vincent? Sorry to wake you, cousin. I waited as late as I could before calling."

Vincent grunted and leaned back in the chair, running his free hand over his face. "What time is it?"

"Five p.m. here. I guess that makes it about two there," Bastien said apologetically.

Vincent scrubbed his hand over his face again, then reached out to turn on his desk lamp. Blinking in the increased light, he said, "I'm up. Were you able to get ahold of that private detective company you said was so good?"

"That's why I couldn't call any later than this. They're on their way. In fact, their plane was scheduled to land at LAX fifteen minutes ago."

"Jesus!" Vincent sat up abruptly in his seat. "That was fast."

"Jackie doesn't waste time. I explained the situation to her and she booked a flight right away. Fortunately for you, she'd just finished a big job for me and was able to put off and delegate whatever else she had on the roster."

"Wow," Vincent murmured, then frowned as he realized what Bastien had said. "She? The detective's a woman?"

"Yes, she is, and she's good. Really good. She'll track down your saboteur and have this whole thing cleaned up for you in no time."

"If you say so," Vincent said quietly. "Thanks, Bastien. I appreciate it."

"Okay, I guess I'll let you go wake yourself up before they arrive."

"Yeah, okay. Hey—" Vincent paused and

glanced toward the curtained windows as a knock sounded at his front door. Frowning, he stood and headed out of the office, taking the cordless phone with him. "Hang on. There's someone at the door."

"Is it the blood delivery?" Bastien asked on the phone.

"Umm . . . no," Vincent said into the phone, but his mind was taken up with running over the duo before him. He'd never set his eyes on such an unlikely pair. The woman was blonde, the man a brunette. She was extremely short and curvy, he was a great behemoth of a man. She was dressed in a black business suit with a crisp white blouse under it, he wore casual cords and a sweater in pale cream. They were a study in contrasts.

"Vincent Argeneau?" the woman asked.

When he nodded, she stuck out her hand. "I'm Jackie Morissey and this is Tiny McGraw. I believe Bastien called you about us?"

Vincent stared at her hand, but rather than take it, he pushed the door closed and turned away as he lifted the phone back to his ear. "Bastien, she's *mortal!*"

"Did you just slam the door in Jackie's face?" Bastien asked with amazement. "I heard the slam, Vincent. Jesus! Don't be so damned rude."

"Hello!" he said impatiently. "She's *mortal,* Bastien. Bad enough she's female, but I need someone who knows about our 'special situation' to deal with this problem. She—"

"Jackie *does* know," Bastien said dryly. "Did you think I'd send you an uninitiated mortal? Have a little faith." A sigh traveled down the phone line. "She has a bit of an attitude when it comes to our kind, but Jackie's the best in the business and she knows about us. Now open the goddamned door for the woman."

"But she's mortal and . . . a girl," Vincent pointed out, still not happy with the situation.

"I'm hanging up, Vincent." Bastien hung up.

Vincent scowled at the phone and almost dialed him back, but then thought better of it and moved back to the door. He needed help tracking down the saboteur out to ruin him. He'd give Ms. Morissey and her giant a chance. If they sorted out the mess for him, fine. If not, he could hold it over Bastien's head for centuries.

Grinning at the idea, Vincent reached for the doorknob.

Coming August 2006

Never a Lady

By Jacquie D'Alessandro

Colin Oliver, Viscount Sutton, is in need of a wife—a demure, proper English paragon to provide him with an heir . . . everything Alexandra Larchmont is not. She's brazen, a fortune-teller and former pickpocket. Clearly they're all wrong for each other . . . Aren't they?

♥

From *The London Times* Society page:

Lord and Lady Malloran's annual soiree promises to be more exciting this year than ever as the entertaining fortune-telling services of the mysterious, much-sought-after Madame Larchmont have been secured. As Madame's provocative predictions have an uncanny knack for accuracy, her presence at any party guarantees its success. Also attending will be the very eligible Viscount Sutton, who recently returned to London after an extended stay at his Cornwall estate and is rumored to be looking for a wife. Wouldn't it be delicious if Madame Larchmont told him whom it is in the cards for him to marry?

Alexandra Larchmont looked up from the tarot cards she'd just shuffled and was about to deal, intending to smile at Lady Malloran, the hostess for the evening's elegant soiree where Alex's fortune-telling services were in high demand. Just as Alex's lips curved upward, however, the crowd of milling party guests separated a bit and her attention was caught by the sight of a tall, dark-haired man. And the smile died on her lips.

Panic rippled along her nerve endings and her muscles tensed, for in spite of the fact that three years had passed since she'd last seen him, she recognized him instantly. Under the best of circumstances, he wouldn't be a man easily forgotten—and the circumstances of their last encounter could never be described as "best." While she didn't know his name, his image was permanently etched in her memory.

She dearly wished that's where he'd remained—not standing a mere dozen feet away. Dear God, if he recognized *her*, everything she'd worked so long and hard for would be destroyed. Did he normally move in these exalted circles? If so, more than her livelihood was at risk—her very existence was threatened.

Her every instinct screamed at her to flee, but she remained frozen in place, unable to look away from him. As if trapped in a horrible, slow-moving nightmare, her gaze wandered down his form. Impeccably dressed in formal black attire, his dark hair gleamed under the glow of the dozens of candles flickering in the overhead chandelier. He held a crystal champagne glass, and she involuntarily shivered, rubbing her damp palms over her upper arms, recalling in vivid detail the strength in those large hands as they'd gripped her, preventing her escape. Out of necessity, she'd learned at a young age how to master her fears, but this man had alarmed and unnerved her as no one else ever had, before or since their single encounter.

The tarot cards had repeatedly warned her about him—the dark-haired stranger with the vivid green eyes who would wreak havoc with her existence—years before she'd ever seen him that first time. The cards had also predicted she'd someday see him again. Unfortunately the cards hadn't prepared her for someday being *now*.

Looking up, she noted with a sickening sense of alarm that his gaze moved slowly over the crowd. In a matter of seconds that gaze would fall upon her.